THE MYTH OF
THE BLITZ

ANGUS CALDER

PIMLICO

PIMLICO

20 Vauxhall Bridge Road, London SW1V 2SA

London Melbourne Sydney Auckland Johannesburg
and agencies throughout the world

First published by Jonathan Cape 1991
Pimlico edition 1992
Reprinted 1994, 1995, 1997

Printed and bound in Great Britain by
Mackays of Chatham PLC, Chatham, Kent

ISBN 0-7126-9820-5

PIMLICO

53

THE MYTH OF THE BLITZ

Angus Calder is Reader in Cultural Studies and
Staff Tutor in Arts with the Open University in
Scotland. He read English at Cambridge and
received his D. Phil. from the School of Social
Studies at the University of Sussex. He was
Convener of the Scottish Poetry Library when it
was founded in 1984. His other books include
The People's War (also available from Pimlico)
and *Revolutionary Empire*. He has contributed to
many Open University courses, notably on
'The Enlightenment', 'Popular Culture' and
'Literature and the Modern World'.

Contents

Plates

19 *The Man on the Ladder*. Photograph by Bert Hardy (Hulton Picture Company)
20 Open-air milk bar in Fetter Lane, EC4, (Syndication International)
21 Quentin Reynolds, BBC Radio broadcaster (© BBC)
22 J.B. Priestly, Leslie Howard, Mary Adams and L.W. Brockington from the BBC Radio programme, 'Answering You' (© BBC)
23 Production still from *Fires Were Started*, directed by Humphrey Jennings (© C.O.I.)
24 Humphrey Jennings rehearsing Myra Hess in *A Diary for Timothy* (BFI Stills, Posters and Designs)
25 'Your Britain, Fight For It Now'. Poster by Frank Newbould (Imperial War Museum, London)
26 Production still from *A Diary For Timothy* (1945), directed by Humphrey Jennings (© C.O.I.)
27 Ed Murrow, BBC Radio Broadcaster (© BBC)
27a LIFE Magazine cover of 23 September 1940 (Photograph by Cecil Beaton, Courtesy LIFE Magazine/Katz Pictures)
28 *Shipbuilding on the Clyde: Bending the Keel Plate* (detail) by Stanley Spencer (Imperial War Museum, London)
29 Production still from *In Which We Serve* (1942), directed and produced by Noël Coward and David Lean (Kobal Collection)
30 Production still from *Mrs Miniver* (1942), directed by William Wyler (Kobal Collection)
31 Production still from *Angels One Five* (1952), directed by George More O'Ferrall (Kobal Collection)
32 Still from *A Yank in the RAF*, used in Frank Capra's documentary film *Battle of Britain* (1942) (Imperial War Museum, London)
33 Winston Churchill among the crowds, from Capra's *Battle of Britain* (Imperial War Museum, London)

For more information about Blitz and related still images see:

Buggins, Joanne, 'An Appreciation of the Shelter Photographs Taken by Bill Brandt in November, 1940', *Imperial War Museum Review 4*, 1989
Foot, M.R.D., *Art and War: Twentieth Century Warfare as Depicted by War Artists*, Headline, 1990
Hardy, Bert, *My Life*, Gordon Fraser, 1985
McCormick, K. and Perry, H.D. (eds), *Images of War: The Artist's Vision of World War II*, Cassell, 1991
Rhodes, A., *Propaganda – The Art of Persuasion: World War II*, Wellfleet (Secaucus, N.J.), 1987
Seaborne, M., *Arthur Cross – Fred Tibbs: The London Blitz*, Nishen Photo-Library 3, 1987
Seaborne, M., *Shelters*, Nishen Photo-Library 7, 1988

Acknowledgements

The author and publishers would like to thank the following for permission to quote extracts from copyright material:

Babs Diplock: 'Battle of Britain War Hero' by Babs Diplock

Martin Brian & O'Keeffe Ltd: 'Verses Written During the Second World War' from *Complete Poems* by Hugh MacDiarmid, vol. 1 (Martin Brian & O'Keeffe 1978)

Faber & Faber Ltd: 'News-Reel', 'Brother Fire' and 'The Streets of Laredo' from *Collected Poems* by Louis MacNeice (Faber 1979); 'East Coker' and 'Little Gidding' from *Collected Poems 1909–1962* by T.S. Eliot (Faber 1963); poem XXIII from *Look, Stranger!* (Faber 1936) and 'Letter to Lord Byron' from *Collected Longer Poems* by W.H. Auden (Faber 1968)

Roy Fuller: 'Soliloquy in an Air Raid' and 'Autumn 1940' from *New and Collected Poems* by Roy Fuller (Secker & Warburg, 1985)

David Higham Associates: 'Is There No Love Can Link Us' by Mervyn Peake from R. Skelton, ed., *Poetry of the Forties* (Penguin 1968); and 'The English War' by Dorothy Sayers from T. Moult, ed., *The Best Poems of 1941* (Cape 1942)

Michael Imison Playwrights: *Peace In Our Time* by Noël Coward (Heinemann 1947)

Methuen & Co.: *The White Cliffs* by Alice Duer Miller (Methuen 1941)

Methuen London: 'Finland 1940' from *Poems 1913–1956* by Bertolt Brecht (Eyre Methuen 1976)

Oxford University Press: 'From an Unfinished Poem' from *The Fiction-Makers* by Anne Stevenson (OUP 1985)

Peters Fraser & Dunlop Group Ltd: 'England, 1941' by Edward Thompson from T. Moult, ed., *The Best Poems of 1941* (Cape 1942)

Sidgwick & Jackson: 'Youth in the Skies' by Herbert Asquith from T. Moult, ed., *The Best Poems of 1941* (Cape 1942)

Acknowledgements

Smith & Smith as literary representative of the Estate of Robert Nathan: 'Dunkirk' by Robert Nathan from T. Moult, ed., *The Best Poems of 1941* (Cape 1942)

Society of Authors as literary representative of the Estate of John Masefield: 'To the Seamen' from *The Nine Days Wonder* by John Masefield (Heinemann 1941)

Preface

This book, commissioned in the early eighties soon after the war for the Malvinas, presents ideas which I began to develop in 1976 in conversation with Cairns Craig, Reid Mitchell and others at the Scottish Universities Summer School. We were more in fashion than we thought. When, in 1980, I became involved with the Open University's new course on 'Popular Culture', I realised fully how 'post-structuralist' thinking by many people was focusing on the role of ideology in society and in history, and refusing to accept the 'innocence' of any narrative, any artefact.

There is little or nothing in this book which I could claim as original, except the perspective from which I have written it: that of a Scot, educated in England, who has lived through the collapse of Labourism, the rise of 'Thatcherism' and what Tom Nairn bluntly called, in his book of the mid-seventies, *The Break Up of Britain*.

I began around 1980 in reviews and articles and papers, well before this book was conceived, to write and talk about 'the Myth of 1940' and 'the Myth of the Blitz'. I did so in a spirit of self-criticism, since I realised that many, perhaps most, readers of my *People's War* (1969) had seen the book as confirming the Myth. Looking it over again, I saw that I had accepted almost without question the mythical version of 'Dunkirk', though elsewhere I flatter myself that I wasn't beguiled.

However, as this present book asserts, the word 'Myth' should not be taken to be equivalent to 'untruth', still less to 'lies'. Clive Ponting's *1940: Myth and Reality*, published as I was completing my work, while not without its uses for enquiring minds, commits this basic error (or so it seems to me). Ponting writes as if exposing scandalous untruths and cover-ups: in fact there is virtually nothing in his book which was not known by scholars, and all interested members of the public, in the sixties.

As I started writing this book, the same pitfall yawned under me. My anger, firstly over the sentimentalisation of 1940 by Labour apologists, then over the abuse of 'Churchillism' by Mrs Thatcher during the 'Falklands War', led me to seek, every which way, to undermine the credibility of the mythical narrative – for instance, by questioning British 'morale'. If I have steered away from the abyss, this is partly because I am reassured, in 1991, that the negative effects of the Myth on British societies have almost worked themselves out.

Most Scots have ceased to regard London as their capital – the question is whether Edinburgh or Glasgow more deserves the title. No inhabitant of Ulster, surely, can now believe that the Second World War had any healing effect on that society. The sacred mystery of the British Constitution is now being widely and very rudely questioned. The generation of Labourites for whom the war was unquestionably a 'People's War' has now passed out of active politics. And 'Thatcherism', never as dominant as so many commentators supposed, is certainly not very popular now. The younger generations of Brits increasingly see the future of their countries in terms of participation in Europe.

So I now regard the 'Myth of the Blitz' as a 'fact', from the past, which, like (say) the Myth of the English Gentleman can be discussed quite coolly. Both myths, indeed, are still ideologically active – not yet, volcanically speaking, extinct. Both are inscribed in a vast number of texts still current, and both condition a great deal of 'common-sense' thinking. But neither has anything like its old dominance.

I write this despite the outbreaks of 'anti-Kraut' rhetoric in England which, with the reunification of Germany looming, disfigured the summer of 1990. The first was prompted by England's appearance against West Germany in the football World Cup semi-final. The soaraway *Sun* newspaper predictably preluded this match with racialist invective: 'WE BEAT THEM IN '45 . . . NOW THE BATTLE OF '90'; 'HELP OUR BOYS CLOUT THE KRAUTS'. Its headline after England lost was 'KRAUT YOU GO!' Then came Nicholas Ridley's hardly more restrained anti-German remarks in an interview which cost him his job as a Cabinet minister, but apparently received quite wide public support. It seems to me that the underlying trend of opinion is better indicated by the *Sunday Sport* of 6 May that year.

The *Sport*, of course, simply invents its front-page stories. The one in question was hilarious: 'HITLER'S BONES FOUND ON BRIT BEACH', with an obviously faked photograph of a skeleton giving a Nazi salute on the sands at Brighton. Amongst the 'theories' advanced by 'experts' as to how it got there was this: 'Hitler's death was fabricated and he lived happily for many years among the gay community of Brighton and dropped dead during a stroll on the beach and was washed out to sea.' While Jews, homosexuals and others might find such levity offensive, the *Sport* is playing on the assumption that Hitler represents the depths of human evil, and is in no way reversing the judgement which the British made during 1939–45.

To identify the *Sport* with the *Sun* as an ideological agent would be quite false. In his regular column, Dave Sullivan ('Speaking on Behalf of the Nation'), who actually owns the *Sport*, attacked Mrs Thatcher and the *Sun*. The Conservatives had just lost heavily, overall, in the local government elections, but press attention had primarily focused on one result, in Wandsworth, where the generally hated new 'poll tax' had been set artificially low. Sullivan commented: '*Every* paper carried news of the borough on its front page . . . The *Sun* even turned that one victory into total annihilation claiming "KINNOCK POLL AXED".' He went back to 1940:

> *Entrenched* PM Margaret Thatcher showed true *Dunkirk Spirit* this week. Not by displaying bravery under fire. But by diverting the nation's attention on to one gun battle . . . while, comparatively unseen, the whole shooting match threatened to *blow* her head off. *The wartime propaganda victory came when military chiefs turned a massive defeat at Dunkirk into a 'miracle rescue' morale booster.*

Rather confusingly, Sullivan went on to praise a British middleweight boxer who had just won the world title for showing 'the *true* meaning of Dunkirk Spirit when he beat *all* the odds . . . ' However, as the accompanying photograph manifested, the boxer in question, Nigel Benn, was black: one could say that by incorporating a 'New British' personality with national tradition, Sullivan was striking a neat blow against racism.

To repeat, the Myth remains ideologically active. But Sullivan clearly credits its 'natural' quality, its definitive truth, no more than I do.

Though I spotted that issue of the *Sport* myself, I have, in my long journey towards a more relaxed view of the Myth, accumulated large intellectual debts, many of which I have no doubt forgotten: to people who tackled me, for instance, after I'd given papers at universities and arts centres. To mention just a few, far too selectively: working with Ian Potts and Jill Peck on their film *Stranger than Fiction*, about Mass-Observation, taught me, at last, something about how camera images work, and it was a pleasure to extend this knowledge by collaborating with Betty Talks on an Open University film centring on W. H. Auden and the GPO Film Unit's *Night Mail*. Reid Mitchell was instrumental, in the last phase of my labours, in getting me to Princeton, where I gave a paper with the same title as this book to the Mellon Seminar on Nationalism and had many rewarding conversations. Reid, by showing me Frank Capra's *Battle of Britain*, affected the final shape of the book: when I got back, I was able, thanks to Ann Fleming of the Imperial War Museum, to look at a shot list of that documentary.

I have particular debts to Tony Aldgate, to Susan Boyd Bowman, to Graham Dawson, to Alastair Thomson, to Jane Fisher and latterly to Nick Cull (without whose guidance I would have made little if any sense of the role of the US press corps in London) and to Mike Seaborne of the Museum of London. I have general debts to many people 'in and around' the magazine *Cencrastus*, set up by Edinburgh students after the Scottish devolution débâcle of 1979, and hope that this book is truly Cencrastoid, in the spirit of the Great Curly Snake of MacDiarmid's poem. My gratitude to Tony Colwell of Cape and to Alison Mansbridge, who edited the book, is not merely formal. Thanks also to Henry Cowper for reading the proofs.

I owe more than I can say to many, many conversations over a dozen years with Dorothy Sheridan of the Mass-Observation Archive, and over quarter of a century with Paul Addison. Neither they nor anyone else I've mentioned has any responsibility for the faults of this book: I hope these two won't mind if I dedicate whatever is worthwhile in it to them.

Finally, apologies to Kate (and Douglas) for all the hassle my writing has caused them . . .

Angus Calder
Edinburgh, 1986–91

I

Myth Making

In the event
the story is foretold,
foremade in the code of its happening.

In the event
the event is sacrificed
to a fiction of its having happened . . .

Anne Stevenson, 'From an Unfinished Poem'

THE 'BLITZ' of, on or over Britain in 1940 and 1941 was an unprecedented experience for the country's people. The subsequent development of nuclear bombs makes it very unlikely that such sustained bombardment could happen again. Though people in other countries – from Spain in the thirties through to Iraq in the nineties – have experienced long periods of aerial bombardment, these have been associated with civil war or accompanied or followed by defeat or invasion. The British have never seen their own 'Blitz' as one example of a widespread twentieth-century phenomenon, as they must, to some extent, have done if Nazi troops had marched into ruined city centres, or even made unsuccessful coastal landings.

Two events just preceding the Blitz have acquired a similar aura of absoluteness, uniqueness, definitiveness – the evacuation of British troops from 'Dunkirk', and the 'Battle of Britain' fought in the air by Fighter Command. They overlap with, are part of, the Myth of the Blitz. Like the Armada when 'God blew and they were scattered', the bloodless miracle of the Glorious Revolution, or the providential triumph of Trafalgar, these were events in which the hand of destiny was seen. As events flattering the dominant particularism within Britain, that of 'Britain' itself, often referred to as 'England', all these have a status denied to Bannockburn, or the Boyne, or Culloden,

I

which, whatever their auras, evoke contestation among the island's people. 'The Blitz' supports a myth of British or English moral pre-eminence, buttressed by British unity.

'Blitz' was named before it happened. Anticipating an attempt by Germany to bomb Britain out of the war, publicists had appropriated the word before 7 September 1940, the 'official' date for the start of the Blitz proper. It came from *Blitzkrieg*, 'lightning-war', applied by the world's press to the swift German conquest of Poland in September 1939,[1] and then to the rapid German advance in France and the Low Countries from 10 May 1940. As heavy bombing of London began in the late summer, the word 'Blitz' became 'almost overnight a British colloquialism for an air raid'.[2] But from the first it suggested more than that. It was instantaneously and spontaneously 'mythologised'.

I don't intend to provide much theoretical argumentation to justify my use of 'myth' and 'mythology' in this book. The word seems to me to impose itself because others don't work. The 'story' of the Blitz has been told many times; I once told it myself, and will summarise it again in my next chapter. Since this story points to events which indubitably happened, and which are pretty well documented, to refer to the 'fable' of the Blitz would be absurd. 'Legend' is nearer the mark – *Chambers Dictionary* tells us that it can refer to 'the body of fact and fiction' gathered around an heroic or saintly personage or, by extension, an heroic event. 'Myth' also suggests untruth, but on a grander scale altogether – according to *Chambers*, its primary meaning is 'an ancient traditional story of Gods or heroes, esp. one offering an explanation of some fact or phenomenon'. My case for applying the word to the Blitz is that the account of that event, or series of events, which was current by the end of the war has assumed a 'traditional' character, involves heroes, suggests the victory of a good God over satanic evil, and has been used to explain a fact: the defeat of Nazism. Furthermore, I can merge with this old definition some of the force of a new one.

Roland Barthes, in his immensely influential *Mythologies* (1957), approached 'myth' semiologically, as a factor in everyday modern life obtrusive everywhere, a 'type of speech'. Though I hope I have learnt something from Barthes and from those whom he has influenced, I don't intend to work with his theory, so to speak, at my elbow. It is, however, useful to me that many of us now understand 'myth' as a relevant term in the discussion of apparent trivialities, like car design or magazine covers, obviously auratic phenomena like the charisma of film stars and politicians, and the projection of events such as the Falklands crisis.

'Semiology', Barthes says, 'has taught us that myth has the task of giving an historical intention a natural justification, and making contingency appear eternal . . . The world enters language as a dialectical relation between activities, between human actions; it comes out of myth as a harmonious display of essences. A conjuring trick has taken place; it has turned reality inside out, it has emptied it of history and has filled it with nature.' If newcomers find these formulations bewildering, I hope this book will help them to sense the value of Barthes' further point:

Myth does not deny things, on the contrary, its function is to talk about them; simply, it purifies them, it makes them innocent, it gives them a natural and eternal justification, it gives them a clarity which is not that of an explanation but that of a statement of fact . . . In passing from history to nature, myth acts economically: it abolishes the complexity of human acts, it gives them the simplicity of essences, it does away with all dialectics, with any going back beyond what is immediately visible, it organises a world which is . . . without depth, a world wide open and wallowing in the evident, *it establishes a blissful clarity: things appear to mean something by themselves.*[3] (My italics)

For a relevant example of a mythological pseudo-explanation posing as a fact I will turn, not for the last time, to cricket, the most 'English' of games and perhaps the most 'mythological'. All followers of cricket are bound to remember the extraordinary series of Test Matches between England and Australia in 1981. Briefly: England began a home series of six encounters under the captaincy of Ian Botham, an all-rounder who had already accomplished feats with bat and ball which were apt for 'legendary' status, but who had latterly been in poor form. Australia won the First Test. The second was a dismal draw. Botham was sacked as captain, though not dropped from the side. The England selectors brought back Mike Brearley as captain. Though not a very successful Test batsman, Brearley had the record of never leading a losing England side at home. He was a brilliant graduate in philosophy with an acute tactical sense.

Even so, halfway through the Third Test at Leeds (Headingley) England were heading for a very heavy defeat, by an innings. At this point the mighty Botham, with help from tail-end batsmen, began to thrash the Australian bowling. This counter-attack took England to the point where the Australians had to bat again, though they needed to score only 129 runs to win. Unbelievably, they were dismissed for 111. Brearley's record remained intact. Botham's was now a fully fledged myth. In the next Test, it was in his role as bowler that he snatched for England another impossible win. In the fifth, he hammered another rapid century with the bat, England went 3–1 up in the series and regained the coveted 'Ashes'. That the Sixth Test was drawn rather tamely did not now matter.

Brearley, most literate of major cricketers, called his book about all this *Phoenix from the Ashes*. In summing up, he turned his thoughts to Hughes, the Australian captain:

> For Kim Hughes, 1981 must have been a desperately frustrating season. With just ordinary luck at Headingley, his team would have won comfortably. Probably there would have been no revival by England after that (though as a country we have specialised in doing badly at the beginning of wars and ending up victorious!).[4]

Cricket has been projected as a 'gentleman's' sport, and it behoves gentlemen to be modest. Brearley does not wish to suggest that he believes his own skill as captain could have 'saved' England. Yet he cannot quite bring himself to put it all down to 'luck'. He evokes a mythological 'fact' which provides an alternative 'natural' explanation. The push of this insinuation is not to assimilate sport with war (after all, the Australians are 'kith and kin' and allies), but war with sport. History is given what Barthes calls 'the simplicity of essences'. It is 'purified'.

Against Brearley's myth that the British begin wars badly, end well, could be set such 'facts' as England's lack of success in the war against Spain after the Armada, the Russian recovery in the Crimean War and the guerrilla successes of the Boers after their conventional forces had been defeated.[5] But as Barthes suggests, myth is invulnerable to mere facts. It 'essentially aims at causing an immediate impression – it does not matter if one is later allowed to see through the myth, its action is assumed to be stronger than the rational explanations which may later belie it'.[6] In this case the 'immediate impression' made by Brearley's statement of a mythological 'fact' of the kind which 'everyone knows' is reinforced by one 'memory' in particular, that of Dunkirk.

The implications of the Dunkirk Myth can be clarified by contrasting it with a superficially similar one. Australians, like the British (whom they tend to dismiss as 'whingeing Poms'), have mythologised a notable defeat: Gallipoli, 1915. In April of that year ANZAC (Australian and New Zealand) forces were landed in the Dardanelles as part of an attempt to open up the Bosphorus and the Black Sea. Australians established a bridgehead at an unsuitable landing place under withering Turkish fire. For months they tussled unavailingly with brave Turks, gaining insignificant ground, until the directors of the war in London decided that the Gallipoli venture had failed, and allied troops were evacuated (December 1915) 'in such an exemplary fashion', one historian tells us, 'that Sir Ian Hamilton's last order of the day reads as though it were in celebration of a victory'.[7]

Australians provided a quarter of the casualties at Gallipoli − 8,587 killed and 19,367 wounded. Their courage won applause from British observers − the novelist Compton Mackenzie, mindful of the classical associations of the area where they fought, wrote that there was 'not one of these glorious young men' who 'might not himself have been Ajax . . . Hector or Achilles'. He admired 'their tallness and majestic simplicity of line'.[8] The world began to realise at this time that Australians had a distinctive ethos, seen not only in Turkey but on the Western Front. Their soldiers were all volunteers, and fought 'without threat of firing squads if they chanced to disobey':

Anzac troops were contemptuous of the narrow discipline to which British troops subscribed and were led by officers who had first shown their qualities as privates in the ranks. Social distinctions between officers and men, so characteristic of the British army, were therefore less pronounced; Australian-born soldiers could not, for instance, be induced to serve as officers' servants . . .[9]

Their combination of fierce courage with disrespect for authority made a strong impression in England. An Anglican parson in Essex, Andrew Clark, noted in his diary in 1917 the remarks of a chaplain back from the Front: 'The Australian troops are splendid fellows, but very independent. They will not take any order which they think unreasonable, from any officer, whatever his rank.' There follows an anecdote, told 'good-humouredly' by a British general who had come upon a party of Australians sleeping and smoking after a march, had ordered them to fall in so that he could inspect them, received no response, repeated his order, was answered by one man 'Fall in yourself, and be damned', saw he'd made a fool of himself, and rode off.[10]

This third-hand tale, whether based on 'fact' or not, is clearly 'mythological'. A myth of Australian identity was being formed out of Australians' perception of themselves in a new, foreign context, British reactions to these 'colonials', and Australian reactions to British reactions. The same parson–diarist, about the same time, reported friction in a local military hospital between an elderly British volunteer nurse and an Australian Sister: 'The other day Miss L.V. pointed her out to a lady visitor and said, loud enough to be heard, "That is the Australian Sister." The lady stared at her somewhat rudely; walked off a few steps; and turned round and stared again. "Gracious me!" said the Sister to a bystander. "Does the woman expect me to hop like a kangaroo?"'[11]

However, the Gallipoli myth of Australian identity projected that quasi-fact, that piece of 'nature', in male terms. It built on the foundations of an earlier mythology of 'mateship'. Russel Ward, the historian, in his influential account of *The Australian Legend* (1958), suggested that it was from images of the outback life of the frontiersman that the presentday stereotype of the Australian derived. He was practical, rough and ready, hated affectation, was always swearing, loved gambling and drinking, was sceptical about the value of religion and of intellectual and cultural pursuits generally; was a 'great "knocker" of eminent people', was fiercely independent, hated policemen and military officers, but was very hospitable and would stick to his mates through thick and thin.[12] Despite the subsequent advance of 'women's liberation', not least in Australia, there is evidence that this macho male myth of national identity is still strong. The burgeoning Australian feature-film industry favours outback locations over the city suburbs in which the vast majority of Australians actually live, and has arguably flaunted macho values in images of the 'Battling White Aussie'.[13] In this case, Peter Weir's film *Gallipoli* (1981) is not a throwback, with its elegiac evocation of two strong, handsome young 'mates' who fight and die in the Dardanelles, but a symptomatic instance of a still–dominant mythology.

The myth of Gallipoli turns *defeat* into *discovery*. C. E. W. Bean, later the official Australian historian of the Great War, wrote in 1915, in the soldiers' *Anzac Book*:

> We only know from good and great
> Nothing save good can flow.
> That where the cedar crashed so straight
> No crooked tree shall grow.

In 1919, Bean proposed that 'the big thing in the war for Australia was the discovery of the character of Australian man. It was character which rushed the hills at Gallipoli and held on there during the long afternoon and night, when everything seemed to have gone wrong and there was only the barest hope of success.' And in 1945, after Australians had again fought bravely, Bean exclaimed that 'The "Anzac spirit" of brotherhood and initiative as shown by our fighting forces and Legacy Clubs is the kind of force to move the world.' As Alastair Thomson (to whom I owe these quotations) comments, in the Anzac–Gallipoli mythology, 'Images of the past are fused with a vision of the future; the individual becomes one with the nation.'[14]

'Gallipoli' as myth represents the *discovery* of a new national identity. It arrives without precedent (Australian forces had never been so committed in large-scale warfare before) and at once attracts to itself the 'mateship' mythology evolved over a bare century and a quarter since the arrival of the first convict settlers in New South Wales. It renders war 'innocent', and 'naturalises' as quintessentially Australian qualities seen at their sharpest (supposedly) in wartime adversity. The Dardanelles defeat was not Australia's — it was suffered by the British Empire, as a result of a strategy decided by the British government. Britons, not Australians, bungled. Hence the Gallipoli myth also crystallises Australian resentment against British condescension towards colonials, and Australians' sense of difference from Britons. It is also intrinsically expansionist: the Gallipoli heroes far from home show the world what Australians are made of, and represent, as Bean put it, 'the kind of force to move the world'.

'Dunkirk', by contrast, involves not *discovery* but *rediscovery*, or *confirmation*. It is not, as 'Armada' and 'Glorious Revolution' once were, a myth for a rising nation. It is a myth for people 'living in an old country', to adapt the title of Patrick Wright's recent book (1985). It does not shrug off defeat, like 'Gallipoli'; it accepts it and sublimates it, adapting old mythology. 'As a country we have specialised in doing badly at the beginning of wars and ending up victorious' is Mike Brearley's revival of a myth already to hand in 1940.

In Arthur Bryant's *Years of Victory*, a narrative, published in 1944, of the war against France from 1802 to 1812, that Tory historian mused over 'England [sic] Alone' in the year 1806: 'It was always the way of England to measure adversity with resolution, and there was no weakening of her purpose.' Without drawing parallels with 1940 — without need to — Bryant noted how 'the Kentish ports', in 1809, 'were filled with militiamen bearing pale-faced ghosts from the transports to hastily improvised reception centres', after the failure of a British expeditionary force in the Low

Countries. 'Twice in eight months had a British army come home in such a plight. It was enough, as a sea captain said, to make John Bull shake his head . . .' And in Iberia, Wellesley retreated after Talavera: 'For even the battle which, in their exultation at their soldiers' courage, the people of England [sic] had hailed as the successor of Agincourt and Cressy had proved Pyrrhic and fruitless.' But Wellesley, the 'Fabian General', remained 'in his calculating, undemonstrative way . . . at heart an optimist. He saw the inherent flimsiness of Napoleon's dominion: its foundations were not sound in time.' Wellesley, now Wellington, wrote in March 1810 that the position in Iberia had 'always appeared to be lost . . . The contest however still continues.'[15]

Other traditions of an 'old country' could be melded with 'Dunkirk'. From the revolutionary Left, Tom Wintringham wrote, just after the evacuation, in July 1940, *New Ways of War*, designed to instruct British civilians on techniques for fighting Nazi invaders. Wintringham had commanded the British Battalion in the International Brigades in Spain during the civil war. He saw Dunkirk as exemplary, when, in his tract, a 'Penguin Special', he suggested a form of 'agreement' to be affirmed by all:

As soldiers, or as civilians who from now on count themselves soldiers, we shall give in the common disciplined effort all our initiative and abilities, including our ability to hang on as our soldiers hung on at Calais and Dunkirk. We will stick by whatever we find to do or are told to do in spite of invasion, bombardment, wounds, hunger or whatever may be the price of victory.

He evoked the spirit of seventeenth-century English revolutionaries:

In this country freedom, made real in new forms, is still as powerful and as heartening as it was in the days when Milton wrote that liberty 'hath enfranchis'd, enlarg'd and lifted up our apprehensions degrees above themselves' . . . Men of the past made our nation by conquering tyranny; like them we shall conquer.[16]

'Gallipoli' signifies novelty, expansion, history-to-be-made. 'Dunkirk', even with left-wing inflexions, signifies reiteration, retrenchment, history-as-made. Barthes argues as if 'mythology' were essentially right-wing, identical in its processes with 'bourgeois ideology'. This is very debatable. But this book will suggest that left-wing interventions in the myth-making process from 1940 through 1941 and onwards contributed to a right wing, or at least 'conservative', effect. While talking like Wintringham about 'new ways of war' and new freedoms, left-wingers ineluctably drew on the existing mythologies of 'an old country'.

Patrick Wright's *On Living in an Old Country* considers 'everyday life, nostalgia and the national past' in contemporary Britain, and discussion of his views may help to clarify my point that 'myth' entails more than 'untrue stories, legends'.

While historiography, quasi-scientific, is a valuable pursuit, and its quest for true or truer 'facts' is amply justified, it arises from 'everyday historical consciousness'. Historians, after all, live in 'everyday life'. (I first heard about the Blitz from my father, who 'was there'. This book is one consequence of his stories.) Everyday life is full of stories. These are concerned with 'being-in-the world' rather than with abstractly defined truth. Such stories have to be plausible, but their 'authenticity', which is a vital ingredient, does not depend on true knowledge. When authenticity collides with 'factual' truth, people in everyday life, even historians trying to work outside it, will often stubbornly resist the latter. (I return to my cricketing example. The mythological power of Mike Brearley's evocation of history would survive any amount of detailed citation of examples standing against his generalisation.)

Historical consciousness has more pressing motivations than scientific accuracy. A Scot can live as a Scot without thinking about, let alone knowing in detail, the calculations which led Robert Bruce to seize the throne, and their legal, social, economic, diplomatic and other contexts; but every Scot chanting at a football match knows that 'Bruce beat the English at Bannockburn'. Historical consciousness, involved with 'stories', helps us to bring our world into order, to 'make sense'. In a homogeneous and static society — say, that of hunter-gatherers in a favourable environment well away from competing groups — people would accept reality ready-made; it would make sense quasi-naturally. But such equilibrium must have been rare over the roughly 10,000 years since agriculture and warfare were invented, and industrialisation and modernisation over the last 200 have made stasis seem abnormal and even 'unnatural', ('I don't see the tide of economic history reversing itself,' one of Mrs Thatcher's ministers announced in February 1986. Since the eighteenth century, Western man has commonly assimilated change not only with 'progress' – which shouldn't be 'reversed' – but with nature: the tide of the sea; although, of course, the tide does 'reverse', change, in either direction, is inevitable.) As Wright puts it: 'The everyday "sense of historical existence" becomes progressively anxious, searching more intently for answers which – in the dislocated experience of modernity – seem to be less and less readily forthcoming.'[17] What Wright calls 'particularisms' – 'us' as opposed to 'them' – confront the 'destabilising demands of social transformation'. The 'sense of national identity and belonging' projected in Britain during the Second World War may or may not be defined in Wright's phrase as 'bourgeois-imperial' (there are objections against so defining it, of a 'commonsense' kind), but clearly Churchill spoke for a 'dominant particularism' lording over the particularisms of marginal groups like Welsh-speakers and subordinated ones like coal-miners. And he spoke through the myths of a particular historical consciousness.

'Everyday life' has been increasingly devalued as the ongoing 'history' of wars and recessions has come to seem something outside it, threatening it. Science, an abstract and universal form of knowledge standing outside 'everyday' life-worlds, has ousted religion. Work and other routines, since urbanisation and industrialisation, commonly have no connection with a person's individuality and seem dictated from outside. In peacetime conditions, nostalgia results, as the rationalised and specialised experience of life every day creates a 'subjective surplus' – there is 'more in' people than can find realisation – and this surplus attaches itself to objects and places and sites which seem to bear meaning in themselves: to 'heritage', to 'history'. But war provides another outlet for that surplus, a counterpoint to 'the routinised, constrained and empty experience of much modern everyday life'. In war, as Wright puts it, 'personal actions can count in a different way, routine can have a greater sense of meaning and necessity . . .'[18]

The 'nation' integrates public images and interpretations of the past. It works by 'raising a dislocated and threatened – but none the less locally experienced – everyday life up into redeeming contact with what it vaunts as its own Absolute Spirit'.[19] This spirit, as Wright's examples show, digests History (particular history) with Nature: not only with particular human nature, but with particular landscape. War, like exile ('Oh, to be in England, Now that April's there'), sharpens within everyday historical consciousness a sense of Absolute National Spirit. Wright quotes a broadcast made on Easter Day 1943 by Peter Scott – son of the famous Antarctic explorer and imperial hero, himself a naturalist and painter of wild-life:

Friday was St George's Day, St George for England. I suppose that 'England' means something slightly different to each of us. You may, for example, think of the white cliffs of Dover, or you may think of a game of bowls on Plymouth Hoe, or perhaps a game of cricket at Old Trafford or a game of rugger at Twickenham. But probably for most of us it brings a picture of a certain kind of countryside, the English countryside. If you spend much time at sea, that particular combination of fields and hedges and woods that is so essentially England seems to have a new meaning.

I remember feeling most especially strongly about it in the late Summer of 1940 when I was serving in a destroyer doing anti-invasion patrol in the Channel. About that time I think everyone had a rather special feeling about the word 'England'. I remember as dawn broke looking at the black outlines of Star Point to the northward and thinking suddenly of England in quite a new way – a threatened England that was in some way more real and more friendly because she was in trouble. I thought of the Devon countryside lying behind that black outline of the cliffs; the wild moors and ragged tors inland and nearer the sea, the narrow winding valleys with their steep green sides; and I thought of the mallards and teal which were rearing their ducklings in the reed beds of Slapton Leigh. That was the countryside we were so passionately determined to protect from the invader.[20]

A naturalist assimilates a mythological 'England' with a mythological 'Nature', in a way that his audience will find perfectly 'natural'. Every sentence of this easy-seeming pronouncement, as I will show, is laden with the mythology of an 'Old Country'; and with a mythology which presupposes and enforces a middle-class view of the world. What is natural to England belongs, literally and figuratively, to the better-off classes.

'St George for England' evokes Shakespeare's *Henry V*, which Olivier was directing (the film was actually shot in Eire) around the time when Scott spoke: St George's Day is the presumed birthday of Shakespeare. England 'means something slightly different to each of us' because 'England' signifies tolerance of individual opinions within an overriding community of feeling. Geordie coal-miners or Hull fishermen, whose views of England might well be more than 'slightly' different, can count themselves part of this England only if they choose to invest in it 'subjective surplus' from their alien everyday experience. Perhaps many such men, or at least their wives, did: 'The White Cliffs of Dover' was the tune most in request from British cinema organists throughout the war. Of course, anyone who had learnt history at any school was likely to remember that Francis Drake chose to finish his 'game of bowls on Plymouth Hoe' when news came that the Armada was sailing towards England, then sallied forth to defeat it. (This is a perfect example of how myth insists on itself against fact. The image was and is quite indelible, though J. A. Williamson himself, the prime scholarly panegyrist of the Elizabethan 'sea dogs', had written in his *Age of Drake*, published in 1938, that while the game of bowls might have been fact – it was first referred to in 1624, when survivors of the event were still living – Drake's famous retort, 'Time to finish the game', looked 'like a myth, for Drake was hardly the man to suggest waste of time at a juncture when disaster might conceivably be averted by minutes'.[21])

I am certain that Scott mentions 'cricket at Old Trafford' (Manchester) rather than at Lord's because he wants to reach out to northern listeners – he doesn't want his England to be merely southern, he wants to suggest that a northern industrial town can also be part of it. I am equally certain that he refers to this ground rather than Bramall Lane (Sheffield) or Headingley (Leeds) because so many middle-class readers admired the writings of Neville Cardus, the *Manchester Guardian* cricket correspondent, for whom Old Trafford was sacred 'home' turf. Cardus had brilliantly accommodated expert sports reporting with the conventions of the 'Georgian' literary essay, and inevitably it had been he who had contributed the volume on cricket to the 'English Heritage' series of books published around 1930.

However, Scott cannot bring himself to refer to 'football at Wembley', let alone 'Rugby League at Wigan'; Twickenham is the arena where England plays international rugby football against Scotland and Wales, and where the annual match between Oxford and Cambridge Universities takes place. Amateur 'Rugby Union' in England was and is a primarily middle-class sport, favoured over soccer in the so-called 'public schools'. 'England' was to do with young Apollos and Hectors from the moneyed classes knocking each other about in a violent, occasionally graceful game, not with northern professionals, paid artisans' wages, playing soccer or professional 'Rugby League' skilfully in front of huge working-class crowds.

The 'English countryside' is a powerful myth although, or because, it can only be evoked vaguely. Scott refers to a 'particular combination' of natural and man-made features which is 'essentially England'. This cannot be northern English land, with dry-stone walls. But what *is* 'essentially England'? The flat Lincolnshire of Tennyson's *In Memoriam*? The more variegated Wessex of Hardy's novels and poems? (When Roman Polanski filmed Hardy's *Tess* quite recently, he found his 'English' landscape in Normandy: I have heard no English watcher of the film remark on this, let alone complain.) Could this 'essential England' be the Marcher orchard-lands of Herefordshire? The wooded Chilterns? There have been, of course, many 'combinations' in England, from the days of feudal strip farming to contemporary 'agri-business'. To quote W. G. Hoskins, master historian of the English landscape, introducing his pioneering study published in 1955:

> No book exists to describe the manner in which the various landscapes of this country came to assume the shape and appearance they now have. Why the hedge-banks and lanes of Devon should be so totally different from those of the Midlands, why there are so many ruined churches in Norfolk or so many lost villages in Lincolnshire, or what history lies behind the winding ditches of the Somerset marshlands, the remote granite farmsteads of Cornwall and the lonely pastures of upland Northampton-shire.[22]

But it is convenient, mythologically, for Scott to evoke the special landscape of Devon. His context in this broadcast has become maritime. Devon was the home of the great 'sea dogs', Drake and Hawkins, Raleigh and Gilbert, who harried the Armada, 'singed the King of Spain's beard', and so forth, in the days of Good Queen Bess (and Shakespeare). It also, as Scott himself knows, provides a home for ducks. Why these ducks, mallards and teal nesting in Devon should be essentially English when their species are found elsewhere in Europe, is a question which myth forbids us to ask. It is quite certain that many English people thought of the local bird-life as especially English, essentially theirs. In the summer of 1940, some 300 bird-lovers maintained a day and night guard not against Nazi invasion, but over the nesting places of a rare bird, the kite. Late in the war, Bernard Miles directed a film comedy called *Tawny Pipit*. Two rare migrant birds appear in an English village. Lest they should be disturbed, military manoeuvres in the neighbourhood are held up. The entire local population conspire to keep off inquisitive ornithologists, by fair means or foul. Mythologically, 'Deep England' could assimilate migrants, just as German classical music was presented virtually as 'English Heritage' during the dark days of war against Germany.

Myth may distort what has happened. But it affects what happens. The 'story' of the Blitz and individuals' own personal 'Blitz stories' were mythologised within 'everyday life' in terms of existing mythologies. It was necessary and inevitable that this should be done. War created conditions in which people could invest the 'subjective surplus' – which in peacetime had found outlets in the arts, in country walks, in nostalgia for 'history' – in an 'everyday life' now suffused with 'history'. Believing that they were 'making history' in harmony with the Absolute Spirit of 'England' (or 'Britain'), people tried to believe as that spirit seemed to dictate. Heroic mythology fused with everyday life to produce heroism. People 'made sense' of the frightening and chaotic actualities of wartime life in terms of heroic mythology, 'selecting out' phenomena which were incompatible with that mythology. But, acting in accordance with this mythology, many people – not all, of course – helped make it 'more true'.

Such a process had worked itself out in other times and places. Myths had been simultaneously generated and reinforced by the realisation (as it were) in action of a synthesis of existing mythologies. We can see this happening in the Thirteen Colonies from the 1760s through to the War of Independence. As Charles Royster has explained things, 'the country's first war both shaped and tested Americans' ideals of national character'. These ideals drew on existing mythologies; on traditions of colonies founded by men who had left Europe to preserve self-government and liberty of conscience; on the cult of the republican heroes of Ancient Greece and Rome; on the 'mental habits customary in evangelical religion', as inculcated by the 'Great Awakening' within the last couple of generations; and on ideals of benevolence and disinterestedness emphasised by evangelical Christianity. 'Everyday life' consciousness was suffused with a sense of history as present and future: the future of the world and of North America depended on resistance to tyranny now:

A song copied into the orderly book of the Second New York Regiment proclaimed, 'The riseing world shall sing of us a thousand years to Come/And tell our Childrens Children the Wonders we have Done.' During the war, when officers started to resign, General Robert Howe reminded them that they were 'actors upon that glorious stage where every incident is to become an historical fact'.[23]

Compare Churchill in June 1940: 'Let us therefore brace ourselves to our duties and so bear ourselves that, if the British Empire and its

Commonwealth last for a thousand years, men will still say, "This was their finest hour." '[24]

But the 'if' was significant. The Thirteen Colonies belonged with a 'riseing world'. Britain in 1940 was an Old Country. The 'subjective surplus' expanded during war went into defending an imperial power which was already in irreversible decline, and national institutions which had tottered into anachronism. The war, and the mythical events of 1940, would become subjects for historical nostalgia on the Left as well as on the Right — perhaps more than on the Right — but the effect of the Myth would be conservative. For the Left it would encapsulate a moment of retrenchment as a moment of rebirth; a moment of ideological conservatism as a moment of revolution. Because Blitz was held to have had near revolutionary consequences, to have somehow produced a 'welfare state', the Myth would divert attention from the continuing need for radical change in British society. The Left would think that in 1940 it had captured History. In fact, it had been captured by it.

'I gotta use words when I talk to you.' We all share the predicament of Apeneck Sweeney. To say that the British Left was trapped and conquered by a myth which it had helped to create is to suggest that it succumbed to the language which it had to use. If we need 'stories' to make sense of our world, then we need words to tell stories — though we also need pictures, from another language of signs, and music also can help.

John Keegan, in his *Face of Battle* (1976), showed us how our understanding of war had been confused by the rhetoric of military historians trying to ride over the piecemeal and often chaotic nature of actual conflict. He also demonstrated how hard it is to come by 'the truth' of the experience of British troops on the first day of the Battle of the Somme, in 1916: 'Even sixty years later, it is very difficult to discover much that is precise, detailed and human about the fate of a great number of the battalions of the Fourth Army on July 1st.' In a phase of intense action, officers wrote up their Units' War Diaries, usually sketchy in any case, days in arrears. Men at the Front could get no overall picture of events, and found it hard to interpret what was going on around them. Officers behind lost telephone contact with the action once men advanced into no-man's-land and high command 'spent most of July 1st in ignorance of how the Fourth Army was faring'. So turning 'what happened' into a 'story' useful to the men who fought, to the relatives of those who died, and to the British at large, was very difficult. Keegan argues that it was the prose writings of poets — Blunden, Graves, Sassoon —

published in 1928–30 which invested 'the experience of the Somme with the importance it still continues to hold', and further suggests that 'from the story of the Somme' the public had 'learnt as much as it ever would about what modern war could do to men, and perceived that some limit of what humans could and could not stand on the battlefield had at last been reached'.[25]

The Great War of 1914–18 could not be mythologised so as to help maintain among Britons enthusiasm for armed conflict or faith in the future of their Empire. It threw up only one individual hero of mythological significance (except, indeed, for certain dead soldier–poets) – and 'Lawrence of Arabia' was an odd, complicated case. After his brave and inventive role in the desert campaign against the Turks, he hid from his own celebrity, changed his name, and joined the RAF as a mere aircraftsman, refusing public honours and appointments. As intellectual, homosexual, and flawed man of action, he fascinated the left-inclined literati of the 'thirties movement' as one who, in Christopher Isherwood's words, had 'suffered, in his own person, the neurotic ills of an entire generation'.[26]

Paul Fussell's *The Great War and Modern Memory* (1975) examines the crisis of language at the Front of 1914–18. 'The problem for the writer trying to describe elements of the Great War was its utter incredibility and thus its incommunicability on its own terms.' It was not that words literally didn't exist – as Fussell points out, the English language 'is rich in terms like *blood, terror, agony, madness, shit*' – but prevalent modes of rhetoric could not deploy such words so as to convey to non-soldiers what was going on. The 'hearty idiom' of imperialistic boys' adventure stories was ludicrously inapposite. The canonical English 'literature' in which many men of all ranks were steeped was more help – richly figurative language from past writers, evoking despair, horror and mortality, could be reproduced as literal:

Finding the War 'indescribable' in any but the available language of traditional literature, those who recalled it had to do so in known literary terms. Joyce, Eliot, Lawrence, Pound, Yeats were not present at the front to induct them into new idioms which might have done the job better. Inhibited by scruples of decency and believing in the historical continuity of styles, writers about the war had to appeal to the sympathy of readers by invoking the familiar and suggesting its resemblance to what many of them suspected was an unprecedented and (in their terms) an all–but–incommunicable reality.

Fussell quotes Alexander Aitken, writing of the scene at the Somme in September 1916: 'The road here and the ground to either side were strewn with bodies, some motionless, some not. Cries and groans, prayers, imprecations, reached me. I leave it to the sensitive imagination. I once wrote it all down, only to discover that horror, truthfully described, weakens to the merely clinical.' The war proceeded in an 'atmosphere of euphemism', used by the authorities to mask the truth, and by the troops to 'soften the truth for themselves'. In an official communiqué, 'brisk fighting' meant that about 50 per cent of a company had been killed or wounded in a raid. Even a tough-minded Tommy would write that a man had been 'hit low down' rather than say 'wounded in the genitals'.[27]

But one effect of the general failure of language was the perverse triumph represented by trench humour. Horror was rendered into 'half affectionate familiarity', as in the trench song about the slaughtered battalion 'hanging on *the old* barbed wire'. What Fussell calls 'the style of British phlegm' involved speaking about war conditions as if they were normal. Horror became 'unpleasant' or 'damned unpleasant'. Flooded trenches had 'a certain dampness'. Letters home by other ranks were characterised by 'almost unvarying formulaic understatement':

Dear Mum and Dad, and dear loving sisters Rosie, Letty, and our Gladys –
I am very pleased to write you another welcome letter as this leaves me.
Dear Mum and Dad and loving sisters, I hope you keeps the home fires burning. Not arf. The boys are in the pink. Not arf. Dear Loving sisters Rosie, Letty and our Gladys, keep merry and bright. Not arf.[28]

As Fussell observes, the language of the Great War – its neologisms, its jargon, its euphemisms and understatements – persisted afterwards, so that 'one result . . . is that the contours of the Second War tend to merge with those of the First'. He quotes a young diarist of 1940 who wrote of going 'up the line' when he returned to London after the weekend: London during the Blitz was the Front Line.[29] But in the mythologising of 1940, the legacy of trench humour – of understatement, joking about the indescribable – was more important than any merely lexical continuity. 'British Phlegm' had its 'Finest Hour' in the Blitz, not only because instances of it made useful propaganda for home and foreign consumption, but also because it had the same kind of use for civilians under bombing as for soldiers under fire: one had to 'keep merry and bright'.

If 'literature' had found no great individual heroes on the Western Front, it had found ways of making a whole class of persons heroic. The image of the phlegmatic, joking Tommy forms part of a spectrum, in which, at the other extreme, 'each soldier becomes a type of the crucified Christ', as when Wilfred Owen described his work as an officer training new troops as 'teaching Christ to lift his cross by numbers'.[30] The Great War thus established precedents useful for those in 1940 who wished to mythologise the entire British people as heroic, and even for individuals trying to reconcile the devastation of their home cities with the mythological needs of ongoing everyday life. In this war, from Dunkirk through to the end of Blitz, horror could not be concealed from the home public. But, except in some parts of London and briefly in a few other places, Blitz was an experience far less extreme than that of soldiers on the Somme, and to 'make sense' of it, to turn it into 'story', was superficially much less difficult. The language of pre-existing mythologies, including the Myth of the Tommy at the Front, adapted itself to events with remarkable 'naturalness' and fluency, and stories were generated with such success that we, born since, have ignored how frightening and confusing the period from April 1940 through to June 1941 was for the British people. Perhaps we simply cannot comprehend that fear and confusion imaginatively. Myth stands in our way, asserting itself, abiding no questions.

In 1976 Miss Vere Hodgson published the diaries she had kept from 25 June 1940 to 16 May 1945. In her foreword, she remarks that 'The events of those years seem like a forgotten nightmare . . .' She was a welfare worker in a Christian 'Sanctuary' in Holland Park, London, and she wrote her diary at her office desk in the evenings when she was on fire watch. She found the nightly air raids intensely distressing. 'Pretty bad' (18 September); 'Very bad night' (19 September); 'An awful night' (24 September); 'the foulest night so far' (25 September); 'Worst night on record!' (26 September). She was not heroic, and didn't profess to be but by 21 December 1940 she was a front-line fighter adept in 'Tommy' understatement: 'Rather a blitzy night now. Something nasty seemed to come down. A new sort of noise.' On 23 December she listened to one of Churchill's broadcast speeches, addressed to the Italian people:

> in the dramatic style that suits him, alluding to Garibaldi, Mazzini and Cavour — and all we did for them. He alluded to Mussolini . . . It was a thrilling speech and made me think our Prime

Minister is really the greatest man we have ever produced in all our long history – except perhaps for Alfred the Great. We have never been so near defeat as we were in June, nor so near invasion on our actual soil. It was just touch and go – and he saved us. A statue in gold would not be too much for what we owe him.[31]

2

'Finest Hours'

This is the year which people will talk about
This is the year which people will be silent about
Bertolt Brecht, 'Finland 1940'

FOR MISS HODGSON, the story of 1940 had become simple. The British had been nearer defeat and invasion than ever before. But Churchill had saved them. Let us hear the story as she might have recognised it.

Britain had declared war on Germany on 3 September 1939 because Hitler had invaded Poland and refused to stop. He had gone too far for Neville Chamberlain, the British Prime Minister, who had striven to 'appease' him. Chamberlain told the House of Commons, 'This is a sad day for all of us, but to none is it sadder than to me. Everything that I have worked for, everything that I have hoped for, everything that I have believed in during my public life, has crashed into ruins.' This gloom was not shared by Winston Churchill, excluded from office for years because his imperialism and warlike disposition were more than the Conservative Party leadership could stomach, but now brought into the government as First Lord of the Admiralty. When he followed Chamberlain to the dispatch box, he hammered out his sentences, according to the *New York Times* correspondent, so that they sounded 'like the barks of a field-gun'. He agreed with Chamberlain that it was a sad day, but spoke of 'the feeling of thankfulness that if these great trials were to come upon our island there is a generation of Britons here now ready to prove itself, not unworthy of the days of yore and not unworthy of those great men, the fathers of our land, who laid the foundations of our laws and shaped the greatness of our country.'[1]

But Chamberlain proceeded as if reluctant to fight at all. Realistically, nothing could be done to help Poland. Britain had to defend its own shipping against German attack. The RAF soon went into action, bombing German ships at the entrance to the Kiel Canal, and suffering casualties. But further 'raids' over mainland Germany were described by the RAF as 'for the purpose of distributing a note to the German people'. Leaflets were dropped, not bombs. Chamberlain declared that the British forswore attacks not only on German civilians, but even on military (as opposed to naval) targets.[2]

British troops were soon in France. Most people expected – and feared – a repetition of the siege warfare of 1914–18. But after the German 'Blitzkrieg' had knocked out Polish resistance in a few weeks, 'sitskrieg' characterised the Western Front. Though Chamberlain rejected peace terms offered by Hitler in October as repugnant to British honour, Britain and France seemed uninterested in making a serious move to defeat Hitler. Only at sea were there real battles – and here Churchill was in charge. In mid-December three British cruisers fought the German pocket-battleship *Graf Spee* in the South Atlantic and forced it to limp into neutral Montevideo. It emerged only to be scuttled. At last Britain had a victory to celebrate. Churchill modestly attributed 'the present satisfactory position in the naval war' to the First Sea Lord, Admiral of the Fleet Sir Dudley Pound:[3] but the public associated it with Churchill. His speech in the Free Trade Hall, Manchester, on 27 January 1940, managed to invent inspiration from five months of 'Bore War' or 'Phoney War':

I know of nothing more remarkable in our long history than the willingness to encounter the unknown, and to face and endure whatever might be coming to us, which was shown in September by the whole mass of the people of this island in the discharge of what they felt sure was their duty . . . The Prime Minister led us forward in one great body into a struggle against aggression and oppression, against wrong-doing, faithlessness and cruelty, from which there can be no turning back . . . So far the war in the West has fallen almost solely upon the Royal Navy, and upon those parts of the Royal Air Force who give the Navy invaluable help. But I think you will agree that up to date the Navy has not failed the nation.

He went on to defend the policy of dropping leaflets, not bombs, on Germany, and to rejoice that the absence of massive war on land had given Britain a 'time of preparation' to strengthen its defences and train its armies. He pointed out that a huge expansion of the labour force was required to make munitions. 'Here we must specially count for aid and guidance upon our Labour colleagues and Trade

Union leaders.' More than a million women would be needed in war industry, but Churchill promised male trade unionists that any 'dilution' of specialised crafts would be temporary – current practices would be fully restored after the war was won. Rousing his audience with references to the brutal treatment by the Nazi conquerors of Czechs and Poles, he concluded:

> Come then: let us to the task, to the battle, to the toil – each to our part, each to our station. Fill the armies, rule the air, pour out the munitions, strangle the U-boats, sweep the mines, plough the land, build the ships, guard the streets, succour the wounded, uplift the downcast, and honour the brave. Let us go forward together in all parts of the Empire, in all parts of the Island. There is not a week, nor a day, nor an hour to lose.

Though 'sitskrieg' continued, Churchill never ceased to be belligerent. In a broadcast on 30 March, he warned that more than 1 million German soldiers were drawn up ready to attack Holland, Belgium and Luxembourg, and that 'at any moment' these neutral countries might be 'subjected to an avalanche of steel and fire'.[4]

Chamberlain was more sanguine on 4 April, when he told the Central Council of the National Union of Conservative and Unionist Associations that the Germans had had their chance in December when they had been better prepared than the Allies. Now Hitler had 'missed the bus'.

But on 9 April the Germans overran Denmark without a struggle and landed sea and airborne forces in Norway. Very soon all the chief Norwegian towns were in German hands. The Norwegian army still held much of the country, and in the third week of April British troops joined them. There was hard fighting in difficult terrain – RAF Fighter Command Squadron 263 flew obsolescent Gladiator biplanes from an improvised base on a frozen lake. But by 3 May it had been necessary to evacuate all British troops south of Trondheim – southern and central Norway were lost. A recent historian of the RAF confirms the impression current in 1940 that 'From the beginning to end the Allied operations in Norway . . . display an amateurishness and feebleness which to this day can make the reader alternately blush and shiver.'[5]

While British forces continued to fight in northern Norway, aiming to control the remote port of Narvik (the final evacuation of nearly 25,000 allied officers and men did not take place till early June), public opinion in Britain was dismayed. An all-party group of MPs, convinced that Chamberlain must go, decided on a trial of strength in the Commons in the debate on the Whitsun adjournment. On the face of it, Chamberlain was invulnerable. His Conservatives and their allies when war broke out had had 418 seats in the House to the 167 held by the Labour opposition, and an overall majority of more than 200. Calls for Chamberlain's resignation by Labour leaders in early May seemed mere gestures. Nevertheless, through the two-day 'Norway Debate', Chamberlain fell.

Chamberlain, opening the debate on 7 May, was heckled by Labour members with cries of 'Hitler missed the bus.' He appeared to try to load the blame for the débâcle on Churchill, announcing that greater powers had been conferred on him to 'give guidance and direction to the Chiefs of Staff Committees', as if this had been true throughout the Norway campaign, then had to admit that it was a more recent development. Attlee, the Labour leader, declared that it was unfair to give Churchill so much responsibility and called on Conservatives to revolt. Devastating speeches followed from two distinguished figures on the government benches. Admiral Sir Roger Keyes, who had been a naval hero in the First World War, spoke for the officers and men of the fighting navy against the incompetence of the naval staff, specifically excluding Churchill from his criticisms. His speech caused a sensation, followed by another when Leopold Amery, a privy councillor and devoted proponent of the British Empire, quoted at the end of his oration Oliver Cromwell's words on dismissing the Long Parliament: 'You have sat too long here for any good you have been doing. Depart, I say, and let us have done with you. In the name of God, go.'

Herbert Morrison, opening the second day's debate for Labour, announced that his party would force a vote. A former prime minister, David Lloyd George, now denounced Chamberlain and, when Churchill rose and declared that he accepted his full share of the responsibility, put it to him that he 'must not allow himself to be converted into an air-raid shelter to keep the splinters from hitting his colleagues'. But when Churchill wound up the debate for the government, he sturdily defended its record, describing Hitler's invasion of Norway as a 'cardinal political and strategic error'. The profit and loss account for the Royal Navy was satisfactory.

The government won the vote by 281:200. But forty backbench MPs on his own side voted against Chamberlain, and perhaps forty more abstained. One-fifth of the Government's total strength had defied a three-line whip, and, as Paul Addison observes, 'Only the most intense outbreak of collective anger' could have produced this unwonted display of disloyalty within the Conservative Party.[6] It was now clear that Chamberlain must resign unless he could persuade

23

either the Tory rebels, the Labour Party, or both, to join a reconstructed government. While negotiations proceeded, shocking news came from the Continent.

In the early hours of 10 May, the German army, as Churchill had foreboded, crossed the frontiers of Holland, Belgium and Luxembourg. The British and French were caught by surprise, and bewilderment persisted as the Germans revealed their new style of 'lightning war'. Airborne landings gave them control of crucial points. Mobile formations of tanks and armoured cars moved rapidly down roads and lanes. Crafty subterfuge was employed, as when some sixty Germans, dressed as mechanics and Dutch soldiers infiltrated Holland in the dark to try to seize the crossings of the Lower Meuse. Rotterdam, declared an open city by the Dutch authorities, was bombed with heavy civilian casualties. The dreaded Junkers 87 Stuka dive bomber tortured the morale of allied civilians and soldiers as German columns poured into France. 'Ironically, it was not a particularly sophisticated aircraft, and was notoriously ungainly in air-to-air combat. But its sinister full-winged silhouette and the banshee scream of its siren helped to make it one of the war's most feared weapons.'

On 13 May, when their forces confronted the French on the Meuse at Sedan, instead of waiting while artillery was brought up to prepare the way for an assault crossing, the Germans committed nearly 1,500 planes, almost equivalent to the total allied air strength in France and Belgium, to attack their opponents' lines 'in the greatest single demonstration of tactical air power that the world had ever seen. By nightfall the Germans were across the river, and the moral disintegration of the French army had begun.'[7]

Chamberlain's fall was equally sudden. Attlee had agreed to ask the executive of his party, meeting at Bournemouth for its annual conference, whether they were prepared to serve under Chamberlain and whether they would serve under someone else. The answer by five in the afternoon of 10 May was no to the first question, yes to the second. Chamberlain gave way to Churchill. It was clear that this change would command enthusiastic popular support.

As early as May 1939, an opinion poll had showed 56 per cent in favour of Chamberlain's asking Churchill to join the Cabinet. As the nation had moved towards war, he had acquired immense moral authority as the one leading politician who had constantly warned against Hitler, demanded rearmament and denounced appeasement. While an equal proportion (57 per cent) approved Chamberlain's prime ministership in a poll taken in April 1940, he inspired at best respect, not enthusiasm. Churchill had profited during the Phoney

War from the fact that only the navy was undertaking glamorous and, in Churchill's word, 'vehement' warlike action. The left-wing popular press had begun to boost Churchill's claim to replace Chamberlain during the first autumn of war. In December a poll had shown that 30 per cent would prefer him to Chamberlain as Prime Minister — and while the latter was preferred by women, elderly people and the better off, Churchill's stock was high with men, with young voters and with the poor: most Labour supporters favoured him. People cheered in the cinema when they saw him in newsreels.[8]

So he came to power as the one man who could inspire and unite the people. Labour and Liberal leaders joined his new War Cabinet. Churchill had referred in his speech in the Norway Debate to Ernest Bevin as a friend of his who was working hard for the public cause, and Bevin, the most powerful man in the British trade-union movement, though he was not at first an MP, joined the government as Minister of Labour. An equally unorthodox appointment made Lord Beaverbrook, owner of the *Daily Express*, Churchill's Minister of Aircraft Production.

On 14 May, the day when the Dutch army surrendered, Anthony Eden, the new Secretary of State for War, gave an important broadcast. He spoke of the new form of warfare which the Germans had employed against the Low Countries — 'namely, the dropping of troops by parachute behind the main defence lines', to cause disorganisation and confusion prior to the landing of troops by aircraft. Eden went on:

> In order to leave nothing to chance . . . we are going to ask you to help us in a manner which I hope will be welcome to thousands of you. Since the war began, the Government has received countless enquiries from all over the kingdom, from men of all ages who are for one reason or another not at present engaged in military service and who wish to do something for the defence of the country. Now is your opportunity. We want large numbers of such men in Great Britain who are British subjects, between the ages of fifteen and sixty-five, to come forward now and offer their services in order to make assurance doubly sure. The name of the new force which is now to be raised will be the Local Defence Volunteers.[9]

Within twenty-four hours, over quarter of a million men had offered their services. Before the end of June, there were nearly one and a half million LDV, all unpaid volunteers. Villages, suburbs, coal-mines, railways, factories, threw up their own LDV troops. Eden had announced that volunteers would be given uniform and arms, but most did not get either for a long time. Men drilled and stood guard with all kinds of sporting guns, pickaxes, spears, truncheons and choppers. But the volunteers were full of enthusiasm and readiness to fight. They relieved the army of such routine tasks as keeping watch over coastlines and vital factories and manning roadblocks. Towards the end of July, they were renamed the Home Guard. As a popular biography of Churchill would put it:

> They were a symbol of Britain's mood, these volunteers who streamed along to enrol while the Allied front in Flanders and Northern France was crashing to ruins beneath the sledge-hammer strokes of Germany's Blitzkrieg. The British were locking their jaws and gritting their teeth. The outlook was black; the hope of checking and defeating this Nazi machine was feeble. But there would be no surrender. Retreat or compromise was simply unthinkable.
>
> That was magnificently expressed by Churchill in the speech he made to the House on 4th June, reporting the course of the war and the miracle of Dunkirk. There are some speeches which are more than words. They are deeds. The stroke of them shapes history.[10]

Dunkerque, or 'Dunkirk' was the port from which, between 26 May and 4 June, British vessels took off about 225,000 British, roughly 110,000 French and some 2,000 Belgian troops. Lord Gort, commanding the British Expeditionary Force, had been confronted with the danger that most of his forces in France would be surrounded and captured by the swift-moving Germans. Withdrawal to Dunkirk meant that British naval power could come to the rescue, and the Luftwaffe proved incapable of preventing the evacuation by bombing, and strafing. Besides Royal Navy ships, many small civilian vessels assisted, and 'the little ships at Dunkirk' at once became symbols of plucky resistance to Nazi might. As another biographer of Churchill, Philip Guedalla, wrote in 1941:

> Those were the burning summer days, when England listened to the distant thunder of the Dunkirk beaches and one officer, as his ship drew in by the dim light of dawn, saw 'what seemed to be vast black shadows on the pale sands – he could not think what they were. As it grew lighter he saw that the blacknesses were enormous formations of men standing, waiting. He saw them thus whenever he entered the pass, coming or going. They did not seem to change; they did not seem to lie down; they stood, with

the patience of their race, waiting their turn.' That fortitude and discipline reaped a miraculous reward, as the worst disaster was averted by the selfless gallantry of rearguards and the young men in the sky overhead and the little ships, the unforgotten, unHomeric catalogue of *Mary Jane* and *Peggy IV* of *Folkestone Belle*, *Boy Billy*, and *Ethel Maud*, of *Lady Haig* and *Skylark*. Just as another challenge in the Narrow Seas had once been met by the Elizabethans, when 'from Lyme, and Weymouth, and Poole, and the Isle of Wight, young lords and gentlemen came streaming out in every smack and sloop' to face the Armada and to tear its threat to tatters, so the little ships of England brought the army home.[11]

An issue of *The War Illustrated*, edited by Sir John Hammerton, came out on 14 June telling 'The Immortal Story of Dunkirk'. It praised the fight which the British Expeditionary Force had put up as it 'Marched to Dunkirk to Glory's Tune'. Under the headline 'AT DUNKIRK TRAGEDY WAS TURNED INTO TRIUMPH' it quoted the *New York Times* on the courage shown at Dunkirk itself 'in such a hell as never blazed on earth before'. The 'soul of democracy' had faced the enemy 'beaten but unconquered, in shining splendour . . . It is the great tradition of democracy. It is the future. It is victory.'[12]

Churchill himself had been rather more cautious when he addressed the Commons on 4 June. He had feared, he said, that it would be his 'hard lot to announce the greatest military disaster in our long history'. He had thought that no more than 20,000 or 30,000 men of the BEF might be re-embarked. But thanks to the devotion and courage of British seamen manning 220 light warships and 650 other vessels, 'A miracle of deliverance, achieved by valour, by perseverance, by perfect discipline, by faultless service, by resource, by skill, by unconquerable fidelity' was manifest to all. And the role of the RAF had been vital: 'We must be very careful not to assign to this deliverance the attributes of a victory. Wars are not won by evacuations. But there was a victory inside this deliverance, which should be noted. It was gained by the air force.' Young men flying Hurricane and Spitfire fighters had proved their superiority even when outnumbered by German planes four to one:

There never had been, I suppose, in all the world, in all the history of war, such an opportunity for youth. The Knights of the Round Table, the Crusaders, all fall back into the past; not only distant but prosaic; these young men, going forth every morn to guard their native land and all that we stand for, holding in their hands these instruments of colossal and shattering power, of whom it may be said that

> Every morn brought forth a noble chance
> And every chance brought forth a noble knight

deserve our gratitude . . .

Though what had happened in France and Belgium was, as Churchill admitted, 'a colossal military disaster', the upshot was that for the moment Britain had on its own soil 'incomparably more powerful military forces' than ever before 'in this war or the last'. This was reassuring to think of when Hitler seemed likely to invade, a possibility confronted in Churchill's famous peroration:

> I have, myself, full confidence that if all do their duty, if nothing is neglected, and if the best arrangements are made, as they are being made, we shall prove ourselves once again able to defend our island home, to.ride out the storm of war, and to outlive the menace of tyranny, *if necessary for years, if necessary alone.* At any rate, that is what we are going to try to do. That is the resolve of His Majesty's Government − every man of them. *That is the will of Parliament and Nation* . . . Even though large tracts of Europe and many old and famous states have fallen or may fall into the grip of the Gestapo and all the odious apparatus of Nazi rule, we shall not flag or fail. We shall go on to the end, we shall fight in France, we shall fight on the seas and oceans, we shall fight with growing confidence and growing strength in the air, *we shall defend our island, whatever the cost may be, we shall fight on the beaches, we shall fight on the landing grounds, we shall fight in the fields and in the streets, we shall fight in the hills; we shall never surrender* . . . [13] (My italics)

In May 1940, 3 per cent of the British people, according to a Gallup Poll, had believed that they might lose the war. 'By the end of the year the proportion was so small that it could not be measured. Confidence in the Prime Minister stood at 88 per cent in July, rose to 89 in October, fell to 85 by the end of the year.' Yet Laurence Thompson, recording this, recalls the realities of 1940, when he was a young soldier:

> A pink cheeked subaltern, fresh back from a course, instructs us that in the event of invasion we are to lay soup plates upside down in the road, which German tank crews will mistake for mines.

When they get out to remove them, we will machine gun them . . . There are in the country fewer than a thousand tanks, most of them obsolete or unserviceable. No division has anything like its establishment of field anti-tank guns. At the current rate of production it will take two months to bring a single division up to strength in twenty-five pounders; and there are twenty-nine divisions. Instead of guns, containers of petrol are mounted beside strategic roads, which as the Germans approach will spray the road with petrol, into which a heroic Home Guard will lob a hand grenade.

While the full truth of British unpreparedness could not be revealed by Churchill or any one, people knew that no smoothly organised, well-equipped defensive forces existed to resist Nazi invasion. Improvisation was the order of the day. Thompson concludes: 'There is no doubt that the British were united, nor is there the least doubt that they found in Churchill an exact expression of their own obstinacy, courage, and refusal to recognise the apparent logic of facts.'[14]

But it seemed to be logic which made the point that everyone had to work harder. Churchill's new Cabinet had received from the House of Commons, on 22 May, an Emergency Powers Act which gave it extraordinary scope for coercion – complete control over persons and property, so that Bevin, for instance, could direct any person to perform any service he thought fit, with wages, hours and conditions set by himself. In July, Order 1305 made strikes and lockouts illegal wherever collective bargaining between trade unions and employers existed. But large-scale direction of labour didn't occur at this stage. Most people were still working in jobs they had voluntarily sought.

Herbert Morrison, the new Minister of Supply, called on Britain's workers to 'Go to it'. Lord Beaverbrook dramatised the crisis in aircraft supply by insisting that Ministry of Aircraft Production contractors worked on Sundays. Bank Holidays and Works Weeks were cancelled. Factories worked twenty-four hours a day several days a week. And the workforce responded in many places. Some people worked continuously for thirty-six or even forty-eight hours without a break, and ten- to twelve-hour shifts seven days a week were normal in sections of 'war industry'.

On 10 June Italy entered the war on Germany's side. On 14 June the Germans occupied Paris. On 17 June, Marshal Pétain, the new French Prime Minister, asked for an armistice. Next day Churchill addressed the Commons with a speech which he then broadcast to the British people. Again he was reassuring about the quantity and quality of the forces now mustered at sea, on land and in the air to defend Britain. He conceded that the Germans had a larger force of bomber aircraft:

> I do not at all underrate the severity of the ordeal which lies before us, but I believe our countrymen will show themselves capable of standing up to it, like the brave men of Barcelona, and will be able to stand up to it, and carry on in spite of it, at least as well as any other people in the world. Much will depend upon this; every man and every woman will have the chance to show the finest qualities of their race, and render the highest service to their cause. For all of us, at this time, whatever our sphere or our duties, it will be a help to remember the famous lines:

> > He nothing common did or mean,
> > Upon that memorable scene.

(The lines are from Andrew Marvell's 'Horatian Ode Upon Cromwell's Return from Ireland' and refer to King Charles I's behaviour on the scaffold.)

Churchill's peroration began:

> What General Weygand called the Battle of France is over. I expect that the Battle of Britain is about to begin. Upon this battle depends the survival of Christian civilisation. Upon it depends our own British life, and the long continuity of our institutions and our Empire . . .

It concluded with his call, already quoted, to make this the British Empire's 'finest hour'.[15]

By 25 June, hostilities in France were over. Britain (with its Empire and Commonwealth) stood alone. This actually came as a relief to many people in Britain. King George VI wrote to his mother that he felt happier 'now that we have no allies to be polite to and to pamper'. The commissionaire of one of the Service Clubs in London cheered a depressed member with the remark, 'Anyhow, sir, we're in the Final, and it's to be played on the Home Ground.' A tug skipper shouted across the Thames to a well-known MP, 'Now we know where we are! No more bloody allies!' And when the Foreign Secretary, Lord Halifax, visited Air Chief Marshal Dowding at the headquarters of Fighter Command, the latter said to him, 'Thank God we're alone now.' On 16 July George Orwell, an enthusiastic

Home Guard member, wrote to an American publisher, 'I actually rather hope that the invasion will happen. The local morale is extremely good . . .' David Low the cartoonist seemed to have summed up the prevailing spirit in Beaverbrook's *Evening Standard* just after the French capitulation: he depicted 'a solitary soldier in a steel helmet, standing on Dover's cliffs and shaking his fist at the blazing vanquished continent. The caption beneath the picture contains only three words: "Very well, alone".'[16]

On 25 June, Vere Hodgson began to keep a diary — inspired, it seems, by the fact that London had had its first air raid the previous night. A German attempt to invade was daily expected, and as Churchill had prophesied, Fighter Command had the key role in preventing it. Churchill's phrase 'Battle of Britain' was applied to the war in the air which began in earnest on 10 July. Charles Gardner, a BBC reporter, was at Dover when German aircraft arrived, and commentated on the resulting air battle as if it were a sporting event. Vere Hodgson thought such broadcasts 'Jolly good!'[17] For some weeks German planes attacked convoys in the English Channel and British aircraft opposed them. On 19 July Hitler offered peace. The BBC, on its own initiative, bluntly rejected it, and Halifax confirmed this rejection three days later. German leaflets giving the text of Hitler's speech were dropped in parts of southern England on 1 August, to the joy of souvenir collectors.

On 8 August a new phase began, as the Luftwaffe attacked targets in south and south-east England. On the 15th it made an assault designed to knock out Fighter Command itself. It claimed to have shot down ninety-nine British aircraft, but the real losses were only thirty-five, and the Air Ministry News Service reported that 180 German planes had been destroyed. There were further huge battles on the 16th and 18th. The RAF was running short of planes, despite inflicting heavy losses on the Germans, but the aircraft industry, under Lord Beaverbrook's control, was pouring out Hurricanes and Spitfires. Beaverbrook had come into office determined to cut red tape and had ruthlessly commandeered supplies for aircraft production. On 10 July he had called on the British people to hand over anything made of aluminium. Even the Royal Family and the War Office turned in pots and pans. And Beaverbrook's 'Spitfire Funds' brought in over £1 million a month from the public, who learnt that any individual, city or group contributing £5,000 would 'buy' a new aeroplane. In August a price list of components was issued — the blast tube of a machine gun, for instance, could be purchased for 15 shillings.

On 20 August Churchill told the Commons:

The whole of the warring nations are engaged, not only soldiers, but the entire population, men, women and children. The fronts are everywhere. The trenches are dug in the towns and streets. Every village is fortified. Every road is barred. The front line runs through the factories. The workmen are soldiers with different weapons but the same courage.

He praised Beaverbrook's 'Genius of organisation and drive' for producing 'overflowing reserves' of aircraft and an 'evermounting stream of production'. And he expressed the British people's gratitude to its airmen: 'Undaunted by odds, unwearied in their constant challenge and mortal danger', they were 'turning the tide of the world war by their prowess and by their devotion. Never in the field of human conflict was so much owed by so many to so few.'[18]

The 'Few', the young pilots of Fighter Command, achieved results broadcast nightly which the British could grasp as they understood Test cricket scores. In mid-August, in Piccadilly, Vera Brittain saw a placard chalked by a newspaper seller:

BIGGEST RAID EVER
SCORE 78 TO 26
ENGLAND STILL BATTING[19]

The risk of death for the young warriors was high — and known to be so by the people of the south-east who saw Fighter Command aircraft crashing in their neighbourhoods: 201 fighter air crew were killed between 15 August and 15 September. Yet these very young men themselves seemed to treat their task as sport. They were cheerful, rakish, disrespectful of service discipline and stuffy conventions. One squadron leader recalled, 'we could be scared to death five or six times a day and yet find ourselves drinking in the local pub before closing time on a summer evening . . .'[20] Herbert Asquith expressed public delight in their spirit in a poem published by *The Times* in August:

> These who were children yesterday
> Now move in lovely flight,
> Swift glancing as the shooting stars
> That cleave the summer night . . .
>
> Old men may wage a war of words,
> Another race are these,
> Who flash to glory dawn and night
> Above the starry seas.[21]

From 24 August, the Luftwaffe began to attack the ring of seven RAF sector stations which were the key to the defence of London. People in and near the capital saw 'dog fights' in the air. On the night of 24 August central London was quite severely bombed. Then, on the late afternoon of 7 September, with the Battle of Britain in the air still undecided, London received a raid on a new scale, which is taken as marking the start of the 'Blitz'.

The docks were set alight. Huge fires blazing in London's East End were seen many miles away. While the Chiefs of Staff issued the code word 'Cromwell', alerting army and (unofficially) Home Guard to the possibility of invasion, and troops kept vigil, the capital's air-raid precaution and fire services were confronted with an immediate task of nightmarish proportions. There were 430 civilians killed and 1,600 seriously injured. Thousands were made homeless. And next night the bombers came back and killed 400 more. The next night, the toll was 370. For seventy-six consecutive nights, excepting 2 November when weather precluded it, London was raided, and usually heavily.

On 15 September (thereafter 'Battle of Britain Day') Fighter Command, which had not recorded any great 'scores' since the German offensive had switched to London itself, broke up a horde of bombers heading for the capital in the morning, then another such in the afternoon. The Air Ministry claimed 185 German aircraft destroyed, for a British loss of twenty-five. As Churchill himself knew within a couple of days, this was followed by the Germans' decision not to attempt invasion in 1940. To the British public it seemed that the battle was still in full swing – on 27 September the Air Ministry claimed 133 German scalps – but though daylight fighting continued throughout October, the Germans had obviously switched their main effort to night bombing.

Mollie Panter-Downes, an Englishwoman who sent a weekly or fortnightly letter from London to the *New Yorker*, recorded on 14 September:

For Londoners, there are no longer such things as good nights; there are only bad nights, worse nights and better nights. Hardly anyone has slept at all in the past week. The sirens go off at approximately the same time every evening, and in the poorer districts, queues of people carrying blankets, thermos flasks, and babies begin to form quite early outside the air-raid shelters. The *Blitzkrieg* continues to be directed against such military objectives as the tired shopgirl, the red-eyed clerk, and the thousands of dazed and weary families patiently trundling their few belongings in perambulators away from the wreckage of their homes. After a few of these nights, sleep of a kind comes from complete exhaustion. The amazing part of it is the cheerfulness and fortitude with which ordinary individuals are doing their jobs under nerve-wracking conditions. Girls who have taken twice the usual time to get to work look worn when they arrive, but their faces are nicely made up and they bring you a cup of tea or sell you a hat as chirpily as ever. Little shopkeepers whose windows have been blown out post up 'Business as usual' stickers and exchange cracks with their customers.

On all sides one hears the grim phrase 'We shall get used to it . . .'

Panter-Downes observed that the East End had suffered most. But the bombers 'made no discrimination between the lowest and highest homes in the City. The Queen was photographed against much the same sort of tangle of splintered wreckage that faced hundreds of humbler, anonymous housewives . . .' Though Buckingham Palace had been bombed twice, damage elsewhere in the West End had so far been slight; however, a bomb which fell in Regent Street and didn't explode for hours eventually shattered glass over a wide area, and 'The scene next morning was quite extraordinarily eerie', with the great thoroughfare deserted by all except police and salvage workers, and the pavements covered with 'a fine, frosty glitter of powdered glass'. Panter-Downes concluded her report:

The behaviour of all classes is so magnificent that no observer here could ever imagine these people following the French into captivity. As for breaking civilian morale, the high explosives that rained death and destruction on the capital this week were futile.[22]

Charles Ritchie, a Canadian diplomat in London, had noted in his diary as early as 5 August that 'English men and women of different classes, localities, sets and tastes are for the first time talking to each other. . . The weather was previously the one subject upon which everyone had fixed for conversations with strangers.'[23] Now bombing mixed the classes together further. Well-off travellers in the London Underground could not miss the thousands of poor people who had turned the tube stations into what Panter-Downes in her report of 21 September described as 'vast dormitories', despite official appeals that they should not be used as shelters. Of the shelters, she wrote: 'The bravery of these people has to be seen to be believed. They would be heart-rending to look at if they didn't so conspicuously refuse to appear heart-rending.' West End stores had now come in for heavy bombing. Whole areas had become unrecognisable and taxi drivers grumbled about the difficulty of finding their way and how hard broken glass was on their tyres — but their grumbles had 'the usual cockney pithiness and gaiety'. On 29 September Panter-Downes noted, 'The courage, humour and kindliness of ordinary people continue to be astonishing.' The Blitz was becoming routine. Everyone ignored air-raid sirens during daylight, unless the noise of gunfire or bombs was uncomfortably near. 'Gieves, the famous military tailor on Bond Street whose shop was completely gutted, ran a stately advertisement regretting that it was necessary to inconvenience clients for a few days, as though the fuss had been caused by a bit of spring redecorating.'[24]

By 27 October, after a spell of especially heavy raiding, 'so vicious that a lesser fighter' than London 'would have been knocked groggy', Panter-Downes was clearly saddened by the 'horrifying' destruction in the capital, and wearied like others by the 'transportation difficulties' which resulted. Nor was she pleased by the 'breezy' tone with which the BBC announced news of raids: 'To someone newly facing grief, the chirpy statement that "casualties were slight" has a way of sounding callous.' She wrote sadly of the destruction of the historic Middle Temple Hall — beautiful carved stone bosses covered in rubble, elegant eighteenth-century doorways and windows smashed, broken stained glass on the choirstalls in the Temple Church. But she went on: 'If history is being torn up by the roots in London, history is also being made. The new race of tube dwellers is slipping a fresh page into the record; nothing has ever been seen like the concourse of humanity that camps underground every night.' People were seen staking their evening's claim as early as eleven-thirty in the morning. 'By five, when the homeward rush hour is on, one walks underground between double rows of men, women, and children — eating, drinking, sleeping, reading papers, and just sitting: all part of the most extraordinary mass picnic the world has ever known.' The authorities were working out a system of permanent canteens.[25]

Meanwhile, the horror of death was mitigated by the spontaneous courage and warmth with which ordinary people strove to rescue and succour their neighbours. Charles Ritchie, on 26 October, was in the heavily bombed area near Lot's Road Power Station, where some friends, Frank and Margery Ziegler, lived. A bomb fell in the next street. Ritchie and the Zieglers rushed to help people get out of the remains of three bombed houses. Afterwards, 'We all went to a pub where a fat landlady, her hair in papers, was offering cups of strong sweet tea, while her husband with a conspiratorial air offered to break the law and give us beer or "take-away ports" although it was two a.m.'[26]

Meanwhile, the Luftwaffe had been devoting some attention to the provinces. On 25 October, 170 persons were killed in a raid on Birmingham, and other places had attacks which seemed significant to local people. It was 14 November, however, that marked the beginning of a new phase of Blitz. That night, the Germans attacked Coventry in force. It was a cardinal centre of British 'war production'. Twenty-one important factories, twelve of them concerned with aircraft manufacture, were severely damaged. Hundreds of retail shops were put out of action. The centre of this medium-sized city (213,000 people in 1938, though swollen considerably since) was gutted. Approaching a third of its houses were wrecked; 554 people were killed.

After this London had a respite – only six major raids and two lighter ones from 18 November to 19 January. But Bristol was 'Coventrated' on 24 November, and Birmingham and Southampton soon received attention on a similar scale. In December, half a dozen more provincial cities suffered, though bad weather limited German attacks. It was by now clear, in any case, that in the provinces as in London, bombing was not going to stop people getting to work. Coventry remained a key centre of war production, and after eight months during which the capital was incessantly 'blitzed' the Ford factory there could claim that absenteeism barely existed.

On 30 December, Vere Hodgson reported 'Terrible Fires' in London the previous night:

> We went up on the roof to look. At Shepherd's Bush flames were leaping, and towards the City they were gigantic. As I walked up the road I could see the smoke. A great red glow filled the sky – I had no need of a torch – I could see every step I took and could have read a book if I had wished. The police said it was Waterloo Station, but the taxi man told Miss Moyes that the City was on fire, and they were trying to save St Paul's . . .

The 29 December raid which produced 'the Second Fire of London' in the City proper had indeed been heavy. But St Paul's, rebuilt to Wren's design after the first Fire of 1666, had been saved this time, and photographs of the great dome riding unscathed over smoke and flame became symbols of British courage and endurance through a remarkable year. Miss Hodgson, like most people, listened to BBC news on New Year's Eve, and in the popular Postscript slot afterwards, 'they gave us some of the phrases of 1940. All the best are by Churchill. We shall never forget them . . . Blood and sweat and toil and tears . . .'[27]

Another 'postscript' to 1940 is needed here. It was still believed that Hitler would try to invade in 1941. Bad weather limited air raiding in January and February, though London and other cities continued to suffer. The second and third weeks of March saw twelve major blows against ports and industrial cities. On the 13th and 14th the burgh of Clydebank, by Glasgow, was so heavily attacked that all but seven of its 12,000 houses were damaged, and 35,000 out of 47,000 people were made homeless. Bristol suffered again. Cardiff and Portsmouth had three and five big nights. On 19 March London suffered its highest casualties yet − 750 killed − and on the two following nights the city centre of Plymouth was levelled.

After another relatively slack period, mid-April brought fresh hammering to Clydeside, Coventry and Bristol. Belfast was 'Coventrated'. Over 1,000 people were killed in London on the 16th, and again on the 19th; 148,000 houses were damaged or destroyed in these two raids, whereas in September the rate had been only about 40,000 per week. But now Plymouth suffered far more intensively even than London, with five heavy raids before the end of the month, until the housing 'casualty' figures came to exceed the total number of houses, as many were hit more than once. Merseyside's turn followed, on eight successive nights in early May. Belfast again, Hull and Nottingham were blitzed. And on 10 May London had its worst ever raid, with 1,436 people killed and 1,792 seriously injured. Westminster Abbey, the Law Courts, the Tower and the British Museum were hit, and the Chamber of the House of Commons was destroyed. A third of the streets of Greater London were left impassable. All but one of the main railway stations were blocked for weeks. Brown smoke blotted out the sun.

Surely invasion must come? But raids over the next few weeks were light. On 22 June the Germans attacked Russia. The Nazis had diverted their main effort eastwards.

And meanwhile, Roosevelt's victory in the US presidential election of November 1940 had confirmed that the world's greatest industrial power would continue to show goodwill to Britain. His 'Lend–Lease' bill passed into law in March 1941, empowering him to

37

give Britain anything it needed on whatever terms he liked. 'Lend-Lease' food arrived in Britain from 31 May — a crucial reinforcement to the nation's diet, and encouraging tangible proof of American support. By the end of 1941, America was fully at war with Germany, and, as Churchill himself saw when news came of Pearl Harbor, Hitler's defeat was virtually inevitable:

> No American will think it wrong of me if I proclaim that to have the United States at our side was to me the greatest joy. I do not pretend to have measured accurately the martial might of Japan, but now at this very moment I knew the United States was in the war, up to the neck and in to the death. So we had won after all! Yes, after Dunkirk; after the fall of France; after the horrible episode of Oran; after the threat of invasion, when, apart from the Air and the Navy, we were an almost unarmed people; after the deadly struggle of the U-boat war — the first Battle of the Atlantic, gained by a hand's breadth; after seventeen months of lonely fighting and nineteen months of my responsibility in dire stress. We had won the war. England would live, Britain would live; the Commonwealth of Nations and the Empire would live . . . Once again in our long island history we should emerge, however mauled or mutilated, safe and victorious. We should not be wiped out. Our history would not come to an end . . . All the rest was merely the proper application of overwhelming force. The British Empire, the Soviet Union, and now the United States, bound together with every scrap of their life and strength, were, according to my lights, twice or even thrice the force of their antagonists.[28]

Churchill, in his war memoirs, patriotically listed the British Empire first among the members of the Grand Alliance in the extract just quoted. Yet until more than halfway through the war, the Empire could boast of no great triumph of aggressive arms. To defeat the Italians in Africa in 1940–41 was better than losing to them, but the British set little store by it. German forces drove British out of Greece and Crete in the spring of 1941. British tanks proved ineffectual against German in the North African desert. Then the Japanese early in 1942 knocked over Britain's Far Eastern colonies — Hong Kong, Malaya, Singapore, Borneo, Burma — like ninepins. In 1942 Churchill was fighting for his political life as discontent swelled at home over Britain's lack of military success, and it took Montgomery's victory at El Alamein in November to secure the Prime Minister's position for the rest of the war.

Throughout the long phase of retreats and defeats until then, the idea that British bombers were hitting the Germans at home was important to Churchill and to many of the British people. The Prime Minister endorsed the policy of attacking the morale of German industrial workers by bombing their homes, which 'Bomber' Harris, Commander in Chief Bomber Command, applied from early 1942. Harris's experimental attack on Lübeck, an ancient German town, late in March, created a firestorm which destroyed half the town. This provoked Hitler to order the so-called 'Baedeker' raids against English towns of historic and cultural significance. Since the summer of 1941, when Hull had suffered several sizeable raids after the main Blitz had ended elsewhere, air attacks on Britain had been only occasional. Now Exeter, Bath, Norwich, York and Canterbury, in April and May 1942, suffered 'Baedeker' raids which, relative to the size of these cities, amounted to full-scale Blitz.

On 30 May, Harris unleashed the RAF's first 'Thousand Bomber' attack, against Cologne. Over 6,500 British airmen were in the sky simultaneously, homing in on one German city; 898 crews claimed to have reached Cologne and dropped nearly 1,500 tons of bombs, some two-thirds of these incendiaries. Huge fires were started. As John Terraine puts it: 'Harris had done what he had set out to do: he had captured the imagination of the British and American public, he had exhilarated his Command, and he had won the unreserved admiration of the Prime Minister, thus saving the bomber offensive for a yet more vigorous future.'[29]

Goebbels, after the Lübeck raid, had feared that weeks of attacks 'on these lines' might 'conceivably' demoralise the German people. In fact, life in Cologne was functioning almost normally (despite 474 killed and over 5,000 injured) within two weeks of the Thousand Bomber raid. Exaggerated British ideas of Bomber Command's success led to still more ambitious plans for rendering three-quarters of Germany's urban population homeless by raids in 1943 and 1944, to kill 900,000 Germans and seriously to injure a million more. This plan was modified because British resources did not permit it. Nevertheless, within the period March 1943 to March 1944, in the operations of Bomber Command, '"independent" strategic air power reached its peak in the Second World War'.[30]

From March to mid-summer 1943 the Ruhr was the chief target. Then Hamburg was assailed in July and August. In Hamburg a huge firestorm was created by incendiary attack on July 27–8. A lake of fire spread over twenty-two square kilometres. Air temperatures may have reached 1,000 degrees centigrade. Vast suction was created; trees were uprooted, people were thrown to the ground or pitched alive into the fires by winds of over 150 miles an hour. In shelters, people were suffocated by carbon monoxide poisoning and their bodies were reduced to ashes. Perhaps 50,000 people were killed, some 40,000 injured. Nearly a million fled. Three-fifths of the city's homes were destroyed. Industry was badly affected. In the words of Generalleutnant Adolf Galland:

> A wave of terror radiated from the suffering city and spread through Germany . . . A stream of haggard, terrified refugees flowed into the neighbouring provinces. In every large town people said: 'What happened to Hamburg yesterday can happen to us tomorrow' . . . After Hamburg in the wide circle of the political and military command could be heard the words: 'The war is lost.'

Albert Speer, in charge of Germany's war production, told Hitler that the armaments industry would collapse if six more major cities suffered such attack.[31]

Yet Hamburg recovered. And the 'Battle of Berlin', four and a half months of raiding from November 1943 to March 1944, was sensed as a British defeat by Bomber Command men taking part, though 9,111 sorties were sent against Berlin itself. This was not a nightly battle of concentrated attrition like the 'Battle of London'. Over the period, nineteen out of the full total of thirty-five operations were against other cities. Bomber Command suffered very severe losses. Awe-inspiring damage was afflicted, on Berlin and other places. But German weapon production rose two and a half times between January 1943 and December 1944. To quote Terraine again:

> As for morale, the story is the usual one; it did not collapse. Berliners could still make jokes; an example which seems to belie all contemporary British estimates of the German situation and character being the café story of an encounter between Goebbels and Goering. Hitler, Goebbels told the *Reichsmarschall*, had hanged himself. 'There you are,' replied Goering, 'I always said we should win this war in the air.' It was not a particularly brilliant joke — wartime jokes seldom are; but the point is that according to British orthodoxy, Germans were supposed not to be able to joke at all, still less to do so under devastating air bombardment, and least of all to joke at the sacred person of the Führer. It was not just the Battle of Berlin that had failed, it was the whole three-year assault on German morale.[32]

Christabel Bielenberg was a British-born German citizen, married to a lawyer who was involved in the secret German resistance to

Hitler. She spent three nights in Berlin that winter under heavy raiding: 'The bombs fell indiscriminately on Nazis and anti-Nazis, on women and children and works of art, on dogs and pet canaries.' She learnt that 'those wanton, quite impersonal killings . . . did not so much breed fear and a desire to bow before the storm, but rather a certain fatalistic cussedness, a dogged determination to survive and, if possible, help others to survive, whatever their politics, whatever their creed.'[33]

Jokes proliferated in Germany about the Luftwaffe's capacity to retaliate:

An ultimatum is going to be presented to the English and Americans. If they do not stop the air war immediately, retaliation will be made the subject of another speech.

May 1950: Discussion in the Führer's headquarters about retaliation. Adjourned, pending a decision as to whether the two aircraft are to fly side-by-side or one-after-the-other.[34]

But between 21 January and 27 March 1944, there were German raids on Britain which, while ineffectual, did involve hundreds of bombers and caused enough damage to lead the British to talk of 'the Little Blitz'. And after the allies' D Day landings in France, the Germans assailed Britain with a novel 'secret weapon', the 'pilotless plane' or 'flying bomb', the V-1. From 13 June to 15 July, over 2,500 of these 'doodlebugs' reached south-east England, and half fell in the London area. During this period, they caused heavy casualties, produced large-scale official and private evacuation, and depressed the morale of a people wearied by war. Then defences against them were improved, and though they continued to come over until the spring of 1944, they were superseded as a serious threat by the V-2 rocket. The first of these exploded in London on 8 September 1944. Eventually 518 of these reached London, and they caused further severe damage, and approaching 10,000 casualties. But nothing compared to the losses finally suffered in and around Berlin in eighteen days in the spring of 1945, as German troops fought the final Russian advance on their capital, and 'between half a million and a million human beings' lost 'their lives, their sanity or their freedom'.[35]

To round this postscript to 1940 off with some more accountancy: during the Second World War, the United Kingdom lost 270,000 men in the armed forces, 35,000 merchant seamen, and approximately 60,000 civilians killed by bombing. This total of about 365,000 was only half the number killed in the Great War of 1914–18, though against this must be set the damage to 4 million houses, and the total destruction of nearly half a million – not to speak of factories, hospitals and schools.[36] However, destruction of buildings and lives never reached levels experienced in large parts of continental Europe.

In the firestorm at Dresden, caused by British incendiary attack on 13 February 1945, which was followed by USA Air Force daylight assault next day, more than 40,000 people probably died, and perhaps more than 50,000.[37] Over the entire war, according to British official figures, 29,890 died through enemy action in London, two-thirds of them in 1940–41. Slightly more died elsewhere in Britain: 30,705. (Total admissions to hospital, most of them seriously injured, totalled 86,182 over the whole country, and a further 150,833 were recorded as 'slightly injured'.[38]) These figures contrast not only with German casualties, but with the appalling rate in Bomber Command itself. Dedicated by High Command to winning the war by destroying German cities, Bomber Command employed over the entire war about 125,000 aircrew, of whom 55,500 were killed. A further 9,838 became prisoners of war, including many wounded; 8,403 were recorded as wounded other than prisoners.[39] It is clear that at least half the Command's men died or were maimed, twice as many in absolute terms as the civilians who died in London air raids.

The courage of these men has never had its due. Public opinion in Britain, even Churchill's own private opinion, recoiled from the effects of RAF 'area bombing' in Germany. Alone among High commanders, 'Bomber' Harris was not given a peerage after victory. Though he thought the casualty rate among his men acceptable, he justly remarked in his memoirs: 'There is no parallel in warfare to such courage and determination in the face of danger over so prolonged a period, of danger which at times was so great that scarcely one man in three could expect to survive his tour of thirty operations . . .'[40] The Few flying fighters in 1940 became and remained mythical heroes. Churchill did not forget Bomber Command in his orations in that year: on 20 August 1940 he told the Commons: 'All hearts go out to the fighter pilots, whose brilliant actions we see with our own eyes day after day; but we must never forget that all the time, night after night, month after month, our bomber squadrons travel far into Germany . . . often with serious loss . . . and inflict shattering blows . . .'[41] The 'blows', at that stage, were wishful thinking; but the courage was real. Bomber crews have never been mythologised, save in one notable post-war British film,

The Dam Busters, which glorified an attack not on helpless civilians but on the water supplies of the Ruhr's war industry. (Unfortunately, this 'brilliant feat of arms' produced no important results.[42])

Bomber Command had to be left out of the Myth of the Blitz, or mythology would have ceased to be efficacious. The heroism of the British under bombardment was quasi-Christian – its great symbol, after all, was St Paul's dome flourishing above the flames. The Myth could not accommodate acts, even would-be acts, of killing of civilians and domestic destruction initiated by the British themselves, however they might be justified strategically. Its construction involved putting together facts known or believed to be true, overlaying these with inspirational values and convincing rhetoric – and leaving out everything known or believed to be factual which didn't fit.

3

No Other Link

Is there no thread to bind us – I and he
Who is dying now, this instant as I write
And may be cold before this line's complete?

Is there no power to link us – I and she
Across whose body the loud roof is falling
Or the child, whose blackening skin
Blossoms with hideous roses in the smoke?

Is there no love to link us – I and they?
Only this hectic moment? This fierce instant
Striking now
Its universal, its uneven blow?

There is no other link. Only this sliding
Second we share: this desperate edge of now.

Mervyn Peake, 'Is There No Love Can Link Us'

THERE IS nothing new about the suppression of evidence, the invention of false evidence, or the distortion of history for propagandist purposes, as anyone knows who is aware, for instance, of how the Tudor dynasty and its apologists successfully turned Richard III, whom a Tudor had deposed, into a mythical monster. Shakespeare's Crookback lives on indelibly, even if local pride within Yorkshire may stubbornly set the last Yorkist king in a better light.

But deliberate distortion of history has thriven particularly in our own century. The best-known examples come from Nazi Germany and from behind the post-war Iron Curtain. Soviet historians dated the start of the Second World War as 22 June 1941. As Joseph Brodsky averred, just before 'Glasnost': 'That the war had already been in full swing in the West for nearly two years has not been public knowledge in the Soviet Union, especially during the last two decades. The only mention the Allies are normally accorded has to do with their reluctance to open the Second Front – implying some

44

sort of complicity with the Nazis, or a malicious desire to see Russia bleed to death.' The Nazi–Soviet Pact of 1939 was not referred to in post-war Soviet fiction. The fact that about 100,000 Romanians fought alongside the Germans in the Battle of Stalingrad was missing from a 1985 issue of a Soviet military encyclopedia – Romania, of course, was then a Warsaw Pact ally. More oddly, Soviet citizens were not told how many Russians died in that battle, or that 20 million Soviet lives were lost in the war overall.[1]

There is no need to belabour such a flagrant and well-known example as Eastern Bloc historiography. But a different process at work in West Germany has not dissimilar practical implications. In 1981 I saw in Frankfurt a public exhibition of photographs illustrating women's life in Germany in the twentieth century. While it did not omit reference to the murder of Jews, it moved through evenly, decade by decade, signalling in its format no great disruptions, as if the thirties and forties were just phases like any other. In 1985, Taschenbuch Verlag published a new dictionary omitting the words Nazi, Gauleiter, Führer, Fascist and Gestapo.[2] What goes on publicly in such cases is akin to the private process whereby 'normal' healthy human beings successfully repress unhappy memories and reorder their own pasts accordingly. Where societies cannot achieve such suppression – where 'history' mythologises mayhem and trauma, as in Northern Ireland – the results can be extremely unpleasant.

In Britain, one could certainly find recent cases where politicians and officials have destroyed documents, misrepresented or invented 'facts', and so forth. But no one has detected evidence of any large-scale 'cover-up' concerning events in 1940–41. On the contrary, one volume dealing with the Blitz in the official series of Civil Histories was written by a distinguished left-wing social scientist of unimpeachable integrity – Richard Titmuss – who had full access to documents during and after the war. Other books in the series were produced on similar terms by historians of high quality with professional reputations either at stake or to make. Since the late sixties, wartime official documents have been freely available under the 'thirty years rule', but even before then wartime civil servants and politicians had written and spoken with every sign of candour about crucial decisions and their contexts. The need for suppression, after all, was much less than in many countries. Britain had not been invaded. No one except a few rather pitiful spies had 'collaborated' with Nazism on British soil, outside the Channel Islands. Whatever the defeats suffered along the way, Britain had won the war.

And had done so while maintaining liberal freedoms of

expression substantially intact. Conscientious objectors to armed service had in some cases been imprisoned. At one stage, pro-Communist intellectuals had been banned from the air by the BBC and a Communist newspaper had been suppressed. Newspapers had submitted to censorship and journalists had been rebuked for straying out of line. But it had always remained possible to protest publicly against these departures from normal freedoms. The coalition government accepted without any sign of hysteria the loss of quite a large number of by-elections. Bishop Bell of Chichester was as free to protest publicly against the 'area bombing' of Germany as Aneurin Bevan, MP, was to criticise Churchill's handling of the war in the Commons. No one was in a position to make a film or a radio programme scathingly critical of the government – but these media were largely in the hands of people who had been disaffected from right-wing government policies during the thirties and were consciously radical in their interpretation of the war and of its implications for peace-time society.

Nor did the Myth of 1940, in some of its most potent expressions, exclude politically contentious matters. In my retelling of the 'story' in my last chapter, I was careful to omit these wherever possible, though I could not have left out the fall of Chamberlain. I was careful to set down no statement which was historically 'untrue', as phrased by me. Historians establish 'truth', or seek to do so, according to a scholarly code which exacts reference to authentic contemporary documents supplemented by credible memoirs and interpreted with the help of sound secondary sources, and I did not knowingly transgress against this code. Nevertheless, I was consciously aiming to express, so to speak, the 'highest common factor' in British mythologising, to provide a version which such an 'innocent' and 'non-political' member of the public as Miss Hodgson might not have quarrelled with, and which would have been rejected neither by a self-conscious Tory, nor by a left-wing member of the Labour Party, nor even by such a pacifist as Vera Brittain. A consensual memory of 1940 was in fact an important basis for the political consensus which was achieved after the war. But over certain details and emphasis it was possible to argue, during the war and later, without disturbing the rock-like 'natural' presence of the Myth.

Confronted in the sixties, as consensus ebbed away, by the question, 'Were people *really* so heroic and self-sacrificing and united in 1940?' any honest veteran would have had to say, 'Well, of course, you got exceptions.' A right-winger might have gone on to inveigh briefly against 'conchies' and confide that he'd never been able to forgive Herbert Morrison, Churchill's Labour Minister of Supply and later Home Secretary, for being a conscientious objector in 1914–18. He could have referred to the 'revolutionary defeatist' line taken by the Communist Party of Great Britain. And a Labour left-winger might quite heartily have concurred with him in deploring the behaviour of CP members: 'Don't think Morrison was right to suppress the *Worker*, but at the time it would have been hard to argue against it – those people could have done a lot of damage.'

But such a left-winger would have augmented the story thus: 'Well, you have to understand that there were people in high places, and lots of them on the Tory benches, who'd never wanted to fight Germany at all. You know, the Cliveden Set, and their pals – people who'd fawned on Ribbentrop the German Ambassador and supported appeasement to the hilt. And that Old Gang, as we called them, were still in the Cabinet after war broke out. It took that disaster in Norway to get rid of Chamberlain and get Labour ministers into the Cabinet, but by then the damage had been done. Look at Dunkirk – good heroic stuff, but behind it a great disaster due to pre-war British governments refusing to realise that fascism had to be fought. Well, under Churchill of course, things improved. The CP had one very strong card, and boy, they played it – provision of air-raid shelters was dreadfully inadequate. Anderson, who was in charge of shelters, was a po-faced right-wing bureaucrat who was completely out of touch with public opinion – but, thank God, we got rid of him and Morrison came in, did a good job. Even then, though, there were still people in high places who thought we should really be fighting Russian Bolshevism – and weren't they sick when Hitler invaded the Soviet Union and Churchill forgot all his own long anti-Communist record and embraced our new and noble ally . . . !'

These left-wing embellishments do not weaken the Myth – they enhance some aspects of it. The British working class and its political leaders are seen as forcing into retreat, through 1940, forces which had betrayed what Churchill would always call Britain's *long* history, of opposition to tyranny. Churchill's own arrival in office expressed the will of the people to 'Go to it' in the correct spirit. The occupation of the London Underground by shelterers becomes a heroic assertion of popular rights against a legacy of inept bureaucracy and Tory rule. And even the CP can be incorporated into the image of 'progressive' or 'anti-fascist' unity. They weren't far wrong about shelters, and after Russia 'came in', they showed by their enthusiasm that they'd always really wanted to fight Hitler. The Old Gang are excluded from 'Unity', but they are seen as anachronistic, increasingly irrelevant, however obnoxious.

So persuasive was this view that the loyalist Conservative retort, 'Well, those Labour chaps opposed rearmament in the thirties, and don't forget how strong pacifism seemed to be – Baldwin and Chamberlain had to take public opinion into account . . .' cut little or no ice in the 1945 general election when, as if on the crest of the wave which had been mounting in 1940, Labour swept into power with a colossal majority.

The left-wing version of the Myth, therefore, can account, or appear to account, for many conflicts and errors and strains and failures abundantly obvious to people in 1940, and of course to any historian. It had for a long time the inherent power of a 'Whig' myth – it explained and legitimated success, as represented by Labour's victory in 1945, the creation of a welfare state, and its maintenance by consensus thereafter. But on what Mervyn Peake's poem of 1941 calls the 'desperate edge of now', how was the 'nightmarish' (Vere Hodgson's word) course of events, day by day perceived? And what aspects of British life did the Myth, as it grew in strength down to 1945, when allied victory finally gave it the last requisite stamp of validation, come to suppress? Because, I repeat, what happened was not a crude propagandist distortion *à la* post-war Bonn Republic, *à la* post-resistance France, *à la* post-Vietnam USA. Desperation on the edge of now was acknowledged in retrospect only as a resolution to fight on the beaches and in the hills: as might indeed have been necessary.

Ironically, Churchill's determination to fight Hitler, 'if necessary, alone', in 1940 hastened the conclusion of the 'long history' of that British Empire overseas to which he was so totally devoted, and made Britain dependent on the United States.

Britain could not afford a long war. In February 1940 the Treasury warned that, 'even if carefully husbanded, British resources could last at the current rate of dollar expenditure no longer than two years'. Yet in August, Churchill and his Cabinet decided to create an army of fifty-five divisions and to expand aircraft production to 2,782 a month by December 1941. To do these things would entail massive purchases from the USA of steel and machine tools, aircraft and aero engines, motor transport and so forth, to the tune of $3,200 million over the next twelve months. The Chancellor of the Exchequer calculated that Britain would exhaust its gold and dollar reserves by December 1940, then go bankrupt. 'This moment of final wreck did not in the event occur until March 1941, when Britain's own reserves were utterly at an end, and payments currently due to America for war supplies could only be met thanks to a loan of gold from the Belgian government in exile.'³

During the Battle of Britain, the USA had been granted ninety-nine-year leases of bases in the Caribbean and Newfoundland in return for fifty old destroyers. This was an important gesture of US sympathy. Five months later, in December 1940, Roosevelt went further. His idea of 'Lend-Lease' was a fine Christmas present for Britain. He asked for powers to provide defence articles to the government of any country whose defence he deemed vital to the defence of the USA, on whatever terms he saw fit. These Congress granted him in the 'Act to promote the defense of the United States', better known as the 'Lend-Lease Act', which it passed on 11 March 1941.

In the short run this made little difference – throughout 1941 Britain still paid cash for most arms obtained from the USA. In the long run, the Act guaranteed that Britain could go on fighting. It also ensured that Britain, as A. J. P. Taylor has put it, would be 'a poor relation, not an equal partner. There was no pooling of resources. Instead Great Britain was ruthlessly stripped of her remaining dollars. The Americans insisted that they were aiding Great Britain so that she should fight Germany and not to maintain her as an industrial power.' Britain 'sacrificed her post-war future for the sake of the war. As Keynes put it, "We threw good housekeeping to the winds. But we saved ourselves, and helped to save the world." '⁴

By 1945, $27,023,000 worth of American military and industrial equipment had come to Britain free of payment. Because of Lend-Lease, Britain no longer needed to earn its own living, nor wage war within its own means and could devote human and industrial resources to the war effort to an extent impossible for any other power. By 1944, 55 per cent of Britain's labour force was in the armed forces or doing war work, compared to the USA's 40 per cent, and British exports had fallen to less than a third of the 1938 figure. Meanwhile, before and after 'Lend-Lease', Britain depended absolutely on US supplies of steel; between 1940 and 1944, despite the attention of U-Boats in the Atlantic, 14,570,000 tons came from America, equivalent to more than a quarter of Britain's own production. In the second half of 1940 steel shipments 'constituted the heaviest single charge on hard-pressed Atlantic shipping capacity'.⁵

Churchill gave to nothing more thought than British–US relations. While still First Lord of the Admiralty, he had begun a private correspondence with Roosevelt, and this greatly expanded after he became Prime Minister, providing, as Taylor puts it, 'the

vital channel for Anglo–American relations throughout the war'.[6]
Roosevelt himself doubted at first that Britain could survive, and
even as he began to believe it could, he was not sure whether the
American electorate would accept war. It was crucial that Britain
should convince US public opinion that it was a gallant and morally
worthy ally, that it could and would survive whatever kinds of
Blitzkrieg the Nazis attempted, and that US assistance was necessary.

Hence any pronouncement by Britons, official or unofficial,
published or broadcast in 1940 was likely to be made by someone
acutely mindful of the USA. This was certainly the case with
Churchill's famous speeches. 'Give us the tools and we will finish the
job', he called out in a broadcast of 9 February 1941 – he was
speaking to the Americans, as it were, over the heads of his own
people, and he had been doing this less explicitly ever since he had
become Prime Minister. His 'Dunkirk' speech of June 1940 was and
is remembered for its stirring promise that the British would fight on
the beaches, in the streets and in the hills, but its actual conclusion
was this:

> and even if, which I do not for a moment believe, this island or a
> large part of it were subjugated and starving, then our Empire
> beyond the seas, armed and guarded by the British fleet, would
> carry on the struggle, until, in God's good time, the new world,
> with all its power and might, steps forth to the rescue and the
> liberation of the old.[7]

His 'Finest Hour' speech of 18 June was designed to rally patriotic,
belligerent feeling in the Commons and in the nation at large, and his
statement that 'we are now assured of immense, continuous and
increasing support in supplies and munitions of all kinds from the
United States' would certainly have helped to dispel faintheartedness.
But his penultimate sentence was an appeal to US opinion itself,
disguised as a friendly warning: 'if we fail, then the whole world,
including the United States, including all that we have known and
cared for, will sink into the abyss of a new Dark Age made more
sinister, and perhaps more protracted, by the lights of perverted
science'.[8]

His broadcast of 14 July 1940 had, by intention or in effect, a
subtler sub-text. He conceded that it was easily understandable that
'sympathetic onlookers' across the Atlantic might have 'feared for
our survival'. He reaffirmed that Britain would never surrender:
'The vast mass of London itself, fought street by street, could easily
devour an entire hostile army; and we would rather see London laid

in ruins and ashes than that it should be tamely and abjectly enslaved.' He went on to stress that he led a government representing 'all creeds, all classes, every recognisable section of opinion', and concluded:

This is no war of chieftains or of princes, of dynasties or national ambition; it is a War of peoples and of causes. There are vast numbers not only in this island but in every land, who will render faithful service in this War, but whose names will never be known, whose deeds will never be recorded. This is a War of the Unknown Warriors; but let all strive without failing in faith or in duty, and the dark curse of Hitler will be lifted from our age.[9]

US opinion – even, or in some cases especially, liberal, anti-fascist, left-wing opinion – was likely to be less than wholehearted in supporting Britain, because that country was seen as undemocratically dominated by antiquated class divisions, and dedicated to the repression of subject peoples in a vast empire which it was selfishly concerned to defend against a rival German imperialism. Churchill's insistence that the war was one of *causes* – the great 'cause' being democratic freedom – his claim that *all classes* were ranged behind him, and his stress on *peoples*, sketched out, as it were, an agenda for sympathetic US journalists in Britain. We shall see later how they followed it. Meanwhile, we may note in passing that Mollie Panter-Downes's epistles to the *New Yorker* served, and were doubtless intended to serve, the aim of convincing US readers that Common People in Britain were united in a Common Cause, that 'unknown warriors' were bravely doing their duty, and that it was for them that the USA should provide help – that such help would not be diverted merely to serve the ends of snobs and exploiters.

On 20 August, Churchill spoke to the Commons on the war situation, and chose to make a rousing climax out of the recent bases-for-destroyers agreement with the USA. He pointed out that:

these two great organisations of the English-speaking democracies, the British Empire and the United States, will have to be somewhat mixed up together in some of their affairs for mutual and general advantage. For my own part, looking out upon the future, I do not view the process with any misgivings. I could not stop it if I wished; no one can stop it. Like the Mississippi, it just keeps rolling along. Let it roll. Let it roll on full flood, inexorable, irresistible, benignant, to broader lands and better days.[10]

There was a lengthy tradition within British thought about Empire of looking to the USA as an 'Anglo-Saxon' or 'English-speaking' ally rather than a dangerous rising rival. Charles Wentworth Dilke, a brilliant young Liberal, had toured the 'English-speaking countries' in 1866 and 1867 and had published a popular book, *Greater Britain*, in which he had argued that 'the English race' could and would dominate the rest of the world for its own good: 'No possible series of events can prevent the English race itself in 1970 numbering 300 millions of beings – of one national character and one tongue. Italy, Spain, France, Russia become pygmies by the side of such a people.' While Dilke believed that Britain would swiftly lose 'manufacturing supremacy' to the USA, as a man of republican views, as well as imperialistic ones, he wrote as if no less pro-American than pro-British.[11] Kipling showed kinship with Dilke's spirit in 1899 when he urged the USA to 'Take up the White Man's Burden' in the Philippines. Churchill's mother had been American. He would make it his task after the war to publish a *History of the English-Speaking Peoples*. In A. J. P. Taylor's judgement, 'he supposed that nearly all Americans were pro-British and that an Anglo-Saxon alliance was in the making. He never understood that even those Americans who wished to defeat Hitler were not equally anxious to save the British Empire.'[12] In fact, US officials were mostly convinced that British imperialism was iniquitous. In the latter stages of the war, the head of the British Foreign Office's Far Eastern Department complained that the Americans were 'virtually conducting political warfare' against the British in Asia.[13] Goebbels tried on behalf of the Nazis to exploit the obvious fact that America, pressuring Britain to concede independence to India, was in effect taking over world hegemony. For instance, he commented on the Anglo–American landing in French North Africa late in 1942 that 'Britain has readily given her consent to this seizure of European property by America, since America is gradually taking over Britain's colonial possessions anyway.'[14]

The greatest single fact suppressed by the Myth of the Blitz is this: in 1940, because Churchill refused to give in, world power passed decisively away from Britain to the USA. And, ironically, the creation of the Myth, by Churchill and others, was intended to secure the US involvement in the war which would produce that very effect. However, the Myth accorded Britain, *standing alone*, a moral victory over Germany. As Keynes put it, Britain 'helped to save the world'. Exulting over this triumph, the British, from Churchill downwards, could ignore the realities of bankruptcy and lost pre-eminence. And this had a valuable side-effect. It defused latent resentment against the USA itself. Had the British public realised that their nation was now a US dependency and that their war effort was destroying the Empire, some might have suffered great confusion of feeling.

There is plenty of evidence that the British public knew, and by implication cared, very little about British colonies. In October to December 1940 the Ministry of Information ran an 'Empire Crusade' campaign in the press: 'At its highest point, after ten weeks of large-scale advertising, under a third of a large sample were aware of the campaign's existence. But of these, only a part remembered what the copy was about. One person in twenty had studied the copy closely in any one week – sufficiently closely to be able to recall at all clearly what it was about.' Even among the upper and middle classes, of whom over a third had read the advertisements, the campaign attracted more unfavourable than appreciative comment. At its end, 'there was no significant improvement in the number of people who knew, for instance, the difference between a Dominion and a Colony'.[15]

This 'Crusade' had been largely the brainchild of an Oxford don, H. V. Hodson, who was director of the Empire Division of the MoI. Its aim, as Ian McLaine puts it, was 'to educate the public about the empire and the commonwealth and in so doing convince them of the moral superiority of Britain's way of ordering the world'. The hope, as Hodson expressed it, was that a 'positive and dynamic faith' in the Commonwealth and its future would replace the 'comparatively negative sentiment of "defeating Nazi Germany"'. So newspaper readers on Sunday 13 October were told, 'We, who are members of the British Commonwealth, hold in our hands the future of the world . . . We are the builders at grips with the destroyers. We stand for healthy unhampered growth, fighting the disease of tyranny.' Whereas the Nazis were creating a 'slave empire', the British Empire was 'a family of free nations . . . the hope of the future'.[16] Clearly this high-flying idealism lacked the force of Churchill's much pithier evocations of 'Empire' as simply a 'fact of life'.

Which is what it was. John M. Mackenzie has argued in his *Propaganda and Empire* (1984) that 'an imperial nationalism, compounded of monarchism, militarism, and Social Darwinism, through which the British defined their own unique superiority *vis à vis* the rest of the world' was the 'dominant ideology' in British society from the late-nineteenth through to the mid-twentieth century. 'Advertising, the theatre, the cinema, broadcasting, the Churches, youth organisations, ritual and ceremonial, the educational system, and juvenile literature of all sorts' spread this ideology throughout life. The British working class, underdogs at home, were reminded, for instance, 'by the containers of every beverage they drank', that they were the fortunate overlords of coloured masses overseas, while 'The great imperial epics of Alexander Korda and Michael Balcon were amongst the most popular films of the 1930s, and they were repeatedly reissued during and after the Second World War.' The complacent habit of superiority 'created what might be called "projected markets of the mind" in Britain, intellectual shells which were only really shattered, like their economic equivalents, in the 1960s'.[17] Only unrepresentative middle-class intellectuals reacted against it. Imperialist ideology not only survived but advanced between the wars, and through the Second.

For instance, V. C. Clinton-Baddeley's very successful version of the pantomime *Aladdin* contained much imperial matter, including a song, 'Mothers of Empire':

> Methinks I see beside the campfire sitting
> Many an Empire Mother at her knitting . . .

This originated in the thirties and was staged by the Bristol Old Vic as late as 1947–8. The imperialistic boys' stories of G. M. Henty, originating in Victorian Britain, were all still in print in 1955. The Empire Day Movement, which could not secure official recognition in Britain until 1916, waxed in power between the wars and reached its apogee during the Second. The King became its patron in 1941, when Empire Day was linked with the war effort as the culmination of War Weapons Week, and the Home Guard and the civil defence services participated in parades and religious events. At the beginning of the war, subscriptions to the movement had barely reached £200. In 1943 they totalled £6,840. In 1944 a Sunday newspaper, *Empire News*, helped sponsor a massive Festival of Empire at the Royal Albert Hall in London. The King and Queen and the two princesses were in a full house of 8,000. Thousands more tried and failed to get tickets. The second half was broadcast to the Empire. Meanwhile the rival Empire Youth Movement, founded by a Canadian, Major Ney, in 1937, held Commonwealth services every year in Westminster Abbey, and these too were often attended by the Royal Family and broadcast. While the American Office of War Information refused Hollywood permission, after 1940, to make any more films about the British Empire (these had been mightily successful in the thirties), Mackenzie argues that the spate of British official films on the armed forces and their campaigns 'gave the Imperial adventure tradition a further boost'.[18]

Mackenzie, I think, goes too far. His conflation of 'imperialism' and 'racialism' with 'monarchism' and 'patriotism' in one dominant ideology oversimplifies a complex cultural situation in which even a non-'intellectual' might be intensely patriotic without sympathising with 'imperialism' in any positive sense. But by showing the great popularity of imperially orientated films, pageants and movements in the forties he does confirm that perhaps *because* of their lack of curiosity about what went on in the Empire, it was something of which millions of Britons approved, and which they took for granted. Its existence confirmed that Britain, outclassed by the USA in population and productivity, nevertheless remained at least equal as a Great Power to any country on earth.

Attitudes to America and Americans, as exposed by studies of opinion during the war, were ambivalent. Before Pearl Harbor, the MoI's Home Intelligence reports showed that while Roosevelt was esteemed, and US help was appreciated, American neutrality was widely resented. The Republic was letting Britain fight the battle for it. America had come late into the First World War, and that still rankled. But Home Intelligence concluded that America was 'not really regarded as a foreign country, to be wooed with praise, but as a close relative, to be chided freely for her shortcomings'. Pearl Harbor provoked expressions of 'malicious delight' that at last Americans would get a taste of war. Home Intelligence noted that 'while the public are prepared to make any sacrifices necessary to help Russia, it is pointed out that they have no such disposition towards America . . . America is "too damned wealthy" . . . '[19]

A Mass-Observation sample survey in February 1942 suggested that three-fifths of Londoners had a favourable opinion of America, only a quarter a hostile one. *Everybody* was in favour of co-operation with the USA after the war, yet now, following British military collapse in the Far East, there was a 'new tendency' in opinion, a 'fear that in any such co-operation we shall be in a *too inferior* position'.[20]

I shall return later to the subject of British feelings towards America. In relation to the mythologising of 1940, the point which I hope I have established is that there was a fund of patriotism identified vaguely with Empire which was inherently right-wing in, so to speak, its gravitational pull, and that this was inherently at loggerheads with public acceptance of alliance with the USA as a subordinate power. Strangely, this meant that left-wing publicists, for whom national power was far less important than justice for the world's poorer people, found it easier than right-wing ones to mythologise in ways favourable to the USA. Half the Mass-Observation sample just referred to thought Americans were 'more democratic' than the British themselves, and Churchill himself was pulled left-ward ideologically by a similar perception, as his rhetoric invoked 'unknown warriors' and 'the forward march of the common people'.

America under Roosevelt – who was very popular in Britain – seemed a 'progressive', even a 'left-wing' country in its domestic policies. In the twenties, British left-wingers had clearly perceived that New York had taken over from London as the prime centre of international capitalism. When Britain's minority Labour government fell in 1931, pressure from US bankers was plausibly blamed: to get a loan from New York, the Cabinet would have had to make cuts in spending unacceptable to most Labour Party opinion. The USA itself at that time had presented a fearsome picture of the results of unbridled capitalism – breadlines bizarrely coexisting with agricultural surpluses. But from 1935, Roosevelt's New Deal began to be inspirational for thinkers on the left centre of British politics. It seemed to represent what 'planning' could achieve without the wholesale overthrow of capitalism.

John Maynard Keynes expressed enthusiasm for Roosevelt as early as 1933, and in the same year Walter Citrine, General Secretary of the Trade Union Congress, persuaded that body to pass a resolution praising FDR. H. G. Wells visited him in 1934 and described him as 'the most effective transmitting institution possible for the coming of the New World Order'. Gradually, more and more British socialists were disarmed by what could be discerned across the Atlantic: Roosevelt's impact seen in a big development of trade unionism; the elimination of company unions; progressive social security measures; and successful public works like those of the Tennessee Valley Authority. In 1939, Jennie Lee, wife of the Labour Left's rising star Aneurin Bevan, was ready to declare, 'There are flags of freedom flying higher and wider in America than anywhere else in the world.'[21]

Even the self-consciously Marxist Left was to some extent won over. Victor Gollancz's Left Book Club, founded in 1936, was a phenomenal success although, or because, it was under Communist Party influence; it appealed to young people thrust left-ward by the spectre of fascism on the Continent, and by 1939 had 57,000 members and 1,200 local groups.[22] Its selectors of titles, besides Gollancz himself, were Harold Laski, the leading 'Marxist' theoretician within the Labour Party, and John Strachey, the chief intellectual guru of the Communist young. Laski's 'Marxism' was a mule crossed with Liberalism. While he could not reconcile it with the New Deal, he announced in 1936 that the USA had 'a chance of showing that there is a genuine alternative to Fascism and Communism'. Two years later he wrote, albeit in the *Chicago Law Review*, not Gollancz's *Left News*: 'If our age emerges satisfactorily from this period of blood and war, I believe that the Roosevelt experiment in America, with all its blunders and follies, will be regarded by the historian as having made a supreme contribution to the Cause of Freedom.' Strachey was expelled from the USA in 1935, but nevertheless revisited it in 1938. He now concluded that the New Deal was a partial model for a transitional *Programme for Progress*, to cite the title of his Left Book Club volume published in 1940.

Between Strachey's arrival at this new opinion and his book's publication, he, Laski and Gollancz had fallen out with the CPGB, over the Nazi–Soviet pact and the 'revolutionary defeatist' line taken by the Party; Gollancz removed the Left Book Club, which was his personal property, from CP control. Nevertheless, Strachey's book carried forward the Party's commitment in the late thirties to a popular front against fascism involving progressives and sincere anti-Nazis from all parties. His aim was to provide a basis in economic theory for socialist collaboration in a political situation after the war, in which the balance of political power would be such that the government represented 'the people' but contained or co-operated with 'forces and parties which were not socialist'. He saw the ending of unemployment as crucial, and presented a 'six-point programme' for action involving the promotion of all kinds of public or mixed investment and enterprise of a non profit-making kind; the lowering of the rate of interest to all borrowers; the redistribution of income by progressive taxation; the payment for greatly increased pensions, allowances and other social services, so long as unemployment existed, with newly created money rather than taxation; the development of a national non-profit-making banking system; and strict public control over the balance of foreign payments. While still claiming to be a Marxist intent on full socialism, Strachey saw this as a programme transitional towards that goal. Having enunciated it, he turned to analyse the New Deal at length.

It was 'by far the greatest programme of public enterprise for pacific purposes' which the world had ever seen. To 'a greater or lesser extent' it had actually carried through the first four points of Strachey's programme, and Roosevelt's devaluation of the dollar was in effect equivalent to the sixth. All the failures of the New Deal were due to the tragic neglect of Roosevelt and his allies to take charge of the US banking system. In short, Britain's leading Marxist theorist was convinced that, had it embodied his fifth point, the New Deal would have represented a perfect equivalent to the transitional policy, towards socialism, which he would advocate *to* the Left Book Club, *for* Britain. He saw clearly that FDR, and even his progressive advisers, didn't want to follow the 'socialist' way of doing things implied by taking control of banks. He discerned that the National Recovery Act of 1933, while producing progressive codes of employment, had basically been a vehicle for cartelisation via trade associations. Yet he praised the manner in which Roosevelt and his allies, by contrast with the socialist Léon Blum in France, had fought back against recession in 1937 – 'the progressive forces of America proved to have greater courage and greater skill than their European equivalents'. He believed that these 'progressive forces' must and would move forward to save the New Deal and transmute it to something better.[23]

America, then, was a land led by a genuine anti-fascist and democrat which had shown how socialism might be feasible elsewhere. So entrenched did such optimism about America become in the non-Communist British Left that even the views of Wendell Willkie, Roosevelt's challenger for the presidency in 1940, as expressed in his *One World* (1943), would be widely approved and quoted in left-wing circles – for instance, his call for 'the orderly but scheduled abolition of the colonial system'.[24] While US anti-imperialism was sometimes so vehement that it annoyed even Fabian gradualists on the right of Labour opinion, it was convenient to invoke in calls for the granting of self-government to India.

And in 1940, approval of America helped the non-Communist Left fight a battle which it saw as all-important against the CPGB and other 'defeatist' elements. The Soviet Union had betrayed the anti-fascist cause, however temporarily and for whatever discernible rational motives, when doing a deal with Hitler in the autumn of 1939. If the USA was far from being the socialist paradise which many had thought Russia represented, it could be made a reason for hope: hope that the Old Gang, Chamberlain and his friends, would be buried by 'progressive' opinion in America as well as Britain; hope that Hitler could be defeated and that, from victory over Nazism, the British people could proceed to create a 'New Order' at home, and help to build one of worldwide scope.

Let us now have a look at what, beneath much rhetoric, went on at 'the desperate edge of now' from September 1939 onwards.

*

What the British people expected in September 1939 was a repetition of the 1914–18 war of attrition and siege on the Western Front, combined with the novel horror of air raids on a huge scale, and perhaps with German gas attacks on civilians. What they experienced was a perturbing phase of anticlimax, during which class divisions in British society were demonstrated and exacerbated as at no time since the 1926 General Strike.

It is conventional to write of the 'intense and genuine sense of national unity' engendered in Britain by the Second World War, of a 'mood of national solidarity and endeavour'.[25] The increased propensity of middle-class persons to vote Labour in the 1945 general election might plausibly be seen as the result of such a 'mood', and the experience of mass evacuation of slum dwellers into respectable areas in 1939–40, and the degree of urban deprivation which it revealed to shocked rural and suburban householders, as 'part of an entire involvement of the worthy middle class with the neglected multitudes brought about by the dislocations of war'.[26] Yet as James Cronin has pointed out, taking election results as a gauge, the period from 1939 to 1951 saw class polarisation in Britain as never before.[27] Labour maximised its working-class support, achieving in 1951 (when it lost) the largest popular vote ever recorded in British electoral history, and still a record. The Conservative Party rallied the middle classes. The Liberal Party, briefly, was almost extinguished, left with a few strongholds on the eccentric 'Celtic fringe'. Without denying that evacuation stimulated the social consciences of many 'worthy' middle-class people, and gave credibility and urgency to projects for social reform, it seems fair to enquire whether it did not also have a bearing on the strong class prejudices so marked in post-war Britain.

Between the world wars official circles in Britain had been obsessed with the role of the bomber in war. As early as 1925, British Air Staff was predicting that casualties in London alone in a new war would begin at the rate of 5,000 on the first day, and settle down at 2,500 a day. It predicted a collapse of morale, and added that there was no possible defence against this sort of attack. This theory of the 'knock-out blow' had continued to dominate Air Staff thinking and to influence government decisions. A novel called *The Gas War of 1940*, by 'Miles' (S. Southwold), appeared in 1931 and prophesied London's destruction:

> In the dark streets the burned and wounded, bewildered and panic-stricken, fought and struggled like beasts, scrambling over the dead and dying alike, until they fell and were in turn trodden

underfoot by the ever-increasing multitude about them . . . In a dozen parts of London that night people died in their homes with the familiar walls crashing about them in flames; thousands rushed into the streets to be met by blasts of flame and explosion and were blown to rags.

Deeply impressed by reports of the horrible effects of bombing in China by the Japanese, Stanley Baldwin averred in the House of Commons on 10 November 1931: 'I think it is well . . . for the man in the street to realise that there is no power on earth that can prevent him from being bombed. Whatever people may tell him, the bomber will always get through.'[28]

In 1937 British experts reckoned that Hitler's Germany, if war broke out, would bomb Britain at once and carry on for sixty days. There would be 600,000 people killed and twice that number injured. Already, air-raid precautions were under way – the Air Raid Wardens' Service had recruited some 200,000 people by mid-1938, and wardens, with police, were on hand to direct British civilians into shelters as sirens sounded in London on 3 September 1939, less than a quarter of an hour after Chamberlain had announced the beginning of war.

But that was a false alarm. And the fact that bombs did not in fact rain down on British cities, while fortunate in itself, provided an awkward context for mass evacuation. On 1 September 1939, one and a half million people were stuffed under a government scheme from cities into 'reception areas'. The scheme was voluntary. About half the schoolchildren from England's 'evacuation areas' left, somewhat over a third from Scotland's: 827,000 children in all, together with 524,000 mothers and children under school age going together, a few thousand expectant mothers, a few thousand handicapped people, and a lot of teachers.

All these were to be billeted on householders in the 'reception' areas. The local billeting officers were in general volunteers with no experience as urban social workers. For various reasons, the scheme was certain to produce social mismatching of hosts and guests. While better-off people were often able 'unofficially' to send children to stay with rural friends, poorer parents could rarely do this. The evacuation areas were mostly zones of high population density, characterised by poverty and overcrowding, where working-class people maintained a higher birth rate than the middle classes, who lived in suburbs deemed less vulnerable to attack. Many poor children knew little or nothing about the countryside. Many well-to-do country householders had had no conception of the ways of life of slum dwellers in London, Merseyside, Birmingham, Glasgow and other cities. Had the Luftwaffe in fact attacked Britain at once, sympathy might have overridden resentment. But it didn't, and a clamour of protests from guests and hosts alike was heard. Billeting officers were 'bombarded' throughout September and October by requests from householders that their evacuees should be removed. In Newbury, Berkshire, for instance, rebilleting averaged forty to fifty transfers weekly. In neighbouring Maidenhead the numbers were higher – 750 transfers in three months. By early November the Education Officer of the London County Council was driven to breakdown and two months' absence from work, after coping with the streams of enquiry and criticism flooding into his office.[29]

The great focus of complaint was the verminous condition and dirty habits of many evacuees. At an extreme, in Bridgnorth in Shropshire, which received evacuees from the notorious Scotland Road area of Liverpool, 70 per cent of the evacuees were estimated to harbour vermin. Skin diseases were sadly common. Many children were very badly clothed and shod. Coming from areas where baths were rare and communal lavatories disgusting, many children lacked modern ideas of hygiene. Children in such a state might be pitied and forgiven, but mothers from the slums seemed to belong to another, and worse, race. R. C. K. Ensor, a distinguished historian, wrote to the *Spectator* from one of the home counties that many of them were 'the lowest grade of slum women – slatternly, malodorous tatterdemalions'. Another historian, W. L. Burn, echoed him in the same journal: only a third of the evacuated women were tolerable; the rest thought of evacuation as 'a cheap country holiday of infinite duration'; and the evacuees were increasing the burdens of middle-class women whose houses were 'chronically understaffed' (that is, short of domestic servants). Town children, Burn continued, represented 'the antithesis of all that the decent patient country housewife' had 'striven to instill into her own children'. A Berkshire Congregational Church journal asked the same question – was there 'any necessity for the spoliation of decent homes and furniture, the corruption of speech and moral standards of our own children . . . '?[30]

As the Phoney War continued, class war abated. The evacuees largely went home – in England and Wales four-tenths of the schoolchildren and nearly nine-tenths of mothers and children under five had retreated by the beginning of 1940. Those who remained would mostly have found billets where they were accepted or even loved. Travis L. Crosby has recently pointed to 'the most significant aspect of the evacuation story . . . Generally speaking, it seems that wealthy and middle-class householders avoided evacuation duty. Working-class inhabitants of the reception areas welcomed the evacuees – or at least tolerated them in a benign fashion.' He quotes a regional administrator for the Women's Voluntary Service: 'We find over and over again that it is the really poor people who are willing to take evacuees and that the sort of bridge-playing set who live at such places as Chorley Wood are terribly difficult about it all.' So far from Christmas inducing feelings of charity and goodwill among such 'sets', it seems that their hostility actually increased as they sought to clear their homes so that they could entertain relatives and friends, or used shutting up house for the holidays as an excuse for forcing evacuees out. In many areas, rural district councils actually 'supported wealthy householders' actions', rather than trying to implement official national policy fairly. In March 1940 a rural district council in Wiltshire wrote to the Ministry of Health refusing evacuees on the grounds that large houses could not be used because 'the servant problem is acute and it would be unfair to billet children on them'.[31]

Middle-class memories of the horrors of September 1939 resurfaced a year later as bombs did begin to fall heavily. Professor Crosby thinks that 'attitudes may have hardened as the raids reversed the flow of drift back and pushed large numbers of evacuees once again into the countryside . . . The billeting controversy remained rooted in class prejudice.' A letter to the *Windsor Express* in October 1940 actually suggested, quite explicitly, 'concentration camps' for evacuees, and local councils in reception areas did actually discuss mass segregation. And even the novel horror of V-1 bomb attacks in 1944 did not stop 'class-engendered hostility' to the reception of evacuees.[32]

Racialism was a subordinate but not unimportant element in this hostility. Many inner-city dwellers, notably in London, were Jewish, and even well-behaved Jews were not acceptable to many 'bridge-playing' persons in reception areas. Seaport cities had sizeable 'coloured' minorities. In a letter actually published in the USA in 1941, in a book called *War Letters from Britain*, the wife of an RAF pilot rejoiced that she had no evacuees herself. She told a friend that they had 'caused more trouble than the Germans. They come from the worst part of Liverpool and the colour varies from black to yellow.'[33]

Gloria Agman was evacuated, aged twelve, from London for a second time after the Blitz began. In a village in the Midlands, between Rugby and Leicester, she and her four-year-old brother were billeted on a couple who ran a pub in addition to the man doing full-time farm work. They were welcomed 'with affection and generosity'. Most of the time village children and evacuees got on well together, but occasionally they formed into hostile gangs:

In the skirmishes between Village and Evacuees, my place was clearly defined; but there were times when both groups united to attack me as a 'rotten Jew'. (Apart from my brother and me, there were only two other Jewish children in the village, and they never once came out to play with anyone.) My defence against this was of limited effectiveness, but it helped to protect me from total isolation and humiliation when these attacks came. I found an ally. My closest friend throughout much of my stay in the village was a half-Chinese girl from London who was exposed to the same experience as mine, except that she was called a 'dirty Chink'. We had a pact. I never called her 'Chink' and she never called me 'Jew'.

Aged thirteen, she won a scholarship and was sent to school in Northampton. Here she was billeted on a 'tight-lipped family, doing their Christian duty but without any warmth'. She pretended to be Church of England herself. This self-protective hypocrisy meant that she could not allow her 'obviously Jewish' parents to visit her. 'And I had to listen in silence to the seemingly unending stream of anti-Semitism which these people directed towards "those filthy Jews" who lived down the road.'[34]

Clearly, evacuation, like other wartime phenomena such as the direction of labour and conscription into the forces, did help to mix people in Britain together as never before and gave a basis for a new degree of mutual respect and understanding, where those people were disposed to be kindly and tolerant. I shall return later to the role of this factor in promoting social reform during and after the war. But heightened social awareness among some sections of the middle classes clearly did not exclude the sharpening of prejudice in others. As Kenneth O. Morgan has written, 'There was much latent anger and passion in British politics after 1945. Mass-Observation data, private surveys by sociologists such as Mark Abrams, and BBC opinion analyses confirmed the very high degree of political commitment, in which voters unhesitatingly proclaimed themselves Labour or Conservative . . . '[35] In July 1948, Aneurin Bevan, the Labour Minister responsible for introducing the National Health Service, made a speech in which he referred to Tories as 'lower than vermin'. Around this period he himself was subjected to extraordinary vilification. He was physically assaulted by an angry member in White's Club. Packets of excrement came through his postbox. He began to carry a stout stick when he went out for an evening walk.[36] Wittingly or unwittingly, the prime promoter of a major social reform aimed to eradicate lice and skin diseases, the very minister responsible for providing better housing for the urban poor, had hit on the phrase most likely to inflame many middle-class householders who had sought to justify their refusal to accept evacuees at the height of national crisis: 'lower than the vermin', they had been identified with the slum dwellers whom they couldn't accept as British like themselves.

4

Celts, Reds and Conchies

> At last! Now is the time with due intensity
> To hew to what really matters – not
> 'Making the world safe for democracy',
> 'Saving civilization', or any such rot.
>
> Hugh MacDiarmid, 'Verses Written
> during the Second World War'

AN INTERNAL 'national problem' lay far less deeply submerged
under the surface of British life in 1939–41 than most historians
have assumed.

Ireland might have been a major problem for the British
government as it had been during the First World War. The Easter
Rising of 1916 had ignited the tinder of nationalism to such effect
that by 1922 an Irish Free State had emerged, though Ulster
remained outside it. The Free State was formally a member of the
British Commonwealth until 1949, but in 1937 its leader, De Valera,
devised a new constitution which gave it, as 'Eire', complete
practical independence. Throughout the Second World War, Eire
was neutral, though its subjects were still accorded automatic British
citizenship if resident on the larger island.

The clandestine Irish Republican Army continued to demand the
reintegration of Ulster with Eire. From January 1939 it conducted a
campaign of violent 'outrages', calling on Britain to withdraw her
institutions and representatives of all kinds from the whole of
Ireland. Public utilities in various parts of England were attacked
with explosives, bombs went off in the London Underground, fires
were started in stores in Coventry. There were tear-gas bombs in
London cinemas, balloon-acid bombs in letterboxes and post offices,
and a device at Madame Tussaud's Waxworks, in the summer,
which blew up King Henry VII. An explosion in Coventry's
shopping centre on 25 August left devastation like an air raid, five
people dead and several more seriously injured, and on the same day

there were more IRA incendiary bombs in Blackpool and Liverpool.[1]
Outrages continued during the Phoney War.

But De Valera and the Dail had responded by stern measures
against the IRA in Eire, internment without trial. Many thoughts of
danger from Ireland seem to have occurred to people in Britain, at all
levels, during the paranoid summer of 1940. Ulster required some
delicate handling. Its Protestant, Unionist government loyally asked
for conscription to be applied there, but Whitehall feared that this
might inflame Catholic and nationalist feeling, strengthen the IRA,
and enrage Irish emigrant sentiment in the USA. So Ulstermen and
women in the services were all volunteers: some 42,000 came
forward during the war, with early peaks in October 1939 and the
summer of 1940. Even more Eire citizens 'went to it' in the British
armed forces – some 50,000 – and the BBC eventually put out a
special series of *Irish Half Hours* for them.[2] And other Irish assisted in
the civilian war effort – 60,000 found work in Britain in 1940–41 and
a further 100,000 in 1942–3.[3]

The possibility that the Germans might try to invade Britain via
Ireland was taken so seriously that four divisions of British troops
were stationed in Ulster by 1941. Belfast received its first significant
air raid on 7 April of that year, when some 100 casualties were
caused; eight days later a further attack killed at least 745 people and
seriously injured hundreds more. Raids early in May caused several
hundred further casualties. Belfast's shelters were probably fewer
and worse than in any other British city. A hundred thousand people
fled to the countryside after the first big raid. Firemen were sent up
from Eire to help. Protestants and Catholics joined in prayer at a
public funeral for 150 of the victims. Then, on 31 May 1941, the
Germans made an absurd navigational error and dropped four
bombs on Dublin, killing twenty-nine people and seriously injuring
forty-five. On balance, Irish neutrality was effectively pro-British.
The Irish and British economies, already closely involved with each
other, were brought still closer. Though the Irish authorities turned a
blind eye on Nazi use of Eire as a base for espionage, that proved
inefficient – and though the Germans in May 1940 sent an agent to
contact the IRA in Eire, he found them so disunited as to be useless.
('You know how to die for Ireland', he told them, 'but how to fight
for it you have not the faintest idea.'[4])

Scotland and Wales were in effect more problematic. It must be
stressed that there are no substantial signs that 'morale' during the
war was ever weaker in these countries than in England. But they
were among the 'buried nationalities' of Europe, to use a phrase
deployed by Tom Nairn, who compares them with Catalonia and

Euzkadi (the Basque country).[5] The German conquest of the Low Countries and France in 1940 was accompanied by a radio propaganda barrage which seemed to people within the BBC to have been spectacularly effective, and had included appeals to Flemish and Breton nationalists. The 'New British Broadcasting Station' operating from Germany and associated above all with William Joyce, 'Lord Haw-Haw', was supplemented at this time with a 'Welsh' freedom station and 'Radio Caledonia', which demanded a separate peace for Scotland.[6] There were good reasons for British public men to be alert to special factors liable to influence morale in Wales and Scotland.

Both contained areas where traditional heavy industries had taken a hammering in the interwar years. Even before the great slump of 1929, a fifth of all British coal-miners were unemployed – and coal was a key industry in both south Wales and Lowland Scotland. A similar decline was seen in shipbuilding, textiles and iron and steel. Thereafter, matters got even worse. In 1932, 36.5 per cent of Welsh workers were unemployed, 27.7 per cent in Scotland – and these proportions were higher than those found in any area of England, or even in Ulster. In certain particular areas the figures were still more horrendous. In Wales, in 1934, '74 per cent of male workers were unemployed in Brynmawr, 73 per cent in Dowlais and 66 per cent in Merthyr'. As for Scotland, 'whereas Glasgow had a total of 89,600 unemployed in 1936, Birmingham, a city of comparable size, had only 21,000'.[7]

Both Scotland and Wales had thrown up nationalist parties between the wars. Plaid Cymru, formed in 1925, had brought together 'nonconformist radicals of the old school', many of them previously pacifist, with certain cosmopolitan intellectuals – one of them the writer Saunders Lewis – who were attracted by Roman Catholicism and by right-wing French Catholic nationalism. The party was at first mainly a cultural pressure group, committed above all to the protection of the Welsh language. But Lewis was a man with some charisma, and Kenneth O. Morgan sees his small party as highly significant of a 'phase of self-examination and self-doubt' in Wales which had important influences on the country's whole culture. By 1939 it had 2,000 members. Its growth had been greatly stimulated by the 'martyrdom' of Saunders Lewis and two other leading members after an incident in September 1936 when they had taken part in the burning of an RAF bombing school in Caernarvonshire to which there had been much local opposition, and had then admitted responsibility. Welsh people of all parties were angered when the Baldwin government moved the trial from a local Welsh court to the Old Bailey, on the grounds that a Welsh jury would probably be biased. No less a Welshman than David Lloyd George wrote of this as an 'outrage' that made his 'blood boil'. The three men were imprisoned in London for nine months after refusing to give evidence in English. There was a mass public subscription in Wales to pay their defence costs. 'For writers and intellectuals', Kenneth Morgan observes, 'the imprisonment of "the three" for an idealistic gesture committed on behalf of nationalist and pacific values had a profound impact.'

The appeal of Plaid Cymru for Christian pacifists was enhanced. Lewis, however, was a man of the Right, 'tinged with anti-democratic and anti-liberal sentiments'. Though he resigned the presidency of Plaid Cymru in 1939, after serving for thirteen years, his party remained detached from 'England's imperialist war'. In August 1940 his successor, Professor Daniel, explained that the war was 'a clash of rival imperialisms from which Wales, like the other small nations of Europe, has nothing to gain but everything to lose . . . It does not accept the popular English view that this war is a crusade of light against darkness. It does not admit the right of England to conscript Welshmen into her army . . . ' The German Abwehr thought of attempting to use Welsh Nationalists as supporters 'on the line of Quisling in Norway or the Breton separatists in France'. Despite the general unpopularity of Lewis's intense brand of nationalism, he received 22.5 per cent of the vote in a by-election in January 1943 for the University of Wales parliamentary constituency (one confined to the institution's graduates) – a striking proof of his prestige in certain intellectual circles.[8]

But a well-informed English patriot casting anxious eyes towards Wales in the summer of 1940 would be more worried by the popularity and militancy of the Communist Party in certain areas. A quarter of the insured working population of Wales was employed in coal in 1939. The Miners' Federation in Wales represented 135,000 miners and sponsored thirteen MPs. Communists were entrenched in its executive council and its impressive president, Arthur Horner, was a Communist. His base at Mardy in the Rhondda Valley had been in the twenties the best-known of the 'Little Moscows' which flourished in Wales, where a whole community had been 'translated into a Welsh sector of a proletarian international with its Young Pioneers, its secular funerals (red ribbons and hammer-and-sickle wreaths) . . . ' By the mid-thirties, the CP was an important part of the informal 'Popular Front', including Labour and Independent Labour Party people, which organised an astonishing demonstration on Sunday 3 February 1935, when, as Gwyn A. Williams puts it, 'the population of south Wales seems to have turned out on to the streets', in a great cry of protest against unemployment and the 'Means Test'. About 300,000 people marched that day – one Welsh person in seven. The CP's moral position was strengthened by the fact that of the 174 volunteers who fought with the International Brigade in Spain, the majority were 'in coal' and Communists: 'To serve in Spain became as much a mark of honour as to have gone to jail for the cause . . . a poverty stricken people gave milk, money and goods to the Spanish republic.' As late as 1945, the Communist Party leader, Harry Pollitt, came close to defeating Labour in the Rhondda heartland of working-class militancy.[9]

In 1938 the Central Committee of the British CP acknowledged the right to self-determination of Wales – and Scotland – and supported the Welsh language. Horner did not go along with nationalism. Nor did he like it in 1939 when the CPGB committed itself after the Nazi–Soviet pact to the view that Britain was fighting an 'imperialist' war. Kenneth Morgan suggests that he 'defied the might of the Comintern in endorsing the war effort'. However, when he expressed his detestation of Hitler to a journalist at the time, and was asked how far he was actually prepared to go in fighting him, Horner hesitated and said 'I stop short at defence.'[10]

And many in the Welsh mining valleys did not like Winston Churchill. It was widely believed in the working-class movement that, when Home Secretary in 1910, Churchill had ordered troops to fire on strikers at Tonypandy in the Rhondda. In fact he 'had at first specifically forbidden the sending of troops, insisting that police be used instead. But he had later authorised the stationing of troops in the valley'.[11] And no class-conscious miner on any coalfield was going to forget Churchill's fierce opposition to the General Strike of 1926. It is no accident that the most memorably vehement of Churchill's critics in the wartime Commons was Aneurin Bevan, who represented a Welsh mining constituency. Even in August 1940, while recognising Churchill's immense popularity, he was warning that 'in a democracy, idolatry is the first sin. Not even the supreme emergency of war justifies the abandonment of critical judgement.'[12]

However, the only Communist Party MP in the Commons was Willie Gallacher, who sat for West Fife, in Scotland, from 1935 to 1951. Like Horner, he was only a very reluctant follower of his party's line of opposition to the war in 1939–41. Nevertheless, he 'pursued an obstructionist policy of attacking the Government on issues such as cheap fares for parents of evacuees; payment of the armed forces; the alleged use of the Home Guard in industrial disputes in Scotland; and the inadequacies of the air-raid shelter system . . . '[13]

Gallacher was a famous veteran of the militant doings in and around Glasgow in 1915–22 which had created the myth of the 'Red Clyde'. Clydeside during the First World War had been the key centre of arms production in the British Empire. It had also seen a great Rent Strike in 1915 – R. J. Morris has recently argued that 'the people of Glasgow collectively and in conjunction with others wrecked an important part of the capitalist system, namely the free market in private rented housing, for ever'.[14] This had been preceded and was followed by impressive strikes by skilled engineers, and vehement anti-war agitation, notably by John Maclean, the leading Scottish Marxist who after the Russian Revolution became Soviet Consul in Glasgow. Maclean was several times jailed. Gallacher and other shop stewards active in the Clyde Workers' Committee were at one stage deported to Edinburgh. After the war, the Clyde Workers' Committee was revived to demand a thirty-hour week, the Scottish Trade Union Congress more moderately called for forty hours and the 'Forty-hour Strike' which ensued worried the Lloyd George government so much that 12,000 troops and six tanks were sent into Glasgow. On 31 January a huge crowd was attacked and dispersed by police in George Square. The Myth of Red Clyde conflated this record of militancy with the election of November 1922, in which ten Labour MPs were returned in the fifteen Glasgow constituencies, and with the image acquired by these 'Clydesiders' of extreme fundamentalist socialists. While some historians agree with Morris that the Myth or legend is not without much basis in fact – after all, Glasgow did become and remain a stronghold of left-wing politics – others have stressed that the Women's Rent Strike and the strikes by engineers were separate, and that 1916–19 saw three years of industrial peace and successful arms production in Clydeside, while Labour's triumph in 1922 had much more to do with the swing of the Catholic vote to the left by the RC hierarchy itself than with the classes in Marxism previously organised by John Maclean.[15]

Be that as it may, myths, as this book has argued, can affect 'fact' by affecting behaviour. Glasgow's shipbuilding industry and the Scottish coal-mines were on the rack of industrial decline between the wars – but both were of key significance again after 1939.

The CP had considerable influence in industrial Scotland. Abe Moffat, who sat on Fife County Council as a Communist from 1924, resigned from it in 1942 when elected president of the National Union of Scottish Mineworkers. Alexander Sloan, secretary of the Union, became Labour MP for South Ayrshire just before the war.

He had been a conscientious objector in the previous world war, joined the Labour Party Peace Aims Group in 1939 and signed their manifesto in October calling for an armistice. He worked closely with Gallacher in the Commons. Like all other sections of the Trade Union Congress, the Miners' Federation of Great Britain adopted a policy of full support for the Chamberlain government against Germany. The Federation's Scottish constituent formally supported 'the war against Fascist aggression'. But its Annual Conference on 4 May 1940 sent fraternal greetings to the Russian miners' trade unions. Its delegate conference on 1 July 1940 called by 61:45 for 'the establishment of a Labour Government and complete removal of elements associated with the Chamberlain Government from important offices in this country'. Sloan, seconding, argued:

> The working classes are fighting because they believe they are fighting for freedom. The possessing classes are fighting for their own interests. Ten per cent of the population possesses 90 per cent of the wealth. France was defeated because 200 families of France possess nearly the whole of the country.[16]

The Independent Labour Party had been an important constituent of the Labour Party until 1932. Its disaffiliation reduced it to a dwindling purist rump with Marxist propensities, though its relations with the CP were intensely hostile. Its figurehead, James Maxton, MP, had been a pacifist agitator on the 'Red Clyde', and publicly congratulated Chamberlain in 1938 for securing the Munich agreement. In practice, as left-socialist opponents of the war, he and his party in 1939–41 had a position akin to that of the CP, but they remained committed to peace after Russia was invaded. Despite this, Maxton and his fellow MPs John McGovern and Campbell Stephen would all be re-elected as Independent Labour Party members in 1945. All three had seats in Glasgow, which was the only area in Britain where the Independent Labour Party, in normal times, retained electoral significance.

But 1939–45 was not a normal period. Even before Labour went into Churchill's coalition in May 1940, the major parties observed an 'electoral truce' in by-elections. Despite its 'Stop the War' line, the Independent Labour Party gained new members, and eventually did rather well in by-elections. At Lancaster in October 1941, at Central Edinburgh in December and again in Cardiff in March 1942, it secured, in the absence of Labour candidates, between a fifth and three-tenths of the vote. While 'independents' of a bellicose populist-Conservative cast did as well or better in the same phase in other parts of the country, there is clear evidence that the Independent Labour Party's virtual pacifism did not make its members electoral pariahs. Even in April 1940, its candidate got a quarter of the poll in Renfrew East, near Glasgow.[17]

A more remarkable by-election record is that of the Scottish National Party. Its predecessor, the National Party of Scotland, had been founded in 1928, three years after Plaid Cymru, which it somewhat resembled in composition, attracting Catholic intellectuals, students, journalists and discontented Independent Labour Party followers: the latter included Roland Muirhead, its first chairman, and its secretary John MacCormick Muirhead, a wealthy tanner whose cash kept the party going, was a devoted pacifist in both world wars who argued that industrial and military conscription of Scots was contrary to the terms of the 1707 Treaty of Union with England, and therefore unconstitutional. In 1934, the National Party merged with the Scottish Party founded in 1931 by dissident Unionists (Conservatives) and Scottish Liberals. It polled 16 per cent in the eight seats which it contested in the 1935 general election. In 1937 the SNP pledged itself to oppose conscription save when carried out by a Scottish government, and when war broke out the chairman of its Aberdeen branch, Douglas Young – a university lecturer in Greek, poet and socialist – duly got himself charged with refusing to register either for military service or as a conscientious objector. Through a long legal battle in 1940 and 1941 Young 'began to attain the status of a martyr'. Privately, he believed that the allies would lose the war and that Scots should prepare to make a separate peace with the Nazi conquerors. He wrote to Muirhead on 1 August 1940:

> The Germans will look around for aborigines to run Scotland, and it is to be wished that the eventual administration consist of people who have in the past shown themselves to care for the interests of Scotland.

Yet in February 1944, Young came very close to winning Kirkcaldy Burghs for the SNP, with 41 per cent of the poll. And in April 1945 the new Party secretary, Dr Robert McIntyre, actually won Motherwell – the first nationalist candidate ever to be elected anywhere in Great Britain.[18]

This success had been prefigured, however, by the remarkable result on 10 April 1940 of a by-election in Argyll. The seat had been held by a Unionist (Conservative). Neither Labour nor Liberals now contested it. The SNP put forward an able candidate, the writer

William Power, who fought on local economic issues. He was not explicitly anti-war, but to oppose a government nominee at all could be construed as unpatriotic – especially as only the day before the poll the Germans had invaded Norway. Nevertheless, the SNP got 37 per cent of the vote – easily their most significant electoral performance up to then.

Soothsaying how Scotland would go in 1940 was therefore problematic. The coming of war cut unemployment to negligible proportions, but created local strains, with many Scottish factories closing down entirely. The Clydeside shipyards, booming with war orders, enjoyed fairly tranquil industrial relations. Nevertheless, after Churchill appointed Tom Johnston as Secretary of State for Scotland in February 1941, the latter was able to use the bogey of Scottish nationalism as a powerful lever for getting what he wanted for Scotland from the Cabinet. Johnston himself belonged to a powerful tradition of support for Home Rule in the Scottish Labour Movement, which went back to the 1880s, but had gradually come to the view that Scotland needed no more than administrative devolution of decisions to the Edinburgh Scottish Office and an end to internal partisan strife. Sir John Reith, fellow Scot and pre-war director of the BBC, heard Johnston say in July 1943 that he was 'very bothered by Bevin and other English ministers who do things affecting Scotland without consulting him. He thinks there is a great danger of Scottish Nationalism coming up, and a sort of *Sinn Fein* as he called it.'[19]

It is worth mentioning here an extraordinary example of the extent to which a respected Scot might distance himself (though without apparent political motive) from England during the war. Edwin Muir was one of the country's leading poets, a middle-aged Orcadian who had once been a member of the Independent Labour Party and had later been attracted to the idea of Social Credit, but was now neither pacifistic, nor communistic, nor fascistic in his sympathies; as for nationalism, he had aroused the fury of C. M. Grieve ('Hugh MacDiarmid') by his suggestion in *Scott and Scotland* (1936) that Scots writers should turn their back on the Scottish tongue and work in English.

His poem 'Scotland 1941' carries not the faintest reference to war, but projects a thesis about purely Scottish history. The Calvinistic reformers, Knox and Melville, had destroyed an idyllic rustic culture and created a 'desolation', crushing 'the poet with an iron text'. The ugliness and materialism of the industrial city had followed – 'Now smoke and dearth and money everywhere . . .' Though the war had reduced 'dearth' by full employment and restricted the use of money by the rich, Muir presents 1941 as merely another post-industrial year:

> [of] spiritual defeat wrapped warm in riches,
> No pride but pride of pelf.

Yet it was the 'perverse' bravery of Scots in the seventeenth century civil and religious wars – 'Montrose, MacKail, Argyle' – which had carved out 'This towering pulpit of the Golden Calf . . . '[20]

Now Muir, 'frustrated and isolated' in St Andrews, and short of money, was an idiosyncratic poet concerned with the timeless and with a preoccupation with the freedom and innocence of an Orkney childhood which contrasted totally with the industrial Scotland where he worked as a clerk for a time from the age of nineteen.[21] But it remains remarkable that he should draw attention, by the date in his poem's title, to his sense of the unimportance of the international context. His attitude was not expressed in action like Douglas Young's, but it too points to the real danger in 1940–41 that in Scotland, and Wales, as in France and Norway, significant people, confronted by defeat, could have reconciled or resigned themselves to it on local cultural grounds.

Wales and Scotland were (and are) very different countries, with almost opposite relationships, historically speaking, to English imperialism. A Welsh dynasty ruling in London, the Tudors, had persuaded the Welsh people into a compromise where independence was largely sacrificed but the Welsh language was preserved. In the eighteenth century, the country had been seized by an evangelical Protestant movement which had in effect divided common folk, largely Calvinistic Methodists, from Anglican, English-speaking gentry, just before English – and Scots – capital had invaded the Welsh economy and industrialised it. Scotland's rulers, on the other hand, had joined in Union with England in 1707 in the hope – richly fulfilled – of a share in the profits of overseas empire. Scottish capitalism had developed independent strength, and the country had retained its distinctive established church and legal system. But while both countries had responded with especial fervour to the call to arms in the Great War, both had seen a striking upsurge of industrial militancy during and after that war, then met economic catastrophe. The danger in both was that pacifistic indifference to the war in some religious, nationalist and socialist circles would coalesce, in practical effect, under the strain of defeat, invasion or heavy bombing, with Communist obedience to the Moscow line. Besides Radio Caledonia and a Welsh 'freedom station', German 'black' broadcasting produced a 'Christian Peace Movement' station in August 1940, while its 'Workers Challenge' station attacked the Labour leadership as betrayers and sneered that the police – 'coppers' – were carrying their guns about but hadn't 'dared to use them against the workers'.[22]

Asa Briggs suggests, in his history of wartime broadcasting, that the Germans 'exaggerated the significance of pacifism in Britain which had undoubtedly assisted them during the period of appeasement before 1939'.[23] And, overall, the record of wartime pacifism paradoxically reinforces the claim implicit in the Myth of the Blitz that the British fought in 1940–41 with unusual unity and in a markedly civilised spirit.

In the thirties, pacifism or pacificism had affected people right across the political spectrum. The horrors of the Western Front in 1914–18 and the new horrors of air bombing revealed by the Japanese in China created very widespread revulsion from war. In 1933, the Oxford Union, representing the nation's junior élite, voted that it would 'under no circumstances fight for its King and Country'. While Canon Dick Sheppard's Peace Pledge Union acquired a membership of 100,000, the Communist Party by the mid-thirties was making 'the fight against war' a central campaigning point, though its line was certainly not pacifist. It supported the Abyssinians in their resistance to Mussolini's invasion. As a leading CP spokesman wrote in 1935:

It is obvious that any victory for Italian aggression would be a tremendous encouragement for German fascism, already threatening the world with war. For Italy to gain any benefit from this war would be to make a new war, starting from Germany, an immediate certainty.[24]

In the summer of 1935, 11.5 million Britons participated in a 'peace ballot' conducted by supporters of the League of Nations, politically middle of the road. Ten to one voted in favour of all-round disarmament and 'collective security'. The Labour Party in its conference that year rejected the pacifism of its veteran Christian Socialist leader, George Lansbury, who resigned, and identified itself with collective security and the League. But the Conservatives niftily outmanoeuvred Labour's effort to seize leadership of pro-League opinion, as Baldwin too presented himself as its champion. Having won the 1935 election, Baldwin cynically turned away from the League and appeased Mussolini. Yet 'appeasers' in government circles might be moved by revulsion against slaughter, as Baldwin himself was. They too, as Arthur Marwick puts it, 'had been "scorched" by war: they would not lightly risk playing with fire'.[25] While the Labour Party abandoned its opposition to rearmament in 1937, and the Conservative government reluctantly began, and went on, rearming, there was no jingoistic relish in either. And when military conscription was introduced from 1939, provision was made for conscientious objection not only on pacifist grounds, which had been accepted in the First World War, but on political grounds.

There was no repetition of the persecution of conscientious objectors which had disfigured British life in 1916–18. Then, objectors who had refused to accept service in the Noncombatant Corps or other work useful to the war effort had been victims of official incomprehension and mass hysteria. Out of 16,000 objectors, more than 6,000 had gone to prison at least once and about seventy had died from their treatment. But the 1,500 unshakeable 'absolutists' had been widely admired for their courage after the war was over, and others, too, had seen that it had been a mistake: they had defended at great cost the individual's freedom of conscience and judgement.[26]

In the event, in 1939, twenty-two in every thousand of the first age-group called up to register claimed the right of conscience and went before tribunals. From registration to registration the proportion of claimants fell – only sixteen in every thousand by 9 March, fewer than six by mid-summer 1940. Altogether, however, 59,192 people claimed objection before the end of the war – four times as many as in 1916–18, but of course 1939–45 was a much longer period. Of these, 3,577 were given unconditional exemption, and 28,720 were registered on condition they took up approved work, generally in agriculture, or stayed in their present jobs; 14,691 were registered for non-combatant duties in the armed forces, 12,204 were turned down altogether. The great majority specified religious grounds. They came disproportionately from the professions and the ranks of self-employed men providing services such as barbers. Individualistic occupations, it seems, bred individualist stances – few miners were conscientious objectors.

Only three out of a hundred, in this war, went to jail for their principles. About a third of those turned down altogether maintained their objection to the length of prosecution or court martial. Their experiences – which quite often involved repeated courts martial – were not pleasant. But there was little real legacy of bitterness, either against 'conchies' or on their behalf. The government advertised its tolerance well. Cabinet ministers attended a memorial service for George Lansbury held in Westminster Abbey. Later, the composer Britten was unconditionally exempted on the grounds that he had a vocation to continue his artistic work, and James Maxton was allowed to broadcast to America.[27]

There was only one period when signs of 'anti-conchie' hysteria were widely evident, and that was in the summer of 1940. When complete 'national unity' was less necessary, before and after that phase, it could be taken for granted, and extended to embrace even conscientious objectors. But with France falling in conditions which suggested general collapse of morale and widespread treachery, people in Britain looked at their neighbours suspiciously, and it was inevitable that some should express strong feeling against pacifists.

There was also strong anti-Communist feeling, nurtured for years not only on Britain's Right but within the Labour Party. It is interesting to consider why so little official action was directly taken against the CP and its members in 1940; after all, the Joint Intelligence Committee, the senior body of British military and civilian intelligence, meeting on 2 May to consider the implications of the Scandinavian débâcle, concluded that German success in Norway and Denmark had been due to the subversive activities of a well-organised 'fifth column' and suggested that, besides enemy aliens, Fascist and IRA supporters, the CP – 'well organised with 20,000 pledged subscribing members – the *Daily Worker* circulation is 90,000' – was a possible source of recruits for such a 'fifth column' in Britain.[28]

Communist Party membership had in fact been rising since the start of the war, particularly in Scotland and the Midlands, and had been reported in a Party pamphlet published in March 1940 to be 'close to 20,000'. *Daily Worker* readership had increased correspondingly; weekly sales of 362,000 in January 1940 (a rise of 54,000 in a year) could have included 90,000, or even more, of individual issues sold at weekends, when volunteer vendors were out in force.[29]

Hence Mary Adams, in charge of Home Intelligence at the Ministry of Information, was perhaps incorrect in asserting within the Ministry that there was no evidence that Communism was gaining ground. The Minister of Information, Sir John Reith, hoped, in a memo of April 1940, that 'with rope the Party may go some way to hanging itself'. Anxious reports on Communist (and pacifist) activity daily arrived at the MoI from the regions. The Party's line, openly published, seemed to imply defence, if not support, of

German actions. But as the Ministry of Home Security told regional commissioners on 27 July, direct action against it would be foolish. In fact there was no evidence from any country which Hitler had invaded showing that the 'fifth column' had drawn on Communists. There was likewise no sign of organised attempts by the Party to slow down or disrupt production in Britain. To repress Communists merely for their political beliefs would arouse accusations of victimisation – and their advocacy of social reform evoked great sympathy. The MoI likewise ca'd canny, doing little directly to counter CP propaganda, and that of 'an improvised and spasmodic nature', as when in March 1940 the regional Intelligence officer in Wales reported that Communists intended to take over a meeting of the North Wales Miners' Federation and the Ministry contacted the Labour *Daily Herald* and Liberal *News Chronicle* to get them to put out adverse publicity.[30]

The Party was protected by powerful commonsense arguments. Firstly its intelligent, dedicated and disciplined members exercised influence in the working-class movement out of all proportion to their numbers. We have noted their strength in Welsh and Scottish coal-fields, but their role in the modern engineering industry which was the basis of so much 'war production' was equally, or even more, significant. For instance, in Coventry, where the aircraft industry expanded rapidly in the late thirties with rearmament, the CP 'played a leading part in the struggle to establish trade union organisation' which 'laid the basis for its central position in the trade union movement during the war'. Its major strongholds were three of the best-organised and highest paid factories, but it had a 'significant presence' in forty Coventry works altogether, including all the largest ones. Its members dominated meetings of local shop stewards and had much success in getting their way on the district committee of the Amalgamated Engineering Union. Jack Jones, the dynamic young district organiser of the other key union organising in Coventry, the Transport and General Workers', worked closely with a leading Party member, Jock Gibson.[31] To attack such a well-entrenched section of the workforce at a time when industrial action was at a record low would have been absurd.

Secondly, it was very hard to separate the CP from respectable members of the Labour Party who had honest doubts about war in general or this one in particular, who were angry or guilty over British imperialism in the Far East, or who shared Communist concern over inadequate air-raid shelters and insensitive social policies. The Conservative Party, riddled with people who would be plausibly branded as appeasers, had hardly moved into war against

Germany without some confusion and agony. Nor had the Labour Party. It required considerable faith in 1939 to imagine that a vicious war which was expected to combine a revival of trench warfare with the wholesale murder of civilians by heavy bombers could possibly be the prelude to a constructive socialist future.

The leaders of the Labour Left, Sir Stafford Cripps and Aneurin Bevan, argued in its organ *Tribune* on 8 September 1939 that it was the 'duty' of socialists to assist 'the anti-fascist forces' while demanding a change of government, working to stop the war degenerating into 'a simple struggle between rival imperialisms' and keeping eventual peace terms ever in mind. On another page of the same issue, Konni Zilliacus, later a Labour MP, declared that it was 'a class war as well as an international war'. A fortnight later, Cripps in *Tribune* defended the Soviet Union's invasion of Poland, and he later presented the Russian invasion of Finland in November as a defensive move. This was too much for the *Tribune* board, though, who a week later denounced the Soviet Union's actions, adding, however, 'We deplore her aggression, but we support her for her socialism.'[32] By March, *Tribune*'s editor, H. I. Hartshorn, suspected of sympathising with the CP line, had been forced out, and under the new editorship of Raymond Postgate, and the leadership of Bevan, the journal gave critical support to Churchill's coalition and attacked the CP fiercely.

Meanwhile, Gollancz, as noted already, had torn the Left Book Club from the control of the CP by April 1940: this meant, incidentally, that the club, whose branches, as Gollancz complained, had tended to become 'bastard CP locals',[33] lost its pre-war aspect of a burgeoning mass movement. His co-editor Strachey moved slowly rather than dramatically away from his former CP attachment. He was not repelled by the Nazi–Soviet Pact, nor by the Finnish war, nor even, initially, by the CP's anti-war line. He claimed that it was the Nazi invasion of Norway which convinced him that the 'inter-Imperialist aspect of the struggle was subsidiary to the necessity to prevent a Nazi world-conquest'. By July 1940 he was publicly berating the CP for its policies in 'the nine months when the revolutionary defeatist line was pursued', imagining wrongly that the 'line' was now changing.[34]

However, Bevan, Gollancz and Strachey did not necessarily carry all the Labour Left with them. CP supporters had influence in many local Labour parties. Not all Party members could slip easily out of the pacifism which they had inherited from 1914–18 or acquired since. The Labour Peace Aims manifesto mentioned earlier, which was signed by twenty-two MPs, including Alex Sloan, was not a very left-wing document (it supported the idea of a Federal Union of Europe, recently quite widely fashionable), but the more than seventy constituency Labour parties and twenty to thirty trades councils which came out behind its call for a truce no doubt found relief in its expression of pacific hankerings.[35]

After the Labour leaders had gone into coalition, most loyal Party members had less difficulty in giving broad support to the war effort. *Labour Discussion Notes*, the organ of a caucus of left-centre intellectuals within the Party (the 'Socialist Clarity Group'), declared in June 1940, 'This war, which originated in capitalist and imperialist conflicts and began under capitalist leadership, is now assuming the character which was implicit in it from the outset – that of a people's war for liberty and social progress against the forces of reaction and monopoly power.'[36]

However, it remained the case that, like Strachey, any leftish member of the Labour Party would find it hard to spot a single argument explicitly advanced by the CP which he or she had not deployed, or considered seriously, at some point since the war began. A witch hunt in 1940 based, for instance, on approval of the Soviet Pact with Hitler would logically have trawled in Cripps among others. In June 1940, Naomi Mitchison, wife of a prominent Labour member and friend of others, and ready to believe that the Nazis would put her in a concentration camp if they won, was confiding in her diary doubts about the morality of the war such as made many, especially women, uneasy: she was shocked to see the *New Statesman* 'going all militarist'. On 7 June she heard the French Prime Minister Reynaud praising in a broadcast the military virtues, and wrote:

> One thinks of people in whom the military virtues are encouraged; after the last war they became Black and Tans. And now? If this is to be a world of military virtues, then my side has lost. Be we not swift with swiftness of the tigress. Let us break ranks when nations trek from progress. We have *got* to have other virtues.

The German conquest of Paris a week later, however, made her feel 'a bit of the real war hate . . . The feeling that one wants to do the same thing to Berlin and all that.' Ruth, a medical student, told her she felt the same: 'Says she thinks a lot of people have been trying to stop that feeling, but it's difficult now.'[37]

A third safeguard for the CP was that any intelligent observer could learn that Party members themselves, while in fact far less likely than the vast majority of Britons to favour any kind of capitulation to fascism, were themselves at least as confused and inwardly divided as Marxists and pacificists within the Labour Party, or as unregenerate supporters of Neville Chamberlain. Nor were their tactics making any distinctive impact, at least before heavy bombing started: they themselves must have realised this.

Harry Pollitt, general secretary of the CP, had reacted fervently to Britain's declaration of war on Germany. Harry McShane, then a CP member, recalled how, after Hitler's invasion of Poland, Pollitt swept into a London bar full of Party members, and cried: 'I have been sitting in the Gallery of the House of Commons, and that old bastard Chamberlain refuses to declare war.' McShane later gathered that at a secret Party meeting which followed, Pollitt proposed 'that a National Government should be formed and that a "man of the people" should be in the Government'. McShane's informant 'added that he had the impression that the "man of the people" should be someone like Harry Pollitt'.[38]

The central committee of the CP at this stage declared that the war could have been avoided if Britain had had a People's Government, that it supported 'all necessary measures to secure the victory of democracy over fascism', but that fascism would not be defeated by the Chamberlain government. By 12 September 1939, the Party had produced 50,000 copies of a penny pamphlet by Harry Pollitt called *How to Win the War*. He proclaimed that 'The Communist Party supports the war, believing it to be a "just war"', though he called on anti-fascists to struggle for a new government in Britain. But the Nazi–Soviet Pact had been signed. On 14 September a Soviet broadcast said the war was 'imperialist' and 'predatory' on both sides, and R. Palme Dutt, the Party's leading theoretician, saw how the wind blew from Moscow. When the CP's central committee met on 24 September, Pollitt continued to argue for full support of the war, and the majority supported him – until Dave Springhall, the British representative at Comintern headquarters in Moscow, arrived with firsthand news of the Soviet line, which was that the war was 'an imperialist and unjust war . . . carried on between two groups of imperialist countries for world domination'. Pollitt still stuck to his guns. When the central committee at last voted on the issue on 3 October, he, Gallacher and J. R. Campbell, editor of the *Daily Worker*, defied the Comintern line, but were outvoted 21:3. Four days later a new CP manifesto declared that the British and French ruling class were 'seeking to use the anti-fascist sentiments of the people for their own imperialist aims'. Pollitt was removed from his post as general secretary and Palme Dutt took over. Campbell was replaced at the *Daily Worker*. Both he and Pollitt were banished to Party work in the provinces. The Party rank and file expressed overwhelming support for the 'new line'.[39]

Noreen Branson, herself a CP member at that time, has argued convincingly that this *volte face* represented not cringing servility towards Moscow, but deep-seated feelings of solidarity with the Soviet Union, suspicion of the British Empire, and disgust over the imperialist war of 1914–18, and over the suppression of the French CP in September 1939. These were reinforced by the exceptional habit of cohesion within the British Party: 'Once a decision was taken, it was your duty to go along with it, even if privately you disagreed; otherwise, it could split the Party.' Hence Pollitt and Campbell, while continuing to believe that the war was worth fighting, publicly recanted their views in the *Worker*.[40] But these men and their comrades were stiff-necked and dedicated anti-fascists. It is impossible to believe that they could have brought themselves to give material or moral assistance to Nazi invaders.

While the war was still 'phoney', the question as to whether it was 'imperialist' remained abstract. Events in the spring and summer of 1940 impelled what Branson calls a 'new approach'. It was 'necessary to make clear that Communists were *not* in favour of surrender to Hitler – something of which they were frequently accused'. As France fell, the central committee called in a new manifesto (22 June 1940) for a People's Government which would make a 'complete break with the interests of the ruling class. The policy of the ruling class has led to disaster after disaster.' It claimed that, 'The same kind of leaders who brought France to defeat are in high places in Britain.' The CP now called for the removal of 'supporters of fascism, the men of Munich' from all commanding positions, and for the arming of the workers in the factories. Nevertheless, John Strachey was wrong in imagining that the 'CP line' had changed. Dutt's theses about the 'imperialist war' remained sacred – as the Party's political bureau stressed in a circular to branches on 15 July which deplored 'tendencies to national defencism' in the Party's current campaign. The Party line was that if the British workers ousted their own ruling class, this would encourage German workers to bring down Hitler.[41]

The CP now set up a front organisation which would gather together 'all those outside the Party who were prepared to support the call for a "People's Government"'. These included local Labour parties which had still opposed the war at the May annual conference, some of which had been disaffiliated, and the MP for North Hammersmith, D. N. Pritt, whose views on virtually all issues corresponded exactly with the CP's, and who had been expelled by Labour. On 7 July 1940 a 'People's Vigilance Committee', which soon became known as 'The People's Convention', was launched at a meeting in London. Pritt – a charming and brilliant lawyer – was its figurehead. Prominent trade unionists who backed the Convention were duly bounced out of the Labour Party, which outlawed it as a CP organisation.

But when, on 12 July, the Home Office formally warned the *Daily Worker* that the Home Secretary was considering whether or not to ban it under the new Defence Regulation 2D 'on the grounds that there is in that newspaper a systematic publication of matter calculated to foment opposition to the prosecution of the war to a successful issue', Professor J. B. S. Haldane, the very distinguished scientist who was chairman of the *Worker*'s board, asked sarcastically, 'What is the *Daily Worker*'s real crime? A very serious one indeed. It is the only daily newspaper which opposes the Government.' When the Cabinet decided to seize and suppress a CP leaflet, 'The People Must Act', the Scottish Office refused to implement the policy on the grounds that it would be illegal. As numerous people were arrested for distributing the leaflet, selling the *Worker* or speaking at open-air meetings, as CP members' homes were raided and documents and books were seized, people who weren't Communists but were concerned about civil liberties were disturbed into sympathy with the Party. The government itself, as we have already seen, recognised the danger implicit in this when Anderson, on 27 July, told the regional commissioners to be careful in proceeding against Communists. And the 'propaganda of events' still further strengthened the Party.[42]

Haldane had led the Party's campaign, from 1937, over inadequate Air Raid Precautions. The onset of full-scale Blitz in September 1940 proved that he and his comrades had not been far off the mark. The CP cry for bomb-proof shelters was reinforced as many Londoners took to sleeping in the Underground railway system. The authorities were so worried by the campaign of leaflets and posters now launched by the Party's London district that police again were sent in to seize them. But Party members played a prominent part in the informal committees which sprang up to represent and organise shelterers, and their clamour proved irresistible. It was not because of controversies over ARP that Sir John Anderson ceased to be Home Secretary in October: the dying Chamberlain's resignation from the Cabinet made a reshuffle necessary. But Anderson's shifting to another post looked to many like the result of agitation against his policies. His successor, Morrison, warned the War Cabinet that he could not counter the CP's campaign if he himself 'adopted a wholly negative attitude towards the provision of deep shelters' – and *de facto* recognition of the public's right to seize the tube stations was now given as the authorities acted to improve conditions in them, and even to expand them by tunnelling.[43]

The bombing of Coventry on 14 November made the CP a propaganda gift. It was 'the turning point for the Coventry Communists'. Their agitation over ARP had achieved some impact while the town had had relatively light raids. Ernie Bevin had come down to address shop stewards. Provoked by hecklers, he is said to have shouted: 'I know you Communists. I know Harry Pollitt. The trouble with you people is – you can't take it.' This, in a 'front-line' city, recently bombed, caused uproar. The Party exploited its position very well when the big raid came: 'Within two days *Daily Worker* sales were resumed. It was the only paper available in the city.' A Communist shop steward has recalled how a dedicated Party man brought a carload of copies up overnight, and arrived at about 4 a.m. By just after daybreak they were on sale in the streets: 'We had a line of people of many hundreds all patiently waiting for their penny copy of the *Daily Worker*.' The Midlands District Committee of the CP rushed out a pamphlet which blamed the city's destruction on 'the big factory owners, the big business and landowning interests', and called for a negotiated peace. The *Worker*'s headline, '1000 CASUALTIES IN "REPRISAL" RAID ON COVENTRY', was clearly intended likewise to push blame towards Britain's 'imperialist' rulers who had ordered raids on Germany. But this 'line' did not prevent the Party from doubling its membership in Coventry, from 70 to 150, by the following June – while the Labour Party's local organisation, shattered by the raid, remained 'inert' and lost many members.[44]

At this very time, in November, the *Worker* successfully launched a Scottish edition, printing 12,000–14,000 copies nightly in Glasgow, according to Branson. Harry McShane recalls a circulation of only 5,000–6,000, but 'rising steadily . . . it appeared that our anti-war line was spreading'. The Party's membership included a high proportion of men in their twenties, and it did not discourage them from accepting conscription into the armed forces, though it did instruct them to destroy their Party cards for their own protection. By November 1940, the *Worker* had a regular page for 'Soldiers, Sailors, Airmen', consisting largely of letters, signed with initials, reporting and complaining about conditions in the services. Its editor, William Rust, claimed at the turn of the year that it had 'become the paper of the forces, passed from hand to hand in barracks, ship and aerodrome'.[45]

On balance, the war seems to have extended, rather than impaired, the CP's scope. To its influence in factories and mines, it now added a prominent role in shelter committees and other *ad hoc* organisations responding to wartime problems which affected ordinary people, and a significant presence in the armed forces. It clearly saw Scotland as an especially promising field for further recruitment. 'The People's Convention' was able to speak to and canalise Britain-wide currents of thought and feeling.

Its manifesto in September 1940 had been signed by 500 people, covering a comprehensive roll-call of the many sections of the Labour movement and adding to them notable figures from the spheres of the arts, intellect and the churches; 265,000 copies were distributed. It called for the appointment of delegates to a national convention, in support of six aims: defence of living standards; defence of democratic and trade-union rights; adequate ARP; friendship with the Soviet Union; a People's Government; and 'a people's peace that gets rid of the causes of war'. The first aim was of wide appeal within the Labour movement; the second could not be contested by liberals; the third played the Convention's strongest single card; and 'friendship with the Soviet Union' was not a bad card either. Public sympathy for Russia had survived Stalin's invasions of Poland and Finland. As Tom Harrisson of Mass-Observation reported, in 1940–41, 'the feeling that Russia was basically sensible, kindly and ordinary, persisted, along with the feeling that there was something mysterious, enigmatical, deeply wise, about Stalin'.[46]

The aims of a 'People's Government' and a 'People's Peace' were shared by the entire Left. Socialists could find them debatable only in terms of tactics and priorities. How could one establish a government representing working people without disrupting the war effort against Hitler? And should a 'People's Peace' be sought before the Nazis were defeated? To such arguments the Convention's organisers replied that popular agitation giving leadership to popular discontent could bring new men to power, and this People's Government would then, by granting immediate freedom to India, introducing socialism at home and setting out reasonable peace terms, so entrance the German working class that it would overthrow the Nazis. Other proletariats would follow suit, and peace-loving socialist régimes would produce stable peace in the world.[47]

The 'capitalist' press kept silent as D. N. Pritt and his colleagues organised towards a grand 'Convention' on 12 January 1941. But when the Convention took place, even *The Times* had to pay attention. It had been scheduled for the Free Trade Hall in Manchester. When this was destroyed in an air raid, the Royal Hotel in London was booked instead. The meeting overflowed into Holborn Hall.

The credentials committee claimed '2234 Delegates directly representing 1,200,000, of which 1,136 delegates represented 1,004,950 in Trade Unions and Factories and in Jobs'. Beside many trade-union branches, eighty Co-operative organisations were represented; 199 'political organisations' (including Labour parties, socialist medical associations, Labour teachers); ninety-one 'Youth organisations'; fifty 'Tenants Associations and Shelter Committees' and so on. There were messages of support from Paul Robeson and from the US novelist Theodore Dreiser. Mao Tse Tung sent 'fraternal militant party greetings' to this convention which represented 'the British working class and toiling masses and all progressive elements', and a future foreign minister of India, Krishna Menon, then resident in London, told the Convention in person that Nehru would have sent his support had the British not recently jailed him: 'We are not impressed by such things as "democratic imperialism", there is no such thing, as there is no such thing as a vegetarian tiger . . . There is no use in asking whether you would choose British imperialism or Nazism, it is like asking a fish if he wants to be fried in margarine or butter. He doesn't want to be fried at all.'[48] Indira Gandhi was also present, in the audience.

It would be impertinent to suggest that those many on the left in Britain who responded with unease or indignation to events in India were merely woolly liberals or willing tools of Moscow. Menon gave living flesh to the idea that Britain was indeed an 'imperialist' power, and one currently acting in India with every appearance of arbitrary injustice. The organisers' claims that the Convention somehow directly represented a million and a quarter people can be dismissed as knowingly mendacious. But there is no doubt that it was a very remarkable event – a huge meeting amid the rubble and bomb sites of London, evoking a very positive response.

Celia Fremlin, one of Mass-Observation's best workers, attended. She had been a CP member, but had resigned over the Nazi–Soviet Pact, and there is no reason to doubt the integrity of her report, which was not written for publication. As she saw it, the great bulk of those present were middle class, with a scattering of upper-middle people ('many of these student and intellectual type') and about 25 per cent working class. Men outnumbered women about 3:1. The attendance was overwhelmingly *young* – the majority seemed to be between twenty-five and thirty-five. There were 'perhaps about twenty soldiers and airmen in uniform'. While there was 'a liberal sprinkling of CP and extreme left-wingers', 'ordinary trade unionists' of 'varying shades of leftish opinion' seemed to Fremlin to make up the 'vast majority'. The spirit of the conference was very friendly, as between platform and audience, and response to the speakers was swift and spontaneous. Menon got an especially good hand, and 'general enthusiasm for internationalism' stood out. 'A marked feature of the proceedings was the fact that applause always followed remarks of ideological or sentimental appeal rather than materialistic.' Talk about wages, food and ARP appealed, it seemed, far less than evocation of 'new opportunities, the possibility of putting the whole of the present mess behind us and starting afresh'. Fremlin detected a 'fair amount' of regret that the extreme Left was so much in control of the Convention: 'There was a large section with the feeling that it is tiresome that whenever any really vital and vigorous political activity arises, the Communist Party always seems to be in the middle of it.' The mood, so far from being defeatist, seemed to Fremlin to be 'one of hope' – a vague hope that a way could be found 'out of the present mess'.[49]

Besides Pritt, and such leading Communists as Pollitt and Dutt, soldiers and clergymen spoke from the platform. Various resolutions were passed *nem. con.*, barely amplifying the original six points. A national committtee of twenty-six was elected: from the CP, Dutt, Horner, Gallacher and Haldane could expect to co-operate harmoniously with the actress Beatrix Lehmann and the 'Red Dean' of Canterbury, Hewlett Johnson.

Significantly, the left-wing press was much more hostile in its reports than the right. The Labour *Daily Herald* and *Reynolds News* attacked the Convention. *Tribune* published an effective onslaught, conceding that the Convention had been a 'great success as a conference', that most of those attending had been 'good honest-to-God workers' and that 'much of what was said was the authentic voice of large and growing bodies of opinion representing genuine, deeply felt and widespread grievances'. Yet it had been 'a fraud, a swindle, snare and delusion'. 'Spontaneous' speeches given from the floor had in some cases been circulated to the press before they were delivered. Those attending were dupes who had 'no idea of the *ends* for which they were being used'. Kingsley Martin, in the *New Statesman*, was more thoughtful. Granted that the Convention was certainly under Communist control, what did the CP propose to use it for? The electoral truce and the absorption of Labour leaders into coalition had left a chance for an alternative leadership:

The CP means to fill that gap. The puzzle is whether they are prepared in their hearts tacitly to aid a German victory with the illusory hope of making a revolution afterwards, or whether they are relying on the RAF to defeat Hitler while they increase their power.[50]

The 'CP line' grew even more mysterious as a result of the government action which followed the Convention. Even before it, on 23 December, Herbert Morrison had proposed to the Cabinet that the *Daily Worker* should be suppressed, along with *The Week*, a more cerebral journal published by a Communist journalist, Claud Cockburn. On the day after the Convention, the Cabinet agreed to this, and on 21 January the papers were stopped. While right-wing and even liberal newspapers approved this manifest restriction on press freedom, the *Daily Mirror* protested and Aneurin Bevan initiated a debate in the House of Commons after which fifteen MPs voted against the ban.

There was further outcry early in March (just after a CP candidate got 15 per cent of the poll standing against Labour in the Dumbarton by-election). The BBC decided not to use People's Convention supporters. These included Lew Stone and a couple of other popular band leaders, Beatrix Lehmann and Michael Redgrave, the star actor. The result was outraged protest from distinguished people who were patently non-Communist. Ralph Vaughan Williams, best-loved of classical composers, withdrew a specially commissioned choral work from the BBC because it had banned the music of Alan Bush, a Communist. Rose Macaulay, the writer, likewise cancelled a broadcast; J. B. Priestley and David Low the cartoonist were amongst distinguished people who wrote letters; and E. M. Forster withdrew all his services from the BBC. Three days after Forster had attacked the Minister of Information at a meeting organised by the National Council for Civil Liberties, Churchill himself led the government's retreat. 'Anything in the nature of persecution, victimisation or man-hunting is odious to the British people', he told the Commons on 20 March; the ban would be lifted. Meanwhile, the Cabinet's recently formed Committee on Communist Activities had decided that 'no action of a general character should be taken at present against the Communist Party', though Ernest Bevin, who sat on it, had toyed with the idea of imprisoning CP intellectuals – reasoning that action taken against the likes of them wouldn't lead to trouble in the factories, though the arrest of CP trade unionists would 'cause discontent among workers who are not themselves in sympathy with Communism'.[51]

Claud Cockburn, who lost his outlets in the *Worker* and *The Week*, recalled the aftermath of their suppression as a 'period of inexplicable political dreariness'. He was consigned to work for the People's Convention as a PRO man:

> Much of the activity of the organisation consisted in what, on a much later occasion, Mr Wilfred Roberts, MP, described to me – he was speaking of a Liberal Party Conference – as 'an attempt to avert a split between the dupes and the fellow-travellers'. The only interest or amusement I ever extracted from the People's Convention was in the reading of a secret report upon it, prepared for the Labour Party or the TUC (I forget which) by some 'expert', a copy of which had been stolen for us from Transport House. From this I gathered that our proceedings, which seemed to me almost totally futile, in reality constituted a serious menace and were a powerful source of political evil.[52]

But Cockburn was one of those 'intellectuals' whom Bevin so despised. Convention supporters in the Amalgamated Engineering Union presumably saw their work as far from futile. In mid-June it was rewarded by a large majority vote at the Union's annual conference for a lifting of the ban on the *Worker*: the same body called for a 'people's government' and a 'people's peace'.

Three days later, Hitler invaded the Soviet Union. The CP's many months of contortion and self-repression were over. The war was manifestly no longer 'imperialist', as it had been in the perturbing days of the Norway campaign, Dunkirk, Battle of Britain and Blitz.

5

Standing 'Alone'

'What are the British trying to do – turn this into a circus or something!'

German artillery major at Dunkirk

Throughout that heroic summer of 1940, and the grim autumn and winter of bombing, informed people were aware that the national 'unity' which Churchill and J. B. Priestley invoked, and which Morrison and Beaverbrook seemed to have found in war industry, was provisional, conditional, and potentially fragile. Latent pacifist feeling was widespread. The Communist Party was invulnerable in its industrial strongholds. Scotland and Wales contained intellectuals and trade unionists whose indefinite attachment to a failing British cause could not be taken for granted. The omission of these factors from generalisations involving British morale is second in importance only to memory's failure to recognise dependence on US goodwill. They are chief among the habits of forgetfulness which permitted, and permit, the Myth to subsist.

By comparison, the Myth can stand any amount of 'debunking' based on the revival or bringing to light of unsavoury military facts. The Myth does not depend for its health on any faith in British military prowess. It can readily ride over proofs that in extremity Churchill and others made errors of judgement or sanctioned morally suspect actions. The more the fallibility of Churchill is emphasised, the more lovable his heroic bearing becomes, and the more superhumanly human he appears. The structure of the Myth depends on the leaving out of certain things. 'Debunking' attention to those which are included merely re-emphasises their central importance.

However, certain 'debunking' points must be made here, if only because they help us to imagine how perilous Britain's position was on 'the desperate edge of now' – how easily the 'propaganda of events' might have played into the hands of the CP and produced pacifistic revulsion.

First, Norway. It was widely known at the time, and has been well established since, that Churchill was largely, even primarily, responsible for that débâcle. He had a taste for reckless adventure which had not been chastened by the Dardanelles disaster of 1915. It was he who had pressed in the war council for an 'amphibious' operation against Turkey, a naval expedition to bombard and capture the Gallipoli Peninsula and press on to Constantinople. Indeed, he had been generally blamed at the time, and had been shunted from the Admiralty to the Duchy of Lancaster, a major demotion from which he took years to recover. Yet after Russia's invasion of Finland on 30 November 1939, Churchill came up with another dangerous scheme: British and French troops should be sent to Finland. On the way they would wreck the iron-mines in *neutral* Sweden on which Germany depended, and seize Narvik, the Norwegian port through which the ore was shipped.

'The Finnish Campaign', as A. J. P. Taylor puts it, 'was Gallipoli again, and worse. The plans, too, were run up in the slapdash spirit which had characterised the expedition to the Dardanelles.'[1] The Norwegian and Swedish governments naturally refused to authorise the expedition, yet early in March 1940 the British War Cabinet decided to go ahead. The folly of entering a campaign against the Soviet Union was prevented by Finland's capitulation on 12 March. But a plan to mine the leads at Narvik remained on the agenda, and Churchill supported Prime Minister Reynaud of France, who pressed for its implementation. It was decided to mine Norwegian waters on the night of 8 April. But as it turned out, allied violation of Norwegian neutrality was covered over by large-scale Nazi aggression as simultaneously German forces moved into Denmark and Norway.

It seems that, as Paul Addison argues, the decision to mine at Narvik was Chamberlain's – he had pushed for it as the least ambitious scheme for action amongst several favoured by the warmongering Reynaud, not believing himself that it would provoke Germany into extending the conflict. However, Churchill himself later claimed credit for pushing the idea through, and he certainly did his best to make the chairmanship of the Military Co-ordination Committee, which Chamberlain had recently given him, a base for actually running the campaign. On this committee, three service chiefs sat with the corresponding ministers. All were dismayed by Churchill's attempts to dominate. According to Colonel Hastings Ismay, the committee's secretary, 'His verbosity and restlessness made unnecessary work, prevented real planning, and caused friction.' A serious political crisis loomed. For a time, Chamberlain himself took the chair. But Churchill's popularity outside Westminster was such that he successfully demanded and got the power to guide and direct the Chiefs of Staff.[2]

All this deepened the distrust of Churchill strongly felt in Whitehall and within the Conservative Party. After Chamberlain's fall in May, 'Churchill faced the remarkable predicament, for a Prime Minister, of having no party to command in the House of Commons'. Chamberlain remained the Conservative leader until fatal illness forced his retirement in October. Churchill's assumption of the mantle at that point seems in retrospect, as Addison says, 'a blood transfusion for an exhausted and demoralised party'.[3] Many Conservatives, however, did not foresee this in May. Harold Nicolson, MP, noted in his diary, on 13 May, 'When Chamberlain enters the House he gets a terrific reception, and when Churchill comes in the applause is less.' The massed ranks of Tory MPs – the Party occupied two-thirds of the House – were still loyal to Chamberlain. Though Labour MPs were glad to cheer Churchill, and though Nicolson felt that 'the House was deeply moved' by Churchill's speech about Dunkirk, the sullenness of the Tory benches towards him was such that a patriotic lobby correspondent felt compelled to warn Chamberlain about the ominous conclusions which foreign diplomats and journalists were drawing. Chamberlain took action. When Churchill made an important speech early in July, the usual Tory silence was broken as the Conservative Chief Whip, Margesson, rose to his feet and waved his followers on to theirs. They began to cheer fervently.[4]

Such behaviour lent credibility to the thesis which became popular in the summer of 1940 that there were 'guilty men' in the Conservative Party, Chamberlain himself the most notable, who had appeased Hitler before the war, who had not really wanted to fight him since war began, and whose apathy (or anti-Communist, pro-Nazi leaning) was responsible for the débâcle at Dunkirk.

When Nicholas Harman in 1980 published a 'debunking' account of Dunkirk, he subtitled his book *The Necessary Myth*. Of course, the best possible face *had* to be put on the evacuation of the British Expeditionary Force: 'If the British told, and enjoyed, and embroidered, some versions of the truth, they did so because that helped them to stay in the war.' As Harman goes on to point out, the truth cannot hurt the British now.[5]

The capture or destruction of the British Expeditionary Force was not part of the German plan. The German target was Paris: 'For the French and the Germans alike the evacuation from Dunkirk was a sideshow.' For the British public, however, it was the crux of the war. They blamed other nations for putting their boys into terrible danger. King Leopold of Belgium was widely denounced for capitulating to the Germans on 27 May – though in fact he had been appealing without concrete effect for support from Britain and France, lacking which the tenacious fight of his troops was hopeless. Harman points out that for the previous ten days three armies had been fighting in Flanders:

> side by side, but with different objectives. The Belgians were fighting to defend Belgium and thought they should surrender if that proved impossible. The French wanted to counter-attack away from Belgium into France, and regarded surrender as a regrettable necessity that might come if that counter-attack failed. The British refused to think about surrender, but planned to get away to England.

Dunkirk had a different significance for each of the allies. It was on the English Channel, next to Belgium, just in France. The Belgians hoped to use it as the base for an operation to drive the Germans out of their own country. The French regarded it as one of their own major towns – a port and a centre of shipbuilding and steel manufacture – and also as a fortified base, easy to supply by sea, from which they could attack the Germans in defence of Paris: 'To ask a French soldier to abandon it was like asking an Englishman to surrender Newcastle.' Yet as far as the British were concerned, Dunkirk was just a convenient place to get out: 'The British alone were to carry through their hope into a plan and then an achievement. But this they were at pains to conceal from their partners.'[6]

From 22 May, the British began to pull troops away from the firing line. It looked as if the Germans could trap them, and they wanted to get out of the trap and escape home. They defied what were tantamount to orders from General Blanchard, the local French commander, and left adjacent French troops exposed on their flanks. They scuppered the plans of the supreme commander, General Weygand, for a counter-attack against German supply lines, which Churchill himself had ordered the British Expeditionary Force to join, and which gave the only chance of aggressive action. The French now had to trek after the British towards Dunkirk. But the French still saw it as a strongpoint on the German rear. Neither they nor the Belgians were informed when, on 26 May, the order went out to start wholesale British evacuation – 'Operation Dynamo'.

When the Belgian army gave in, the British, without consulting the French, moved into the gap which it left south-east of Dunkirk. The Germans in turn moved in where the British Expeditionary Force had been. And seven French divisions, 'half of the French First Army', were left cut off near Lille.[7]

The British public liked to imagine that the gutless collapse of the French had left no alternative to evacuation. In fact, the French troops around Lille held out so bravely, until all their ammunition was gone, that the Germans in tribute to them allowed the survivors to keep their weapons for the ceremonial parade of surrender. It was the morale of the British Expeditionary Force which was at rock bottom.

As they engaged the Germans in Flanders after 10 May, 'Neither at headquarters nor at the fighting front did the British know what had hit them.' British Expeditionary Force military intelligence was understaffed. Radio communication was inadequate. It was in a context of confusion and dismay that the British Expeditionary Force developed the habit, which spread back to Britain, of blaming defeat on the poor morale of their allies and on grossly exaggerated conceptions of the role of fifth columnists. Bewildered and bad-tempered, British troops behaved on occasion very poorly. It was an accident that the Grenadier Guards, on 15 May, shot up elements of the Belgian army retreating towards them, and inflicted quite heavy casualties. But belief that the British had been 'betrayed' thereafter provided an excuse for looting food and drink from the local population, and for summary execution of supposed fifth columnists. As Harman comments, 'It is small wonder if local civilians were eager to see the back of them – even if the replacement was to be the German army, whose propaganda had plenty of material to work with.' While some soldiers figured bravely in rearguard actions, 'too often' the British collapsed. One frank account published during the war described a 'disorderly mob' of British soldiers running away because of a false report that German tanks were at hand and 'looking (if the truth be told) very much like the popular conception of the Italian army'. One thing which frightened the British soldiers was the fear of capture. They assumed that, like themselves, the Germans had been ordered to take no prisoners. While SS troops did cold-bloodedly murder 170 British prisoners in two separate incidents, this was after men of the Durham Light Infantry had killed a great many (perhaps 400) SS men who were legitimate prisoners of war.[8]

The order to head for Dunkirk and home was a great relief to the British Expeditionary Force. And 'Operation Dynamo' was indeed a triumph, though hardly a miracle: the evacuation had been planned in advance, and the weather was favourable. The radiance of the triumph – which involved many acts that can fairly be called heroic – is stained in retrospect by the fact that it also involved 'methodical deception' of the French. While the latter were planning to make Dunkirk a redoubt, the British began days before the fight to ship non-fighting personnel out of the port. Though reserves were hastily sent from Britain to defend Boulogne as late as 22 May, they evacuated within two days on the basis of false reports that the town was untenable, without giving notice to their French allies, and after some had attempted to drink the place dry. The Royal Navy thoughtfully sank a blockship in the harbour mouth, which ensured that the French, fighting bravely on, could be neither supplied nor taken out by sea. 'Politically, Britain encouraged her friends to fight on. Meanwhile her soldiers were disengaging from the fight.' On 25 May Lord Gort, commanding the British Expeditionary Force, was formally ordered to deceive the French about his intentions. Churchill himself was involved in disguising from Reynaud what was going on. On 29 May, by which time 'Dynamo' had lifted 72,000 British soldiers across the Channel in three days, Admiral Abrial was astonished to receive a complaint from Gort that French soldiers were trying to embark too, on equal terms with their allies. This was the first that Abrial had heard of the evacuation. At this point – with a third of the British already gone – the allies reached agreement: French troops were to be taken off in equal numbers with British. But the French went on defending the port's perimeter. The British in practice sailed first. In the end, most of the French troops did get away, outnumbering British embarkees from 1 June onwards. But the soldier who emerged as leader of the Free French, General de Gaulle, was convinced by this episode that the British would always choose the open sea rather than Europe – 'Perfidious Albion'.[9]

Another people with some cause to feel aggrieved was the Scots. The 51st (Highland) Division had been detached to serve under French command on the Maginot Line. They fought on through the Dunkirk 'miracle'. Afterwards, French troops evacuated through the port went back to resume the battle in France, and Britain's only two formed divisions went with them. Further miniature 'Dunkirks' eventually got most of the British troops out of French west-coast ports. Altogether, 558,032 were brought back to Britain during the battle of France – and 368,491 were British. But the Highlanders, cut off with a large contingent of French at St Valery En Caux, could mostly not be evacuated, because of fog, and 8,000 of them passed into captivity after surrender on 12 June. They would have no place in the Myth of 1940.

But Dunkirk was indeed a great escape. Between 27 May and 4 June about 186,600 British soldiers and 125,000 French were taken across the Channel. And this was hailed as a triumph for the English volunteer spirit. Early in July, Victor Gollancz published *Guilty Men*, the most famous political tract of the war, by 'Cato', the pseudonym of three Beaverbrook journalists – Michael Foot, a socialist, the Liberal Frank Owen and Peter Howard, leader of Buchmanite moral rearmament – who were united in contempt for Chamberlain and his pre-war Cabinet colleagues and determined to brand them as responsible for British military unpreparedness. This opened with an evocation of the scene at Dunkirk:

> A miracle was born. This land of Britain is rich in heroes. She had brave daring men in her Navy and Air Force as well as in her army. She had heroes in jerseys and sweaters and old rubber boots in all the fishing ports of Britain. That night the word went round . . . In all the south-east ports of Britain there was not a man or a boy, who knew how to handle a boat, who was not prepared to give his own life to save some unknown, valorous son of his country who had faced without flinching the red hell of Flanders in the cause which he knew to be his own . . . For almost a week the epic went on. The little ships dodged their way up the waters and hauled over their sides the soldiers who waded waist deep, shoulder deep to safety.[10]

A few months later Gollancz published an account of 1940 by another Beaverbrook journalist, Hilde Marchant, who had been at Dover to see the troops come home. Like other press persons and publicists, she confirmed that during the 'miracle' the navy had been assisted by 'an armada of fishing boats, steamships, barges and pleasure steamers' manned by 'our rough-rugged coastal seamen – ordinary fishermen in jerseys with yachting club initials across their chests' and 'the men who in a peace-time summer would be standing on a Southern pier shouting "Bob trip in the *Saucy Jane* to see the sights"'. Volunteers had come from Norfolk, Suffolk and the Yorkshire ports:

> They went in, a line of cheeky arrogant little boats to sit like wrens on the edge of the battlefield, to be picked off by the German guns, as they grabbed men on to their fishing decks . . . Always we knew we had men like that, men who said little, but went backwards and forwards for sixty, eighty, a hundred hours, throwing sea water over themselves to keep awake . . .[11]

And so on. Account after account appeared in similar terms. No heroic story of 1940 was better confirmed by eye witnesses.

And yet, as Nicholas Harman shows, the received story was grossly misleading. Few members of the British Expeditionary Force owed their passage to 'little ships' manned by civilian volunteers. The crews of the pleasure steamers and fishing vessels which operated from the beginning were members of the Royal Naval Reserve, 'as much part of His Majesty's armed forces as any peacetime civilian recruited for the duration of hostilities'. It is true that 'the ships which carried the largest number of soldiers out of Dunkirk were entirely civilian, with civilian crews . . . ' These were passenger ferries, which in peacetime had plied between Britain and the Continent or other islands in the British archipelago. But they were hardly *little* ships: the *Scotia*, for instance, was built to take 800 passengers from Holyhead to Ireland, and on 29 May packed about 3,000 troops aboard from Dunkirk pier. On the following day, believing wrongly that the Luftwaffe had succeeded in closing Dunkirk port, the navy diverted ships to the beaches, where small vessels were needed to take men off to bigger ships at sea. But these were not crewed by enthusiastic volunteers, nor could they have been. The evacuation was still a secret. Owners and crew of ships registered in the Small Vessels Pool at Sheerness for service as necessary had no information about the operation they were summoned to join. The beach operation was in fact a sanguinary muddle, as motorboats and rowing boats laden with soldiers in sodden battle dress dug into the sand, so that the men had to get out, push off and start all over again: 'It was infuriating for the soldiers, who cursed what they saw as the incompetence of the seamen. It was agonising for the masters of the bigger ships offshore, as they waited for the arrival of the next load – or for the arrival of the bombers.'[12]

Next day, the 31st, was in fact the last on which large-scale evacuation from the beaches was attempted. Tiny wooden 'bawley-boats' from Essex – normally used to fish for shrimps and cockles – were conscripted, but even the skill and courage of their sailors did not stop these ancient vessels grounding on the sand, and they were taken off beach work and sent to act as ferries in the harbour. Meanwhile, the Small Vessels Pool had assembled a large number of tiny craft for 'special tows' – they were tied in strings behind larger ships. Their owners stayed at home. The idea was that soldiers would man them. But very few actually made it across – the tug of the ropes tore them up – and the few motorboats which did get to the beaches broke down.

Some other 'little ships' had more success – flotillas of pleasure-fishers from Ramsgate, launches from Southampton. But the fishing fleet of Rye in Sussex collectively refused to go, and the navy had to commandeer small craft in Devon whose owners would not volunteer. Even southern crews of the Royal National Lifeboat Institution mostly failed to come forward when asked, and the navy had to man their vessels. But as Harman points out, this does not prove that the vaunted heirs of Drake and Grenville were cowards. When civilian sailors were told of the importance of the operation, they normally offered to serve at once. But 'nobody can volunteer until he has been told there is something to volunteer for' – and the British people were not fully informed about the evacuation until the six p.m. radio news on 31 May:

> Before the secret was lifted 72,000 soldiers left from the beaches, mostly in craft manned by the Royal Navy, or by the soldiers themselves. After the secret was lifted, when civilian volunteers began to come forward, 26,500 were rescued from the beaches. The contribution of civilian volunteers to the success of the Dunkirk evacuation was gallant and distinguished; but it was not significant in terms of numbers rescued.[13]

Even Churchill, in his epic speech of 4 June, did not refer to the 'little ships'. But he did, strangely, give credence as well as credibility to exorbitant reports of Fighter Command's exploits against the Luftwaffe over Dunkirk, including the impossible claim that a squadron of Boulton Paul Defiants – a misdesigned fighter which had no forward-firing guns and placed its crews in fearful danger – had shot down thirty-seven enemy planes without loss. This was on a day when in fact the Germans lost only eighteen planes on all fronts. While deliberate misrepresentation was probably not involved in this story – pilots in the heat of battle often misread what they see – there is no doubt that deliberate propagandist distortion disfigured the authorities' 'news management' of the evacuation. It was found to be counterproductive, and thereafter government and BBC stopped telling lies. Soldiers, after all, had eyes in their heads, and bitter tales to tell when the 'undefeated army' got home – including complaints of inadequate air support, which were not badly founded since Dowding, the head of Fighter Command, had fought and won a battle against Churchill himself in mid-May to prevent too many of his planes and men being committed in France when he foresaw that they would be needed to defend London.[14]

The desperate 'Battle of Britain' in which Dowding commanded will always retain the aura of a unique episode – the first and still the only decisive battle fought in the air (though some German authorities doubt that it should be termed a battle at all). It is no legend that Fighter Command, by staying in the air, preserved England from German invasion. The 'cricket scores' attributed to the Few were inaccurate, but not deliberately rigged. The Luftwaffe's largest loss on any single day was seventy-six on 15 August; the Air Ministry News Service claimed 180. The most authoritative recent figures indicate that the Luftwaffe during the battle lost 1,882 planes, and Fighter Command 1,017. The German figures of course include bombers as well as fighters (and it was much easier to shoot down a Stuka or Dornier than a Messerschmitt 109). If we throw in the losses of British Bomber and Coastal Commands involved in the fight for national survival, which John Terraine estimates at 248 aircraft, then the ratio of 'scalps' is still roughly three to two in the RAF's favour, and the same applies to air crew killed. Terraine feels able to conclude that the battle was an 'entirely glorious occasion for the Royal Air Force', clouded only by the dismissal of Dowding and the transfer of Air Chief Marshal Park, who had commanded the crucial No. 11 Group under him, before the end of 1940.[15]

It does not 'debunk' the Battle of Britain to point out that the best German fighter, the Messerschmitt Bf 109, which was at least equal to the Spitfire and considerably superior to the Hurricane, could never spend more than thirty minutes over British soil: the Germans were not equipped with long-range killer planes, but if they had had the sense to fit external 'drop tanks' to their fighters the result of the battle might well have been very different. British aircraft design, flying skill and tactics were adequate to ensure a decisive victory over a more experienced and previously triumphant air force, and to deprecate that achievement would be absurd.

Nevertheless, 'real life' does not provide tidy examples of unadulterated heroism. Certain adjustments to the received story may now be made. They concern the weather, the supply of fighters, and the morale of Fighter Command.

When the prowess of the Few is recounted, brilliant summer weather is evoked – vapour trails crossing clear blue skies as delighted civilians watched the dog fights from below. In fact, although May and June 1940 were warm, dry and sunny – temperatures reached 90 degrees Fahrenheit in the latter month – July (before the battle reached Britain's inland parts) was cool and wet. August brought average sunshine and temperature. September began well, but turned cool after the first week. This was not irrelevant to the RAF's success. 'Normal' weather over England is uncertain weather. The average English August increased the

Luftwaffe's problems. If German planes flew under cloud, anyone looking up could see them. If they flew above cloud, fighters still higher up could spot them easily. But to fly in the cloud was dangerous and made accurate navigation and bomb-aiming impossible.[16]

However, weather conditions which on balance favoured the defence could not have helped Fighter Command much had the supply of fighters faltered. German intelligence in Britain was mercifully inept. Not only did it fail to grasp the way the British fighter defence was organised, with radar in a key role, it mistook the Supermarine aircraft factory at Southampton (not at all a difficult target to reach), which was, until the height of the battle, the only works manufacturing Spitfires, for a factory making bombers, and ignored the crucial significance of the world-famous Rolls-Royce works at Derby, one of only two places producing the Merlin engines which powered both Spitfires and Hurricanes. Even so, by mid-August losses of these two key fighters were exceeding the number available in storage, and this trend increased ominously until early September, when it was reversed, largely thanks to the operations of the Ministry of Aircraft Production's Civilian Repair Organisation, which put 4,196 damaged planes back into the line between July and December. A third of the aircraft issued to fighter squadrons during the battle were in fact salvaged, not new.[17]

Beaverbrook has commonly been praised for what Churchill described as his 'personal force and genius' in busting bottlenecks which had impeded supply of fighters, turning a production shortfall of 282 aircraft in February into an excess over target of 291 in August. Jennie Lee, a former Labour MP, was surprised and pleased when Beaverbrook, the 'arch-appeaser' of 1938, called her in to help with his production drive, and in her memoirs, published in 1980, she paints again a familiar picture of her boss: the man who 'was not a gentleman', who 'had not been to the right schools', who abhorred red tape and long memos, and won the Battle for Britain because he was 'ready to starve the Army and drown the Navy . . . provided he got all the planes and spare parts through to the fighter pilots on time'. Her own job was as a kind of trouble-shooter. For instance, she would 'go to any factory where the workers stopped work once the sirens warned of approaching enemy planes' and tell people to ignore the government instructions to seek cover. She was also asked to detect causes of delay if essential deliveries were not made on time. She cheerfully connived in acts of piracy – as when Beaverbrook heard from her that men were rushing back to their homes from a certain factory when the sirens sounded because their families did not have adequate shelters, and promptly commandeered cement destined for elsewhere so that proper protection could be provided.[18]

However, statistics show that it was in April, before Beaverbrook came to office, that actual production of fighters first exceeded plans, a surge accelerating when Churchill created the Ministry of Aircraft Production for him in May.[19] While Beaverbrook's flair for publicity (which was in no way impeded by his ownership of three popular newspapers) undoubtedly dramatised most successfully the need for the highest possible aircraft production, there is little doubt that his buccaneering methods were in the long run dangerous. Aircraft production doubled in mid-1940, but fell back in the last quarter of the year. By the time Beaverbrook left the ministry in mid-1941, his crude technique of 'carrot planning', whereby unrealistic production targets were set in the hope that bottlenecks would be burst in the effort to meet them, was contributing mightily to public loss of faith in 'war industry' both inside and outside the factories.

Nor was the 'Dunkirk Spirit' which he fostered an unequivocally desirable phenomenon. Some factories worked twenty-four hours a day, seven days a week. Bank holidays were cancelled. An experienced industrial correspondent claimed that it was common-place to meet people who had worked continuously for thirty-six hours on special rush jobs. The results of the manic spurt came as no surprise to experts on industrial health, who knew from First World War experience that a twelve-hour day produced no greater output in the long run than a ten-hour one. Production rose by a quarter in the first week after Dunkirk – but by the fifth week was practically the same as before. Ernest Bevin, the Minister of Labour, saw the danger. At the end of June he insisted on ordering the restriction of hours worked by women and young people to a sixty-hour week of six days, and he strongly recommended the same limits for men. Yet excessive hours continued to be demanded in the munitions industries, 'despite the conclusive evidence that such demands lowered efficiency and raised the rate of absenteeism'.[20]

In 1940 only 941,000 man-days were lost through strikes, as compared with 1,354,000 in 1939. But in 1941 the figure rose again to over a million, and in 1942 the pre-war total was actually exceeded. Dunkirk and the Battle of Britain did not destroy the mutual antipathy of workers and management characteristic of large sectors of the industry. Jennie Lee recalls a moment in 1940 when 'several workers said they wanted a private word with me. "That bugger", they told me, "is a bloody Nazi." They were referring to the factory owner. What in fact was happening was that work had come to a standstill because material that should have arrived from

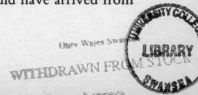

the United States was at the bottom of the sea.' But the manager was wholly unable to communicate to them his own zeal for winning the war.[21] And Mass-Observation, surveying the discontents of war industry in 1942, saw a kind of nostalgia for 'Dunkirk days' as part of its malaise:

> Instead of keeping up a steady optimum, people were allowed to descend from the peak of furious endeavour without being guided on to any plateau. Since then, the various organs for leading public opinion have demanded periodic peaks. The normal human mind is not adjusted to a peak-to-peak effort . . .

It was, however, adjusted to the notion that when you were tired you needed time off. Absenteeism, notably higher than pre-war, was 'the workers' relief before the fatigue state'.[22]

RAF fighter pilots were also human beings, and in most cases very young ones. I should now offer complete a quotation from one of them of which I gave part in Chapter 2 (page 32). Squadron Leader 'Minnie' Manton recalled:

> I don't think any of us (and I was older than most) really appreciated the seriousness of the situation. When we could be scared to death five or six times a day and yet find ourselves drinking in the local pub before closing time on a summer evening, it all seemed unreal . . . [23]

Peter Townsend, a young squadron commander at the hard-hit Croydon airfield at the climax of the battle, likewise recalled:

> The greater issues were beyond us . . . Action and more action was the only antidote against the deadly, crushing fatigue creeping up on us . . . Our dispersal point, with ground crews' and pilots' rest rooms, was in a row of villas on the airfield's western boundary. Invariably I slept there half-clothed to be on the spot if anything happened. In the small hours of 24 August it did. The shrill scream and the deafening crash of bombs shattered my sleep. In the doorway young Worrall, a new arrival, was yelling something and waving his arms. Normally as frightened as anyone, not even bombs could move me then. I placed my pillow reverently over my head and waited for the rest. Worrall still had the energy to be frightened. I was past caring. It was a bad sign; I was more exhausted than I realised.[24]

Inevitably, morale under such stress was variable. 'Chivalry' was attributed to Fighter Command's young men. It was not a virtue attuned to the rigours of mechanised warfare, though some RAF pilots did vow to disobey such instructions as were in force from 14 July, ordering them to shoot down German floatplanes painted with red crosses which were aiming to rescue aircrew from the Channel. Pilots with rank, reputation or influence made sure that they avoided flying in the dud planes which every squadron suffered from, and that they got the services of the best technical staff: 'The green pilots got the slack and inferior ground crews, and the inferior aircraft, and they were shot down.' But by the climax of the battle, experienced men were a dwindling minority, and, as in Townsend's case, their own battle-worthiness was becoming suspect as fatigue took its toll.[25]

By then Fighter Command was full of complaints and bad feeling. At top level there was the controversy over tactics between Park of 11 Group and Dowding on the one hand, and Leigh Mallory of the more northerly 12 Group on the other: the latter favoured the commitment of fighters to attack in 'big wings'. Park saw that to protect the vital 'sector airfields' properly the Germans must be hit as early as possible, and there was no time to form up 'big wings'. But flyers under him who might have agreed were perplexed and annoyed by his order that they should concentrate on shooting down bombers and avoid fighter-to-fighter contact: a wise but unchivalrous command. On the other hand, by 30 August, whole squadrons were disobeying orders which demanded they intercept Messerschmitts, flying deliberately away from the enemy. And on that crucial day, 15 September, when the morale of exhausted Fighter Command men was at its lowest, on the very brink of victory, Johnny Kent, sent in to take charge of 92 Squadron, was appalled when some of his Hurricanes turned for home at the sight of Messerschmitts.

Well before this time, relations between pilots and ground staff had in some cases been very strained. At Warmwell in Dorset civilian cooks refused to get up early to provide breakfast for aviators. The squadron's commander cooked breakfast for his men himself; he was then rebuked by the station commander when the cooks complained about the dirty dishes, and was told never to use the kitchen again. Manston, an airfield perched on cliffs by the Channel in Kent, suffered a 'twelve-day martyrdom' under bombing during which it was, in Townsend's words, 'the scene of the finest and the most abject in human nature'. When the Luftwaffe attacked in force on 12 August, hundreds of airmen went down into the shelters and stayed there, despite threats and entreaties by their officers. Local civilians took the chance to loot damaged buildings of RAF tools and spares. The luckless 264 Squadron which flew Defiants was stationed there: they were helpless against the 109s when they valiantly rose up under attack from Stuka dive bombers which on 24 August finally put the airfield completely out of action. But Manston was not the only field where men spent weeks cowering in the shelters. Civilians employed to deal with bomb craters, who had been doing nothing until the action started, now refused to work during air-raid alerts. RAF personnel had to combine the job of filling craters with their other duties. As Len Deighton, noting this, goes on to observe, 'Even the less glorious moments of the Battle retained their class-conscious character . . . This war in the air belonged to Varsity men, with technical school graduates as travelling reserves.'[26] Ground staff taking shelter while officers Carried On foreshadowed the relationship in London between tube dwellers and 'varsity' men in Whitehall. Similar class cleavage marked British industry.

Amongst about 3,000 men who flew for the RAF in battle, over 80 per cent were from the UK. But there were also many men from Europe and the Commonwealth – the former, exiles who hated the conquering Germans; the latter, often men who had paid their own fares to England to join the peacetime RAF. Commonwealth casualties were disproportionately high. In a period when average air-crew fatalities in Fighter Command were 17 per cent, nine out of twenty-two South Africans and fourteen out of twenty-two Australians were killed. Of the 'top ten' fighter pilots, those accredited with fourteen or more victories, one was Czech, one Polish, two were New Zealanders, one Australian – only five were British. (Taking the war as a whole, it seems that only two of the top eight RAF aces were British: the others were from Ireland, France and the Dominions.[27]) Nevertheless, the enduring image of the Battle of Britain would be of a young Briton fresh from public school or varsity soaring into combat with upper-class slang on his lips. The reputation of Oxford and Cambridge had been tainted before the war by resentment felt by unemployed workers against 'toffs' and by crusty Tories against 'long-haired' youths who were prone to pacifism and communism. The Battle of Britain helped to reglamorise England's traditions of expensive private education.

Babs Diplock was in the WAAF during the war, and a factory worker after. Forty years on she collected and published poems she had written in response to various life experiences. With her permission, I reprint one here. It seems to me to project very clearly a sense of class distance from the boys in blue mingling with sympathy and admiration and recollection of the horror of war. It is an honest tribute from a contemporary (she was nineteen in 1940) to the courage shown by part of her own generation. In another poem she asserts her own role, as one of 'the lasses in blue' who mended aero engines and did 'a man's job', not 'For the lads' but '*with* them'; but the role of technicians in the WAAF is not part of the Myth of the Battle:

Battle of Britain War Hero

On a summer's day
you sat opposite me
in a Tea Shoppe near the sea.
You had no hands
but you managed well
as far as I could see.
Plastic fingers on each metal hand
coped well with food
and I wondered how they would do
with silver sand
on our sunlit beach
with buttons and shoes
and the toilet
and holding your baby
and loving your wife
in bed
and did you mind me staring?

Were you I wondered
one of the Battle of Britain 'FEW'?
Did you in another age say
WIZARD PRANG and BOMBS AWAY?
I search your face for a clue.
Did everything used to be
PUKKA GEN in 1939?
Did you see the HUN
at TWELVE O'CLOCK
as you flew in the English sun?

Your face is so guarded,
a tight sad mask.
I don't want to intrude
but I've got to ask,
was it ALL dear friend
A JOLLY GOOD SHOW
so very long ago?

(I did have tea in a tea shoppe . . . in Eastbourne, and I did see a badly disfigured man at a nearby table. I knew his burns were 'war' burns . . . they always look the same . . . lips thin and stretched and the eyes in shrunken sockets. The skin a pattern of burn marks purple and white on grey skin. I tried to see him as he once was. One of the young gladiators we all adored in the war years. As a wartime WAAF I saw and knew many of these. Their odd jaunty language was a cover for their deep fears and sorrows when comrades had a 'wizard prang' and didn't survive. How easily they are forgotten. We have already forgotten the young men of the Falklands . . . But through this small poem I will not forget the glorious young men of my war.[28])

If Babs Diplock and her WAAF colleagues have been discarded from the 1940 story as unmythworthy, so, in effect, has Sergeant Pilot Josef Frantisek, the ace who probably made the highest score of anyone. A Czech Regular airman, he had flown from his own country after German occupation, fought for the Polish air force, escaped via Romania (despite being interned there) and won the Croix de Guerre flying with the French. The RAF placed him in a Polish squadron. He died as the battle was ending. He is hardly a household name in the country over which he fought his last dogfights. But at least he was not among the thousands of anti-Nazi European exiles who, at this time, were interned in Britain, and whose treatment tells us something about the state of British morale between 9 May 1940, when Hitler invaded the Low Countries, and 7 September, when heavy bombing of London began.

There is abundant testimony to demonstrate that the British in the summer of 1940 demonstrated remarkable *sang froid* and phlegm.

Mollie Panter-Downes assured *New Yorker* readers after the surrender of Belgium and the first news of Dunkirk that, in London, 'the calmness of the average non-military citizen' was 'magnificent . . . The public remains amazingly cheerful . . . The success of the new Defiant fighting planes . . . has raised everyone's spirits considerably.' While she noted a couple of weeks later that there were 'urgent and frightening problems to think of at the moment (such as how to induce stubborn East End mothers to evacuate their children so that the defence of England will not be delayed by tragic fleeing hordes like those which blocked the roads out of Brussels and Paris)', after the fall of France she felt able to write:

It would be difficult for an impartial observer to decide today whether the British are the bravest or merely the most stupid people in the world . . . The individual Englishman seems to be singularly unimpressed by the fact that there is now nothing between him and the undivided attention of a war machine such as the world has never seen before. Possibly it's lack of imagination, possibly again it's the same species of dogged resolution which occasionally produces an epic like Dunkirk. Millions of British families, sitting at their well stocked breakfast tables eating excellent British eggs and bacon can still talk calmly of the horrors across the Channel, perhaps without fully comprehending even now that anything like that could ever happen in England's green and pleasant land.[29]

Herbert Agar, a distinguished journalist and one of a caucus of American 'warmongers' which met at the Century Club in New York to discuss how to get their nation into the fight, was impressed by a Gallup Poll taken when France fell: 'only three percent of these astonishing people thought they might lose the war'.[30] But as Panter-Downes implied, such confidence at such a juncture might be tantamount to stupidity. Another American journalist, writing in 1960, described the conversation in a pub in 'front-line' Kent that month: 'This was a period when the English habit of considering war as a series of small personal affronts tried the nerves of foreigners in their midst.' There were grumbles about tea rationing and disrespectful remarks about the appointment of the Duke of Windsor to govern the Bahamas. 'Of the prospects for survival and victory, nothing.'[31]

Charles Ritchie, the Canadian diplomat, had visited Dover on 2 June, in the latter stages of the Dunkirk evacuation. The war was close enough here: as he walked on the pier, a destroyer limped into harbour with its stern blown clean off by a bomb. Other warships, British and French, carried French soldiers. A tug debouched German prisoners:

While the procession of prisoners and wounded moved by, the Tommies who were guarding the pier remained silent . . . About the cliffs the eternal gulls circled. Two little girls were shrilly calling to each other from their bicycles as they rode in and out of the small gardens in front of a row of houses at the foot of the great bluff of cliff behind the docks. These docks, and in fact the whole of Dover, are now within range of German shell-fire from Boulogne. But the life of the town is going on just the same. We could see the groups of old ladies coming out of church after eleven o'clock service and standing for a minute to chat in the sun.[32]

Vera Brittain, a pacifist, wrote at the time an account of a visit to Hyde Park on 4 August 1940. Whatever meteorological records show, for her it was 'one of the hottest and sultriest' days of an 'ironically perfect summer'. She also remembered it as the twenty-sixth anniversary of the outbreak of the First World War, but found that for Londoners it was, more pertinently, 'the Sunday before the Monday which in normal times would be August Bank Holiday. Although work, tomorrow, is to continue as usual, the British determination to celebrate a holiday somehow is obvious to the most casual spectator.' The crowds were out to hear the speakers at Hyde Park Corner proclaiming their political and religious opinions with as much freedom as in peacetime: the Salvation Army and the National Secular Society; the Catholic Evidence Guild – and the Ministry of Information. Passing behind the MoI's stand, 'a group of Welsh miners singing hymns in unison temporarily drown the efforts of the speaker to assure his audience that all empires but the British Empire have been built upon domination'. Next to the Peace Pledge Union, an Anti-Fifth Column League speaker held forth, denouncing Lord Haw-Haw as a cowardly rat and Hitler as a dirty murderer. The crowd listened with 'mild amusement', as if 'children slain in Hull and Hamburg' were unreal to them. 'The sound and fury of the orator's hatred do not in the least represent the feelings of the majority, who regard Hitler as a dangerous but pitiable lunatic . . . ' Brittain could 'not help wishing' that Hitler and Goebbels could see in that crowded park 'the vast London population' which they had 'so often described as panic stricken'. She too worried about whether 'our national equanimity' might be too closely related to 'apathy, inertia, lack of foresight and failure of imagination'.[33]

Yet none of these could be charged against the Mayhew family, scions of the joint vice-chairman of Colman's, the famous mustard manufacturer. Six young Mayhews and two Howarth cousins served in the war and kept in touch via a family 'Budget' – each writing letters for family consumption, which Beryl, Lady Mayhew, circulated to all from the family house in Norfolk. Of her step-sons, Christopher was prospective Labour candidate for South Norfolk, serving in the army; Pat, a Christian Pacifist, had joined the army as an ambulanceman and had received the Military Medal for his bravery at Dunkirk, from which he had escaped in an open rowing boat, upon which Christopher wrote: 'It is the most delightful incident of the war so far. One's faith is simultaneously strengthened in democracy for allowing Pat to object; in the Army for decorating an objector to itself; in Pat himself; in religion for helping him not to run until the time came.' But Pat now went through a crisis of conscience, and applied for a commission as a combatant soldier. Meanwhile, young Paul's turn was coming up: he was in the RAF, about to be trained for service in fighters. As they all awaited invasion, Beryl, who kept busy with voluntary work, wrote that she found the crisis 'quietly but deeply exhilarating . . . I wouldn't change places with anyone in history.' Yet she hardly had time to think about the war: 'I'm either much too busy making sure pyjamas will be finished as promised or 1001 odd jobs attended to, or else as on Sunday evening Dad and I are paddling in the lake taking off weed and scum, turtle doves crooning in the woods behind us, a family of baby ducks catching flies by the island, and a kingfisher over in the alders – peace incarnate.'[34]

Gulls wheeled over Dover cliffs; kingfishers darted in alders; Britain awaited invasion with quiet confidence. Thus, it is clear, was the 'finest hour' prepared for. So why were thousands of innocent aliens interned? Why were people in high places obsessed with the danger of a British fifth column?

It seemed important fairly to represent here the mass of evidence showing how tolerance and apparent equanimity persisted in Britain during the summer of 1940, as it helps to explain why the persecution of aliens and the scare about traitors were haltable before they did too much damage. But there is also ample evidence, familiar and unfamiliar, to indicate widespread fear and paranoia bordering on panic. Perhaps the weather seemed so 'perfect' because sunlight contrasted with inward ongoing nightmare. Certainly, the apparent persistence of everyday normalities which pleased commentators, worried them, or had both effects at once, must have involved an element of delusion brought about by the contrast between *any* peaceable, pleasant behaviour and the horrors heard of from the Continent, which might shortly be visited upon Britain.

The evidence of widespread abnormality was easily available to Laurence Thompson in 1966, though he discounted it in his account of *1940: Year of Legend, Year of History* with the remark that 'Unity was not quite complete.' He notes that spy mania prompted those Local Defence Volunteers who were used as armed sentries to kill or wound a number of motorists, not always after calling them to a halt. 'Some of the British, excitable in the early summer of 1940 as nesting blackbirds, easily convinced themselves of the truth of the wildest rumour. Elderly ladies bravely followed trails of sky blue wool which, they believed, had been laid to guide parachutists across the country.' General Ironside, Commander in Chief Home Forces, proposed 'to turn a certain Captain Orde Wingate loose in Lincolnshire with a posse' to hunt down traitors, complaining that 'it is extraordinary how we get circumstantial reports of 5th Column and yet we have never been able to get anything worth having. One is persuaded that it hardly exists. And yet there is signalling going on all over the place and we cannot get any evidence.' The *New Statesman*, that left-wing journal, believed equally devoutly that there must be a fifth column, and deplored the 'liberalism of Home Office officials' which held them back from suppressing fascism thoroughly. As Thompson puts it, proven Nazi sympathisers were 'few, and uniformly petty', and German intelligence about Britain was particularly bad.[35] But these facts were not clear at the time, and many people credited absurd rumours that 'Lord Haw-Haw', broadcasting from Germany, was so well equipped with information that he knew when local public clocks stopped.

In fact, an MoI investigation established in January 1941 that 'no case' had been discovered 'in which Haw-Haw or any German wireless made predictions regarding a specific place or announced any detailed facts which . . . could not have been obtained through an explicable channel'. But rumour itself was a danger to morale. Churchill, on 5 July 1940, instructed the MoI to mount a campaign against it, and the distinguished art historian Sir Kenneth Clark was put in charge of an ill-fated campaign by poster, on radio and in the press which launched the 'Silent Column'. With what Ian McLaine neatly dubs 'lumbering jocularity' the public were introduced to typical rumour-mongers and tittle-tattlers – 'Miss Leaky Mouth', 'Mr Knowall' and 'Mr Glumpot' – and instructed, 'TELL THESE PEOPLE TO JOIN BRITAIN'S SILENT COLUMN'. It was further suggested that rumour-mongers should be reported to the police, though only 'as a last resort'. Coinciding with a number of prosecutions against individuals for spreading 'alarm and despondency', this campaign went down badly with the public, who construed it as a campaign against free speech, and Churchill swiftly announced its abandonment (without admitting his own responsibility). At first sight the 'Silent Column' episode provides further evidence for the predominance at this time of British tolerance and phlegm: people wanted free speech as normal.[36] But what it may represent most strongly is a reflex of revulsion against earlier, very widespread, fifth-column mania.

At the outbreak of war a number of Germans living in Britain – some, but far from all, with Nazi sympathies – were interned in a holiday camp in Essex. Soon afterwards, early in October 1939, tribunals all over the country began to consider the cases of all 'enemy aliens' in Britain – that is, people of German and Austrian origin. They were to be sorted out into three categories: 'A' for those who were definitely dangerous and should be interned; 'B' for people who need not be interned but should be subject to restrictions; and 'C' for harmless persons who could remain at liberty. C class covered long-term residents in Britain of good character, and the scores of thousands of refugees who had fled to Britain to escape Nazism. The work of categorising these 'enemy aliens' was finished by the spring of 1940. Out of 73,800 cases considered, only 600-odd were recommended for internment; 64,200 were placed in Category C, and 55,460 of these were classified as 'refugees'.[37]

The phrase 'fifth column' had originated, it seems, in October 1936, when Franco's associate General Mola had threatened the Republican defenders of Madrid with the boast that, besides four columns of soldiers ready to march on them, he had a fifth already in the city itself, prepared to rise and fight for Franco. It was a phrase already in the air early in 1940 when the *Sunday Dispatch* – owned by Lord Rothermere, himself an open supporter of fascism before the war – began a scare campaign against aliens in Britain linked with another against Communists. After the Nazis invaded Norway in April 1940, 'the *Dispatch* invoked the Fifth Column to attack all its favourite targets simultaneously'. Hitler, it alleged on 14 April, had a 'fifth column' in Britain 'made up of Fascists, Communists, peace fanatics and alien refugees in league with Berlin and Moscow'. The conscientious objectors in the Peace Pledge Union constituted 'an underground political force' endangering 'the very life of the nation'. Other newspapers now took up the *Dispatch*'s theme – that Hitler, before attacking a country, created a fifth column to undermine it from within. A correspondent on the respected *Daily Telegraph* used it to explain Hitler's success in Norway – a 'Trojan Horse' had been built, by bribery, infiltration and treason, to admit the Nazis. However, despite a growing chorus from press and MPs, Mass-Observation at this stage found among ordinary people little understanding of the term 'fifth column' and almost no spontaneous support for interning refugee 'aliens'. Anderson, the Home Secretary, was determined to avoid it if possible.[38]

But after 9 May, his position became untenable. The military authorities insisted on the internment of all adult male 'enemy' aliens living in the south-east and east of Britain – from Hampshire to Nairn – and the Cabinet backed this policy. Arrests were duly affected on 12 May. An unfinished housing estate at Huyton, near Liverpool, was hastily surrounded with barbed wire, and from 17 May it began to fill up with internees. There was no furniture, no towels and very little soap and toilet paper in the estate, which in that 'ironically perfect' summer was deluged with rain so that the field around became a sea of mud. Though nearly half the men interned there were over fifty, and many were ailing, there was a shortage of medical supplies.

Worse was to follow. The British ambassador to the Netherlands, Sir Nevile Bland, had returned and reported on the 'fifth-column menace', which he now linked to the new fear of German parachute troops. 'Every German or Austrian servant in Britain' was, he alleged, 'a real and grave menace.' When Hitler gave the order, there would be 'satellites of the monster *all over the country*' who would at once embark on sabotage and attack 'civilians and military indiscriminately . . . ALL Germans and Austrians, at least, ought to be interned at once.' Anderson anticipated the inevitable and ordered the internment of all Class B aliens throughout Britain.[39]

German generals were vastly amused to gather that Britain was possessed by baseless fantasies about fifth columns, and Lord Haw-Haw was soon exploiting the scare by sending spoof instructions over the air. Nevertheless, real grounds for concern emerged when an official of the US Embassy in London, Tyler Kent, and a young British woman named Anna Wolkoff were arrested and charged with passing military secrets to Germany, and a Conservative MP, Captain Maule Ramsay, was alleged to be implicated. The case was proven. The Cabinet's attention was sharply drawn to the far Right of British politics.

Ramsay had founded the anti-Jewish, anti-Bolshevik Right Club, with about 300 members. Similar views were propounded by the Link, founded in 1937 by Admiral Sir Barry Domville, a former director of Naval Intelligence. The Anglo-German Fellowship was less paranoid, and socially up-market; it had attracted literary and aristocratic admirers of Hitler. The largest concentration of anti-Semites was still found in the British Union of Fascists, founded by Sir Oswald Mosley in 1932, which entered the war with (MI5 estimated) 8,700 members. As recently as July 1939, 20,000 had flocked to a British Union of Fascists rally in London. Nevertheless, Anderson, with impeccable liberalism, had insisted that there was no positive evidence that the Union was unpatriotic and would help the enemy: the *New Statesman* was correct to suggest that the Home Office was reluctant to move against the Right. However, Regulation 18B, which permitted the government to detain anyone suspected of endangering public safety, was now amended to cover those 'likely to' imperil it, and Mosley, Captain Ramsay and fifty-seven others were arrested and imprisoned by 20 May. Further arrests, including

Domville's, followed; at a peak at the end of August, 1,428 people were detained under 18B – not all fascists or fascist sympathisers.[40]

As news from the Continent worsened, the pressure from the War Office and press to intern more aliens intensified. Churchill gave his weight to it, and seems to have initiated, in Cabinet on 24 May, the idea of deporting all internees from Britain. Control of the 'alien' question was passed by the Cabinet on 27 May to a new Home Defence (Security) Executive chaired by Lord Swinton. Anderson had lost. On 31 May chief constables were informed that they could now intern any German or Austrian in Category C whose reliability seemed doubtful.

The entry of Mussolini into the war on 10 June at once made 'enemy aliens' of 19,000 Italians in Britain. The chief role of this community had been to tickle the British palate, with everything from high-class West End restaurants to fish-and-chip and ice-cream shops in Scotland. Now they were easy targets for xenophobia. Of the 4,000 suspected 'Fascists' arrested in two weeks, some were probably glad enough to escape from possible mob fury.

On 11 June, Naomi Mitchison heard that in Campbeltown, near her home in Kintyre, 'the three Italian shops had been broken up. The old man had been rather rash, saying that England needed a totalitarian government and so on, but the younger ones were all decent, good citizens who gave money to charity and paid their taxes . . . one of the youngest generation was in a mine sweeper.'[41]

The tragedy of the interned Italians, however, did much to generate revulsion against the new, unbridled, internment policies. Many were respected and popular local figures; some had been explicitly anti-fascist. Several hundred of them were sent to what was probably the worst of the improvised camps – a derelict cotton factory, 'Warth Mills', at Bury in Lancashire. It was filthy; its roof let in the rain. Food was bad, sanitation appalling. Some blankets were verminous. Rats scuttled among the remains of the mill machinery.

Now the Cabinet learned that Canada had agreed to accept 7,000 male internees. On 1 July, a conscripted ocean liner, the *Arandora Star*, sailed from Liverpool with well over 1,000 German, Austrian and Italian refugees aboard. North-west of Ireland it was torpedoed by a U Boat. A Canadian destroyer picked up survivors, but roughly a third of the 478 Germans on board had died, and two-thirds of 712 Italians.

The German dead included well-known socialist opponents of Hitler. The secretary of the Italian League of the Rights of Man perished. The press – Labour *Herald* as well as Tory *Express* – compounded Britain's disgrace by printing reports which suggested that many lives had been lost because aliens on the ship had panicked, cowardly Germans punching and kicking feeble Italians in their haste to get to the boats. These stories were simply untrue. The truth was that the *Arandora Star*, with a load of 1,564 internees and crew, had lifeboats sufficient for only 1,000. Despite this, there had been no fighting and little panic.[42]

Nor would those Britons who had known the Italians easily credit the tales of their moral turpitude. Colin Perry, an eighteen-year-old who lived in the Surrey suburb of Tooting, wrote in his diary:

Azario, the man who owned the pet stores at the bottom of our road, has lost his life on the *Arrandora* [sic] *Star*. It was only a few short weeks ago that my brother, Alan, took our canary to him to have its nails cut . . . We used to be slightly amused at his long, straggling hair, his stooped shoulders and his characteristic Scrooge appearance. Then Italy entered the war. The pet man – as we called him – an Italian subject who had lived peacefully in Tooting for forty-two years, was immediately taken off in a police car for internment. His last words to his wife and daughter were: 'I shall never come back' . . . It just seems incredible that an old man who kept a pet stores in Upper Tooting Road has suddenly been snatched away, to forfeit his life in the Atlantic.[43]

Tom Johnston, though regional commissioner for Scotland, was powerless to prevent the 'tragedy' of an Italian merchant in Edinburgh who had spent all his adult life in Scotland, whose family were serving in the British Forces and who loathed Mussolini. Together with the Scottish Lord Advocate, Johnston 'bombarded the army authorities. But by the time we had convinced Security of the sheer injustice of its action the Italian had been "lost".' He too went down with the *Arandora Star*.[44]

Other drowned internees were known in governing-class circles: Zangiacomi and Maggi of the Ritz, Zavattoni of the Savoy, and several more who were prominent in London cuisine; also P. M. Salerni, an Italian engineer who had been doing important work in the British aircraft industry, had lived most of his life in England and had a British-born wife. The Ministry of Aircraft Production had lobbied unavailingly on his behalf. Yet Beaverbrook's own paper, the *Express*, continued the anti-alien campaign.

Three other ships carrying deported aliens did reach Canada, where the puzzled authorities found themselves guarding such 'dangerous' characters as Jewish schoolboys and left-wing German merchant seamen. One ship, the *Dunera*, sailed for Australia on

10 July. The 2,550 internees aboard included over 400 survivors from the *Arandora Star*. These included some Category A pro-Nazis, but all the rest were B or C. The commander of the military guard, Lieutenant Colonel Scott, put on record his view that the Nazi Germans on board were 'of a fine type, honest and straightforward, and extremely well disciplined', whereas his Jewish charges were subversive liars, demanding and arrogant. His soldiers plundered the internees they guarded of anything they could find of the least value. One of their charges recalls how they seized suitcases as they shepherded internees aboard: 'Those who were carrying their watches had them taken off them by the soldiers. There wasn't much you could do about it.' A senior seaman offered to look after internees' valuables in a case under his bunk, but they never got them back. Eventually the British government had to pay out over £30,000 in compensation. The *Dunera* narrowly missed a torpedo on the way, while conditions on shipboard were hardly, if at all, better than those endured by convicts on the same route 100 years before.[45]

The Cabinet did not yet know of this scandal. But by 18 July they had had enough of alien-baiting, which had caused so much obvious injustice – chronically ill persons seized and interned in rough conditions, relatives ignorant of whereabouts, genuine anti-fascists and Jewish refugees imprisoned with equally genuine Nazis. It transferred responsibility for the detention camps from the War Office to the Home Office, ordered an inquiry into the selection methods used for the *Arandora Star*, and halted internment at 27,200.

Of these people, 7,350 had been deported and 650 drowned. The remainder were scattered in camps throughout Britain,. with the biggest concentration by far on the Isle of Man, which was now virtually a prison island, with a camp for British 18B internees, two camps for 'enemy alien' women, two for Italians, and one for German and Austrian men. The Government had requisitioned seaside boarding-houses and surrounded them with barbed wire. An astonishing galaxy of talent was gathered at Hutchinson's Camp in conditions which they were able to make tolerable. Most of the inmates were 'assimilated' middle-class German and Austrian Jews (though there were oddities such as a circus entertainer originally from Bremen who had been heavily decorated fighting for Britain in 1914–18, had risen to Company Sergeant Major, but had never been naturalised, and twin brothers from Scotland, coal-miners, born during a brief stint their father had done in a Ruhr pit, whose nationality had never been regularised). A rich artistic and intellectual life flourished.

Sixteen painters and sculptors of repute in Hutchinson's Camp protested in a letter to the *New Statesman* (24 August) that art could not live behind barbed wire. But Kurt Schwitters, the co-founder of Dadaism, made collages out of everything to hand – cigarette packets, ripped-up lino, seaweed and so on. 'His *pièces de résistance*', a fellow internee recalls, 'beyond doubt, were sculptures fashioned out of stale remnants of porridge, which he assiduously collected from breakfast tables. They had the colour of Danish blue cheese and exuded a faintly sickly smell. Alas, they did not survive long; the mice soon got at them.'

In Hutchinson's, distinguished scholars helped set up a camp university. There was also a technical school. Fine musicians provided camp concerts. Onchan Camp nearby also seeded art exhibitions, lectures, chamber music, and had its own weekly newspaper. In these two camps, 'the general mood of the internees was on the whole reasonably buoyant'. Conditions in Central Promenade Camp in the centre of Douglas were much poorer. Dr Bell, Bishop of Chichester, visited it and denounced it in the House of Lords on 6 August: the 'unforgettable depressing picture, seeing men of high quality wandering aimlessly about behind high palisades of barbed wire'. Another observer, Mary Hills, thought conditions worse than at Wandsworth jail.[46]

By now, liberal and left-wing opinion was outraged by what had happened. Nor was Conservative opinion unaffected by a widespread revulsion in late July and August at the threat to civil liberties posed by 'police state' methods. The demise of the 'Silent Column' was one symptom of this; so was the rather ridiculous furore over 'Cooper's Snoopers', the social researchers of the Wartime Social Survey who were studying public opinion, quite inoffensively, for the MoI.

I have argued that morale (however defined) remained potentially volatile thoughout 1940. But a positive tendency can be discerned between the time of Dunkirk – when Sir Nevile Bland's broadcast of 30 May had inflamed what François Lafitte, who studied the aliens' case at the time, described as 'panic' affecting 'a large section of the public' – and late August, when one of the younger Conservative MPs, Major Cazalet, said resoundingly in a House of Commons debate:

No ordinary excuse, such as that there is a war on and that officials are overworked, is sufficient to explain what has happened . . . Horrible tragedies, unnecessary and undeserved, lie at the door of somebody . . . Frankly, I shall not feel happy, either as an Englishman or as a supporter of this Government, until this bespattered page of our history has been cleared up and rewritten.[47]

Anderson himself on this occasion freely admitted that 'most regrettable and deplorable things' had happened. Already, internees were being released. By 13 February 1941 over 10,000 were free. Thousands went straight into the British army's Pioneer Corps. As late as October that year, there were still over 3,000 Category C refugee men and women behind barbed wire, but, gradually, all but a handful were freed before the end of the war.[48]

In the First World War the gutter press had had its own way over 'aliens'. It is to the credit of Churchill's Cabinet that at the height of national emergency it pulled back before internments passed the 1914–18 total of 29,000, and reversed a policy which had been shown to be cruel and senseless. A cynic might suppose that it did so because it was frightened of the effect of unpleasant revelations on the Jewish, German and Italian communities in the USA. No doubt this factor did cross ministers' minds. But François Lafitte, whose bitterly critical, very well-documented Penguin Special on *The Internment of Aliens* came out in November 1940 and sold approaching 50,000 copies, wanting to use this very factor to bring pressure on the government for further relaxation, was forced to admit that American publicity had not been bad: ministers had 'been lucky, because the big American papers do not wish to make things awkward for them'.[49]

I believe that the turnabout on aliens represents the calming and hardening of morale, not least in official circles, as the Battle of Britain traced its patterns on southern English skies (when these *were* clear). It is an example of how the myth-making process (which would eventually ensure that the 'bespattered page' of which Cazalet spoke was rewritten with the aliens as an unimpressive footnote) was in itself conducive to good behaviour. Here was Britain Alone, fighting for democracy and freedom against totalitarianism. And men like Cazalet and Bishop Bell believed that 'she' must fight with clean hands, jealously preserving the liberties which permitted Lafitte to write and publish an anti-Establishment best-seller.

The evidence of a Gallup Poll is that even in July, only 43 per cent of the public wanted all aliens interned, as compared to 48 per cent who wanted harmless and friendly ones to be spared.[50] I once placed that 'only' the other way round. But considering the panic-making tendencies of Bland's broadcast in the midst of terrifying events, and the barrage of anti-alien propaganda put out by newspapers – of which the proprietors and journalists (especially those of Rothermere and Kemsley) were manifestly hoping, by inflaming racialist 'patriotism', to atone for their support for appeasement and worse before the war – I now think that the figures represent a modest triumph for traditions of British liberalism over such hateful propaganda as the article in Rothermere's *Daily Mail* which 'reported' from Canada on 12 July:

> In Montreal a shopkeeper told me that he is convinced that Hitler drove out the Jews and political opponents with the express purpose of sending Gestapo agents among them to the Christian countries that took them in. 'Where did so many of them get so much money to live on?' he said. 'Poor refugees – huh! All they have to do is say Hitler was mean to them and we take them in and feed them and half of them are spies.'[51]

6

Day by Day

Who can observe this save as a frightened child
Or careful diarist? And who can speak
And still retain the tones of civilisation?

Roy Fuller, 'Soliloquy in an Air Raid'

THE BLITZ (the bombing of 1940–41) exists for any curious person in an uncountable proliferation of published accounts and published and unpublished documents, as well as in the tape-recorded or filmed memories of 'talking head' survivors. No archive of such abundance exists for any other 'major event' in British history. It can be asserted with complete confidence that no 'big secret', no nasty fact or set of facts which could invalidate the Myth, will ever emerge: no such secret could possibly have been 'covered up'. I recall the frisson of shock (and excitement) which I experienced in the sixties when, as a young researcher, I first read the then-unpublished reports by Mass-Observation for the government on morale in provincial towns under bombing. This was not what I'd learnt from published sources – here were people panicking, people in despair. Yet my own father had bravely published, in 1940–41, as much as could be said at the time (quite a lot) to suggest the confusion and demoralisation of bombed out people confronted with inadequate post-raid services, let down by the authorities. And it was not long before the Big Facts were clear to me: none of the incidents and public reactions which Mass-Observation described contradicted the Big Facts that British society and its institutions remained intact. British 'war industry' continued to expand, American supplies continued to enter through the horribly stricken western and southern ports – Liverpool, Plymouth, Portsmouth, Southampton – which the Royal Navy continued to use.

That many *small* secrets will always be hidden is indubitable. Successful after-raid looters have not written their memoirs.

Cowardly people in local government have not advertised their shame. Yet the memoirs and documents which do exist testify so abundantly and frankly to panic, to horrified revulsion, to post-raid depression, to antisocial behaviour, that the general pattern is plain, and new particulars, however interesting for the inhabitants of such-and-such a town to which they relate, or to the families of those involved are, from the historian's point of view, redundant.

As still more 'careful diarists' are published, as yet more 'components of the scene' (to quote another poet) are arrested from the fallible memories of millions of survivors, as the media and the oral historians continue to mine a seam that appears to be nowhere near exhaustion, every new 'fact' or 'memory' slots into the Myth. There is nowhere else for it to go, within the parameters of our present consciousness. The Myth that the British were Bombed and Endured stands, supported by the Big Facts.

Poets in this war were driven towards the Little Facts, towards the posture of 'careful diarists'. Actual diarists writing about events and feelings in the year from May 1940 to May 1941 were already able to slot their 'components' into a recognisable 'scene'. There was, to begin with, considerable scepticism about BBC Radio News and about the newspapers. Rumours were commonplace. What was actually seen by an individual often contradicted what was said to be happening. But gradually the 'careful diarist' was likely to take for granted a broad overview supplied by: the speeches of Churchill and Ernest Bevin; the broadcasts of Priestley; the BBC News – and perhaps the left-of-centre pages of *Picture Post* and the sturdy, heroically simple cartoons of the great David Low. There were also numerous, admittedly propagandist, films shown in the ever-popular cinemas, and, as publishers found time and paper to get them out, a large number of books about the Blitz in particular; collections of Churchill's speeches; biographies of Churchill. For a literate, thinking person, the personal 'morale problem' was thus: day by day you either believed the evolving Myth (which showed at each stage how Britain was invincible), or you relapsed into scepticism and fears. When you recovered from such an aberration, the Myth had already moved ahead to help you onwards.

This pattern can be found in two types of source unpublished at the time and clearly untampered with afterwards: the Home Intelligence Reports of the Ministry of Information, and material, including diaries, given to Mass-Observation by volunteers and employees, used fitfully by Mass-Observation in its investigations and then left untouched for several decades.

The director of Home Intelligence at MoI was Mary Adams

(1899–1984), one of the most remarkable women of the twentieth century. Daughter of a farmer, she had grown up after his death in great hardship. After getting a first in botany at University College, Cardiff, she became a Cambridge don, leaving in 1930 to join the BBC, first as adult education officer, then as the first woman TV producer in the world's first TV service: she was in charge of education, political material, talks and culture. After the war she held senior posts in BBC TV. According to the *Dictionary of National Biography*, 'She was a socialist, a romantic communist . . . a fervent atheist and advocate of humanism and commonsense.' It is important to note that these impulses held each other in check; also that she was married to a Conservative MP, Vivyan Adams – an anti-Nazi and social reformer. She brought to the work of surveying morale – on which she became the key authority in government circles – a will to beat Hitler controlled by habits of academic and scientific caution, and an exceptionally wide range of intellectual and political contacts.

Home Intelligence Reports[1] – the initial title was 'A Summary of Public Opinion of the Present Crisis' – began on a daily basis on 18 May 1940. After well over a hundred of these, Home Intelligence switched to producing weekly reports, beginning with the period 30 September to 9 October, when London's initial ordeal was still at its height. By late November, presentation had evolved so that the reports had an almost scholarly air. There was certainly no shortage of material from which to compile them. In 'Weekly Report by Home Intelligence – No. 8' (18–25 November) no fewer than thirty-seven different 'references' were listed. Few members of the public can have come near to guessing how many friends or strangers might be reporting on them to the government or to independent organisations aiding government. The regional information officers in various 'provincial' centres probably saw other bigwigs for the most part, but their club-room impressions were augmented by:

1 Summaries of the newspaper press prepared within the MoI itself, reports of the MoI's 'Anti-Lie Bureau', and grievances voiced through MPs and combed from the papers of *Hansard*.
2 Reports from the Postal Censorship – these might result from examination of hundreds of thousands of letters. Also Telephone Censorship summaries.
3 Reports from police duty-rooms relayed by chief constables.
4 Reports by Mass-Observation (independent, though regularly retained by MoI) and the government's own Wartime Social Survey.

5 BBC Listener Research reports and other material supplied by the Corporation.

6 Reports from the firm of W. H. Smith, which owned a very large chain of newsagents, notably at railway stations: their managers, through travelling superintendents, supplied information about comments and gossip concerning the war.

7 Reports from the managers of the large chain of Granada Cinemas.

8 Information from a wide range of organisations, including the Citizen's Advice Bureaux, the Women's Voluntary Services, and the right-wing Economic League, which interested itself especially in Communists.

9 Rather intriguingly, Scottish Unionist Whips' intelligence reports (coming from those responsible at Westminster for keeping Conservative MPs from north of the Border in line), and special fortnightly reports from the regional/intelligence officer, Scotland, based in Edinburgh.

It has never been suggested that Mary Adams was a woman incapable of judging and correcting her own biases; in any case, she could not have looked through such a mass of material on her own, nor withheld access to it from colleagues. There is no doubt that the daily reports rushed out down to the end of September are somewhat impressionistic – but surely any dire threat to morale would have been detected? It is true that Adams was prepared to show such things to friendly US journalists in order to cement their conviction that Britain would fight on. But she was under no compulsion to do so: these documents had a heavily restricted, secret circulation. (The meeting within MoI on 27 September, at which Adams agreed to produce weekly reports specifying selected sources, laid down that these were to be 'used as a guide for action by the departments of the Ministry concerned with publicity at home', and *not* to be circulated outside it, except that 'extracts without comment affecting other departments may be issued where action appears requisite'.)

It emerges from a draft memo in Adams's papers how Home Intelligence created the reports. All incoming material was 'carefully and completely read' by two assessors who produced abstracts and summaries. They then compiled a report, of which the final version was written in conference with Adams herself. The 'final interpretation', she could claim, was produced by three people, each of 'entirely different outlook', all of whom aimed at objectivity.

The early daily reports convey rather excitingly the sense of public opinion reacting to a multiplicity of news and pressures, many of which dropped out of the Myth and were largely forgotten. Churchill's broadcast of Sunday 19 May aroused entirely 'favourable' comment, though its effects were 'still apparent' on Tuesday, and these included worry over its serious implications among about half of 150 people interviewed house-to-house in London. On 23 May there was an 'excellent reception' for the Emergency Powers Bill, which effectively suspended all civil liberty for the duration of war. Both xenophobic 'anti-alien' feeling and wild rumours of airborne invasion abounded. On 24 May there was 'the usual crop of rumours about "hairy-handed Nuns", parachutists, etc.,' plus one beauty (as it seems now) about 'a house full of blind refugees which [sic] were alleged to be in possession of machine guns'.

By 25 May, as allied collapse in France became evident, Home Intelligence was reporting 'increasing confusion . . . bewilderment and disquiet'. It was already in the habit, perhaps partly conditioned by Adams's political impulses, of indicating that upper- and middle-class morale was frailer than that of working-class men. A theme of its 1940 reports was serious public concern about the danger of invasion through Eire – this had surfaced before the end of May. Soldiers evacuated from Dunkirk were by 30 May 'talking freely about their experiences, particularly in pubs. The effect of this is not good.' Such talk would have included far from baseless stories about inadequate British Expeditionary Force equipment, poor RAF fighter support and *sauve qui peut* flight to the ships by officers. But on the 30th, optimistic press reports about the evacuation were said to have produced 'a general calmness, allied with a new feeling of determination'. Next day, the return of the British Expeditionary Force was credited with giving 'great emotional relief' and producing elation. 'Relief and elation', Home Intelligence reported, continued on 3 June, and by the 4th, Dunkirk was 'accepted as a "Victory", as a "lasting achievement . . . "' and Home Intelligence was worried that morale was 'too high', based on 'an inadequate realisation of the facts of the situation'. The popularity of J. B. Priestley's classic Dunkirk broadcast of 5 June was strongly registered, though it is curious to note that, according to his Home Intelligence underlings, the Minister of Information, Duff Cooper, was, by 'general view' at least, rated the best of all radio propagandists; his growing 'fan following' was reported from Newcastle (11 June) amongst, especially, the working classes. This polished socialite seems an improbable rival for Priestley, but it appears that his attacks on Italy went down well with 'less sophisticated working-class feeling'.

One could go on right through the summer reports plucking out interesting pieces of detail. But it is enough to register here some of the daily verdicts on morale in general: 'gloomy apprehension', at least in middle-class circles and amongst women after the fall of France (17 June), 'cheerfulness' re-emerging by 27 June, by when early, light bombing raids by the Luftwaffe had been received calmly in various places; then, after a period of 'cheerfulness and determination', real dismay over the German occupation of the Channel Islands. Through this period, the great public enthusiasm for evacuating children to the Dominions suggests that people expected worse to come: it was somewhat dampened when the *Arandora Star*, carrying refugees to Canada, was torpedoed early in July. But throughout that month 'cheerful'. . . 'little change' . . . 'morale is high' recur in general assessments, even if by 24 July Home Intelligence felt constrained to note that the 'high pressure' under which factories were working had produced 'signs of fatigue'. By mid-August, revealing consistently high morale seems to have begun to bore Home Intelligence itself: its daily reports became shorter. On 15 August it declared that morale continued to be 'high' and that 'intensified' air raids had been taken with 'calmness and courage'. Next day it reported, 'Many people in Scotland are now awaiting impatiently "for their turn to come", and a first glimpse of a spitfire [sic] chasing a Dornier.' From London, where daytime raids were now common, the message was that 'people on the whole are excited rather than apprehensive'.

What Home Intelligence took to be a general mood of confidence and determination was not even affected by the withdrawal of British troops before Italians in Somaliland – 'Fancy, the Wops, it's disgusting.' In fact, an implication which emerges strongly from the whole Home Intelligence series is that the more British civilians felt involved in the war at home, the less bad news from overseas fronts interested or affected them: the massive air raids of May 1941 would therefore neutralise somewhat catastrophic news from the eastern Mediterranean. According to Home Intelligence, the long standing controversy over when sirens should be sounded to warn of raids – sometimes they came too late, sometimes no bombs followed – was not enough to dampen high spirits.

It is crucial, perhaps, to the understanding of behaviour in bombed Britain to notice the following pattern:

1 From June onwards, *light* raids and warnings were experienced over many areas.
2 By August, during the Battle of Britain, London was experiencing frequent raids which were 'heavy' by earlier standards, though trivial by those set on 7 September.

3 Other cities experienced really heavy bombing only weeks or months after reported behaviour in London had fixed a key figure in the Myth, the 'Cheerful Cockney', firmly on a pedestal as a model for others to follow.

Now, it is the case that MoI-directed 'Home Propaganda' could help to create such a model of approved behaviour. But the Home Intelligence reports suggest that its salient features – including, by August, enhanced 'neighbourliness' shown after raids – were believed to have emerged spontaneously. Individual cases displaying cowardice, defeatism and selfishness could be treated as exceptional, once the test of 7 September and the week or so following had been endured. The exceptions may occasionally strike a late twentieth-century reader coming upon them as very impressive indeed. But the overall paradigm never had to shift to accommodate them: the tube shelterers, for instance, could quite quickly be incorporated as good, gutsy, essentially orderly Cockneys. This case, however, involved a continuing 'left-ward' shift in the paradigm, as the government appeared to concede that its previous shelter policy had been misguided. To the element in the Myth which already firmly attributed the troubles of the British Expeditionary Force in France and the RAF's shortage of planes to the 'Guilty Men' of pre-war Conservative governments was now added the notion that the 'people', improvising bravely and brilliantly, were fighting the Luftwaffe without much direction from above. All triumphs of fire-fighting, rescue, post-raid feeding and so on belonged to 'us', the people; all bungling was due to 'them' – unpopular ministers, boneheaded bureaucrats, gutless local government personnel.

If the general analysis above is correct, then the key period of British adjustment to bombing occurred, in London, not *after* 7 September but *before* that date. Conditions in August were very much less frightening than pre-war forecasts had indicated. But they were severe enough, in a number of places, to generate patterns of response and adaptation which would be generally useful later.

A 'Special Interim Report by Home Intelligence: AIR RAIDS: Reactions and Suggestions: July–August 1940' summarises what Adams and her team made of the situation just before the great night attacks on London began. It asserted that people were worried by sirens, and in many cases angry about the apparent inefficiency of warning systems, but rapidly became insouciant if no bombs dropped. Continuous loss of sleep, however, could be a problem – as in Bristol, which had many night 'raids' without bombs, and where people tended not to bother to go to inconvenient shelters. There were 'evidences of growing strain especially among women and children' and the Communist Party was beginning to 'make political capital out of siren and shelter difficulties'. However, Home Intelligence concluded: 'There is no need to "improve morale", but there should be more appreciation, encouragement, congratulations and explanation.' The writer of the last sentence quoted might have been remembering the 'increasing' criticism from Wales reported by Home Intelligence on 24 August, 'that this region is not always mentioned in our raid communiques [sic] when it should be. . .'. Local pride was already strongly involved in post-raid reactions.

Home Intelligence began to register the steeply mounting impact of raids on London in its report of Monday 26 August. London had 'come through a weekend of extensive raids with courage and calmness . . . East Enders experiencing screaming bombs for the first time expressed great fear but did not panic.' Next day: 'Determination has not weakened, but our reports show a definite increase in apprehension . . . The realisation that night raids may persist throughout the winter is bringing despondency.' On the 28th, growing effects of loss of sleep were generally reported but, in London, 'Great neighbourliness was evident.' However, on the 30th, Home Intelligence concluded that morale was 'higher in the provinces than in London', where 'in some districts' people had latterly expressed 'considerable apprehension'.

It may be that the crucial adjustment in London was made in the week which included the first anniversary of the outbreak of war. On that day, Tuesday 3 September, Home Intelligence felt able to report that people 'apparently' were adjusting to sleeping through raids. On Friday 6th, 'The public continue to take the bombing in good heart . . . An increasingly fatalistic attitude towards the effects of bombing is reported, and this appears to be coupled with a high state of morale . . . Co-operation and friendliness in public shelters are reported to be increasing.' (So, also, were 'cases of blatant immorality in shelters'!)

Hence, Home Intelligence's reports after 7 September can retain a businesslike, even blasé, manner. On Monday 9th, it found 'little sign of panic and none of defeatism' in the East End, though it did notice ugly anti-Semitic feeling coming to the fore. Jews of the area provided a convenient scapegoat. If people from the East End evacuated themselves to the Kent hopfields or headed for London's terminus stations, this was because they were 'thoroughly frightened', not a result of 'defeatist feelings', Home Intelligence concluded on 10 September. There was heavy 'unplanned evacuation' from the East End and London generally, but this (as Home Intelligence would stress later) was no bad thing for 'morale' if it meant that people of fearful disposition whose presence as workers wasn't essential went, leaving behind the brave and the needed.

On 12 September, Home Intelligence felt able to report that morale was high, particularly in London, and that people were much more cheerful. Home Intelligence did not attribute the shift to Churchill's latest speech – 'well received but not so enthusiastically as usual', since people who had convinced themselves that no invasion would happen disliked being reminded that one was still possible. The main morale-boosting factor, in London, was that after several days when it had seemed that no defence against bombers was being offered, a noisy anti-aircraft barrage had at last opened up: ' "We'll give 'em hell now" is a typical working-class comment.' On the 17th, Home Intelligence reported that morale in London was 'steady' and that most people were settling down to the 'new air-raid life cheerfully'. Car drivers were 'giving lifts more readily'.

According to Home Intelligence, people outside London received an exaggerated impression of the damage which the capital was suffering. But 'if London can take it, so can we' was a common response (18 September). There was anger reported from Merseyside next day, however; Liverpool had been bombed by day with no RAF fighter cover apparent. 'Liverpool considers that for its size its losses have been as heavy as London's, and that it should have appropriate fighter protection.' (Ironically, the rumour circulating in the north-west that East Enders had petitioned Churchill to end the war would be more than matched by one about a pro-peace demonstration in Liverpool itself during its 'May Blitz' of 1941: of all such figments of gossip, the 'Liverpool peace demonstration' would probably be the most durable, believed in even by sensible, scholarly persons decades later.)

By 21 September, after just two weeks of severe Blitz, Home Intelligence was serene. 'Yesterday's cheerfulness' was maintained. 'In London conversation is almost exclusively about air raids; it is gossipy, not panicky, and is centred in personal matters. There appears to be very little relationship between the "bomb at the corner of our street" and the war as a whole.' Interest in war news was 'very low'. In the invaded tube stations, 'People are orderly, officials humane.'

By 8 October, when Home Intelligence issued the first of its weekly reports, the less excitable and impressionistic format was matched by a calm analytical posture. 'Morale in general continues good . . . People now seem to be living from day to day.' Some 120,000 letters investigated by Postal Censorship, and over 100 incoming reports each based (Home Intelligence claimed) on between 1,000 and 2,000 interviews, yielded no evidence weighty enough to contradict such generalisations. 'From Dundee', Home Intelligence reported, demonstrating its easy geographical comprehensiveness, 'comes the sentiment – "if only they would give us a turn, they might give London a night's rest".'

Whether this was actually said by an idiotic civic dignitary or a drunk in an hotel bar – indeed, whether anyone actually said this at all – was, and is, completely immaterial. 'Provincial' journalists, recently taken on a tour of London so that they could adjust their previously 'overdrawn picture', had certainly imbibed as they went around the view now shared with Home Intelligence by US journalists, Crown Unit film-makers, politicians of all parties and Londoners themselves, that *in general* Londoners were cheerful, and their gritty behaviour a wonder for the world to admire. The paradigm was firmly established. And if morale was anywhere less than wonderful, this was not because (for instance) corpses blown to pieces and collected piecemeal in sacks, or beloved children horribly burnt, were depressing matters to be aware of; it was because the authorities weren't doing enough, or doing the right things, for the heroic People. The basic story was scripted, and could now be transferred *en bloc* to any other city.

While the institution of the George Cross for civilian bravery would recognise the heroism of individuals, feelings that Hull, say, or Sheffield had never had sufficient recognition for its 1940–41 ordeal would persist as long as survivors lived. A letter from Mr F. J. Mansfield, published by *Bristol Labour Weekly* (22 January, 1943), would foam furiously about the MoI's official account of the Blitz, *Front Line*:

Frankly, I am greatly disappointed with the Bristol portion of this publication for the world. There are several errors in describing our losses during the blitzes, and apparently no mention is made of the raids we had prior to the general blitzing of the country. I think I am right in saying we began with raids in June 1940 – weeks before London. And what about the two mass day attacks on a neighbouring suburb of Bristol, if Croydon gets mentioned? . . . And again, our 12½ hour blitz receives no mention.

Paradoxically, such envy of London would *reinforce* London's status as Metropolis and emphasise the paradigmatic character of its inhabitants' experience. Thus Mr Mansfield is not denying that London 'Took It'. But Bristol, he feels, Took It before London, and, later, Took blitzes of London-like ferocity. For every such 'provincial' chauvinist, the point was to prove that your city was *as brave* as London.

So on 4 November Weekly Report no. 5, noting the 'continued cheerfulness' of Londoners could add that bombs on Coventry had produced a similar response to that of the capital, and generalise safely: 'It seems that the reaction of an urban community to heavy bombing is fairly consistent.' A 'large group' of 'jittery people of all classes' fled, or, to put it more kindly, 'evacuated themselves'. The more nervous of the remainder went at night to the 'safest place near at hand' – in London, the Underground stations, in Coventry the countryside where they could sleep in villages, fields, woods, cars, charabancs. There would be complaints about inadequate air defence and demands for deep shelters (fanned by the CP), but 'petty grumbling' would vanish. 'The morale of most people is affected by severe bombing, and improves quickly when raids slacken.'

Grumbles were rife among the British people: Report no. 6 chose to interpret these as evidence of *good* general morale. Prices were rising, people were dissatisfied with pay in the services and in industry, 'billeting problems' between evacuees and hosts were back with a vengeance, raid victims faced problems getting compensation. But the latest Gallup Poll indicated that 80 per cent were confident that Britain would win. Report no. 9 (4 December) asserted, 'In general morale continues steady and there is a general feeling that we shall win in the end, but only after a long struggle. In no less than 82 out of 88 returns from railway bookstalls, are the public described as "being confident of final victory".'

One could selectively extract from these winter reports plenty of counter-mythic detail: many people in the poorer districts of Bristol talking about being let down by the government and of the possibility of a negotiated peace; a great increase in listening to German radio; 1,167 votes for a Christian Pacifist candidate in a by-election in Northampton, where the winning Tory got 16,587 (no. 10, 11 December); 'Rapidly increasing grumbles' about food (no. 11, 18 December). But such items seem insignificant when set beside the authoritative conclusions of Dr P E Vernon, Director of Psychology at Glasgow University, on individual reactions to air raids. From this and other evidence, Home Intelligence concluded that the number of psychological casualties in the raids had been 'astoundingly small'. Up to 10 per cent of the population could normally be expected to cave in to 'nervous illnesses' when circumstances gave them an honourable excuse: hence the serious problem of 'shell shock' in the armed forces. The government had anticipated the problem while preparing for war by setting up two special psychiatric hospitals near London. But in practice, the suicide rate fell and 'psychological' casualties in London and elsewhere were very few. Home Intelligence suggested that whereas on the battlefield psychological breakdown permitted physical escape from danger, Blitz conditions ruled this out. 'The refuges from bombing (the country and the deep shelter) are reached, not by having a breakdown, but by having sufficient determination to get there.'

A quarter of London's population (as Report no. 14 revealed) might have left the city by November 1940. Big surges (up to 35 per cent) in population in safer places that were easily accessible – such as Hertford, Aylesbury, Reading, Gloucester – and in remote parts such as west Wales, might suggest where many of these had gone. But there were many other reasons, including the dispersal of industry, for people to move out; and resentment of rich self-evacuees or hostile treatment of poor ones were not signs of social order collapsing, but rather of the persistence of class resentments, abundantly present, but well contained, in Britain during the thirties.

Class war on Clydeside worried Home Intelligence, who paid special attention to the area. MoI's office in Edinburgh reported in December 1940 (WR no. 9) signs of unrest in Scottish industry after 'a long period of quiet' and linked this to Communist penetration. Another report from Edinburgh at the end of February (WR no. 21) said that tales of slackness by workers and bad management were 'common'. 'Difficulties in industrial relations on Clydeside', strong class feeling, bad transport and poor management were held to explain a Communist vote of 3,862 (Labour 21,900) in the Dumbartonshire by-election held at this time. But when the area had its first heavy raids in mid-March, Home Intelligence found a 'striking similarity' to the initial response in London's East End, except that Glasgow came out 'if anything, slightly better'. There was 'remarkably little grumbling' afterwards, and the engineering apprentices who were on strike (primarily, it seemed, over higher rates of wages paid to government trainees) 'offered their services in any post-raid work'. In Clydeside a week later, Home Intelligence reported 'a sense of relief at having been able to stand up to the ordeal'. By early April it could be stated that 'In Glasgow, as an apparent result of the raids, there was much greater interest in and enthusiasm about the news than is usual' and 'A new feeling of partnership with the English blitzed cities . . . '

Around this time (31 March) the MoI produced 'Advice on the Preparation of Broadcasts', about conditions in badly-blitzed towns.

'Those who remain in the town', this remarked primly 'often show a considerable amount of "cheerfulness" which is often thought to be synonymous with "high morale". Joking is common.' Such scepticism anticipates that of the scholar, decades later, who suspects that journalists and others mythologising the Blitz were often deceived by high spirits of the kind generated by crises, which proverbially 'end in tears'. The sensible advice was that broadcasters should never generalise about the state of morale, as many listeners would find themselves to be exceptions, and people would resent a 'standard' being set up which they knew to be 'impossible'. It was important to 'shift attention from the present to the future', emphasising 'rebuilding, reconstructing, replanning . . . The future will be *better* than the past.'

Two points emerging from this can conclude our survey of the contribution of Mary Adams and her collaborators to the solidification of the Myth. Firstly, such people were not complacent, or easily fooled. If they presented, week in, week out, a positive view of British morale, this was presumably because their nationwide remit permitted them to distinguish temporary and local crises of opinion from general and repeated patterns. Scary Mass-Observation reports suggesting depression in Portsmouth or despair in Southampton referred to exceptional cases. London was a very large city, and an outbreak of panic, anti-Semitism or defeatism in one quarter of its East (or West) End was far from enough to determine morale in general.

Secondly, the irresistible left-ward impetus of the Myth at this time is clear. While Mary Adams was glad to encourage it because of her own political impulses, she and those who thought like her certainly did not create it. *Of course* people could not be expected to endure daily and nightly discomfort, the smashing of landmarks and of whole communities, increasingly austere standards of living and uncomfortable accommodation without some promise of a better future. And this would have to be Planned.

Mary Adams liked and admired Tom Harrisson, the co-founder and, by the time of the Blitz, sole director of Mass-Observation, and she defended him against his critics inside the MoI. But she and her assistants certainly did not accept Mass-Observation's views on morale under bombing unhesitatingly. Had they done so, their daily and weekly reports would often have made disturbing reading.

In December 1940, Harrisson went to Southampton with an employee of the Ministry of Food. This man wrote a report, and on the copy of it in the Mass-Observation Archive, Harrisson's hand has noted that the Minister of Food, Lord Woolton, 'took this to the Cabinet'. The document asserted: 'It seems likely that the almost total destruction of provincial towns will continue. There is no time to lose if the despair and suffering at Coventry and Southampton are to be mitigated elsewhere.' It claimed, 'That morale generally is deteriorating is the view of the Intelligence Branch of the Ministry of Information.'[2]

In fact the Weekly Report at this juncture announced 'no marked changes of morale'. What was the Ministry of Food man (Lionel Fielden, no mean writer) up to, perhaps with Harrisson's connivance? Surely he was campaigning in the struggle for improved post-raid services, led in the press by Ritchie Calder of the *Daily Herald* and *New Statesman*. Fielden was arguing that covered post-raid 'feeding centres' were needed around every city, with sufficient alternatives to obviate the risk of all being bombed simultaneously.

Likewise, Mass-Observation's report of 14 August 1940 on the government's '"Stay Where You Are" Leaflet' (File Report 349) was not innocent of polemical direction or of self-interest. To take the latter aspect first – it was crucially important to Mass-Observation, dependent financially on continued government commissions, to establish that its methods of questioning and observing yielded information about what went on in public opinion 'below the surface'. Thus, this one declared: 'In previous reports we have frequently asserted that while civilian morale is superficially good, it was not firmly based. But this conclusion had to be reached partly by intuition and partly by a study of what happened in France and Belgium. There was no direct evidence that people were likely to panic extensively in case of invasion.'

But, lo and behold, when the new government leaflet advising people to 'stay put' in the event of invasion was tried by Mass-Observation on '320 persons in an urban and rural area' (probably part of London, and Worcestershire), it yielded evidence that people *would* panic. By more than three to one, people were critical of the leaflet. There was a great deal of comment to indicate interviewees' lack of confidence in their own or other people's ability to 'stay put': 'Usually specific spontaneous reference was made to panicking and refugeeing.' Mass-Observation attributed this to all the publicity given to refugees in France. It then ticked off the MoI for the inadequacy of its propaganda and alleged that the schoolmasterly tone of the leaflet raised hackles. This was a favourite Mass-Observation polemic. If its views were credited at all, they should help guarantee further commissions for Mass-Observation, the organisation best equipped to test the submerged opinion towards which effective propaganda would have to be directed.

I do not allege that Harrisson and his coadjutors were cynics profiteering in the crisis. Harrisson was manifestly a patriot and anti-fascist, and his criticisms of 'Home Propaganda' were generally shrewd and hence constructive. Polemic and unconscious self-interest – closely allied – may, however, have distorted Mass-Observation's use of findings from what now seems a very small sample (for a start, if these interviews were conducted on doorsteps by day, as seems likely, those expressing opinions were unlikely to include an adequate proportion of active young and youngish people engaged on 'war work').

However, 'components of the scene' could indeed look so very bad as to seem to justify fears of likely panic. A very young but extremely intelligent paid Mass-Observer, Nina Masel, reported from an East End base during the raids. As the big night raids began on 7 September she was joined by four more Mass-Observation 'investigators'. What they said and heard, Mass-Observation could not refrain from pointing out, confirmed the conclusions of its 'Stay Where You Are' report. People *weren't* staying. Immediately after the bombs on the afternoon of the 7th, people began quitting the area. Mass-Observation estimated that as many as six out of ten had abandoned certain streets – some of them untouched by bombs – by Monday evening. While the press 'sentimentally proclaimed' that old people refused to leave their 'beloved homes', it was in fact mostly older people who were going:

> The whole story of the last weekend has been one of unplanned hysteria . . . Of course the press versions of life going on normally in the East End on Monday are grotesque. There was no bread, no electricity, no milk, no gas, no telephones . . . The press version of people's smiling jollity and fun are gross exaggeration. On no previous investigation has so little humour, laughter or whistling been recorded. (FR 392: Report on Evacuation and other East End Problems, 10.9.40)

Many 'refugees' from the East End headed to Paddington station and on to Oxford. A sharp (again very young) paid Observer, Len England, reported from there on 19 September, when the city was reckoned to hold up to 20,000 'refugees'. The impression which they had brought with them that London was 'a mass of smoking ruins' had got across to local people, so that when England mentioned that he was going back there, 'practically everyone was astonished: they seemed to have no idea that even parts of London were still habitable'. (FR 412: Evacuees in Oxford)

But other 'components' in the same archive suggest why Home Intelligence, surveying the whole 'scene', was able to take a positive view of morale. Using Mass-Observation material, we can work from 'periphery' to 'core' of the Blitz experience.

First, the diary, kept for Mass-Observation, of a woman aged twenty-three, living in Monmouthshire and working as a statistician in an engineering works producing valves.[3] Because she kept her Mass-Observation diary from the outbreak of war, we know a lot about her. Because she sent her diary in by instalments, we know that she had no chance to note and 'correct' inconsistencies or impose hindsight on the material by revision or editing. She was a Cambridge graduate, engaged to be married to a young doctor. She was earnestly left-wing, and continued to attend Left Book Club meetings despite her distaste for the Communist line taken by the chief speakers. When bad news from Norway began she wondered (10 April) if she would be 'put in a concentration camp' because of the LBC books she owned. Two days later, feeling 'an awful coward', she wrote to say that she wouldn't attend any more LBC meetings – 'a friend' had advised her that it wasn't safe.

Her reactions in May confirm that the *early* summer weather of 1940 was indeed glorious, and show how generalisations about public opinion can completely exclude deviant experiences: she was so preoccupied with cycling round Wales with her Jack that it seems she hardly noticed the fall of Chamberlain. On 19 May, after another trip to meet Jack in Shropshire, she wrote:

> This has been such a wonderful spring and the trees are so lovely, and, in spite of the war, I've enjoyed it all immensely. I listened to Churchill's speech when I got back. It was a fighting speech and rather depressing. To my mind a nation under Nazi rule for a short period would be better than a nation completely wiped out if we intend to fight to our last man rather than surrender.

However, on the 23rd she could express surprise at her own cheerfulness: 'I suppose that I have a strong trait of the English belief that we shall muddle through somehow.'

But she remained uncertain about the ethics of fighting the war. On 24 May she noted that part of the King's speech was 'hypocritical . . . He spoke of our policy of freedom, justice and peace but we hardly followed those ideals in the way we acquired our Empire, nor in the way we have governed it since.'

Three days later: 'If we have got to give in to Germany, I almost think it would be better to do it now, though I hate the thought of defeat as much as anyone. But I think that I hate the thought of mass slaughter even more.'

Gradually, the excitement of 'living on a besieged island' began to resolve such doubt. By 9 June, after Dunkirk, she was expressing frustration that no one in the area wanted her help in the evening – she'd 'willingly help a farmer, or at a canteen, or with evacuee children'.

The French surrender was a blow – 'In the afternoon people were feeling that we had better give in.' But, though she knew perfectly well that over-long hours of work were counter-productive, she kept wanting to do more.

Air-raid warnings began in mid-June – 'yellow every night for a fortnight' – so she was asked to sleep at the works once a week. By early August, when a threat of strike by the workforce unless they got a Bank Holiday as usual prompted the sudden announcement of a day off, she could sound like a confirmed, even Blimpish patriot: 'One hears a lot about the keenness of the British worker to increase war production. None of that spirit is shown among our men.'

Her diary during this phase, however, suggests the very lively response which raids and the constant threat of raids provoked in her. On 17 August:

We had to take Vi to Cardiff. We were caught in a raid half-way there, but they let us go on with only our headlights. I felt rather as though I was living in a film. There was a full moon, which gave the cold light one gets in night drives on the screen. We were stopped six times to show identification cards, and once or twice we saw bursts of anti-aircraft fire.

On 29 August, 'there was quite a pretty fireworks display over Newport'. On 13 September: 'Miss Jones burst into my room this morning saying "We've brought a plane down! Isn't it thrilling?" A plane was caught by the Newport balloon barrage last night and crashed in flames. Unfortunately, it crashed into the only house I have visited in Newport, killing the two children who were sleeping downstairs.'

What with brief meetings with her fiancé and worries about her parents in south-east England, she was surely living at a high emotional pitch. All the more striking, then, that in her replies to Mass-Observation's September 'Directive' questionnaire, presumably written at the end of the month, she stressed how 'normal' everything had become again. She now slept 'very happily' through the warnings and didn't worry about bombs, though her lodgings were in a bungalow with no shelter. Her replies next month were aloof and disapproving about the apathy she detected in her corner of Wales – typists 'as far as is possible . . . unconscious of the war', workmen unabashed when their defective valves caused aircraft parts to be scrapped, young men thinking of conscription only as an inevitability like going to school. Unusually for the time, her politics were moving right-ward – to admiration of Churchill as *war* leader and moderate support for Labour's *post-war* policies. The rest of her war was anticlimactic – marriage to Dr Jack, some months as a happy housewife, then years of boredom in office jobs during which her husband was posted to India. Inevitable, one muses, that some people in her kind of situation would come to look back on the summer of 1940 as a heyday of glorious life. But the main reason for introducing her case here is that it illustrates how a potentially 'unreliable' component of public opinion – Marxist, left-wing, inclined to pacifist impulses – emerged after a prolonged though light exposure to Battle of Britain and Blitz conditions, as a rather conventional patriot deploring the lack of war spirit in others.

Perhaps her censure of Monmouth people was excessive and more shared her alertness than she conceded. But another 'Directive' reply, to the September questions, from an auto-didactic steel worker in Ayrshire, suggests that outside London and the south-east indifference to the war was possible. This man saw 'no change' in the mental attitude of his fellow workers. He himself read 'as usual' but cared less for the radio than before, 'not because of the propaganda but because of the bad reception, a general complaint here'. He lived in a top flat, had no shelter, had never tested his gas mask and never carried it. 'We wouldn't know that there was a war on if we were not told, except for hearing the siren 13 times, so uneventful is even the siren that I didn't get out of bed the last four times.'

The MoI would have worried about his attitude. Yet surely the areas of relative calm where people carried on as usual were an important factor in balancing public opinion? It is likely that most Ayrshire workers would have rallied to defend the land of Kyle celebrated by Robert Burns had they seen any need to do so; but, according to Mass-Observation's respondent, there was nothing to get excited about.

However, when our next Observer, Bill Lee, a teacher in his late twenties, was returning from Cumbria to his home in suburban Middlesex on 15 August 1940, he was 'momentarily' thrilled on that clear warm evening to hear the siren sound All Clear, 'as the war seemed such a remote thing in the Lake District, and the blackout was slackly observed in Keswick'. Travelling in and out of central London over the next few days, he was in a good position to see freshly how citizens were adapting to raids. Very many calmly ignored government advice to take shelter, as he did himself on 16 August when, after a warning had sounded, he phlegmatically finished his anchovy toast in the ABC teashop in Charing Cross Road, walked across to a News Theatre and got so engrossed in the screen that he soon forgot there was a raid on.

Warnings and 'light' raids were now a commonplace in the straggling suburban lanes of Middlesex. Lee's elderly parents, by 22 August, had decided not to bother to go to the shelter next door after the siren unless guns were fired or bombs dropped.

A week later, Lee was at a Promenade Concert in the Queen's Hall, listening to Brahms's First Symphony, when at about nine p.m. a man in evening dress hurried through the orchestra and Sir Henry Wood stopped conducting. 'Immediately there came from the audience a sound like mingled laughs and groans, with a few claps. The man announced that the siren had gone and asked anyone who wished to leave to do so at once. Here came loud applause.' Apparently, no one left. The concert resumed after a couple of minutes. In the interval quite a number of promenaders (though fewer than usual) went out to sit on the steps of the church next to Broadcasting House. There were not many people in the streets, but taxis swooped about. The second half of the concert passed without incident. When it finished at ten twenty-five, Lee found that Piccadilly tube station was closed, as always in raids, but pushed on 'through crowds' to Leicester Square, brushing off a prostitute on the way.

The tube out to Hillingdon took twenty minutes longer than usual. Walking home alone, well after midnight, Lee became aware of searchlights probing for a raider overhead. Then came a sound such as he had never heard before; followed by another of the same. He flung himself to the ground. The bombs were half a mile away but sounded much closer, 'great explosions with no end of depth and body, much louder than [he] had expected bombs to be'. Getting up and finding no cover in sight, he sprinted to the bottom of the hill. Only thirty yards from home a voice called, 'Is someone there looking for shelter?' He was so terrified that he plunged into the garden of a house occupied by Women's Auxiliary Transport service personnel and thence into their shelter – a V of trenches covered with zinc sheets, sandbags and earth. There were six or eight young women there in the pitch dark, with six inches of mud underfoot.

They were in high excitement, having scrambled out of bed in night clothes and dressing gowns when bombs had made their house rock – 'all scared . . . but keeping it down pretty well'.

A young man with certain opportunities in mind might have lingered, but after a few minutes, with the sound of 'the plane' much less, Lee moved on to the shelter which his parents used, found the dense atmosphere unpleasant, went to his own house, put a kettle on . . . Then 'the plane' came back, so he turned off the gas and went and hid under a downstairs bed with cotton wool in his ears and rubber between his teeth. It is striking that Lee was convinced that there was just one German bomber up there, unchallenged by anti-aircraft or night fighters, wheeling around picking off one target in the area after another. Such paranoia or solipsism was a factor in the process by which people under bombing were driven away from the larger issues of the war to concentration on their own local patch. Presumably the raiders (probably plural) were looking for one of the RAF stations in the area.

'The plane' came back twice while Lee was making cocoa for himself and tea for others. On the second occasion he thought 'Bugger that, I'm not going to let this cool' and took the tea through the hedge to the shelter next door. Very tired, he' nevertheless couldn't sleep. He went out several times to chat to the air-raid wardens, one of whom remarked 'After another night or two of this we should be all done up', and finally went to bed at three-thirty a.m., half an hour before the All Clear. In the morning a tradesman told him that three bombs had fallen on houses in Hillingdon, just over half a mile away, and one lad of eighteen had been killed.

Next evening, at home, Lee simply typed on (a report for Mass-Observation) after the sirens sounded, despite heavy noises. However, his sleep was disturbed by the sound of 'Nazi' planes and distant thuds. Coming back by tube on Saturday 31st, Lee found that no one took much notice when the siren wailed: 'No stir, little talk. It's a hot day. Near Rayners Lane Station tennis and cricket are going on as usual. (A bomb fell here a few nights ago.)' That night, Lee learned a little more about aircraft. Thinking he heard a 'Nazi' plane about nine p.m., he went out and saw an aircraft 'with lights on coming down calmly into Northolt aerodrome'. So the 'broken throb' of a plane's engines was not, as he had thought, 'characteristically Nazi'.

Lee's pattern of reactions – indifference, sudden fear, curiosity, calm adaptation – was probably that of many young or youngish people under 'light' raiding. Reports by other paid and unpaid Mass-Observers in the same file, made after the bombers had invaded

Greater London seriously, in mid-August, bring out the almost holiday-like atmosphere: neighbours in Battersea out in the streets on 15 August after the All Clear sounded, laughing as they chattered to each other; people in Whitehall on the same day ignoring wardens' encouragement to take shelter; an hour frittered away next morning in a government office as workers swapped memories of what they did while the sirens sounded.

It was Croydon aerodrome which had been the centre of attack on the 15th. Walking in Putney with her boyfriend that evening, an Observer saw the sky to the south-east 'full of heavy black smoke clouds'. From Putney Bridge, looking along the river, 'There was a dull orange glow in the sky, on the horizon, which spurted into great brightness every few minutes.' But in Streatham nearby, when the siren went that evening, commuters simply walked home from the station at the same pace as usual. At Ealing Broadway, when the All Clear sounded, some 200 people were seen pouring out of public shelters and 'everyone looked calm and cheerful' though obviously annoyed at interrupted journeys home. A middle-class man laughed and said: 'Look at terrified Britain.' Upper-class folk in Kensington told an old Etonian observer how they had reacted to the sirens. One young woman had felt compelled 'to hand out brandies to everyone in the flat'; another had filled her handbag, at once, with cigarettes; a man's reflex had been to take the whisky bottle off the table and put it on the floor.

On the 16th, young Len England went to report for Mass-Observation on the damage in Croydon. There were several bomb craters near the aerodrome, houses and factories had been damaged, shrapnel had broken roofs over a wide radius and white chalk dust covered the area. But apparently the big fire (seen in Putney) had been in Wandsworth and had involved tyres. The general impression given by people in Croydon was that it had been quite a show, and they'd have been sorry to have missed it. Outside a house in Purley Way which had been severely damaged, an Air Raid Precautions man was clearing up wreckage with a broom. The woman who owned it called out in a mock-serious tone, 'Don't you mess about with my flowers, I'm keeping them extra special to give Hitler a bouquet when he comes over.' Journalists would not have to *invent* examples of post-raid humour.

It is interesting to think how differently one might read these and many similar reports, had the Germans later used gas. As the Myth developed, the gas mask became an irrelevance: it is hard to remember that responsible citizens were supposed to carry them, and one's eye tends to glide over references to people actually doing this.

A sudden gas attack in September? Millions caught without their masks? The phlegm and insouciance of the British people would then seem still more tragic than that of the inhabitants of Dresden who had come to believe by 1945 that their city would never be heavily bombed.

7

Formulations of Feeling

Since Munich, what? A tangle of black film
Squirming like bait upon the floor of my mind
And scissors clicking daily, I am inclined
To pick these pictures now but will hold back.
Till memory has elicited from this blind
Drama its threads of vision, the intrusions
Of value upon fact, that sudden unconfined
Wind of understanding that blew out
From people's hands and faces, undesigned
Evidence of design, that change of climate
Which did not last but happens often enough
To give us hope that fact is a façade
And that there is an organism behind
Its brittle littleness, a rhythm and a meaning
Something half-conjectured and half-divined
Something to give way to and so find.

Louis MacNeice, 'The News-Reel'

O NE COULD now proceed deeper into the 'core' of Blitz
experience – into huge and squalid East End shelters, into
mortuaries where attempts were made to identify the dead from
fragments of their corpses, into great fires, destruction of beloved
buildings, into the maimed lives of victims such as (to pick one at
random) the woman in a 'comfy' shelter in Clydebank in March
1941, who remembers playing cards with friends as suddenly a bomb
not even heard blasted her brother through the door, tore her friends
to pieces, smashed a concrete roof down on her mother's chest,
crushed her father, and left her buried under her dead friends for
eight and a half hours. 'I was paralysed from the waist down . . . my
mother was killed . . . my friends were killed. . . my father and
brother survived.'[1]

But many hands, including my own, have illustrated that 'core' of horror and not infrequent heroism. Without a sense that at certain places, on certain nights, carnage and wreckage were like that of a town besieged and breached, though almost all the protagonists and victims on the ground were civilians, we might have a Myth of 1940, but no Myth of the Blitz. That civilian 'morale' survived exposure to conditions often as frightful as those of battle is what guarantees, mythically, that the British people, as a whole, deserved to save Europe and defeat Hitler. Because they held out and Hitler was eventually defeated, one cannot counterfactually select from contemporary reports by careful observers, not for publication, like the Mass-Observation material just discussed, all the remarks and glimpses of behaviour that suggest poor or volatile morale and dismiss the rest as wishful thinking.

The jokes of the (mostly) Cheerful Cockneys were incessantly quoted. Photographs established in various ways the normality of 'good morale'. Photography, of course, is never free of ambiguity. In his memoirs, the great Bert Hardy of *Picture Post* cheerfully admits to having fabricated stories and pictures for sale to newspapers and magazines before the war. But it seems that, even if he had needed to, he would have been ashamed to fake Blitz pictures when he went into the East End: 'After having taken so many "laid-on" pictures, I almost hesitated to photograph scenes like the girl in the clothing workshop still at work on her sewing machine, in case it didn't look "real" enough.'[2]

This *Picture Post* item (see Plate 14), however, could be decoded to yield other meanings than Hardy's own preferred propagandist message, that it illustrated the 'tremendous' spirit of the people. Photographers between the wars – including some, like Bill Brandt, often thought of as 'documentary' – had been greatly influenced by surrealist practices. The oddity of Hardy's picture is that the remaining glass in the workshop window might be seen as the angelically shimmering cape of the Air Raid Precautions man outside, whose upper body it covers with apparent exactitude. And this distracts attention from another detail which might strike someone looking for literal rather than surrealist significance: it is true that one woman is working at her machine, but there is no one at the machine next to the glass, nor (we finally notice) at a third machine in the foreground. Why shouldn't the caption read: 'East End Workshops can now produce only one third of their previous output, due to raids'?

When a young Mass-Observer, Jack Atkins, who had left London before the Blitz started, returned towards the end of October, he found Londoners' morale higher than that in Birmingham, which he had visited: 'Considering what they have been through they appeared to be remarkably cheerful and friendly. It was much easier to talk to strangers than it had been formerly, and the worse the conditions the more laughter there seemed to be.' He complained, however, that, 'All new experiences today seem to be spoiled by *Picture Post.*' He hadn't been in the tubes since their appropriation as deep shelters, but 'they were exactly like what he had imagined and seen pictures of'.

Further refinement would occur, with Henry Moore's celebrated drawings of the tube shelterers. Odoriferous slum dwellers, frightened small businessmen, these cannot be: they are an image of Humanity itself, in heroic repose.

The mature Lucien Freud might have produced something 'human' yet sadly credible out of these sleepers. Not until Bacon's 'Three Studies for Figures at the Base of a Crucifixion' were exhibited in London just before the end of the war would even well-informed lookers at art-works see proof that at least one British artist had held in his vision its horrors: what it does to human bodies, minds and emotions. Bacon's half-human, half-animal figures cramped into a strangely shaped, low-ceilinged space, more extremely claustrophobic than even the 'Morrison' shelters latterly used in Britain, suggest mutilation, anguish, hatred and gluttony.

An historian cannot damage the Myth without appearing petulantly wilful, because the Myth soaked deeply into the very first-hand evidence which he must come to at last if he wishes to destroy it. The artist or the writer, who can (most can't) step outside conventional discourses and paradigms, is in a position to defy the Myth's status as an adequate and convincing account of human feeling and behaviour. Very few writers during the war, or in nearly half a century since, have come close to the radicalism of Bacon, or even matched the side-step of Louis MacNeice.

MacNeice's poem, 'The News-Reel', written in mid-war, expresses with both eloquence and caution the challenge and hope involved for citizens as they tried mentally to order their war experiences. The process by which some images are put together as newsreel, others lost on the cutting-room floor, is a metaphor for the working of memory which reminds us that memory is, in plain fact, profoundly affected by cinematic images created and selected by film-makers. MacNeice is 'inclined' to hold back from finalising his personal 'newsreel' until the 'organism' behind the facts appears. Its presence (a quasi-divine one – but MacNeice was neither believer nor idealist) is suggested by that 'sudden unconfined/Wind of understanding' which briefly gave hope that 'fact' was a façade. There *should*, the poem implies, be some significance in that sense of uplift which transfigured crisis for many in 1940–41. But we must wait for it to emerge.

MacNeice, himself a British propagandist during the war, clearly wasn't convinced that the rapid and largely spontaneous creation of Myth had done the job for good and all. A sceptical, albeit anti-fascist, Ulsterman, he wrote some memorable Blitz poems which stand up better than any others on the subject precisely because they work outside the Myth's paradigm. In 'Brother Fire', written late in 1942 when allied victory had come to seem inevitable and repression of naughty ideas was perhaps less exigent, the blaze of London is ironically acclaimed. In a way we willed it, as children want bonfires:

> Did we not in those mornings after the All Clear,
> When you were looting shops in elemental joy
> And singing as you swarmed up city block and spire,
> Echo your thoughts in ours? 'Destroy! Destroy!'

Just before Hiroshima, MacNeice wrote 'The Streets of Laredo', a still more sardonic poem, playing off the American ballad, in which 'Laredo' is the London of Wren, Bunyan and Blake, now burning. Familiar elements of Myth – the fireman, the Cockney, the architectural past, and the literary heritage – are virtually burlesqued. Finally, 'The voice of the Angel, the voice of the fire' tells the narrator:

> O late, very late, have I come to Laredo
> A whimsical bride in my new scarlet dress
> But at last I took pity on those who were waiting
> To see my regalia and feel my caress.
>
> Now ring the bells gaily and play the hose daily,
> Put splints on your legs, put a gag on your breath;
> O you streets of Laredo, you streets of Laredo,
> Lay down the red carpet – My dowry is death.[3]

These macabre poems are grounded in MacNeice's secularised Calvinism. Consciousness gives us knowledge that time and the universe are vast, and individual fates within them arbitrary: one thing is certain, which is that we all die, and no way of dying, no threat to life, is perhaps more significant than any other. MacNeice's 'good nature' and romantic sentimentalism strive (as in 'The News-

Reel') to get beyond despair; but when, as in 'Brother Fire' and 'The Streets of Laredo', he lets the skull beneath the skin emerge clearly, the results are strangely refreshing and bracing.

They may be contrasted not only with his friend Dylan Thomas's bombastic consolation in the famous 'Refusal to Mourn the Death, by Fire, of a Child in London' ('After the first death, there is no other'), a poem which does not refer to bombs but in 1945 would certainly have seemed to, but also with T. S. Eliot's subtle digestion of the Myth into 'Little Gidding', the last of the *Four Quartets*, which came to represent Old Possum's major war work.

I have written elsewhere[4] about the *Quartets* as public poems with a propagandist function, and will mostly content myself with summary here. Eliot, a British citizen since 1927, but born in Missouri as a member of a distinguished New England family, had achieved a dominance in 'English letters' and a prestige in Church of England circles which interacted with his inherited sense of public duty as he found that the structure of 'Burnt Norton' (1935) could be replicated in three further *Quartets*. The repeated themes of the 'Quartets' are 'universal', 'religious', 'timeless' – including Time itself, Art and the search for spiritual health. As many critics have shown, they can be read coherently without any reference to the Second World War at all. 'Burnt Norton' has no topical or 'political' resonance whatever. But the imagery of 'East Coker' (published Easter 1940), 'The Dry Salvages' (February 1941) and 'Little Gidding' (October 1942) belongs in great part very much to 1939–41.

'East Coker' opens, usefully for the Myth, by evoking a 'timeless moment' in a Deep English village where medieval or Tudor peasants are imagined dancing in communal harmony. Its last section, in which Eliot speaks of the struggle to write good verses, was written during the Phoney War, but expressed an attitude which must have struck readers in mid-1940 as highly appropriate to their situation (my italics):

. . . And so each venture
Is a new beginning, a *raid* on the inarticulate
With *shabby equipment* always deteriorating
In the general mess of imprecision of feeling,
Undisciplined squads of emotion . . .
There is only the *fight* to recover what has been lost
And found and lost again and again; and now, under conditions
That seem unpropitious. But perhaps neither gain nor loss.
For us there is only the trying. The rest is not our business.

The poet's attempt, with inadequate personal means, to re-create the splendour found in poetic tradition, is oddly similar to that of Home Guards drilling with broomsticks, 'trying' against all odds, submitting to military discipline and leaving 'the rest' to Mr Churchill.

Clearly, Eliot could not have intended this effect – his military imagery relates at most to the experience of a conscript army. But it is impossible to believe that the choice of subject and treatment of 'The Dry Salvages' were in no way influenced by Britain's predicament in 1940. The Battle of the Atlantic – convoys of US supplies defended against U Boats – was of paramount significance. Eliot, though ex-American, had high prestige in literary circles in his native land, as he was fully aware. It in no way derogates from his integrity to suggest that his sudden decision to revert for material to the Mississippi of his earliest childhood and the New England waters of his happiest sailing days was at least partly triggered by a 'propagandist' imperative. He wrote 'The Dry Salvages' extremely fast. Its first readers would surely have read its fourth section as a most moving prayer for British seamen at risk, for the women who had seen sons and husbands 'setting forth and not returning' and for the souls of dead mariners.

Over 300 British merchant ships were lost to U Boats or air attack in three months down to May 1941. Nor would Eliot's invocation, in Section III, of Krishna's advice to Arjuna on the battlefield – the incarnated god says it is Arjuna's duty to fight, even against his own kin, and the fruits of his action are not his business – have failed to intersect with the thoughts of conscientious Christians worried about the ethics of RAF bombing of Germany.

It is in 'Little Gidding' that Eliot produces a representative working of the Myth to stand beside Churchill's speeches, the broadcasts of Priestley and Ed Murrow, and famous productions of the Crown Film Unit. The place of the poem's title, in Northamptonshire, was the site of an Anglican community which briefly gave refuge to Charles I as he fled to surrender to the Scots and was soon after sacked by Parliamentary troops. What the voice of the poem's first section is overtly saying is that the place represents 'the world's end'. But so do many others – 'the sea jaws' (in which Royal Navy and merchant sailors are drowning), the 'desert' of North Africa (in which Britons are fighting Rommel) or a bombed 'city':

> But this is the nearest, in place and time,
> Now and in England . . .
> Here, the intersection of the timeless moment
> Is England and nowhere. Never and always.

1 Laura Knight (1877–1970) produced strong images of women at war. Daphne Pearson (left), a clerk at WAAF headquarters, received the George Cross for saving the life of a pilot, at great risk to her own, in May 1940.

2 Dorothy Coke, an Official War Artist, shows Women's Auxiliary Transport members in a gas-mask drill exercise.

C'est l'Anglais qui nous a fait ça!

3 'War's Greatest Picture'
was the *Daily Mail*'s caption
when it published Herbert
Mason's classic image of
St Paul's Cathedral (above)
riding the 'Fire of London' on
29th December 1940.

4 A German poster for
France by Theo Matejko (left)
blames the English for the
destruction.

5 Compare the St Paul's
image with the drawing (right)
of a scene by the city wall of
Boulogne, 1940, by German
artist Josef Arens.

23. Destroyed portion of redeployed French units
City Hall of Boulogne

6–7   Air Marshal Barratt on the wing of a Hurricane epitomises Fighter Command derring-do. In fact RAF fliers were entirely dependent on the women in the Operations ('Ops') Rooms.

8–9 In Moscow's Mayakovsky Metro Station (left) shelterers enjoyed more spacious and gracious premises than Bill Brandt's Londoners (below) on the underground platform at Elephant & Castle.

10–11 The Ministry of Information commissioned the German-born photo-journalist Bill Brandt to depict shelterers in November 1940; a set went to President Roosevelt. Some images are very famous; these are not, for they don't fall into 'The Myth of the Blitz'. The couple (right) under a quilt in the basement of a West End shop might come from some wacky Hollywood comedy. (Below) People sleep in the bowels of a Bloomsbury book business.

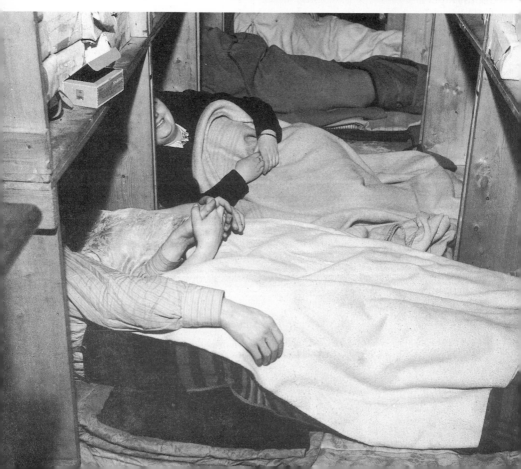

12–13 Brandt shows a Sikh family (above left) sheltering in an alcove at Christ Church, Spitalfields. Bert Hardy rivalled Brandt, a warmer photographer. *Picture Post* used his images to show that 'London Could Take It' – (right) a man works on his income tax return in the ruins of his East End home.

14 Hardy's image below, 'surrealistically', might have been called 'Angelic Transfiguration of a Warden in E1'.

15–20   P.C.s Arthur Cross
and Fred Tibbs systematically
photographed air-raid scenes
for the City of London police.
Tibbs just happened to be passing when the Salvation Army

headquarters fell down on 11th May 1941. Leonard Rosoman's nightmarish painting, *A House Collapsing on Two Firemen*, recalled an experience he had himself survived. Jacko, the martyred fireman in *Fires Were Started*, was hardly braver than Bert Hardy, who climbed to photograph 'The Man on the Ladder' for *Picture Post*. On the morning after, firehoses still lay in Newgate Street while folk were carrying on as usual in Fetter Lane. Was the amusing placard 'faked' by the photographer or his editor?

21 Quentin Reynolds (left) in sentimental mood.

23–24 (Right) Teamwork, again, is asserted in the documentary film *Fires Were Started*, directed by Humphrey Jennings, seen below with the pianist Myra Hess.

22 (Below) At a rare moment, three key figures in British propaganda are seen together, J.B. Priestley (left), Leslie Howard (centre) and Mary Adams (right) 'share a joke' with Canadian broadcaster L.W. Brockington (foreground).

25   'Deep England' – Frank Newbould's poster was intended to stiffen the resolve of servicemen.

26   Filming Humphrey Jennings's *A Diary for Timothy* (1945).

Inside the image, on the magazine cover:

LIFE

AIR-RAID VICTIM

SEPTEMBER 23, 1940   10 CENTS
YEARLY SUBSCRIPTION $4.50

On the building: BOVRIL

27–27a   Ed Murrow, who towers over two friends in Trafalgar Square,
reinforced the potent effect of Cecil Beaton's photograph for the cover of
Life (23rd September 1940).

28–29 Painters and film–makers stressed 'team work'. Stanley Spencer (1891–1959) depicted shipbuilders on the Clyde (top) and Noël Coward's film *In Which We Serve* (1942) showed naval ratings and their officers as staunch comrades under duress.

30 (Right) Bombs transfigured suburban England in William Wyler's Hollywood film *Mrs Miniver*. A clergyman memorialises raid victims as martyrs of the 'People's War'.

31 John Gregson and Jack Hawkins in George More O'Ferrall's *Angels One Five* (1952).

32–33 In Frank Capra's U.S. documentary *Battle of Britain*, some shots came from feature films, like the Fighter Command 'Scramble' from Hollywood's *A Yank in the RAF*. But Capra's image (below) of Churchill smiling among his people is 'true' newsreel.

The sound doctrinal point that one might as well pray anywhere is completely overidden by the patriotic surge of 'England . . . always'.

Section II is probably the most powerful, and certainly the most complex, work of poetry related to direct experience of the London Blitz of 1940–41. Eliot served as an air-raid warden early in the Blitz, and as a fire-watcher on the roof of Faber & Faber, the publishing firm of which he was a director. The poem is easily available, in many editions and anthologies, and there is no need here to show, detail by detail, how closely this section refers to phenomena typical of Blitz – from the 'Dust in the air suspended' of its opening lyric to the 'blowing of the horn' at the end which suggests the siren sounding the All Clear. Yet all is so deftly handled that I know a sensitive reader (and distinguished historian) who was astonished when I demonstrated in a seminar that the 'patrol' of the speaker who meets a 'familiar compound ghost' in a Dantesque setting replicates that of a warden pacing the London streets after the Luftwaffe had raided and caused fires in 'three districts'.

The ghost's 'compound' includes Hamlet's father; Dante's old master Ser Brunetto; Mallarmé; Swift; Milton and W. B. Yeats, who had died in 1939. The language given to him, echoing or alluding to these figures, represents in itself with memorable authority the power of tradition in poetry as Eliot conceived it. For him the tradition is not 'English' only but 'European'. Bombed London is the site on which European tradition is reaffirmed. But in the rest of 'Little Gidding', the timelessness of *England* and the 'peculiar genius' of *English* people are strongly affirmed.

History, in effect, is over: 'now and England'. The quarrels of the seventeenth-century civil war (and, by extension, all struggle and faction in the English past) don't matter any more. Charles I and the regicides who cut his head off 'Accept the constitution of silence/ And are folded in a single party'. They were, we are told in Section III, 'United in the strife which divided them'. History is a 'pattern of timeless moments', one of which is 'now and England'. The fire of the Blitz is like the fire of Purgatory. And eventually (Section V):

> . . . All shall be well and
> All manner of thing shall be well
> When the tongues of flame are in-folded
> Into the crowned knot of fire
> And the fire and the rose are one.[5]

I can understand why people who take Eliot very seriously as a religious poet find a reading of the last three *Quartets* as 'propaganda' deeply offensive. They are about 'eternal matters'. There is no way that their last five lines, just quoted, can be read as a descriptive statement about secular society in 1942. They speak of Christian hope for a timeless and paradisal state. There is ample evidence that the *Quartets*' many wartime readers loved the poems because they meditated about matters other than war, 'above' the daily news bulletins. So how can I argue that 'Little Gidding' provides one of the definitive versions of 'the Myth of the Blitz'?

I can do so because the poem, without literally stating them, appears to *endorse* central elements in the Myth extremely strongly.

'History is now and England' chimes with Churchill's 'this was their finest hour'. The folding 'into one party' of past factions suggests Churchill's mighty, triumphant coalition. Bombardment – or at least the fire which it generates – is equated with purification: Blitz makes people *better*. And because, with their 'peculiar genius', the English people have turned out to be especially good, 'all shall be well'. There is no doubt that when Eliot refuses in Section III to 'summon the spectre of a Rose', he is referring to the factional Wars of the Roses. But the Rose is a favourite symbol of England. In the Myth 'fire' and 'Rose' come together in so far as the latter represents the flowering of English unity amid the flames which never destroyed the dome of St Paul's. In the pattern of its symbolism, in the equation of 'History' and 'England', 'Little Gidding' supports the Myth all the more powerfully because so few of its readers (or so it seems) have ever thought of relating it to the war at all.

Compared to Eliot's achievement, attempts by lesser poets to stamp their art on the Myth while it was being created seem as conceitedly trivial as the activities of the fly in La Fontaine's fable, which, darting around the horses, imagines that it pulls the huge coach up-hill. Embarrassment is now triggered even by a poem, 'To the Seamen', written by the competent, much-loved and certainly sincere Poet Laureate, John Masefield:

> Through the long time the story will be told;
> Long centuries of praise on English lips,
> Of courage godlike and of hearts of gold
> Off Dunquerque beaches in the little ships.[6]

Herbert Asquith's Battle of Britain poem 'Youth in the Skies', already quoted, takes the Churchillian rhetoric about chivalrous fighter pilots to a vapid extreme of euphemism:

> Old men may wage a war of words,
> Another race are these,
> Who flash to glory dawn and night
> 'Above the starry seas.

These verses, which appeared in *The Times* in August 1940, were dutifully collected by Thomas Moult, to whom fell the tricky task of editing *The Best Poems of 1941*, the latest volume of a twenty-year-old series which, by including English-speaking authors from both sides of the Atlantic, had 'kept bright' the links between Britain and the USA. 'Thus the present endeavour by the leaders of thought to establish a closer political and economic union of the two great Western commonwealths had for a prelude the already united poets' contribution', Moult wrote in the introduction.

This was hardly apparent from Dorothy Sayers's 'The English War', reprinted by Moult from the *Times Literary Supplement* and rejoicing in a moment:

> When no allies are left, no help
> To count upon from alien hands,
> No waverers remain to woo,
> No more advice to listen to,
> And only England stands . . .
> And all the tall adventurers come
> Homeward to England, and Drake's drum
> Is beaten through the Straits.

But Sayers's infatuation with the Sea Dogs was fully matched by one of Moult's chosen American poets. Robert Nathan's 'Dunkirk' originally published by *Harper's Monthly* in March 1941, is a short narrative, lavishly echoing Newbolt, Alfred Noyes and Masefield, about a boy who comes home from school and, with his fourteen-year-old sister, sails a tiny ship across to Dunkirk where they pick up fourteen men. They bring them home through an 'English mist' which baffles the Stuka dive bombers over the Channel:

> For Nelson was there on the *Victory* . . .
> And guns were out on *The Golden Hind* . . .
> The old dead Captains fought their ships.
> And the great dead Admirals led the line.
> It was England's night, it was England's sea.

Moult also trawled in much less clichéd and sensitive responses to the mythical events of 1940 (he collected poems published between July in that year and June 1941). But their very thoughtfulness and modesty expose why the Myth-making capacity of poets in this war (contrasting with the Great War) would be extremely limited. They suggest, on the one hand, the partial, specialised character of each individual's experience in this varied and complex struggle, on the other, the reluctance of decent persons to indulge in patriotic, bombastic and all too falsifiable prophecies of Triumph, Peace and Universal Justice. This kind of thing could be left to Churchill, who did it with the appearance of complete conviction.

Edward Thompson's 'England, 1941' from *The Listener* disturbingly inverts an element of the Myth. The beloved landscape 'turns traitor'. Familiar symbols of 'Deep England' stretching back to prehistory – the white horses cut in chalk, 'the Ancient Man' – are now signalling to the enemy:

> And this brook, whose waters flow
> To push the wheel and rock the mill-pond's freight
> Of sleepy lilies, beckons in the foe
> To wreck the hamlet it beguiled to rise!

Yet this rather subtle poem remains within the paradigms of the Myth. Like all the Myth's products, its reading will depend on the large fact: either defeat, in which case the verses are prophetic but slight; or victory, which makes it into intelligent whimsy.[7]

One young poet, Roy Fuller, virtually avant-garde, attempted in several wartime poems overviews as magisterial as those of his own master, Auden's 'Spain' and 'September 1, 1939'. An accountant of Marxist proclivities, Fuller was not called up until April 1941. He found that joining the navy on the lower decks (though he finally became a mechanic in the Fleet Air Arm) 'extricated me from the great problem of the thirties – how to live and write for a class to which one didn't belong'.[8] In 'Autumn 1940', before this experience, he produced an impressive but rather bombastic version of the Myth in its left-wing aspect. The 'real', the poem announces, has at last reached England from 'Spain and China', as 'rubble and fear, as metal and glass'. The Blitz, for this young Marxist, brings 'relief'; the shells and the bombs are objectivities outside the 'deathly self' of the bourgeois:

> Death is solitary . . .
> But where the many are there is no death,

> Only a temporary expedient of sorrow
> And destruction; today the caught-up breath –
> The exhalation is promised for tomorrow.

The very violence of the moment guarantees 'changed tomorrow'.

Fuller's 'Soliloquy in an Air Raid' is a more thoughtful and troublesome poem. The predicament of the soliloquising poet is its main topic:

> Inside the poets the words are changed to desire
> And formulations of feeling are lost in action
> Which hourly transmutes the basis of common speech.

He sees the Blitz as a challenge to the current resources of 'common speech' and to the English verse tradition, now 'sunk in the throat' between the opposing voices of the old (capitalism) and the new (socialism). His Marxist perspective aligns him with what Paul Fussell and John Keegan would later show us about the failures of language in 1914–18, and sets him counter to Eliot's Christian confidence in the endurance of tradition, as where he asks the questions, already quoted:

> Who can observe this save as a frightened child
> Or careful diarist? And who can speak
> And still retain the tones of civilisation?[9]

The reluctance of the better young poets, Fuller excepted, to tackle overviews and large themes is a point on which all who have read through wartime magazines and anthologies seem to be agreed. Robin Skelton in his thorough anthology of *Poetry of the Forties* quotes approvingly another anthologist, Ronald Blythe, as remarking: 'The great thing was not to pretend, or proffer solutions or to be histrionic. Each poet spoke as wholly and truthfully as he could from out of the one inviolable spot of an otherwise violated order, his own identity.'[10] Reasons for this are not hard to find. The trench poets of the Great War – Owen, Sassoon, Rosenberg – had exposed the horrors of battle definitively. A younger generation believed with them that war might be necessary, but that pre-1914 heroics in verse about it were contemptible.

Furthermore, this new kind of war – heavily mechanised, often fast-moving, scattering conscripts south into Africa, east into far parts of Asia – had an impersonal character and a vast complexity which defied representative verse statement. The 'careful diarist', as

Fuller had shrewdly anticipated, was the most plausible model for poets, presenting their 'components of the scene' (a phrase from one of them which Blythe used as title for his anthology).

That poetry can have extraordinary myth-making power is demonstrated by the case of Wilfred Owen, whose effigy and imagery still domineer over conceptions (as purveyed by television) of what the Great War 'was like'. So my detour, as it might seem, into discussion of an art form which, except through Eliot, made very little short-term or long-run impact on memory of 1940–41, is actually helping to establish a most important, though negative, point.

8

Fictions

A bad raid last night with heavy civilian casualties, as usual, in the densely populated port areas. I was sent this morning to investigate the reports of panic, and frantic crowds running through the streets crying, 'give us peace' . . . In Santa Lucia . . . I saw a heart-rending scene. A number of tiny children had been dug out of the ruins of a bombed building and lay side by side in the street. Where presentable, their faces were uncovered, and in some cases brand-new dolls had been thrust into their arms to accompany them to the other world. Professional mourners, hired by the locality to reinforce the grief of the stricken families, were running up and down the street, tearing at their clothing and screaming horribly.

Norman Lewis, *Naples '44*

THAT DESCRIPTION of reactions to a Luftwaffe air raid in the Second World War obviously doesn't refer to Britain. Norman Lewis, then a British Intelligence officer in Naples, presents in his diary, with brilliant terseness, a scene in that city in March 1944. Neapolitans have their own way of coping with death. Lewis does not commit the racist solecism of finding their behaviour absurd and barbaric.

His own worst experience of being bombed came some weeks later, when he had been 'dining' on the crude delicacies available in that famished city with a friend and a couple of local women. The British officers were reluctant to use the shelters provided for tenants of the block of flats 'for reasons of face', the women refused to go down without them; bombs began to fall, the ceiling came down, the whole building 'began to heave and sway as if in the tremors of a moderate earthquake'. Their 'hair, skins and clothing were coated with lime-dust. No one spoke, and neither girl showed any sign of fear.' But after the All Clear, when they went down into the street, Lewis found they 'were all chattering loudly in a childish and pointless fashion'.[1]

The behaviour described in this passage is such that no one would

153

notice if it were slipped into some collage or anthology of Blitz experiences from Britain. It is reasonable to assume that some reactions to bombing are not specific to any one cultural background, and may be found in many parts of the world. But recognising this does not prevent retrospective embarrassment over Douglas Wilkie's report in the *Herald*, published in Melbourne, Australia, on 19 January 1942:

> Europeans here have given up talking about 'white' and 'coloured' races – these Europeans are proud to be trying to help Asiatics show the world that Singapore can take it . . . Singapore island's three-quarter million Asiatics can take it. They have taken it with a smile when the Japanese dropped bombs indiscriminately on the outlying native suburbs and villages, killing innocent civilians whom Tokyo threatens nightly to 'liberate', blasting nothing but precious gimcrack furniture and savings of a coolie's lifetime . . . The European ARP workers who braved death alongside Singapore's splendid body of Asiatic wardens, roof-spotters and fire-fighters have learnt things not easily forgotten. European women shielding children in the same shelter with Chinese mothers, who have exchanged smiles of relief as a stick of bombs passed a few hundreds of yards away, have discovered many things which will not vanish when Singapore's ordeal has passed.[2]

Of course, it didn't 'pass': the city soon fell. Nor was Wilkie reporting accurately. During the raids that January, in which 600 Singapore civilians were killed, 1,512 injured, defence was badly organised, and Asian workmen ('coolies'), so far from Taking It, were prone to disappear from their jobs when Japanese broadcasts and leaflets threatened air raids. They had good cause: very little had been done to provide shelter for them. Yet without an idea of what really happened, any fairly experienced Blitz-reader would surely sense untruth in Wilkie's account. It blatantly imposes on a different situation rhetoric originating in the London Blitz, substituting 'European' for 'middle-class' and 'Asiatic' for 'working-class'.

Wilkie's report is 'fictional' in a clearly pernicious way: it distorts experience in order to provide a heartening story. However, it should not be supposed that Lewis's diaries, as edited many years later by the distinguished novelist who wrote them, are, by contrast, providing unmediated truth. One's delight while reading Lewis's *Naples '44* is much like that sparked by a superb work of fiction with a large but still select cast of vividly drawn characters. Experience is shaped artistically: Lewis's book rings as true as a good novel, one which gets behind the clichés of journalism and the stereotypes of bad fiction to expose fleeting and ambiguous emotions, inadmissible reactions, the complexity in human nature which makes ethical distinctions between collaborator and partisan, cautious Appeaser and British Bulldog, inane optimists (in the autumn of 1940) and thoughtful and fearful citizens, ultimately so hard to draw.

A vast quantity of fiction has dealt with Britain's Second World War. Valiant efforts have been made to sort it into classes by Holger Klein.[3] I propose now to take certain post-war novels bearing on 1940, and to see how the ways in which they acknowledge or counter the Myth may illuminate the Myth's structure and the capacity, if any, of fiction writers to disturb it.

Leslie Thomas's *The Dearest and the Best: A Novel of 1940* appeared in 1984. Its author, born in Wales in 1931, must remember the year of Dunkirk and Blitz directly. However, he researched for the novel carefully, and provides a bibliography of eighteen titles. His book centres on the Lovatt family, who live in a Hampshire village by the sea. They are upper middle class. Robert, who fought in the Great War, 'principled and quite often pompous', is a Tory patriot prone to thank God he is 'an Englishman, not British but *English*'. He is chairman of the parish council, in charge of ARP and inevitably, when it is mustered, commands the local Home Guard. His eldest son, James, is an army officer who returns in a grim mood from the Norway campaign and is seconded to work for Churchill himself. The younger, Harry, is in the navy. All three happen to be together, with the village's Home Guard, in a sandbagged emplacement on the jetty, aiming to bring down a low-flying German, when the plane comes up from inland and neatly drops its bomb, killing James and crippling Robert. This is the moving final climax of the book, as Battle of Britain is shading into Blitz.

Thomas provides a great range of vivid episodes, arising from the family's varied experiences. Besides risking, quite successfully, a fictional presentation of Churchill, he commendably brings in the difficult matter of the interned aliens: James involves himself honourably in assisting one of them. The comic potential of the Home Guard is well exploited and the human limitations of the male Lovatts are kept sharply in view. James's affair with a female American newspaper reporter is the least convincing element in the book. She is represented as a loner with ample time to go to concerts and make trips and love with James: in fact, as will be illustrated later, the US press in London characteristically hunted in packs. Overall, though, Thomas's novel is a very honourable attempt to reconstruct, without false heroics or condescending farce, the texture of life on the south coast 'Front Line' in the summer of 1940.

His handling of Dunkirk, however, demonstrates how stoutly the Myth resists demystification by sensitively conceived fiction. As we have seen, that story *always* included generally admitted negatives. After the British Expeditionary Force men came back with their stories, no one writing about the retreat and evacuation could have got away with putting a radiant heroic gloss over all. Only the maritime operation could be represented as a typical triumph of British naval tradition. Organisation was good; but there was something preciously extra – 'The lifting', as John Masefield put it, 'was a wonderful improvisation by the seamen of this people.'[4]

Thomas presents Dunkirk through Harry, sent by the navy into the French port to organise embarkation, and Robert, who sails across in a friend's small paddle steamer to help with the 'lifting'. From the first viewpoint we confront 'a mess'. In the bombed and burning town, a naval officer briefs Harry and others:

> I'm afraid the whole damned thing is terribly difficult and it's not made easier by the fact that the brown jobs are thoroughly fed up with the entire story. There are soldiers all over this town lost, some drunk, some half crazy. It will be your task to round them up . . .

Harry, pushing 'deeper into the stricken streets' begins 'to realise what a widespread and undignified defeat had been inflicted upon the British Army'. He finds a party of Royal Engineers about casually to set fire to half a dozen military vehicles, drunk to the eyeballs, incensed by the desertion of their officers. He has barely rallied them when 'a gang of staggering British soldiers, maddened, drunk, all pride lost, defeated in every way', comes into view, one wearing women's clothes, another a woman's hat, two more wheeling a dead man in a barrow. The transvestite threatens Harry with a pistol . . . But these too accept naval authority, along with the hope of getting out and getting home.

The paddle steamer *Sirius*, with Harry's father in its crew, does useful work before it is crippled by the Luftwaffe at a point when it is carrying a mixed load of Senegalese Africans from the French army and German prisoners of war. While this odd combination produces farcical conflict, there is no doubt that we are to take *Sirius*, as its very name nudges us, seriously. So, while Thomas is very hard indeed on the British army, his narrative emphasises the heroic role of the navy, and pays tribute to the legend of the Little Ships. The Myth, on balance, is reinforced.[5]

It is remarkable that even the gifted Derek Robinson, committed (as his scholarly postscript makes clear) to a wholly 'revisionist' view of the 'Battle of Britain', cannot, in his *Piece of Cake* (1983), escape from the paradigm. In fact, this powerful book demonstrates particularly well how 'debunking' the Myth component by component ensures that you end up with the same pattern. 'There was a lot more to the Battle of Britain than the legend suggests', Robinson writes at the end of the 'Author's note' in which he justifies the way he has told his story. 'By exaggerating the triumph of the RAF, and by deflating the performance of the *Luftwaffe*, the legend has given Fighter Command both too much and too little credit. The truth is fairer to everyone.' Why 'too little credit'? Because, presumably, as Robinson shows in the novel, the balance in the air was still *more* heavily against the RAF than the earliest heroic accounts suggested, its pilots more youthfully accident-prone than tradition allowed, its commanders more confused and divided than was apparent even to outsiders not very long after the event.

Clean, simple yet convincing heroic accounts exist against which Robinson's book can be set. Richard Hillary's *The Last Enemy*, published in 1942, was a best-seller during the war itself. Hillary flew a Spitfire in 1940, was horribly burnt in the cockpit, was given plastic surgery by the remarkable McIndoe, returned to the RAF and died in a training accident, aged only twenty-three. His autobiographical but fictionalised book is remarkably mature. What 'dates' in it is its moralising: the author presents himself as an egotist interested only in self-fulfilment, who is finally convinced that 'no man is an island' and that he must identify with Humanity in general by the experience of seeing a woman die after he has helped to extract her from the ruins of her blitzed home. Her last words, after drinking from his brandy flask, are, 'Thank you, sir. I see they got you too' – his face still shows the ravages of fire. This moment itself is well handled and very moving, but its effect is spoilt by the remaining pages of the book, in which he commits himself to write for his dead RAF comrades a book addressed to Humanity, 'for Humanity must be the public of any book':

> If I could do this thing, could tell a little of the lives of these men, I would have justified, at least in some measure, my right to fellowship with my dead, and to the friendship of those with courage and steadfastness who were still living and who would go

on fighting until the ideals for which their comrades had died were stamped forever on the future of civilisation.[6]

Had he been spared, this very gifted writer would surely have learnt to avoid such rhetorical excess. As it is, he told a compelling story very well, using understatement and silence as key devices. (Silence, for instance, when he mixes in London West End society and becomes close to the fiancée of a dead RAF friend while his face and hands are still subject to McIndoe's further ministrations: it is up to us to remember that this poised socialite and eloquent talker must create countless shocks on his public appearances.)

A merit of the pages describing Hillary's days at Oxford, his RAF training and his active service in the Battle of Britain up to his incineration is that they dress powerful simplifications with superficial sophistication and complexity. Understatement is cleverly used to characterise the narrator, Hillary, as a man who is deeper than he cares to let on. This 'idle' Oxford undergraduate, besides coming close to a rowing blue, and flying in the University Air Squadron, is also an effective student journalist, widely travelled, with a grasp of French and German. At his college, Trinity – 'a typical incubator of the English ruling classes before the war' – kindred souls are held together by 'a common taste in friends, sport, literature, and idle amusement, by a deep-rooted distrust of all organised emotion and standardised patriotism . . . '[7] The dead friends he will evoke at the end being mostly Varsity men, his book will serve subtly to vindicate the English ruling class and its Oxbridge 'incubators', of which he initially appears dismissive. Meanwhile, the left-wing intellectuals among the student body, accused of 'adolescent petulance' in Hillary's early pages, will finally be discredited by the agonising dilemma of one of them, David Rutter, a pacifist who, when Hillary sees him after his burning, is irreconcilably torn between his principles and his impulse to join in the struggle.

The point of the struggle is neatly made clear by Hillary's account of an experience in Germany in 1938. He joins an *ad hoc* crew of Oxford oarsmen which extracts from the German government permission to row in a regatta at Bad Ems for 'General Goering's Prize Fours'. They arrive with no boat – a friendly German, the *only* friendly German, finds them one in the nick of time. They face five 'elegantly turned-out German crews' with 'set, determined faces':

Looking back this race was really a surprisingly accurate pointer to the course of the war. We were quite untrained, lacked any form

of organisation and were really quite hopelessly casual. We even
arrived late at the start . . .

They are trailing by five lengths up to the halfway mark:

> But it was at that moment that somebody spat on us. It was a
> tactical error. Sammy Stockton, who was stroking the boat, took
> us up the next half of the course as though pursued by all the fiends
> in hell and we won the race by two-fifths of a second. General
> Goering had to surrender his cup . . .[8]

Hillary's appealing account of RAF training in Scotland does not
gloss over the matter of silly accidents in training, but presents a
friendly picture of the young would-be pilots, as a very mixed body
of people. They became, as Hillary presents it, a case apart,
inarticulate in the mundane world. 'It is only in the air that the pilot
can grasp that feeling, that flash of knowledge, of insight, that
matures him beyond his years . . .' On the ground, 'He wants only
to get back to the Mess, to be among his own kind . . . He wants to
get back to that closed language that is Air Force slang.' Indifferent
to war news, pilots read 'not literature but thrillers, not *The Times*
but the *Daily Mirror* . . . They like to drink a little beer, play the radio
and a little bridge.' But they do not stand aloof from the technicians
who service their planes, working with them in 'easy comradeship';
and some of them, including Hillary, devote their time off to playing
games with Scottish child evacuees . . .[9]

Granted the almost monastic virtuousness of Hillary's dedicated
pilots, it is not surprising that they fight the Battle of Britain, those
who get there, in a clean, inspired way. The Germans, of course,
make things easy because of their 'mass psychology'. They are very
good at prearranged manoeuvres, confused and ineffectual once
these are disturbed. Even their planes are so constructed that the
crews are 'always bunched together, thus gaining confidence and a
false sense of security'. On his very first sortie in a Spitfire out of
Hornchurch, Hillary destroys a Messerschmitt 109 – other kills by
him follow, as he casually intimates. During August and September
the RAF is hard-pressed, but Hillary's squadron swiftly learns how to
counter German tactics, and when the Germans attack Hornchurch,
apart from four men killed in a lorry and a network of holes on the
landing surface there is 'nothing to show for ten minutes really
accurate bombing', and this is 'striking proof of the inefficacy of
their attempts to wipe out our advance fighter aerodromes'. (Hillary
has forgotten the destruction by bombs of three Spitfires which he
vividly described two pages before.[10])

As August draws to a close, the squadron shows 'no sign of strain' (despite casualties), and Hillary is personally content:

> If I felt anything, it was a sensation of relief. We had little time to think, and each day brought new action. No one thought of the future . . . At night one switched off one's mind like an electric light.[11]

Hillary and his kind might enjoy a good meal in a West End restaurant, we infer, but had no time for hard drinking, heavy wenching and other immoralities.

Another heroic yet plausible version of pilot behaviour can be seen in *Angels One Five*, released in 1952, one of the greatest box office successes among many popular British war films of its decade. While it stands up better to reviewing than the coarsely epic *Battle of Britain* of 1969 (with Laurence Olivier as Air Chief Marshal Dowding), its modesty now seems excessive. Seven years after victory, the film doesn't have to explain the context of its action: quotations from Churchill screened at beginning and end are enough to evoke the whole well-known story. Centred on just one Fighter Command aerodrome, it establishes the Battle of Britain as a family event. The station is a family, with Group Captain Small (Jack Hawkins) as its father and Nadine (Dulcie Gray), the wife of Squadron Leader Clinton, as its mother. The technical staff are Cheery Cockneys ('Cor, chase me round the 'angar') but the women in the Ops Room almost all have high-carat upper-class accents as do most of the flyers. Humphrey Lestocq as Batchie copes impressively with the concentration in his lone person of all the famous irreverence and high spirits of the Knights of the Air, with his cricketing and public school metaphors and air of rakishness. Otherwise, the pilots behave on the whole like prefects in a well-ordered educational establishment, with just two moments of ritualised horseplay. (They are seen rolling around in a heap on the floor of the Mess, with the group captain well submerged; later they chair Pilot Officer Baird home from his first kill, chanting carefully bowdlerised RAF songs.)

Tension in this almost idyllic community is provided less by the never-seen Germans than by the actions and personality of a newcomer, from the Volunteer Reserve, Pilot Officer Baird. He is a stereotyped Scot, acted by John Gregson with such conviction that he runs the risk of being as boring and embarrassing as the equivalent would be in real life. A medical student before the war, he is pompous and formal, extremely shy, diffident and self-punishing; he is a good theoretical flyer who makes mistakes in practice.

Nicknamed 'Septic', he plays chess between sorties and drinks Drambuie in preference to bitter. But Mother Gray and Father Hawkins like and encourage him, and are seen (with the whole female Ops Room complement) to be deeply grieved when, hit from behind by a cowardly Messerschmitt, he dies in the cockpit of his Hurricane, his last poignant radio messages received at the very time when he should have been meeting upper-class English Rose Betty (somewhat round-shouldered, but jolly sweet) for their First Date.

The aerodrome has been bombed. The girls in the Ops Room have shown they can Take It. There is no suggestion that this battle belongs solely, or even chiefly, to the young Knights of the Air. What is foregrounded is the brilliance of British Method, based on 'radiolocation' (radar). Baird dies, not in the air, but over Ops Room radio. There are only brief (though efficiently devised) episodes in the air: we see much more of the Ops Room, and stress is laid on the strain felt by Squadron Leader Clinton (Cyril Raymond) in charge of that, rather than any weariness among the pilots. The Ops Room girls plot accurately the course of battle. The Ops Room guides pilots intelligently to their targets. Outnumbered six to one or so by the Hun, the RAF family are seen to be defeating 'him' by superior discipline and method. When, in the final frames, Mother Gray hangs up a light in the ruins of her bungalow at the end of the runway to guide any benighted stray pilot safely home, we are perhaps to think of a gesture towards the faint hope that Baird might yet somehow return; but the image has much wider force – any pilot's goal is the domestic family happiness from which he is a temporary absentee.

What is one to make of the film's conception of Baird? His extreme Caledonian stiffness makes the stiff-upper-lip English public-school types seem relatively wild. As poignant representative of the Fallen Few he incorporates probity and chastity; as Scot he shows that the Battle of Britain wasn't just a south of England affair. But perhaps his main effect is to demonstrate the wisdom and cherishing power of the RAF family: he is an awkward child, but, carefully directed, rewards his parents, who grieve over his loss especially.

Derek Robinson's *Piece of Cake* is a kind of sequel to the same writer's *Goshawk Squadron*, which made his reputation in 1971. That book presents the activities of the Royal Flying Corps in France in 1918 in terms of sordor, black comedy, and futility. Major Woolley's brutal training methods are designed to disabuse his flyers of any notions about chivalry and fair play, and to instil in them the idea that their job is to kill Germans. Not out of the top drawer – a football follower with a Midlands accent - Woolley is clearly more or less mad. Robinson's ruthless realism presents him with an acute problem of closure. A colossal casualty rate picks off good, bad and ugly RFC men alike, so a conventional 'happy ending' is wholly impossible, and any kind of 'point' would be hard to educe. Robinson makes Woolley go soft. In the air, he starts thinking about his mistress, not the Germans. His resulting death, which concludes the book, ironically vindicates his own callous ideology.

Piece of Cake is far longer, taking a squadron of Hurricanes all the way from the outbreak of war to 7 September 1940, when the Germans break through in force and bomb London. The Hornet Squadron's experiences of 'phoney', then disastrously real, war in France occupy more of the novel than the 204 pages out of 667 (in the paperback) given to the Battle of Britain. Though having 'popsies' is much alluded to, there are only three significant female characters in this *épopée*. Two are teachers in France (one herself English) who marry Hornet Squadron members. The lively French girl is killed in a road accident trying, against the tide of refugees, to meet her husband after the squadron has flown from its old base. The other becomes the focus of misogyny, haunting the base in Kent after her husband fails to return, being accused of bringing bad luck, and shoved away. Only the rather thinly conceived Jackie Bellamy, a US presswoman, long attached to the squadron, with a nasty habit of querying the RAF's claims, is there at the end to vindicate at least the intelligence of the non-flying sex. So much for *Angels One Five* and its strong emphasis on (supposedly) feminine values . . .

And so much for Richard Hillary. The ex-public-school types in Hornet Squadron are variously oafish, stupid, callow, neurotically disturbed or (in one case) positively evil: 'Moggy' Cattermole is a relentless practical joker, liar, bully and thief with homicidal propensities which make him (Robinson's text insinuates) just the right type to be a fighter pilot. Willy-nilly, after destroying most of his pilots in horrible ways, minutely described, with uncannily precise technical know-how, Robinson, resisting closure, is bound to suggest a kind of 'point' by his selection of those who are still alive in the last pages. We do not know for certain that 'Mother' Cox, stranded out in the Channel but drifting towards land, will survive. He is half Jewish, notably quieter, more sensible and more decent than most of his mess-mates. 'Pip' Patterson, the rather dour and detached but over-imaginative Scot has, we know, landed safely away from the raid at a base in Essex used long before by the squadron. CH3 (Chris Hart III), the Squadron's ever-critical American, is diving into battle on the last page, following his leader

Fanny Barton, a New Zealander who has achieved authority despite awkward personality problems.

The last Englishman, evil Cattermole, has been killed by a Messerschmitt on the penultimate page. As we review the book in our minds, we remember that the best marksmen and pilots the squadron ever had in the battle were a Czech Communist and an anti-Semitic Pole, both now dead. The young Englishmen, apart from the horrible Moggy, seem flimsily unsuccessful compared to colonials, Yanks and Europeans. CH3, the rich young American who has already flown against the Luftwaffe in Spain, has, in the course of the book, been vindicated in his contempt for chivalric motivations and for pretty flying formations. Readers are perfectly clear that even up-to-date Hurricanes are vastly inferior to ME 109s and that Fighter Command by early September has been reduced to a shambles. As Jackie Bellamy has pointed out, what's saving Britain is its navy. The Germans, so inferior in ships, can't risk cross-Channel invasion. But Fighter Command can't stop the Luftwaffe getting through to London.

Robinson, though, is up against the Big Fact. He can expose, with complete justice, the gross exaggeration by the RAF of numbers of Germans brought down; he can demonstrate his virtuosity by making somehow tolerable page after page of silly RAF backchat linked with pointless and sometimes cruel horseplay; he can emphasise stresses and fatigues which destroy men's judgement and set us up to mock the crumbling organisation of Fighter Command. But he cannot end with the Luftwaffe winning: because it didn't. Barton and CH3 may not be chivalric young Englishmen, but they are still in the air fighting at the end, as indeed their whole groggy Command was. Robinson's book is very exciting and often, in gallows-humour mode, very funny. But its conclusion with an 'Author's note' indicates that he could not quite drive his overview of the Battle of Britain successfully home in fictional shape. By concentrating entirely on a squadron exposed in east Kent, Robinson can accentuate horror and chaos. However, he cannot counteract his reader's knowledge of the Big Fact, which at times makes his approach to the battle seem wilfully cynical. Nor, apparently, does he think that an overall 'debunking' would be valid. 'Dowding has, quite rightly, received credit for his handling of the Battle', his 'Author's note' gratuitously concedes.[12]

Battle is generally an all-male affair. That must be Robinson's justification for giving women so little to do in his novel, which is sexist, one feels, by default. A much older book, Nicholas

Monsarrat's *The Cruel Sea* (1951), seems sexist virtually by intention. Alan Munson summarises the evidence thus:

> Sailors are undermined by bad marriages and bad sex, unfaithful women harm the war effort itself. Apart from Ericson's wife and Lockhart's girl-friend, every woman described in the novel is unfaithful or harmful. A promiscuous actress laughs at the news of her husband's death, a seaman goes absent hunting for his wife, a young officer catches venereal disease. The men in this novel fight two battles: one at sea against U-Boats, another at home against women.[13]

Monsarrat's book – famously and very successfully filmed, with Jack Hawkins, as Captain Ericson, making his casting seem inevitable – retains considerable power. Like Robinson, he can make technical detail vividly interesting. As Captain Ericson and First Lieutenant Lockhart patrol the seas from 1939 to 1945 guarding convoys against U Boats, first in the *Compass Rose*, then in the *Saltash*, their travels yield many strong incidents, of which Monsarrat handles the most sickening and macabre particularly well. The novel cannot be dismissed as merely a matter of dated Union Jack heroics. However, the merits of its best passages are not the reason for discussing it here. I mention it because its negatives, silences and exclusions help to illuminate certain highly positive characteristics of the Myth of the Blitz – which is warmly inclusive.

Monsarrat celebrates all-male life on shipboard – the dogged courage of men whose lives are at risk day after day, month after month, year after year. Homosexuality among sailors is hardly unknown. Monsarrat allows only a single hint of its existence. And yet such contentment as we are supposed to feel at the end of the novel is because two men have survived with honour, fully in tune with each other, After Lockhart has learned of the death of his Wren fiancée in a meaningless accident, Ericson watches him 'with compassion' that is 'very nearly love'. Lockhart in turn feels 'enormous affection' for the captain with whom he reviews the war on the final pages.[14] One feels that Monsarrat – whose ruthlessness in condemning men to death for weak dalliance with the other sex is, as Munson points out, shown in the passage where *Compass Rose* sailors, after the corvette is sunk, struggle in the cruel sea – has disposed of Lockhart's sensuous Julie Hallam in order that the pure, platonic love of captain and Number One shall shine forth in the finale without competition. (Ericson clearly lost interest in sexual relations with his dull wife years ago.)

Monsarrat's mythologised Battle of the Atlantic stands in defiance of the Myth of the Blitz. Not only women (and Americans), but also British civilians in general, are treated with contempt and ridicule. British workers are idle and incompetent. The black market in petrol at home disgusts brave men sailing oil tankers in the Atlantic. Glasgow mid-war has for Lockhart 'the same futureless air' as he had found in 1939, with its 'inward-looking, pallid faces'.[15]

Such virtues in the English as the Myth of the Blitz extols are here concentrated amongst men on shipboard, together with one crowning virtue, expressed in Ericson's view of his crew, mostly made up of volunteers and conscripts:

'The sea in their blood' meant that you could pour Englishmen – any Englishmen – into a ship, and they made that ship work and fight as if they had been doing it all their lives, catching up, overtaking, and leaving behind the professionals of any other nation. It was the basic virtue of living on an island.[16]

On a particularly dangerous convoy run to Gibraltar, Ericson's *Compass Rose* picks up great numbers of survivors from other vessels that have been sunk. Typically, none of the twenty Wrens embarked on one of them are permitted by Monsarrat to survive. So the rescued people cramming *Compass Rose* are all male: fourteen Merchant Navy officers and 121 others – 'Seamen, firemen, cooks, Lascars, Chinese'. It is worth quoting the account of night in the fo'c'sle at some length:

The place was crammed to the deckhead: men stood or sat or knelt or lay, in every available space: they crouched under the tables, they wedged themselves in corners, they stretched out on top of the broad ventilating shafts. There were men being sea-sick, men crying out in their sleep, men wolfing food, men hugging their bits of possessions and staring at nothing: wounded men groaning, apparently fit men laughing uneasily at nothing, brave men who could still summon a smile and a straight answer. It was impossible to pick one's way from one end of the fo'c'sle to the other, as Lockhart did each night when he made the Rounds, without being shocked and appalled and saddened by this slum corner of the war: and yet somehow one could be heartened also, and cheered by an impression of patience and endurance, and made to feel proud . . . Individuals, here and there, might have been pushed close to defeat and panic, but the gross crowding, the rags, the oil, the bandages, the smell of men in adversity, were *still* not enough to defeat the whole company. They were all sailors there, not to be overwhelmed even by this sudden and sustained nightmare.[17]

With a very few words changed – 'deckhead . . . fo'c'sle . . . sailors' replaced, say, by 'ceiling . . . shelter . . . Londoners' – this could *almost* be an account from one of the 'worst' shelters early in the London Blitz. But not quite. It is very hard to imagine a situation where the occupants of a shelter with over a hundred in it could have been exclusively male. A typical account of the crowded tube station, the sordid public shelter or the overflowing rest centre will in fact emphasise the presence of women and children.

The Myth of the Blitz welcomes almost all comers. It has awkward dealings with race (the presence not only of many Jews but of 'coloured' and Asian residents in the East End produced remarks in passing by journalists and others which now seem embarrassing). But the Myth usually tells us that *anyone* – old, young, rich, poor, female, male – could be an heroic front-line fighter in 1940–41. The *Daily Express* correspondent in the Blitz, Hilde Marchant, quoted a soldier patrolling the Thames Embankment during a raid: 'We feel a bit ashamed of ourselves when we see it's the women and kids fighting the war for us.'[18] Even if she improved in this case on a less striking remark, such thoughts were familiar at that time. This makes Monsarrat's handling of the Merseyside Blitz all the more starkly indicative of the male chauvinism of the Myth of the Battle of the Atlantic which his book in many respects develops successfully.

Compass Rose returns frequently to Liverpool. By 1941 it seems, we are told, to 'belong to' that city, where its sailors have married or established their wives. Chief Petty Officer Tallow has regularly taken his colleague Chief E. R. A. Watts to be fed, while on leave, by his widowed sister Gladys in Birkenhead, and it is understood that Watts, a widower, will marry her once the war is over.

In May of 1941, the ship comes in to find devastation in and around the docks. Bob Tallow and Jim Watts, unable to get through to Gladys by phone, go to Birkenhead. There is little left of the street where Gladys lived. They find her house 'a heap of dust and rubbish'. From ARP workers they learn that two dead women were brought out of it. They go to the Warden's Post for confirmation of their fears . . .

The remarkable thing about this passage of some four pages is that not one woman is reported to be seen in devastated Birkenhead. Male rescue-squad members, male wardens are given voices. 'Children' play in the rubble of Gladys's house. But the tough seamen get the hard news, and laconic sympathy, from males in uniform, not female neighbours. There are to be no tears, no cups of tea, no gossip, so Monsarrat, consciously or not, has decreed.

In contrast, Helen Forrester's very well researched *Three Women of Liverpool* (1984) is a most effective novel presenting the Merseyside May Blitz from female perspectives. It does not exaggerate the active role of women in Civil Defence, but the heroine, a plain thirty-nine-year-old 'spinster', Emmie, released from a long sentence of caring for aged parents, works in a canteen for sailors alongside other women, some of them upper-class volunteers. She is there when it is bombed, and her long ordeal trapped in a vault before she is rescued, carefully and most vividly realised, gives the book a very strong climax.

Written four decades after the events which it fictionalises, Forrester's novel is unselfconsciously honest about working-class Merseyside. An admirably devoted Irish Catholic air-raid warden is also a black marketeer: his children, presented with sympathy, are as ill-trained and verminous as evacuees from Merseyside were so often alleged to be. Post-raid looting is several times referred to; also, ghoulish sightseers clustering round an 'incident'.

Forrester does not have enough subtlety to make the most of the grudging accommodation with Catholic neighbours which the raids force on Emmie's intensely Protestant and houseproud sister-in-law, Gwen, but the issue of sectarianism is squarely faced. In no way is the Blitz glamorised or its horror treated lightly. It is seen throughout in terms of work – at the climax the skilled work of technicians (it is a telephone engineer who by fluke locates the buried Emmie), of former builders and coalminers in the rescue squad shifting intricate rubble to get to her. And also the housework which obsesses Gwen, and the labour of women feeding sailors.

Overall, this warm and intelligent novel provides as plausible a reconstruction of the Blitz – using the new freedom to write about sexuality enjoyed in the later twentieth century, not available during the war – as any reader could wish. It doesn't disturb the Myth one iota. It ends like a wartime film, with Emmie, out of hospital, enjoying a Sunday outing with her merchant-sailor fiancé, who is about to return to the cruel sea, or, as she thinks, to 'the god-damned Atlantic'. She is resolved, when fully healed, 'to try for a job in munitions', so she can 'send a bit back to the Jerries with her best compliments'.[19] In 1942 or 1943, of course, no film-maker or novelist could step outside the war and create closure there. Why doesn't Forrester do so?

One speculates, as with Derek Robinson, that the effort of

detailed, horrific reconstruction raised too many issues for glib long-term resolution. There is also this feature of the events gathered in the Myth: that they have such heroic intensity that exploration of characters' fates beyond them can only generate anti-climax. 1940–41, the Finest Hour, invests all active, courageous, and half-decent participants with glory. Forrester would have undermined the status of her people by showing them watching the Coronation of 1953 on television, or reminiscing together after J. B. Priestley's TV documentary *1940* made for the twenty-fifth anniversary of the Battle of Britain. And the disturbing point would emerge that 1940 was *not* the end of history, that memories of it would become tangled in post-war 'austerity', in fifties 'affluence', in sixties 'permissiveness', in the widening realisation during the seventies that Britain had for some time been a distinctly second rate power.

The problem of closure can be further illuminated by considering two very different novels by distinguished writers.

The Belfast Blitz of April 1941 was particularly gruesome and, from the German point of view, effective – the hardest of all 'provincial' blitzes to mythologise adequately. Little needs to be said here about the pervasiveness of sectarian division in Ulster. More men from neutral Eire's twenty-six counties volunteered to serve in the British forces than stood forth in Northern Ireland, where the British government dared not demand conscription for fear of inflaming Catholic Irish feeling. The Home Guard in Ulster was effectively barred to Catholics by the Protestant majority who controlled the parliament which ran this mini-state within the UK. Craigavon, the Prime Minister, had successfully pleaded for contracts for Belfast's shipbuilding and aircraft industries. These made the city a natural target for Luftwaffe raids, yet the Northern Ireland government did little to provide protection. When Coventry's ordeal made the danger clear, it was too late. Belfast was still badly short of shelters in the spring of 1941.

Air defences were so feeble that two of the six German planes which made an exploratory raid on 7 April and killed thirteen people actually switched on their navigation lights over the city. On 15 April, 180 more followed. The fire service was ill-equipped. Faced by conflagration and chaos, the Minister of Public Security rang Dublin for help. Daring German displeasure, De Valera obliged, and thirteen fire appliances set off north. The driver of one of them would always remember Belfast as a place of devastation, with 'human bodies and dead animals lying all over the place'.

Official statistics eventually showed 745 lives lost – many more than in Coventry's big raid. Next day, a thick fog of smoke, ash and dust covered the city. The Germans came back on 4 May, killed only 150 more people, but did so much damage in the port area that Harland and Wolff's shipyard was not back in full production for six months.

'Trekking' to sleep outside Belfast assumed colossal proportions – up to 100,000 people. 'Every industry or factory listed on the Luftwaffe's target indicator chart in the previous November' was destroyed or seriously damaged. The Northern Ireland Cabinet now considered improved ARP. It gave priority to working out how to safeguard the large statue outside the Parliament building of Carson, the defiant Protestant politician who had prevented Home Rule for a united Ireland.[20]

Brian Moore, future prize-winning novelist, served in Belfast ARP during the big April raid, and his novel centring on it, *The Emperor of Ice Cream*, is semi-autobiographical. Moore's own Catholic and Republican father was a distinguished surgeon, young 'Gavin Burke's' is a Republican solicitor. This fine novel, full of witty and incisive detail, is unsparing in its account of the Blitz, in which Gavin, against his British-hating father's wishes, works as an ARP regular. Wearing wellington boots and yellow oilskins, Gavin is set to work coffining corpses in the morgue; 'In the stink of human excrement, in the acrid smell of disinfectant, these dead were heaped, body on body, flung arm, twisted feet, open mouth, staring eyes, old men on top of young women, a child lying on a policeman's back, a soldier's hand resting on a woman's thigh . . .' At least Gavin doesn't have to work on, or even look at, 'the pieces', attended to in a back room. 'He thought of old films he had seen . . . But this was no film. There were no ugly corpses in films.'

His own family has fled to Dublin. Gavin returns to an empty house, windows broken, 'condemned' as 'unsafe'. To his extreme surprise, his father appears. He has come back from Eire, worried about his son:

In the candlelight, he saw that his father was crying. He had never seen his father cry before. Did his father know that the house was condemned, did his father know that everything had changed, that things would never be the same again? A new voice, a cold grown-up voice within him said: 'No.' His father was the child now; his father's world was dead. He looked over at the wireless set, remembering his father, ear cocked for England's troubles, pleased at news of other, faraway disasters.

Gavin realises that he himself has risen to adulthood:

> His father seemed aware of this change. He leaned his untidy gray head on Gavin's shoulder, nodding, weeping, confirming. 'Oh Gavin,' his father said, 'I've been a fool. Such a fool.'

Though this literally deals only with an individual's development and one father–son relationship, the novel pushes us to see this ending as prophetic of the future of Ulster. Protestants and Catholics have been bombed indiscriminately.

The young IRA supporter who flashed a light deliberately to guide the bombers has been seen repenting bitterly. Moore has seized hope from the Irish Blitz experience and brought Belfast under the umbrella of the Myth. Just as in London, class differences were reportedly subdued, so in Belfast sectarian feeling is chastened.[21]

Moore published his novel in 1965, when prospects for harmony in Ulster seemed good. By the end of the decade they would be in ruins. For all the quality of the writing, *The Emperor of Ice Cream* seems betrayed and diminished by Moore's attempt at a closure which would relate the Blitz to the sixties and beyond.

Robin Jenkins, who provides in *Fergus Lamont* perhaps the most powerful evocation of Blitz in Scottish fiction, is lured into positioning the raids on Clydeside in 1941 as if at the end of Scotland's history.[22] The book's first-person narrator dies in 1963, as we learn from a concluding 'footnote' by his son, 'within hours' of completing this 'autobiography'. The last twenty pages of the novel describe the return of Lamont, in 1941, to his home town, 'Gantock'. His persona has been intriguingly complex and inconsistent: he is proletarian radical, pseudo-aristocratic snob, soldier and poet. He confronts his old teacher, Calderwood, an erstwhile socialist rebel now 'screwed up and shrunken' with disillusionment:

> Yet any of his pupils in Kidd Street school nearly thirty years ago would have recognised him at once. Even the least sensitive of us then had been aware that though he wanted to love us he could not: not because of our academic shortcomings, or because some of us stank through not washing often enough, but because he had seen us developing into eager conformists, indolent and cowardly acquiescers in the iniquities and inequalities of society.

The two drink whisky. Calderwood tells Lamont, 'The best thing that could happen to our beloved native town, Fergus, is for a few bombs to fall on it.' He cites the recent case of a back-street abortionist jailed for three months by a sheriff who 'chose the occasion to deliver an impassioned harangue about the sanctity of human life, and this in the midst of a war which he thoroughly approves of . . . ' Pressed by Lamont to agree that 'humanity is not all stupid and vile', Calderwood will only concede, 'You could never have written such good poetry if you had been able to think things out to their nihilistic conclusion. Then you would have had to remain silent. Like me.'

When guns begin to fire, bombs to fall, Calderwood argues that as a patriot, Fergus should desire that the Germans should miss the shipyards – important for victory – 'even if it means that they hit instead tenements crowded with women and children, some of them known to you'. Lamont rushes out of the house and stands shaking his fist: 'I did not know at whom or what. I felt no hatred of the young German airmen doing their loathsome duty, and for the people of Gantock, at that moment suffering terror and pain and death, I felt only pity and love.' Throughout the novel, Lamont seems to embody problematic, divided Scottish 'identity'. 'Love', the last word of his memoirs, seems to redeem both poet and people at the moment of Blitz. But after that there is nothing in the life of Lamont except the eccentric loneliness reported in asides during his narrative. Between 1941 and 1963, either Scotland has no history or Lamont has ceased to relate to it.

Interpreting this strange novel is difficult. It is typical of Jenkins's rigorous approach to abiding moral problems that he should leave Calderwood's cynical logic – 'war is the greatest abortionist of all' – unquenched by Lamont's irrational love for Gantock people, who, he says, 'believe that the war is being fought for something more important than life itself'. This, it could be argued, takes the Clyde-side Blitz outside the paradigm of Myth and makes it merely an instance, suitable as the basis for a debate about philosophical questions long troublesome within Western culture.

But the implication that Scotland's history is concluded by its integration, through the Clydeside Blitz, into the UK's 'people's war' is naggingly present. As basis of closure, the bombing of Gantock seems involved with the positive significance, the fulfilment, of the book's puzzling yet representative narrator: the moment might be compared with Lewis Grassic Gibbon's withdrawal from history, in the early thirties, of his representative Scots heroine Chris Guthrie, 'Chris Caledonia', at the end of his great *Scots Quair*, as another case where a major Scottish novelist seems to leave his nation without a meaningful independent future. In such a reading, Jenkins's book acknowledges the Myth's power to integrate all the

UK with metropolitan experience: Gantock, Taking It, is inspirational, as London's ordeal had been inspirational. That human fineness is revealed by and excited by night bombing is taken for granted, because London's response proved it.

Most differently, R. F. Delderfield's *The Avenue Goes to War* (1964), the second volume of the immensely popular *Avenue* saga, attempts to incorporate 1940–41 incident of mythical stature into the mesmeric, unstoppable soap-opera-like flow of incident among the outer-suburban middle classes who are, in Delderfield's eyes, the quint-essential continuators of Englishness and English history. The book, which takes Avenue-dwellers from 1940 to 1947, is based on a blatant sleight of hand: the Avenue, literally a long road of semi-detached houses stretching away on the edge of London, the city to which many of its people commute, is purported to constitute a 'community'. Furtive covert lives, adulteries, black market operations, which give rise to lively incidents, confirm that in fact people here *don't* really have much in common or know much about each other. A random bomb, bringing ARP into action, is insufficient to create a community where none has existed, as Delderfield unwittingly shows by the way he summarises the carnage: 'Soon the casualties were tabbed, and driven away, two from Number Thirteen, three from Number Fifteen, three more in Number Seventeen, four from the remaining houses, a total of twelve human sacrifices to a madman's dream of world conquest.'

If the Avenue can be said to have its own higher values, they are probably distilled in the reverie of nice young Judy, resuming, now that his wife has left him, her childhood romance with rather tragic Esme – 'that dear familiar dream, of a white wedding in Shirley Church, the ecstatic honeymoon in Bournemouth, or Felixstowe, and the triumphant return to the semi-detached on the Wickham housing estate, with the baby in the pram on the lawn, the lawn that Esme would mow each Saturday afternoon, while she prepared his tea in the trim little kitchen'.

Delderfield's optimistic sensibility, which converts the RAF in which Esme serves into 'one huge, sprawling, joke-cracking, grousing family', invests a bereaved city clerk with the tradition of Alfred the Great and Agincourt:

People like Harold, who had worked thirty years in one job and carried their modest salaries back to the Avenue every Friday,

were not likely to be bowled over by a single, personal tragedy . . .
Harold would survive, and so would all the other people of the
Avenue, and crescents of the suburb, no matter how battered and
scattered were their homes and possessions, when madness had
run its course across the Channel.[23]

Delderfield's rhetoric has the sickly flavour of complete, obtuse
sincerity. An enormous readership could accept it because they, like
him, took the Myth for granted. Of course a commuter was
naturally heroic. The valour of such men, struggling in to work, had
been duly celebrated by writers and film-makers during the Blitz.
London's suburbs had been, somehow, glorious in war. As we shall
see when we inspect John Boorman's vastly more intelligent *Hope
and Glory*, a film set in very similar territory to Delderfield's Avenue,
the Myth is at its least destructible where it might seem rather weak,
in its incorporation of areas only lightly scattered with bombs, where
communities could not rise to confront challenges because communities didn't exist.

'Suburban values' and the suburban life-style, created in the new
housing estates of the interwar period, did have in 1940 a flourishing
future ahead of them. Ravaged by the Luftwaffe or not, the
working-class areas of British cities were due to be devastated by
town-planners; while, in the sixties, poor people were shifted from
'communities' into tower blocks, the suburbanites who despised
them continued to mow the lawn every Saturday, make tea in trim
little kitchens, and keep up with the ever-more-affluent Joneses.
More successful elements in the working class sought and acquired
similar private amenities. The role assigned by the Myth to the
'Heroic Commuter', whether picking his way, briefcase in hand
through the rubble or donning the warden's tin helmet, the Home
Guard's uniform, related to a thriving stratum of society. Delderfield
flattered this stratum with his optimism about its historic destiny.

Boorman grew up in this stratum and by his own account,
prefacing the script of his film, detested its values:

I was born at No. 50 Rosehill Avenue, Carshalton, a monotonous
street of those semi-detached suburban houses of which *four
million* were built between the wars. My father bought the house
with a deposit of £50 . . .

To shoot his autobiographical film, Boorman reconstructed
Rosehill Avenue on a disused airfield at a cost of three-quarters of a
million pounds:

In point of fact, our 'Street' set looked much more like one we moved into in Ewell when I was two years old, such are the composites of movies and memory. Council estates were springing up around Rosehill Avenue, rehousing London's slum dwellers. My parents, like other home-owning semi-dwellers, had only a murky view of their place in the class system, but an acute sense of gentility which was affronted by council houses . . . My father . . . was not a snob, certainly never despised those below him, but he deeply respected his superiors, felt threatened if things and people were not properly in their places. He was a sentimental patriot, a passionate royalist, a dogged Tory . . . Voting Conservative was a way of reassuring himself that he was not slipping into the dreaded pit of the working class.

Boorman goes on to meditate about the historic implications of 'the rise of this semi-suburbia' in which he is still ashamed to have been born:

They all missed it (or got it wrong) – the academics, the politicians, the upper classes. While they worried about Socialism and Fascism, the cuckoo had laid its egg in their nest and Margaret Thatcher would hatch out of it . . . Where did it come from, this new class? Some had slipped down from the middle class; most were dragging themselves up from the working class . . . Most of the children I knew had no interest in where they came from, no memory of family history. We viewed each other with suspicion, kept ourselves to ourselves. Privacy protected our uncertainty about how to behave . . . The private, inward looking world of the nuclear family was taking shape . . . In these streets there were no places of work, no schools, no shops, no churches, no sport, no pubs. During the day the men and the young were syphoned out to business and to learn; the wives were left to clean and polish, listen to the wireless and dream.

War, as Boorman shrewdly suggests, gave frustrated, uncertain suburbanites a chance to 'vault over their embarrassments into the arms of patriotism'. And the ever-generous Myth had plenty of room for them.[24]

Hope and Glory (1987) is a very well-made film, scrupulously produced, splendidly cast, beautifully photographed. And the hedonistic fullness and credibility of its reconstruction is one reason why it does nothing to counter the Myth, of which Boorman, as his preface shows, is fully aware. Reconstruction generates nostalgia for periods wholly out of reach of living memory: when many in the audience can still remember the period, and all can still see streets much like that in Boorman's set, this effect is bound to be even stronger. Those Were, indeed, The Days.

Furthermore, the beautiful young boy, Sebastian Rice Edwards, who plays 'Bill' (Boorman himself) so touchingly, is the witness whose point of view controls ours. He can sense, as children do, adult inanity and hypocrisy; but he cannot pass comment on suburban values, convey the points which Boorman makes so sharply in his preface. Consider one delicious sequence. 'Clive' (Boorman's Tory, ex-Indian army father) has volunteered to fight again. The performance of Clive is superbly 'alienated': the actor cast, David Hayman, is well known to be in fact a working class Glaswegian and committed socialist. He is seen teaching Bill, with solemn fervour, how to bowl the cricketer's 'googly', a famously deceptive ball disguised as a leg break but spinning in the other direction:

BILL: It's like telling fibs.

CLIVE: That's it. When you tell a lie you hope to get away with it. When someone else does, you want to find them out. A good batsman will spot a googly. A good bowler will hide it. Always remember that, son.

The next scene shows Clive going away to war. As his mother closes the door, Bill stays outside:

BILL: Dad! Dad!

(CLIVE, now some twenty yards away, looks back. BILL throws the cricket ball and CLIVE catches it neatly. He smiles and marches off down Rosehill Avenue. BILL is puzzled as CLIVE shows no sign of returning the ball. He calls after him.) Dad!

(CLIVE is now eighty yards down the street. He suddenly turns, smiling broadly, and with a prodigious throw he sends the ball in a high arc towards his son. BILL juggles his position, cups his hands, gets under it as the hard, heavy ball hurtles downwards. At the last moment he loses his nerve and jumps back, letting the ball thump into the lawn. He looks towards CLIVE, full of shame. BILL is relieved to see that his father has turned the corner.)[25]

From an adult viewpoint, Hayman/Clive's behaviour could be seen satirically, or even made sinister. His talk about lying casts doubt on the supposed code of gallant sportsmanship integral to the sacred game of cricket; to throw a hard ball towards a small boy whom it might hurt quite seriously and then to turn and stride on hardly shows due paternal care. This is the kind of man who might, in the British Expeditionary Force, have shot Belgian civilians as suspected fifth columnists, not out of viciousness but from ethical and mental confusion. But from Bill's point of view he is Dad, whom he lets down by muffing the catch. The effect of the sequence is gently comic. Later in the film, the boy will get his father out with a googly and all will be artistically and emotionally harmonised. ('CLIVE: I'm proud of you.')

The flow of wartime incident in *Hope and Glory* is clearly not intended to show Rosehill Avenue in any heroic light. The patriotism of schoolteachers is held up for mockery. Bill's sister becomes pregnant by a Canadian soldier (who will eventually go AWOL to marry her, so that, too, will be harmonised). When bombs fall, this is both exciting and very frightening: one neighbour is killed. In the aftermath, Boorman provides some remarkable scenes involving what might be called 'juvenile delinquency', in which young Bill is caught up.

Here it is worth mentioning one of the very best post-war fictions about the Blitz, Robert Westall's *The Machine-Gunners*, published as a 'children's story', but not fairly to be imprisoned in that category. It confronts with great imagination and wit the serious problem of 'juvenile delinquency', a rise of which was only to be expected when war disrupted schooling, preoccupied adults, fractured families and broke down social control. Westall himself, pursuing the matter after publication of *The Machine-Gunners* had brought him a large number of letters from adults, edited a volume of reminiscences, *Children of the Blitz*. His own memories are particularly interesting on the subject of the Prime Minister:

Churchill – big Winnie – was the lad for us. We all wished we could be Winnie. What our gang-leader did for our gang, Winnie did for Britain. It was the marvellous way he insulted the enemy gang-leaders . . .

Winnie appeared in the comic strips, too (though King George VI never did), always smiling, two fingers up, entirely in control. He frequently colluded with ever-victorious comic-strip heroes like 'Big Eggo', 'Desperate Dan' and 'Lord Snooty' . . .

We saw him not as a great, distant war leader, but as a naughty irrepressible super-child who could do anything.[26]

This puts into interesting perspective the 'antisocial' behaviour of children in Boorman's film and Westall's novel. On the face of it, juvenile bad behaviour must be non-mythical, if not counter-mythical: its existence seems to defy the Myth's insistence that bombs enhanced caring and social cohesion. Yet in so far as children were caught up in the war in their own way, and mimicked adult militancy, their actions might be reconciled with the Myth. Some of Richmal Crompton's stories about the wartime exploits of her ageless naughty boy William could be republished in 1972 in a collection called *William the Hero* . . . The title isn't quite ironic.

The *Machine-Gunners* is set in a vividly realised Tyneside in a phase of heavy bombardment and fear of German invasion. (Effectual chronological telescoping is neatly managed, and admissible in a work of fiction.) A souvenir-hunting schoolboy and a gang of his friends take illegal possession of a machine gun with live ammunition from a crashed German bomber. Stealing material from various places, they build with great care and success an emplacement for it. They are ready to fight German invaders, but as their gang loyalty deepens, the whole adult world also becomes a 'kind of enemy'. Their only adult allies are a simpleton and a German flier, Rudi, who parachutes unnoticed from a shot-down plane and is drawn into their alternative family. (One of the gang is a 'motherly', though tomboy, girl.) They are eventually flushed out, in a moment of dangerous farce, by Polish soldiers whom they mistake for Germans and on whom they fire. As the Poles hand over to British authority, the bemused children prepare to fire their gun at the advancing local adults, and are brought to reality only when one of their members, with a pistol, wounds Rudi, who is going forward to explain the position. The gang are taken into custody by their parents, 'never to be all together again . . .'

Westall, most admirably, refuses to harmonise what has happened with a predictable closure on *Just William* lines. It is true that the children have built a fine emplacement, and, as one father defiantly says, shown lots of guts: their preparedness to meet the foe is in its way a model demonstration of the 'fight them on the beaches' spirit. But one of them, Clogger, an incomer from Glasgow, has displayed, to their disturbance and awe, the 'hard' ethos of that city's violent underworld. They have all been deceitful, disobedient and dangerous. If we continue to side with them it is because we can sympathise with their alienation from pompous, incompetent and hypocritical adults.

At the very end, one adult turns to Nicky, in hiding, at first presumed dead, since a bomb killed his widowed mother – a child with no parent to take him into custody:

'C'mon son', said the police sergeant to Nicky. 'You're going to tell me all about this. You're a cut above the rest of this riff-raff, you know. *Your* father was a ship's captain. God knows what he'd have said.'

Nicky took a deep breath.

'Get stuffed,' he said.[27]

Nicky's words, the last in the book, refuse the reader permission to incorporate 'the machine-gunners' into the Myth. With its sympathetically-portrayed German character and its anarchistic play with received ideas and conventional values, Westall's book achieves a mid-war closure which leaves us free to see, behind the Myth, problematic human nature. As with mythical narratives, the action has been so intense that the future could enter only anti-climactically. Respectable lives lie ahead, one assumes, for most of the gang. But the values of 'respectability' are contested, provocatively, by the 'Churchillian' gang spirit of the delinquents. A 'Churchillian' element is detached from the Myth and redirected to wreck the ideal of social coherence and self-disciplined good behaviour at the Myth's centre.

The shape of John Boorman's narrative rules out such Tolstoyan radicalism, even though the last images of the film will be of children celebrating deliriously when they find that their school has been bombed flat. Bill, exploring ruins, is trapped by a gang of boys. Its nasty leader, Roger, tells him that it is their 'territory'. Bill is inducted into the gang and joins them in an 'orgy of destruction' in a newly bombed house. The gang provide their HQ with expensive furniture, a wireless and a cocktail bar, where they smoke, drink beer and entice a passing girl to let them look inside her knickers. At home on leave, Clive sees his son running wild in the rubble, but does not intervene. From this, though, Bill is whisked by accident into idyll: the family's home burns down – an ordinary fire, not a bomb – while they are all out. When Bill next day finds Roger and the gang looting his own home, he punches him in the face. For the rest of the film the family stay with eccentric Grandfather George in his large house up-river on the Thames, an arena for pranks and jollifications, where cricket can be resumed, where Dawn has her baby: all shall be well.

Living with Grandfather means a sharp break from Rosehill Avenue and its values. The charming idiosyncrasy of these final scenes derives from the unique history of Boorman's own far-from-ordinary extended family. Yet we haven't escaped from the Myth's paradigm, which contains the earlier episodes comfortably. The

Shepperton scenes in *Hope and Glory* bring forward new elements in the Myth: English eccentricity, English love of boats and water, English landscape . . . My next chapter will look at the ways in which self-conscious propagandists – honourably – used such elements to give the Myth, which was spontaneously developing, definitive and durable shape. I should end this one by saying that I like Boorman's film very much. I was born, in 1942, in a suburb adjacent to Carshalton. I share his sense of shame about such origins and can see, I think, how it was nevertheless impossible for him not to re-create his youth with such roundness and love that the warm motherly Myth settles on his film like a nesting bird.

9

Deep England

Some of the damage in London is pretty heart-breaking but what an effect it has had on the people! What warmth – what courage! What determination. People sternly encouraging each other by explaining that when you hear a bomb whistle it means it has missed you. People in the north singing in public shelters: 'One man went to mow – went to mow a meadow.' WVS girls serving hot drinks to firefighters during raids explaining that really they are 'terribly afraid all the time!' . . . Everybody absolutely determined: secretly delighted with the *privilege* of holding up Hitler. Certain of beating him: a certainty which no amount of bombing can weaken, only strengthen . . . A curious kind of unselfishness is developing . . . We have found ourselves on the right side and on the right track at last!

Humphrey Jennings to his wife, 20 October 1940

As this quotation from Britain's most remarkable wartime maker of official films amply shows, it is quite wrong to think of the 'propagandists' of 1939–45 as being like post-war advertising copywriters, or as clearheaded ruthless traffickers in cleverly worked-out lies and half-truths. Dr Goebbels himself worried a great deal in private about how things were going for the German cause, with which he identified himself completely. When Humphrey Jennings used the singing of 'One man went to mow' in a sequence of heartrending brilliance in his film *Fires Were Started*, he was releasing in artistically shaped form something which he remembered from the autumn of 1940, and which had meant a great deal to him personally.

Paradoxical as it may seem, much of the most effective propaganda about 1940–41 – the speeches of Churchill, the broadcasts of Priestley and Murrow, the films which Jennings and others created for the Crown Film Unit, the cartoons of David Low - remains more impressive as literary and artistic production than almost all independently conceived poems, prose and artworks which address the Battle and the Blitz. This is not cynically to imply that Nazi and fascist equivalents may have equal strength: propagandists for Britain expressed humane values and the claims of human beings to individual and communal freedom, and these remain more than acceptable causes.

Of course, each of the propagandists just named had a very strong individual personality, and peculiar preoccupations: Churchill's delight in the broad sweep of history, Priestley's in innocent holiday fun and games; Murrow's memories of Wobblies in the lumber camps and their hero Joe Hill, 'who never died'; Jennings's troubled obsession with finding some interior essence of Britain. But all could draw on resources amply present in 'English' culture and English language, and on images of England and conceptions of Englishness developed so fully between the Great War and the Second that they had the aura of 'natural' existences rather than ideological constructs.

To demonstrate the importance for propagandists of the English literary tradition is so easy as to be unnecessary. Blitzed Londoners became Dickensian; the cause of freedom was Milton's; Donne's assertion that 'no man is an island' echoed; the cadences of Gibbon and Macaulay could be heard in Churchill's; Kipling's soldiers had joined the Home Guard, along with Hardy's Wessex villagers. (One rather surprising instance is worth noting: Professor Patrick Parrinder has pointed out to me that when Churchill in 1940 spoke about the 'life of the world moving forward into broad, sunlit uplands' he was probably indebted to H. G. Wells's phrase 'the uplands of the future' in *The Discovery of the Future*, published in 1902. The great man was a fan who corresponded with Wells over forty years, and perhaps owed to him much of his delight in the potential of science and invention.)

The creativity of English cultural tradition was not exhausted. Between the wars, two distinct and, indeed, largely antagonistic tendencies had enriched it: on the one hand, that represented by 'Georgian' poets and essayists and by certain painters, graphic artists and composers; on the other, that of 'left-wing' and 'avant-garde' intellectuals and artists seeking to reconstruct national taste and character. Priestley came from the 'Georgian' camp, whereas Jennings represented the 'Auden generation'. That their visions of 1940 overlapped suggests that the power of wartime experiences to draw together people who would previously have had nothing polite to say to each other has not been exaggerated.

Both Georgians and Audenisers were much obsessed with English landscape and countryside. Neither school gave thought to the crisis of British agriculture in the period, from which the Second World

War rescued it, preparing it for an era of mechanisation and prosperity. The decline of rural crafts in the face of mass production struck a nerve; less so the pauperised condition of farm labour.

The terrain under literary, pictorial and musical contestation might be described as follows. There was a Green and Pleasant heartland, 'Deep England', which stretched from Hardy's Wessex to Tennyson's Lincolnshire, from Kipling's Sussex to Elgar's Worcestershire. It excluded, self-evidently, the 'Black Country' of the industrial Midlands and the north with its factories and windswept moors. It included those areas of the Home Counties around London which had not been invaded by suburban development. Parts of Kent, for instance, were 'deeper' than anywhere, but areas of the county close to London were commuter territory.

Suburbia, and the life-style identified with it (the little car kept in the garage for trips at weekends), had paradoxical effects. On the one hand, there were still fresh air, green woods, attractive riverbank scenes, fine old manor houses, within areas staked out for suburbia: a taste of 'country' pleasures was close at hand for many. Furthermore, the little cars, like charabancs from the cities, made it relatively easy for urbanites to penetrate and enjoy parts of Deep England hitherto hard of access. (Britain was far behind the USA in car ownership – with just 1,157,344 in 1930 compared to over 23 million in the land of Henry Ford: but that was still a quicker start than anywhere else in Europe, and over a million private petrol-driven vehicles already represented profound social change.)[1] Drivers venturing into quiet, 'unspoilt' places meant that their purportedly timeless beauty was, of course, vulnerable.

Meanwhile, the march of suburban buildings, commonly with 'traditional' Tudorbethan elements in their design, such as fake beams, literally obliterated cherishable scenery. John Boorman's suburb, Carshalton, developed over territory where the Pre-Raphaelite painters had once sought inspiration from nature. 'Ribbon development' along arterial roads was another blow to those used to, and indeed fond of, the railways which had transformed transportation and cut through every part of Deep England in Victorian days. The steam train had for many become an icon of Deep Englishness; the Baby Austin couldn't be that. To some lovers of English countryside, recent developments seemed catastrophic. H. J. Massingham, a townee journalist who became a country dweller, inveighed with all the fervour of a convert against developments since the Industrial Revolution, which he saw as a disaster which had 'destroyed the true England'. He disliked not only new housing developments, but also town people who 'dropped out', as we now say, to fiddle with 'arts and crafts' in rural places. The countryside for him was properly 'a source of our daily bread and the indispensable foundation of our national well-being'.[2] Suburbia, its enemy, was 'detached from all other cultures, detached from everything'.[3]

Yet probably suburb dwellers formed part of the large public for Massingham's books, which between 1930 and 1950 he published at a rate of more than one per year. Perhaps some readers were attracted by an element of scientific rationality in his writing – his concern for what we now know as 'ecology'. In the autumn of 1940 his latest book sturdily confronted the heroic population of the Green and Pleasant Land in their Finest Hour with an apocalypse caused, not by bombs, but by building. In Buckinghamshire, where he himself lived, 'the bottoms and the alluvial strip' had been 'more heavily urbanised than the less fertile summits'. He cried out sorrowfully, 'Only a handful of Englishmen regard this phenomenon as a tragedy for England, but a truth is not cheated by evading it, and one day by no means in the distant future that tragedy will close, like *Hamlet*, in a harvest of catastrophe.'

Meanwhile, he found a little consolation in the fact that nearly thirty stone curlews had convened at their local meeting ground in the first October of the war and that the craft of the bodger, creating chair legs with a pole-lathe, still survived, if tenuously, in the Chiltern woods.[4]

Judging from the frequency with which such images appeared in films and newspapers, the spectacle of huge shire horses drawing ploughs and the craft of stooking and stacking hay with pitchforks, had a considerable appeal for large sections of Britain's over-whelmingly urbanised or suburbanised population. Hiking and rambling were popular with the working classes: the Ramblers' Association was in fact left-wing, and organised demonstrations to keep open rights of way. But even manual workers seem, when seeking in the country side an escape from everyday conditions, to have ignored its primary function. Men and women laboured in the countryside to produce food. Those best at it were unlikely to be smock-wearing 'yeomen' (though ironically the 'yeoman farmer', in a sense, was making a comeback: in 1910 only 10 per cent of farmland in England and Wales was owner-occupied, but the effect of high duties and taxes, which suddenly broke up great estates, was such that the proportion rose to 36 per cent in 1927, about three-quarters in 1973.[5]) Farmers were on the whole worldly people who maximised gains as best they could. One would not guess this from most of the outpouring of books in the years before and during the Second World War which celebrated the English countryside.

As Howard Newby has pointed out, 'real English countryside', in the 'idyllic sense', has been 'located only in the minds of those engaged in the search for it, on a few calendars and chocolate box lids – and in the wholly misleading paintings of John Constable'. Constable painted after 'improvement', including enclosure, had transformed England. Newby notes that 'the eighteenth century landowner, through the agency of his hired landscapers, invented what we have now come to accept as picturesque natural beauty', and, in the process, 'provided a decisive break between ideas about nature and beauty on the one hand and a functional countryside on the other', still marked in our own day.[6]

Alex Potts has incisively analysed the values which were attached to the English countryside between the wars. He distinguishes the charabanc trip taking, say, East Enders from London to Epping Forest – a highly sociable outing – from the 'cultural ideal of an intensely personal "away from it all" immersion in the beauties of "unspoiled" countryside'. This middle-class aspiration opposed itself both to the vulgarity of bus trippers and the 'crass materialism and mindless socialising of the very wealthy country-house set'.

The countryside's attraction for middle-class people, Potts argues, lay 'precisely in its distance from immediate social and material interest'. Middle-class people, feeling marginal, members of social groups with no 'Heritage', wanted to 'possess a true inner identity' more valuable than the merely external 'social persona'.

From the later Victorian years down to the First World War, Potts continues, the notion of 'race' and 'stock' was paramount in nationalism: 'Englishness was an essence residing in a race which was to be found in its purest form in the country, preserved by an honest and traditional way of life.' (A harmless version of such thinking is easily found in Massingham.) But in the inter-war period, 'a nationalist ideology of pure landscape' came into its own. Theories of racial identity were transferred to the inanimate landscape.

The new medium of photography was exploited by the wave of countryside books which followed H. V. Morton's best-selling *In Search of England* (1927). The camera, skilfully positioned at the right time, could produce images of extraordinarily trim, lush and fertile farmland 'set off by small controlled pockets of picturesque shrub and tree, excluding any implications of shabbiness or the unkempt'. This paradigmatic view of what the 'real England' was like supplanted, between the wars, 'Claudian parklands, Welsh mountains, and Derbyshire dales' – ousted, in fact, the dominant traditions of landscape painting in England since the eighteenth century, and even the authority of the great J. M. W. Turner. Victorian taste had favoured river, harbour and coastal scenes which could be made to look like old Dutch paintings, dramatic hill and mountain views, and plangently 'romantic' perspectives of desolate marshes, empty woods, cold winter afternoons.

Critics and artists in England in the twenties and thirties opened up an art-historical dead end and proclaimed it to be the highway of English landscape tradition. The work of late eighteenth-century and early nineteenth-century watercolourists, and their contemporary John Constable, was thus canonised, and gave a basis for emulation, in spirit if not in technique. 'English landscape' was brought down from Turneresque heights, and tamed. Its essence was located in the southern counties. The Blakeian visions of early nineteenth-century Sussex by Samuel Palmer also influenced some painters.[7]

J. B. Priestley, a city-bred northerner but a resident by choice of Deep England, was typically generous to the variety which actually characterises the island's scenery when he introduced a 'pictorial survey' by various hands called *The Beauty of Britain*, published in 1935. But he emphasised repeatedly the common characteristic of 'exquisite moderation'. There were genuine mountains in the Lake District, but you could climb two or three of them in a day. You could wander alone in the remoter parts of the Yorkshire Dales. 'Yet less than an hour in *a fast motor* will bring you to the middle of some manufacturing town *which can be left and forgotten just as easily as it can be reached* from these heights.' (My italics)

A car, he observes, 'will take you all round the Peak District in a morning. It is nothing but a crumpled green pocket handkerchief.' The essential English landscape 'looks like the result of one of those happy compromises that make our social and political plans so irrational and yet so successful. It has been born of a compromise between wildness and tameness, between Nature and Man.' Priestley goes on to discuss the suburb. There is a 'great deal to be said' for it. 'Nearly all Englishmen are at heart country gentlemen. The suburban villa enables the salesman or the clerk, out of hours, to be almost a country gentleman.' But 'against' the suburb, he has to say that suburbs 'eat into the countryside in the greediest fashion' and that it 'might be better if people who work in the cities were more mentally urban, more ready to identify themselves with the life of the city proper'. Having delivered himself of these rather dangerous remarks, he reverts to 'that exquisite balance between Nature and Man', and becomes ineffably nationalistic:

We see a cornfield and a cottage, both solid evidences of Man's presence. But notice how these things, in the middle of the scene, are surrounded by witnesses to that ancient England that was nearly all forest and heath. The fence and the gate are man-made, but are not severely regular and trim – as they would be in some other countries. The trees and hedges, the grass and wild flowers in the foreground, all suggest that Nature has not been dragooned into obedience. Even the cottage . . . looks nearly as much a piece of natural history as the trees: you feel it might have grown there. In some countries, that cottage would have been an uncompromising cube of brick which would have declared 'No nonsense now. Man, the drainer, the tiller, the builder, has settled here.' In this English scene there is no such direct opposition.[8]

Priestley, the socialist, gives this cottage no occupant, nor does he wonder about the size of the occupant's wage, nor ask if the cottage has internal sanitation and running water. His countryside exists only as spectacle, for the delectation of people with motor cars. Of course, he does not specify where this ideal cottage may actually be found outside paintings, nor name the foreign countries where no wild flowers (it seems) grow near the dwellings of agriculturalists. Had he been upbraided with these sins of omission, being a man of quick mind, warm heart and fluent pen he would of course have dashed off a piece welcoming the recent improvement in conditions for rural workers, or deploring their continued exploitation in some areas by the 'tied cottage' system. It is characteristic of this versatile circus artist, swinging from rope to ideological rope before jumping off to stand steady and erect on the back of some sturdy horse of cliché, from which he will proceed to defy a few tame ruling class lions, that he can harmonise every kind of contradiction into very readable 'Georgian' prose.

Priestley also wrote a foreword to *The Heart of England*, published by the same firm (Batsford) in the same year. The author, Ivor Brown, was a Scot. Priestley, the indefatigable light essayist, appears here not as Jolly Jack but as Grumpy Jack. Brown, as an outsider, is far too kind to suburbia, Priestley says – 'I do not see men and women of character emerging in any great numbers from this Americanised urban life' – and Brown flatters the English by dwelling upon their political good humour and tolerance which, Priestley avers, largely derive from mere apathy.

Brown himself is both tolerant and thoughtful. He is not uncritical of English suburbia – 'Far too many of the new "estates" are a welter of sham Tudor villas, without style or dignity of any kind.' He doesn't like the shortage of public buildings – public houses, even, are scarce. But he is kind about that way of life which involves the 'tiny garden', the 'midget' motor, the 'ubiquitous' radio, plus the tennis and clubs, bowling greens, evenings out at the cinema and occasional nights on the town.[9]

Brown's thoughtful, semi-detached appraisal of England reminds one at times of George Orwell, then a far more obscure writer. When I interviewed J. B. Priestley in the mid-sixties, he asked me, gloomily and rhetorically, why everyone now talked so much about 'this man Orwell'. '*I* said', he went on, 'everything that Orwell said, but people don't talk about *me*.' Priestley was in a sense correct: notions corresponding to most of Orwell's characteristic ideas can be found in one part or another of Priestley's enormous output. But Priestley never pulled them together into arguments and stories and images which people would find haunting. I offer this anecdote because one does indeed find a degree of consensus among numerous writers in the late thirties about the essence of the English character. It relates to the 'moderation' of the English landscape, as Priestley chose to regard it, and to the 'tolerance' which Brown, amongst others, associated with the character of Anglican religion, which, he argued, typified the capacity of 'the English mind' to 'accept foreign doctrine without becoming doctrinaire'.[10] An Anglican cleric, Dean Inge, in a volume of essays on *The English Genius* edited by Hugh Kingsmill which appeared in 1938, claimed that Christianity was stronger in Britain than in any other European country. Church attendance figures would have suggested otherwise, but for Inge they were immaterial: 'Ethically, we are still a Christian nation.' The 'typical Englishman' is 'humane', moved to 'violent indignation' by cruelty, 'stoic in repressing his feelings', contemptuous of those 'who give way to emotion'.

He is, by intention at least, just, and will not take an unfair advantage:

> 'Fair play' for him is a duty which should govern his conduct in almost every relation of life. Most of these principles are integral parts of the ideal of a gentleman, which is recognised everywhere as our chief contribution to ethics, and which is very far from being the standard of one class only.[11]

In a different book from this, I think I could show how the 'ideal of the gentleman' as a classless phenomenon was crystallised by a Scot, Samuel Smiles, in the aftermath of the Crimean War and in the interests of peace between the classes: Smiles stated polemically – and influentially – what was implicit in such novelistic creations as George Eliot's Adam Bede and Dickens's Joe Gargery. Priestley's idea, though, that every Englishman is a *country* gentleman at heart points to the importance of the village in so many presentations of 'Englishness'. The ideal village – it may be in Sussex, or in the Cotswolds, or in Jane Austen's Hampshire – contains a pleasant Anglican vicar, an affable squire, assorted professionals, tradesmen and craftsmen, many of whom will be 'characters', plus a complement of sturdy yeomen and agricultural workers learned in old country lore. It has a green, on which the village team plays cricket, with the squire or his son as captain. It has an annual flower show – this was one tradition which greatly moved H. J. Massingham because it was 'virtually the only survival of the communal village festivals that were older than the Feast of Flora' – and under 'the great marquee' rich and poor, 'natives and strangers' mingle in a reawakening of 'Gothic democracy'.[12]

P. G. Wodehouse, whose fictions (steadily aimed at the vast American market) must have powerfully influenced US perceptions of 'English character' between the wars, had a great deal of fun with the various elements of the ideal village. But the vision survived his parodistic games with it. Certainly there must have been villages which approximated closely to the ideal, if one overlooked rural slums, incest, and so on. American tourists can still, if so disposed, find places in Deep England which will cater for their fixed idea that the manorial village is 'typically English'; when Andalusian singing is offered to tourists in (Catalan) Mallorca as 'typically' Spanish, and 'Tudor' feasts are advertised in Edinburgh's Royal Mile, what is deemed 'typical' of anything can be created almost anywhere.

One of W. H. Auden's several distinctions was that he rudely rejected the notion of Deep England which had acquired a hold. He begins a poem of 1934:

> To settle in this village of the heart,
> My darling, can you bear it? True, the hall
> With its yews and famous dovecote is still there
> Just as in childhood, but the grand old couple
> Who loved us all so equally are dead;
> And now it is a licensed house for tourists,
> None too particular. One of the new
> Trunk roads passes the very door already,
> And the thin cafés spring up over night.

The sham ornamentation, the strident swimming pool,
The identical and townee smartness,
Will you really see as home . . . ?[13]

His verse of the thirties, while rarely preoccupied with landscape,
offers shocks to Georgian nature-tasters. From the top of the
Malvern Hills (Deep England is especially sacred here, haunted by
the shades of Langland and Elgar), Auden's speaker hears 'saxophones
. . . moaning for a comforter' and refers to the great west country
cathedrals as 'luxury liners laden with souls'. He admired instead the
dour scenery of the north, and in his 'Letter to Lord Byron' (1936)
mockingly extolled it, together with that of the Black Country, near
which he himself had been brought up:

> There on the old historic battlefield,
>   The cold ferocity of human wills,
> The scars of struggle are as yet unhealed;
>   Slattern the tenements on sombre hills,
>   And gaunt in valleys the square-windowed mills
> That, since the Georgian house, in my conjecture
> Remain our finest native architecture.
>
> On economic, health, or moral grounds
>   It hasn't got the least excuse to show;
> No more than chamber pots or otter hounds:
>   But let me say before it has to go,
>   It's the most lovely country that I know;
> Clearer than Scafell Pike, my heart has stamped on
> The view from Birmingham to Wolverhampton.
>
> Long, long ago, when I was only four,
>   Going towards my grandmother, the line
> Passed through a coal-field. From the corridor
>   I watched it pass with envy, thought 'How fine!
>   Oh how I wish that situation mine.'
> Tramlines and slagheaps, pieces of machinery,
> That was, and still is, my ideal scenery.[14]

Auden's spell-binding effect on his own generation of intellectuals is
well attested. His intellect seemed vast, his verse technique was
beyond question brilliant, and his revolt against the values of the
upper and middle classes was timely after the débâcle of the Great
War and in an era of novel political creeds which had in common the
intention of transforming society. His impact on the precocious

Benjamin Britten, some years his junior, is audible in the latter's cycle 'Our Hunting Fathers', which sets a poem by Auden and other verses chosen by Auden. First heard at the Norwich Festival in 1936, in one of the heartlands of squirearchical Deep England, it was deliberately intended to annoy the local gentry. (It also upset Britten's mother.) Auden had found a seventeenth-century hawking song. After the harvest, men fly birds at small creatures over the bare fields. One of the birds named is 'German', another 'Jew': Britten emphasises this. The English countryside is the scene of persecution.[15]

In another collaboration of that year, the two men worked on the famous documentary *Night Mail* for John Grierson's GPO Film Unit. Grierson, a Scot with a fervent belief in the educative potential of documentary film, had originally set up the Unit to serve the Empire Marketing Board. The Post Office had taken it over. Its reward was a string of remarkable films produced by a talented creative team of men (no women!) who included the experimental New Zealand artist Len Lye and the avant-garde Brazilian director Alberto Cavalcanti, as well as more conventional film-makers. Basil Wright and Harry Watt were in charge of *Night Mail*: Auden provided verses, Britten music.

Night Mail represents very well the counter-Georgian tendencies in the sensibility, at this time, of younger intellectuals. Its remit is to explain how letters are taken by train from London to Scotland. It gives an efficient account of the routines involved, using lightly dramatised documentary techniques, employing real postal workers to act themselves. The narrator's excitement mounts as, in the dark, the train enters the industrial north, a land of romance: Auden's famous verses finally take it over the Border into morning, and Scotland.

The documentaries supervised by Grierson, and those inspired more or less by his principles but executed outside his Unit, were not meant to be about England, Englishness, Britain and such matters. But they did develop approaches out of which wartime film-makers could create images serving to include dirty, decayed but vital industrial England in the overall image of the country for which men must fight and die. Other forces in English culture contributed, including the commercial cinema.

The anti-aesthetic character of northern industrial townscapes had been compounded by the effects of depression and mass unemployment. Not all of Deep England got off lightly, but fresh prosperity came to much of the south-east in the thirties with the new 'light industries' and the suburban life-style to which their products related. Over large areas of the north (and Wales, and Scotland) unemployment reached catastrophic heights and remained very high as the depression receded. Since its results were very often, for individuals, emigration or demoralisation, it was not the seedbed of revolution which leftists thought it should be. The 'national' coalition put together in 1931 won comfortably in the 1935 election: it was utterly dominated by the Conservative Party. However, the conditions prevailing in the north had awkward implications for the social cohesion of Britain and its governability. Sympathy for 'northern hunger marchers' was by no means confined to Communists and socialists.

Hence the commercial film *Sing As We Go*, directed by Basil Dean and released in 1934, has a significant place in cultural history. It is based on a story by – who else? – J. B. Priestley, the master harmoniser of social discords. It stars Gracie Fields, the very popular Lancashire singer. At its beginning, the closure of a cotton mill in Lancashire throws out of work not only Gracie but Hugh, the manager's son. Gracie leads the dismissed workforce out of the mill with linked arms, with a chorus of the film's title song. Gracie then goes to Blackpool, the great holiday resort of the era, in search of seasonal employment, gets into a variety of amusing situations, but is on hand to lead the workers back in when the mill, thanks to a wonderful technological innovation, is enabled to reopen. The film's ideological import is transparent: the unemployed can still be cheery, find other jobs, have fun; the management are really on their side; and somehow everything will come right in the end. But it pioneers in giving a lively and positive character to the industrial workforce and its female members and in providing a voice (however unconvincing now) in the cinema to the north: Launder and Gilliatt's *Millions Like Us* (1943), about 'mobile women' conscripted into 'war industry', is a weightier movie by far but probably owes something to Gracie's precedent.

Meanwhile, the conscience of intellectuals from the public-school and Oxbridge-educated professional classes had been stirred by the plight of the mysterious industrial north. Old Etonian George Orwell's *Road to Wigan Pier* was by far his most successful book before *Animal Farm*; its documentary account of life in a coal-mining area played on the guilt of Left Book Club members. Likewise, Tom Harrisson, a Harrow-and-Cambridge product, returned from living on a South Sea Island with people whom he chose to present as 'cannibals' with the conviction that he was an 'anthropologist', and proceeded to Bolton, Lancashire, to dwell with the natives there and survey their strange customs. His project came under the aegis of Mass-Observation, which Harrisson founded, together with the poet Charles Madge and the latter's friend Humphrey Jennings, early in 1937. Some dozens of students, writers and artists went north for longer or shorter periods to work with Harrisson in Bolton. It may seem absurd to suggest that places like Manchester and Leeds, intensely and justifiably proud of their own local traditions and their place in national life and history, needed to be brought into the mainstream of consciousness of English identity by young Oxbridge types who thought you could observe northerners as you did birds or New Hebrideans. But northern businessmen, trade unionists and local historians did not manage the BBC or the Ministry of Information or film propaganda: Oxbridge graduates did.

Auden himself left for the United States before war started and made it clear that he had no intention of coming back. But his close friends MacNeice and Britten, who were also in the States, returned (though Britten, as a pacifist, could not express his love for his native land very actively). It was a favourite right-wing *canard* of the early war years to imply that Auden's 'cowardice' and lack of patriotism typified those who had looked to him for leadership: it was, in fact, from his followers that he had fled, disliking his own position as artistic–political guru. In practice, the intellectuals who had identified themselves as anti-fascist by supporting Republican Spain, preponderantly got over their pacifistic or Leninist qualms and served the British war effort with conviction.

Such experimental tendencies in thirties artistic production as literary documentary, *vox pop.* radio, socialist pageantry, and even surrealism, adapted perfectly well to the service of the war effort, while Marxist scientists did very valuable war work.

Tendencies in painting in the thirties are of interest here. British art had seemed to 'lag behind' exciting developments on the Continent. In 1933 the distinguished painter Paul Nash (1889–1946) led a short-lived group, Unit 1, which gathered together the sculptors Moore and Hepworth and the painter Ben Nicholson along with others interested in abstraction in art and 'un-English' ideas. These people were actually drawn to different foreign ideas: while Nicholson's work related to the constructivists, Nash was attracted towards surrealism. A younger generation developing in a climate much affected by Marxism would gravitate towards neo-realism. There was a lot of life in avant-garde British painting at this time; it was very diverse, and generalisations hardly convey it.

However, transactions between avant garde artists and 'landscape' are worth exploring even at the cost of excessive generalisation, such as we might complain of in Ian Jeffrey's summary:

During the nineteen twenties, while memories of the Great War were still vivid, artists and writers envisioned Britain sometimes as a pastoral haven and sometimes as a multi-coloured pleasure garden. They continued to do so during the 1930s, although at the same time new images of landscape were established: in these the countryside increasingly featured as an orderly worked terrain of farmland and quarry.

Jeffrey detects a sense of retrospective threat in landscape depictions: the nightmare of the Great – and mechanised – War was associated with a loathing of the industrial Midlands and north and fear of modernisation.[16] Yet Nash – whose own images of the disaster of 1914–18 had been as powerful as any – was one of those attracted, in spite of the general tendency, towards modernist forms.

There was a market for representations of England-as-idyll such as Alfred Munnings provided. There was also a market for bold poster art. Smoothed and refined modernist forms suited the selling of cars, cigarettes and other items associated with the 'fast' life-style of the well-to-do.

The success of E. McKnight Kauffer as a poster artist showed that such commercial work could be not only lively but somehow distinguished. The Shell Oil company, fuelling the new motor vehicles, had a corporate problem of conscience and a potential 'image' problem: cars and lorries destroyed the purportedly idyllic peace of Deep England, a point long mythologised in Grahame's ever popular *Wind In The Willows*, where the outrageous Toad goes poop-poop here and there in an automobile.

Shell in 1930 announced that it would not advertise on roadside hoardings, and was duly praised for its stand by a leading arbiter of taste, Clough Williams Ellis. The company commissioned from serious artists bills to be stuck on lorries, with such legends as 'Everywhere You Go You Can be Sure of Shell', and 'See Britain First on Shell'. These depicted English 'beauty spots'. Thus Kauffer drew 'Stonehenge' – and Paul Nash painted 'Rye Marshes'. Ben Nicholson and Graham Sutherland were other avant-garde artists who contributed posters.[17]

In 1934, the company launched a series of *Shell Guides* to the English counties, with the poet John Betjeman as general editor. These provided further opportunities for artists: Paul Nash worked on *Dorset* (1935), John Piper on *Oxfordshire* (1938). Piper was at that time, conspicuously, involved in abstract painting. Charles Harrison has deduced that from the mid-thirties Piper was preoccupied with 'finding means to make the technical mannerisms of Modernist painting serve a fashionable interest in picturesque architectural detail or "gothick" landscapes'.[18] Commissioned as an official war artist in 1940, he served by producing images of bombed churches in London, Coventry, Bristol and of the blitzed interior of the House of Commons. His war work would also include landscapes and pictures of intact country houses.

Nash, a far weightier artist, reconciled the attraction of English landscape with those of abstraction and surrealism. Certain prehistoric sites in Wiltshire where stone circles could still be seen offered shapes which were 'naturally' like forms favoured by modernists. Discovery of them in 1933 led Nash to embark on a series of paintings which presented Deep England at its deepest. His interest in continental surrealism flavoured such work after a time, but English landscape remained a recognisable presence in it. His dreamlike image from 1940, of an English sky crossed with the vapour trails of fighters, executed as an official war artist, is one example among many demonstrating that 'surreal' imaginings of the thirties had literal counterparts in 1940. What could be more 'surreal', for instance, than a blitzed, eviscerated bourgeois dwelling with a bloated barrage balloon floating above it?

By 1940, then, both Georgian and avant-garde currents in English culture had provided ample verbal and visual materials from which Myth could be swiftly fashioned. To enhance them, there was distinctively 'English' music available, thanks to the rise of a nationalist school. Though Elgar's style was heavily influenced by German music, marches and other pieces by him were well known and readily identified as patriotic. Parry, in 1916, had set William Blake's poem 'Jerusalem' for the 'Fight for Right' organisation: the aim was to stiffen resolve among the public against the temptation of a 'premature peace'. By 1924 a musical dictionary could refer to it as a 'new National Anthem'. It was taken up by the Women's Institutes in 1924 – but also by the Woodcraft Folk a few years later: these were the Co-operative Movement's socialist counterpart of Baden Powell's imperialistic Boy Scouts. Meanwhile, Vaughan Williams, a most patriotic Englishman in spite of his Welsh name, had developed an idiom which could accommodate in modern orchestral works elements derived from the English past which appeared to give them a uniquely English flavour: the music produced in the era of the Tudors, who though (or because) Welsh seemed most Deeply English of all dynasties; and the tunes which he and others had discovered in the 'folk-song revival' of the turn of the century. 'Greensleeves' or 'Jerusalem', or a snatch from Elgar's 'Pomp and

Circumstance' marches, or the tune of a 'folk-song' much used in schools could instantly signify 'England' on a sound track.[19]

By the time war broke out in September 1939 the myth of the Blitz had been all but scripted. We can see this in the GPO Film Unit's early war effort *The First Days* (1939), written by Robert Sinclair and using four of the Unit's directors – Cavalcanti, Harry Watt, Pat Jackson and Humphrey Jennings.

This film claims to give 'a picture of the London Front'. No bombardment from the air had occurred, of course. But as the first air-raid *warning* sounds Londoners file calmly into shelters. The friendliness of air-raid wardens is emphasised, used to point to a general phenomenon. 'Friendliness – It has become the war-time equipment of all Londoners.' A dramatised exchange of talk between strangers in a shelter follows.

This is a volunteers' front. 'Filling sandbags is everybody's business', and volunteers from both damp basements and luxury flats Go To It. A generation of young men reared to despise the 'bogus romance of the battlefield' are going into uniform 'willingly'. In the East End, the Cockney Spirit is rampant – here is a 'patient world, of adaptability and enterprise'. Nurses are knitting in hospital, waiting for casualties . . .

This 'front' is a 'civilian front' dominated by the 'Cockney voice of London'. The city's people are famous all over the world. 'This is not twilight that has come to England, it is dawn, and dawn we hope for more than England.'

The Myth is ready, like raw pizza dough. It won't take long to cook once spicy ingredients are arranged on it. When J. B. Priestley makes *Britain at Bay* with the GPO Film Unit for the Ministry of Information, in the summer of 1940, he has fresh flavours to hand.

The Americans will see this one. They respond to History. We begin with waves breaking on a beach (the island race), move on to Deep English shots of haymaking: 'For nearly a thousand years these fields . . . have been free from foreign invasion.' Cutting to scenes from industrial towns, we point out that at least 'they are ours'. Near even the blackest towns, we say, there was always lonely peaceful countryside – until this war came. Shots of Germans drilling, Germans invading other countries, refugees on French roads, accompany an attack by Priestley on the Nazis. 'This has left Britain alone, at bay', he says as we return to the White Cliffs of Dover. 'The future of the whole civilised world rests on the defence of Britain', by the armed services, and 'by all of us'. Shots follow of people 'hurrying to man this island fortress', factory workers drilling as

Home Guard, ARP men in action. The *voluntary* nature of such effort is stressed. The script finally quotes Churchill – 'We shall fight on the beaches.'

A structural feature of the Myth is emerging. Perhaps two columns of opposites will clarify it:

England (Britain)	Germany
Freedom	Tyranny
Improvisation	Calculation
Volunteer spirit	Drilling
Friendliness	Brutality
Tolerance	Persecution
Timeless landscape	Mechanisation
Patience	Aggression
Calm	Frenzy
A thousand years of peace	The 'Thousand-Year Reich' dedicated to war

It will be seen that each presumed characteristic of the Germans is (and has to be) opposed by a strong English opposite. A penalty is involved. The English, conquerors of a vast empire, famous once all over Europe for the violence of their politics, the clarity of their philosophical thought and their innovations in business and technology, must now be portrayed as gentle, pacific until provoked, and temperamentally at odds with merely rational thinking, with careful organisation, and with new-fangled machines. They fight not for their own Empire, their own interests, but for freedom all over the world. Spitfire pilots will help to give a more positive, warlike air to this self-image, but even they will be engaged in defensive action.

While Churchill's matchless rhetoric could help sustain a will towards the aggression necessary to win the war, there is implicit in the developing Myth an understanding that England will be fully itself under a new, peacetime dispensation, in which qualities of friendliness and co-operative assistance, emphasised in war, will determine peacetime social relationships. So Priestley, as intimate Sunday-night broadcaster, has the difficult job of sustaining such hopes without creating frustration and, indeed, a yearning for peace.

In his autobiography, published in 1962, Priestley was not very forthcoming about his activities as propagandist in 1940. Rather characteristically, he says that his broadcasts to the British people were ridiculously overpraised in such a way as to nudge one to suppose that his unpublished and, at home, unsung broadcasts to the

USA must have been quite something. The overseas broadcasts, he states firmly, were his 'chief task on the air'. He broadcast several times a week, always late at night, 'to America, the Dominions, and in fact through recordings transmitted every hour or so, to all parts of the world where English was understood'. He had a gratifying postbag from Canada and Australia in particular. The call to give an extra Blitz broadcast to Canada saved his life in September 1940 when the section of the Langham Hotel, by Broadcasting House, where he would have been sleeping was 'sliced off by a bomb'.[20]

The BBC initiated a series of 'Postscripts' to the nine p.m. News, in which well-known speakers were to explain events in a reasonable way, admitting British shortcomings and avoiding 'exaggerated propaganda'. Priestley was brought in during the Dunkirk crisis because the Corporation, worried about lower-class morale, wanted a 'contrast in voice, upbringing and outlook' to the public-school educated RP speakers who dominated the airwaves. He was first given the Postscript slot on the Wednesday after the evacuation from Dunkirk was completed; thereafter, he occupied it frequently over several months, usually on Sundays: a total of nineteen broadcasts between 5 June and 20 October. His audience averaged 31 per cent of the adult population over this period, and he received 1,600 letters from members of the public.[21]

Home Intelligence's Weekly Report no. 5, for 11 November, remarked: 'From a great number of sources there are reports of strong feelings because J. B. Priestley's broadcasts have stopped. His views on social reform appear to be shared by the great majority.'[22] However, they inflamed an influential minority in the Conservative Party to great rage. His first sequence of Postscripts ended at his own request: he was, understandably, very tired. In November, he made it clear that he wanted to come back with a series of talks which would be more or less overtly 'political'. The press had widely deplored his absence from the air. Even Graham Greene, who had produced a satirical portrait of him (as 'Savory') in a pre-war novel, wrote in the *Spectator*, 'For those dangerous months when the Gestapo arrived in Paris he was unmistakeably a great man.' But when he reappeared after the Sunday News on 26 January 1941, a deputation from the 1922 Committee of Tory back-bench MPs protested to the Minister of Information, and Churchill himself complained that Priestley's views on 'war aims' differed from his own. Priestley after this broadcast received 1,000 appreciative letters and 200 which were critical. As the series proceeded, BBC listener research showed that one of the Postscripts was approved by seventeen listeners out of twenty. After eight Postscripts, Priestley was taken off and replaced by the lively, independent-minded but right-wing A. P. Herbert. He refused to come back later to do 'occasional' Postscripts and it was widely assumed that he had been banned from the air.[23]

The very strong right-wing reaction against Priestley's 1941 broadcasts highlights the contrasting fact that in the summer of 1940 he wasn't thought to be more 'controversial' than other broadcasters. The public for his novels and plays – a very large one – was certainly for the most part middle class. His credentials as a sturdy patriot had been established by his popular travelogue of 1934, *English Journey*, and various celebrations of English landscape and character since then.

His Yorkshire vowels probably were, for many working-class listeners, a relief from 'posh' voices on the airwaves; but plenty of people shared them whose views were far to the right of his, and they cannot have been the sole or even main cause of his success. Taking his own word for it, though, it may be that features of his Bradford upbringing had helped make him a plausible 'voice of the people'.

Priestley's family had a tradition of manual work in Bradford's woollen industry, but his father had become a teacher. His father's political stance, as a member of the Independent Labour Party, meant that Priestley was exposed to a brand of socialism motivated by intense ethical concerns and indifferent to Marxist analysis. He was to remember it as 'liberalism with the starch left out'. In retrospect, the Bradford community was one 'where to a youngster the social hierarchy was invisible'. The wealthy owners of the mills did not live in the town and if they had come back, Priestley believed 'a lot of men wearing cloth caps and mufflers would still have called them Sam and Joe'.[24]

Priestley's impatience with theoretical socialism and his inbred egalitarianism were associated with a passionate nostalgia for the Edwardian England of his boyhood. The Myth of a Golden Age of peaceful, golden afternoons can be found elsewhere among writers of Priestley's generation – in the elegant prose about cricket and music by another northerner, Neville Cardus, and in certain passages by George Orwell. It exists in obverse to the horror of the Great War trenches: before, innocence; after, disillusion. Priestley served in the army in France and barely survived. He did not write poetry or fiction about this experience: in his memoirs, he emphasises the fact that it instilled 'class feeling' into him – bitterness against the 'boneheaded' officer class which had killed his friends by its sheer stupidity. Though he became a wealthy professional writer and lived by choice in hierarchical Deep England, rarely returning to his native West Riding, a heartfelt animus against Conservative upper- and upper-middle-class elements would give his political utterances bite.

However, the notes struck in his famous Dunkirk Postscript were calm and national pride, the two reinforcing each other: 'Now that it's over, and we can look back on it, doesn't it seem to you to have an inevitable air about it – as if we had turned a page in the history of Britain and seen a chapter headed "Dunkirk" . . .?' 'Nothing', he said, 'could be more English than this Battle of Dunkirk, both in its beginning and its end, its folly and its grandeur. It was very English in what was sadly wrong with it . . . But having admitted this much, let's do ourselves the justice of admitting too that this Dunkirk affair was also very English (and when I say "English" I really mean British) in the way in which, when apparently all was lost, so much was gloriously retrieved.' The Germans couldn't have achieved such an epic – 'That vast machine of theirs can't create a glimmer of that poetry of action which distinguishes war from mass murder. It's a machine – and therefore has no soul.'

The opposition of British improvisation and inspiration to German calculation and mechanisation was to be integral to the Myth. The navy's use of pleasure steamers to bring the British Expeditionary Force home was a gift to Priestley, the celebrator in fiction of innocent fun of the fair, music halls, seaside concerts. So was the fact that one of them was called the *Gracie Fields*, which enabled him to imply that the industrial north, whence Gracie the woman came, was involved in spirit in this south-eastern operation.[25]

Priestley's next Postscript, on Sunday 9 June, worked the oppositions of the adolescent Myth with sturdy, definitive simplicity. The loveliest spring and summer weather in memory – 'I'll swear the very birds have sung this year as they never did before'; 'twinkling beeches and the stately nodding elms' in the south of England countryside around Priestley's home; 'the round green hills dissolving into the hazy blue of the sky'. Remembering the terrible war news. Imagining the 'peaceful and lovely' English scene torn apart 'to reveal the old Flanders Front, trenches and bomb craters, ruined towns, a scarred countryside, a sky belching death, and the faces of murdered children'. Reminding himself that the landscape 'was there long before the Germans went mad, and will be there when that madness is only remembered as an old nightmare'. The anti-German invective which follows is, like so much in these broadcasts, a model for later writers. Simply and vividly, without grandiose phrases or obvious rhetoric, it characterises the German machine:

perhaps at this very moment, *thin-lipped and cold-eyed* Nazi staff officers are planning, with that mixture of *method and lunacy* which is all their own, how to project on to this countryside of ours those half-doped crazy lads they call parachute troops. This land that is ours, that appeals to us now in all its beauty, is at this moment only just outside the reach of these *self-tormenting schemers* and their millions who are used as if they were *not human beings but automata*, robots, mere 'things'. They drop them from planes as if they were *merely bombs with arms and legs*. They send them swarming forward in battle as if they were not fellow-men but death-dealing dolls, manufactured in Goering's factories. (My italics)

Priestley goes on to contrast a German propaganda film, *Baptism of Fire*, about the invasion of Poland, with the British film *The Lion Has Wings*: 'Our film didn't take itself too solemnly', but the German one had 'not a glimmer of humour or fun, or ordinary human relationships. It's all machines and robot stuff.' And of course such lack of humanity in them ensures that the Nazis will lose. 'What they don't understand . . . is that men also have their hour of greatness, when weakness suddenly towers into strength; when ordinary easy-going tolerant men rise up in their anger and strike down evil like the angels of the wrath of God.'[26]

This would become a staple of formal and unofficial British propaganda. Compare the conclusion of John Strachey's *Post D*, published by Gollancz in 1941, a moving, lightly fictionalised account of the author's experiences as an air-raid warden in London. At the end, Ford, Strachey's third-person version of himself, writes 'a sort of invocation to Hitler': 'Pay attention, Hitler. You have scattered the nations; you have easily deceived the statesmen, the generals, the bankers, the diplomatists.' But now Hitler is up against 'a different kind of people':

You have encountered the unemphatic and the unassuming. It is not that they have done anything, nor ever can do anything, that you need fear − except one thing; they have survived. They have had the temerity to survive your bombs. Moreover, and this is serious for you, they have become not less, but more, themselves. They have become less, not more, like you: they have become less, not more, neurotic, unbalanced, fierce, cruel and suspicious . . . Make haste, or their quietness will echo round the world; their amusement will dissolve Empires; their ordinariness will become a flag; their kindness a rock, and their courage an avalanche. Make haste. Blot them out, if you can.[27]

Strachey's rhetoric was certainly directed at US opinion – his book was published in America as *Digging for Mrs Miller* – at a time when that had to be convinced that Britain could and would fight on though no decisive counter-offensive against the Germans was possible. But the British themselves had to be convinced that they could not only survive, but win. And Priestley's message of June 1940 – that the Nazis were *incapable* of conquering British humanity and British humour, linked to the immemorial properties of the English landscape (as, later, they would be to London's long and proud history) – was a crucial complement to Churchill's ringing calls for heroism on the part of every man, woman and child. People might very well doubt if they were capable of heroism. But most could feel that they shared in such invincible 'national traits' as fairmindedness, kindness and 'sense of humour'.

Priestley's broadcast of 16 June took up a topic which would tickle that sense of humour for decades: he describes his first outing with the Local Defence Volunteers, not yet renamed the Home Guard. He cannot yet acknowledge on the air the most comic feature of this force – its near-total lack of martial equipment. Rather, he makes the group, with its 'cross section of English rural life', typify Deep England: 'Even the rarer and fast disappearing rural trades were represented – for we had a hurdle-maker there; and his presence, together with that of a woodman and a shepherd, made me feel sometimes that I'd wandered into one of those rich chapters of Thomas Hardy's fiction in which his rustics meet in the gathering darkness on some Wessex hill.' The phlegmatic calm of these rustics – 'simple but sane men' – derives from immemorial habit: the countryman 'sees this raiding and invading as the latest manifestation of that everlasting menace which he always has to fight – sudden blizzards at lambing time, or floods just before the harvest'. The situation really is frightening – these homes in the valley below where 'our womenfolk' knit as they listen to the news might be bombed at any moment. Searchlights are seen, sirens heard, from 'our two nearest towns' – bombs, gunfire. But after the All Clear Priestley feels, he says, 'a powerful and rewarding sense of community; and with it too a feeling of deep continuity'. He ends by reciting Hardy's 'In Time of the Breaking of Nations'.[28]

The left-leaning politics which begin to feature in Priestley's scripts from 23 June onwards are therefore soaked in traditionalist values. The Nazis represent modern corruption – 'the darkening despair of our modern world, shaping itself into one vast dark face – a German dark face . . .' In any country falling under their domination – by implication, even in Britain – there will be kindred elements ready to collaborate: 'Let the Nazis in, and you will find that the laziest loudmouth in the workshop has suddenly been given power to kick you up and down the street . . .'[29]

On 30 June, he complains that the war isn't being fought in the right spirit by the nation's rulers: 'Sometimes I feel that you and I – all of us ordinary people – are on one side of a high fence, and on the other side of this fence, under a buzzing cloud of secretaries, are the official and important personages: the pundits and mandarins of the Fifth Button! and now and then a head appears above the fence and tells us to carry our gas masks, look to our blackouts, do this and attend to that.' The war shouldn't be so dreary: 'I'd have bands playing everywhere, and flags flying, and as much swagger and glamour as the moment will stand.' The British are 'still, as we always have been, at heart an imaginative and romantic people'. The bureaucrats – 'Complacent Clarence, Hush-Hush Harold, and Dubious Departmental Desmond' – are contrasted with 'Two Ton Annie', evacuated from a mainland hospital to the Isle of Wight, where Priestley lived, at the outbreak of war: a fat, sick woman, but an 'indomitable lioness' roaring out repartee 'like a raffish old empress'.[30]

'Two Ton Annie' and the rustics in the Local Defence Volunteers preluded a string of cheerful images: a duck and her ducklings on a pond in Hampstead Heath late at night – she has asked no bureaucrat's permission to be there, and is mentioned to represent the 'creative energy' which opposes Nazi 'death worship'; Churchill digs Bevin in the ribs in the House of Commons – the two halves of the English people and English history, aristocrat and working man, sit side by side; then, after a week of heavy bombing on London, 'the Dome and Cross of St Paul's, silhouetted in sharpest black against the red flames and orange flames . . . like an enduring symbol of reason and Christian ethics . . .', while the Cockney spirit of Dickens's Sam Weller burgeons. A giant pie, there ever since Priestley can remember, is still to be seen through the boarded-up window of a bomb-damaged shop in Bradford, 'every puff and jet' defying 'Hitler, Goering and the whole gang of them'.[31]

Priestley's gift for bringing big ideas together with homely examples is well exemplified by his Postscript for 11 August. It begins:

The other day I saw two thousand people push aside what remained of the meat pies and fried plaice and chips they'd had for lunch, lift their eyes and ears towards an orchestra consisting of four young women in green silk, and then, all two thousand of them, roar out: 'Oh Johnny, Oh Johnny, How You Can Love'. And having paid this tribute to Johnny and applauded the four young women in green silk, these two thousand people, who were mostly young and feminine, and very natty in their coloured overalls, returned – much heartened – to another five or six hours' work at their machines.

He goes on to describe a 'grimmer, more masculine' engineering works nearby where men attend machines for 'ten to eleven hours a day', then 'rapturously' listen to a small concert party, 'The Night Howls', telling old jokes. Such tribute to these contributions to gaiety and relaxation by Basil Dean's ENSA organisation, 'joining songs and high jinks to hard work', establishes Priestley's non-élitist stance. But the government should go further, to sponsor 'great symphony orchestras peeling out the noblest music, night after night, not for a fortunate and privileged few, but for all the people who long for such music'. As well as 'comedians in the canteens' there should be productions of great plays. The 'quality of our life' should be raised. 'No burden, it seems, is too great for the people. Then there can't be too rich and great a reward for the people.'[32]

What Priestley is implicitly advocating is the systematic state support for the 'high' cultural forms which would indeed begin during the war and eventuate in the creation of the Arts Council of Great Britain. The 'politics' of Priestley's broadcasts were non-partisan, as he hotly insisted. But their left-ward impulse was all the more insidious for being expressed so commonsensically, without clichés or jargon. The war is an episode in the 'breakdown of one vast system and the building up of a better one', in which 'ordinary decent folk can find not only justice and security but also beauty and delight'. The 'change from property to community' is implicit in the united struggle against Hitler. Why shouldn't 'working men' take over the gardens of rich people who have fled to America? The young men fighting unselfishly for everyone in the RAF deserve job security after the war and Priestley takes from his postbag the views of one of them, a former salesman, who doesn't want to go back to the 'old business life', with its cut-throat competition, after the co-operation and the spirit of 'giving' he has experienced in the Force. Nazism is conflated with greed, privilege and 'despair' – 'hope' is found in communitarian values, which flourish already everywhere in Britain 'among the decent common folk'. All that is needed to bring about a just society is the active involvement of such 'folk' in running their own lives, through a revitalised democracy.[33]

Alderman Roberts of Grantham and his daughter Margaret Hilda can hardly have been among Priestley's horde of admirers. But the demotion of 'free enterprise' in favour of communitarianism was always latent in the Myth's structure, in its basis in opposition of 'English' (or 'British') values to those attributed to Nazism. That Conservative ministers, with support from press magnates, elements of 'high society' and business interests, had 'appeased' the 'Nazi bullies' was another major reason why the developing Myth often assumed a radical, socialistic character.

It could however be given a right-wing, imperialistic character, and its anchorage in English landscape and English history made this quite easy. Arthur Mee, the evangelical Christian imperialist who edited the *Children's Newspaper*, brought out a collection of his own articles – *Nineteen Forty: Our Finest Hour* – which received four printings between January 1941 and March 1942. The style is coarse and strident, whereas Priestley's is thoughtful and calm, but the sentiments are often very similar (note, in the quotation which follows, another example of the phrase 'thousand years'):

It is not in parliaments that this country is herself; her spirit lives in her deep silences, in her little hills and dales. It lives in those enchanting haunts where William Blake strolled piping down the valley wild and John Wesley rode on horseback talking to the people on the village greens. Here Peace has made her home for a thousand years and here it seems as if nothing could break the spell of the little island with its far-flung power.

Only the words 'far-flung power' involve un-Priestley-esque sentiment. Under the spell of his own rhetoric, the Christian Mee, in an article called 'It Will Never Be The Same Again', sounds as socialistic as Priestley:

the thought that we are not as others, the willingness to die rich while so many live poor, the reluctance to bear our share of the burdens, the scorn for those who seek to improve their lot, the belief that some are born to toil and some to rule, the idea that wealth gives rights and that those with power can use it as they please – all these must die in that new world which is now being shaped in the furnace of sacrifice and suffering and death.[34]

Nevertheless, in the same year Mee published his *Book of the Flag: Island and Empire*, aimed at a youthful readership and replete with ineffable boasting. All the good things in the modern world (including, bizarrely, 'The Monroe Doctrine which has made America safe for democracy') can be attributed to 'the most successful colonisers the world has known' – not least 'the idea of playing games, especially cricket which has in it the core of something which cannot live with narrowness and pettiness and selfishness. We have led the way with gardens, one of the chief sources of human delight.' Mee even seeks to convince his readers of the 'wonderful' fact that England is set exactly 'in the middle of the earth' – this is apparent, he alleges, if we take a globe of the world. England is 'a place of hope and refuge for the race of men, a central shining beacon on the earth. Freedom's Own Island, yes, but Nature's too.' Her 'green carpet is the loveliest in the world. Her rivers flow through the fairest landscapes. Her little lanes bring us to scenes unmatched in any country in the world.' A five-page aerial survey of the island includes nine lines about Scotland, less than one line about Wales . . . [35]

It is a relief to turn from such outpourings to the *Dandy Monster Comic* annual for 1941, where there is just one strip referring to the war. Desperate Dan, that unshaven cowboy and eater of cow pie who lives in a terrain more like lowland Scotland than Texas, tries to knit himself a jumper out of wires using telephone poles as needles. Inadvertently, he creates a chain, which he agrees to sell to a sea captain who needs it for his anchor. When Dan throws it to the boat, it sinks. He fishes it out, holds it upside down to empty the water out, throws it back into the sea – where a U Boat sinks it. Using his chain as a lasso, Dan hauls ashore not only the British boat but no fewer than three U Boats. A naval gentleman, observing this, gives him a £50 reward. 'Frizzle mine Aunt Von Fanny, Danny der Desperate has our goose cooked', says a German submariner. Dan remarks, 'I guess old Addie will feel pretty sick over this.' [36] Mee, fortunately, was not without competitors in the juvenile market.

Radio propaganda could no more credibly employ Mee's nationalistic ego than it could revel in biff-bang comic heroics. One of Priestley's most significant colleagues among broadcasters to the USA was Leslie Howard, very well known as a star of the prodigiously successful *Gone With The Wind*. Leslie Howard Steiner (1893–1943) was the son of a Hungarian Jewish immigrant, but returned to England when he could have lived safely and lucratively in the USA, and made himself more than useful to the national effort as broadcaster and film-maker until German fighters, probably directed to destroy him personally, hit the plane in which he was travelling over the Bay of Biscay on his way back from a lecture tour in Spain and Portugal.

Howard was certainly not identified with left-wing ideas, but his one Postscript for the British audience received a significantly more favourable response, according to BBC listener research, from working-class than middle-class people. He directed and starred in the feature films *Pimpernel Smith* (1941) and *The First of the Few* (this latter about the 'boffin' R. H. Mitchell who had designed the Spitfire but had died before the war). Both were enormous box office successes, both developed elements of the Myth. In both, Howard, remarkably, played an *intellectual*, with heroic, even romantic qualities. With his blond good-looks, pleasantly cultivated accent, dry humour and rather absentminded air, Howard's screen image could merge the typical Englishman with the typical intellectual. As Aldgate and Richards remark in their survey of British Second World War cinema, with his 'dreamy, other worldly air' he represented the 'visionary aspect of Englishness', suggested by the music of Elgar and Vaughan Williams, and apparently seen in action in the persons of such eccentric heroes as Lawrence of Arabia and Orde Wingate.[37]

In *Pimpernel Smith* Howard plays an Oxford archaeology professor with a secret life: he rescues anti-Nazis from pre-war Germany – artists, intellectuals, scientists. His courage and gentle humour go along with the message that England is fighting to save *civilisation*, high culture, intellect. According to one set of rankings, Howard rose from being the nineteenth most popular British star in 1940, to the second by 1942. Meanwhile, the London *Daily Mail* in July 1940 had described him as 'Number 2 public speaker to J. B. Priestley in the overseas service'. The BBC valued his 'great success in the American transmission' very highly – when Priestley dropped his transatlantic broadcasting in the autumn of 1940, Howard's going on seemed 'particularly important'. Between 16 July 1940 and 7 August 1941, he gave twenty-two talks on the North American Service.

He knew the USA very well, and stressed to listeners there that he had spent 'most of his adult life' in their country. He described for them a Battle of Britain airfield, the work of the Observer Corps, the maintenance of 'business as usual' in London, frankly (as it were) raising question of the extent to which his own talks were propaganda. The British, he said, were very bad at propaganda, and took it up only 'cautiously, politely and with a painstaking rectitude'.

He was an appropriate person, vaguely aristocratic as his screen image was, to grasp the thorny problem of US dislike of British class distinctions as represented by such institutions as the monarchy, the House of Lords and Oxbridge. Britain was democratic, he explained

over the air in mid-August 1940, but he defied anyone to prove this –
'for it is a paradox, and our constitution is not a document like that of
the United States, it is simply an instinct in the minds of the English,
an instinct which governs their laws, their institutions and their
behaviour'. He insisted in other broadcasts that Britain shared in the
principles of the US Declaration of Independence and Lincoln's
Gettysburg Address. The principle of *tolerance*, which Britain stood
for, was 'one form of that freedom for which the Greeks fought at
Marathon, and Bruce's Scots at Bannockburn, and Elizabeth's
English in the Channel and the French at Valmy, and the American
colonists at Saratoga'.

So the English, or British, in their own special way, stand for the
universal spirit of liberty. Pressing this point – and he seems to have
made such points seem convincing – Howard abdicates, as it were,
on behalf of his countrymen, the purportedly moral rule of Empire.
Paradoxically, English institutions somehow represent the spirit of
Scots, and of French and American revolutionaries, who fought
against English power. This may have some kind of emotional
coherence, but intellectually it is hardly convincing. Paradoxically,
the man who was so good at playing English intellectuals expresses
to US listeners a mystical, anti-intellectual, conception of English
character. The English are marked, he tells them in mid-October
1940, by:

> qualities of courage, devotion to duty, kindliness, humour, cool-
> headedness, balance, commonsense, singleness of purpose. But
> there is a master quality which motivates and shines through all
> these – that of idealism. Mind you, you have to be smart to spot it.
> The English do their best to conceal it, and they succeed pretty
> well . . . In my case it is the Englishman in me that is able to
> unearth it and the American in me that is able to stand off and
> marvel at it.[38]

Freed from its usual validating links with Deep English landscape,
team games and flower shows, we have here, surely, the wholly
ineffable concept of Englishness at the heart of the Myth: distillation
of the post-Smilesian concept of the Gentleman.

It is as elusive as the relationship between English nationalist music
and English landscape: you *feel* that if you are English, to adapt
Howard; you *recognise* it if you're not. Concluding this section, I
cannot resist citing a deliciously 'English' exchange between the
composers Julius Harrison and Elizabeth Poston, transmitted to
North America on 29 September 1941. The BBC 'plugged' English

music in its broadcasts abroad, including Harrison's *Bredon Hill*, a rhapsody for violin and orchestra not heard nowadays but apparently 'in the mould of Vaughan Williams's *The Lark Ascending* of a quarter century earlier', and certainly much admired by other composers of the school, Moeran and Ireland. It was given its 'first world performance' on radio beamed at North America and introduced ecstatically by the announcer as 'witness to the eternal spirit of England. Julius Harrison, Worcestershire born of generations of countrymen, lives in sight of Bredon Hill.'

Bredon Hill features in one of A. E. Housman's most melancholy and effective poems, but Harrison, talking to Poston about his piece, did not mention that particular inspiration. He recalled writing the piece and playing it to Poston on the piano when she was staying with him:

J.H. And we drove on a perfect summer afternoon high up in that lovely countryside of mine and had a picnic tea in sight of Bredon Hill.

E.P. Yes – and I felt how really you had caught the essence of that English scene and put it into your music, and that you had written a real Rhapsody.

J.H. Yes, I think so – because it grew out of itself in my mind from all those scenes I have known all my life. After all, we musn't forget that this part of Worcestershire speaks of England at its oldest. It is the heart of Mercia, the country of Piers Plowman, and it is the spirit of Elgar's music too. If I've been able to catch something of all this then I'm indeed glad . . .

E.P. Yes . . . It's all in your music.[39]

10

Telling It To America

> Here they were, the people who rule a fourth of the globe . . . They
> had been imperialistic and had exploited, they had subjugated, but
> down in the Tubes of London they were demonstrating that they
> could take the same sort of punishment they had handed out . . .
> They were a tough generation of Englishmen and I admired them
> in the shelters. They had Elizabethan fire in their guts.
>
> Ben Robertson

NEGLEY FARSON was among the American journalists – well over
a hundred of them were in London during the Blitz – who had
no difficulty in accepting that there was a link between the Deep
English landscape and 'the strength of this marvellous country'.
Farson was one of several important writers – John Gunther, Walter
Duranty and Vincent Sheean were others – whose reports on the
European crisis were distributed for syndication by the North
American Newspaper Alliance. But his book, *Bomber's Moon*, one of
the first to cover the Blitz, published by Gollancz in January 1941,
seems to have been aimed initially at British readers. Farson, from
September 1940, had toured London with an artist, Tom Purvis,
whose drawings provided the book with nearly fifty illustrations. It
is particularly well written, with a restraint lacking in most Blitz
writing at that time. Farson had known England for a quarter of a
century and was able to put what was happening into long
perspective. However, *Bomber's Moon* is rich in what had already
become clichés, especially in Cockney jokes. And his evocation of a
small west-country town provides a version of Deep England
mythology which is more interesting in its details than most, but
includes the statement that, 'In rural England you feel the deep,
uncorrupted things which give this country its staying power. These
people take a calmness from their affinity with peaceful things.'[1]
  Quentin Reynolds of *Colliers Weekly Magazine*, typically, was less
mystical, more direct. He describes going to a village in Kent in the

autumn of 1940. The local pub was 'three hundred years old . . . Up the road was the village school; across from it the village church and here the pub. These three things are symbols of what England is fighting to maintain. The pub in many ways is more important than the other two; it is the place where men gather to speak their minds. The pub is the symbol of free speech in England.'[2]

A basic problem for British propagandists addressing the USA was that Americans who had a Disneyland conception of England as a country of villages, green fields and Wodehouseian eccentrics could not swallow the class hierarchy implied in these images (and, of course, strong in reality).

Alice Duer Miller's poem *The White Cliffs* was a publishing sensation in both the USA and Britain in 1940–41. In America, more than 300,000 copies were sold. The actress Lynne Fontanne broadcast the poem over the NBC Blue Network and Jimmy Dorsey recorded a highly popular song relating to it. In Britain, eight printings were called for in a few months. *The White Cliffs* tells the story of Susan Dunne. This American girl visits England in 1914 and marries a young aristocrat who dies in the war. Now Lady Ashwood, she takes her son to the States, is shocked by prohibition, gangsters and political sleaze, and returns to England, which, alas, is a land of class distinctions and appeasement. Her son joins the services when war breaks out, and if she loses him it will be in a great cause.

This synopsis makes clear that the poem, which is conventionally but not incompetently written, is not simple-minded propaganda. (When, after long wrangles with the Office of War Information, MGM turned it into a Hollywood feature, it was forbidden to export it, except, rather oddly, to liberated France and Italy.[3]) Susan is ambivalent about England – loving the cultivated English voice with its 'pure round "o's"', but loathing the arrogance of its users. Even Miller's view of English patriotism is hardly dripping with affection:

> . . . Englishmen
> Will serve day after day, obey the law,
> And do dull tasks that keep a nation strong.
> Pale shabby people standing in a long
> Line in the twilight and the misty rain
> To pay their tax, I then saw England plain.

Her eventual resolution of doubt into support for England's war effort is based on the idea that the founders of the USA were English – 'Never more English than when they dared to be/Rebels against her' – and that the seed of the tree of Liberty 'was English':

I am American bred,
I have seen much to hate here – much to forgive,
But in a world where England is finished and dead,
I do not wish to live.[4]

There is no suggestion in the book that war is breaking down English snobbery: it implies that England has to be supported in spite of gross faults in its society, and might even have provided grist for the mill of shrewd isolationists.

One strong card which isolationism had in hand was provided by the widespread belief that cunning British atrocity propaganda had lured the USA into the Great War. Aware of the strength of this feeling, the British government was now extremely cautious in its approach to propaganda in the States.

A small British Library of Information already existed in New York. In 1939 a secret government inquiry was set up to devise a more ambitious policy. This was done on the basis of 'direct and detailed consultation' with Edward R. Murrow, the London–based European director of the Columbian Broadcasting Service. It was resolved that 'the British should merely feed information into American channels, cultivating . . . the makers of American opinion and particularly the growing number of American broadcasters in the United Kingdom'. By August 1939 a structure was ready. The News Department of the Foreign Office, which would continue to brief US correspondents, would be backed up by an American liaison unit in the BBC and a small American Division of the Ministry of Information.[5]

The very ineptitude of the MoI in the early months of war, when its amateurish staff was faced with the problem that there was little war news of interest, may have done Britain a favour. Referring to the first minister, *Time* magazine said: 'If Lord Macmillan's first task was to undo Britain's reputation for cleverness, he could not have done it more brilliantly.' In any case, Chamberlain was not sure what he wanted from the USA – he wrote to his sister in January 1940: 'Heaven knows I don't want the Americans to fight for us; we should have to pay too dearly for that if they had any right to be in on the peace terms.' Events thereafter, which made USA help completely essential, transformed British 'informational' operations both at home and in America. It was helpful that Churchill himself, even before May 1940, had been a popular broadcaster in the USA. As Nicholas Cull summarises the developments which followed his accession to the Premiership:

During the critical period of 1940 and 1941, practically all America's news about the war passed through London and was accordingly shaped by the publicity and censorship structure of the British Government, or indirectly by the partiality of the press corps. The flow of information from London established the picture of a new, dynamic Britain, and a struggle increasingly based on moral issues; these same ideas were reflected and rearticulated in the indigenous American mass media, creating a new paradigm for the American public and ultimately redefining conceptions of America's role in the world. The old culture of isolationism and the policy responses associated with that culture had given way to a new culture of war and globalism many months before Pearl Harbor.[6]

In so far as the Myth of the Blitz did not evolve spontaneously (and I have argued that in great part it did), it was a propaganda construct directed as much at American opinion as at British, developed by American news journalists in association with British propagandists and newsmen – and was all the more strongly accepted by Britons because American voices proclaimed it. It could therefore be said that the most important single figure in its dissemination was Edward R. Murrow, who, as we have just seen, had helped the British government pre-war to set up the procedures whereby his colleagues would receive official war news.

Murrow was a man of unquestionable integrity, completely committed to the ideals of broadcasting as a public service and of journalism as truth-telling. In a broadcast from London to the USA at the outbreak of war, he said:

> I have an old-fashioned belief that Americans like to make up their own minds on the basis of all available information. The conclusions you draw are your own affair. I have no desire to influence them and shall leave such efforts to those who have more confidence in their own judgements than I have in mine.[7]

In spite of this, there is not the least doubt that Murrow, during and after the summer of 1940, used his broadcasts consistently to influence US public opinion away from isolationism.

Murrow's wife, Janet, actually took a job in the MoI. His relationship with the BBC, which was committed to truth-telling but was of course highly selective with 'the truth', was so close that he was virtually on their strength: night after night, he would sit into the small hours talking to the scholarly Scot, who was the BBC's news editor, R. T. Clark. (But, as he told BBC listeners on one of the occasions when he broadcast to them – he was sitting beside his friendly rival Fred Bate of NBC – he was his own editor: 'There's one big advantage we have, and that is that no one can rewrite or change our material.'[8]) We can picture him in his flat in Hallam Street near the BBC singing 'Joe Hill' to his wife's piano accompaniment for the pleasure of Clark, Alan Wells (the foreign editor of the BBC Home Service, a close friend of the Murrows killed in the Blitz) and maybe Jan Masaryk, the exiled Czechoslovakian leader. He and Janet were frequent guests at 10 Downing Street, and John G. Winant, who, during the Blitz, replaced the anglophobic Joseph Kennedy as US ambassador, was an old friend. After 'Lend-Lease' went through, important Americans visiting London all resorted to Murrow as the most reliable source of information.[9]

He was regarded with some awe by many of the American press corps in London, whose numbers swelled after the fall of France. Eric Sevareid, a CBS colleague, would recall the impression which Murrow had made on him before the war:

> A young American, a tall thin man with a boyish grin, extraordinary dark eyes that were alight and intense one moment and sombre and lost the next. He seemed to possess that rare thing, an instinctive, intuitive recognition of truth.

This initial admiration never dimmed. In his memoirs (published in 1946, when both men were still under forty), Sevareid hailed Murrow as 'the first great literary artist of a new medium of communication'.[10] Murrow's older friend Vincent Sheean (whose articles from London were taken by the North American News Agency) likewise wrote about him, in a book published in 1943, as if he was already confirmed to be one of the great men of history – 'dark and taciturn and often beset by gloom', he 'was at the same time capable of sustained hilarity and high spirits: the range of his moral orchestra was great'.[11] Murrow's British co-workers also fell under his spell: reserved by American standards, he seemed refreshingly free and easy to them.

Murrow's dedication and energy are almost frightening to read about. Several times knocked down in London streets by bomb blast, he refused to enter an air-raid shelter unless it was in search of a story. Chain-smoking as always, he drove through the Blitz in his small British car, checking casualty reports, since he never worked from official handouts; he paced the streets of the city not only as a reporter but as a fire warden; yet he maintained close contact with

European governments in exile, consorted with Cabinet ministers and important Labour politicians – and broadcast up to four or five times a night. To colleagues he seemed, as one of his biographers puts it, 'the iron man of the blitz, living on adrenalin, black coffee, and cigarettes . . . his six-foot-two frame down to 150 pounds'.[12]

Murrow's father was a farmer – not poor, as he liked to imply – who owned 320 acres in the North Carolina Piedmont, but had been tempted to the North-west to work as a locomotive engineer in the lumber industry. 'Ed' himself had worked in the frontier lumber camps as a youth and was heard on occasion to wish that he'd never left them: his egalitarianism was fed by memories of men in the epic Wobbly movement, whose activities brought a taste of revolution to Seattle in 1919. At Washington State University, however, his chief interest was in 'speech'. His platform skills brought him election as president of the National Student Federation in 1929, and in that capacity he travelled to a congress in Bucharest in 1931 and had a foretaste of sinister changes in Europe.[13] In 1937 he went to London as CBS's European director. The role of the foreign correspondent speaking on radio was about to enter a literally heroic phase. By 1940, CBS, NBC and to a lesser extent their rival, the Mutual network, had 'established the broadcast correspondent as a staple of the American news scene. The small group of men and women', (David H. Hosley goes on), 'were as good as any radio or television correspondents since, and they were a key element in the Golden Age of Radio.' A *Fortune* poll in 1938 had shown that listening to radio was America's favourite leisure activity – preferred by 18.8 per cent as compared with 17.3 per cent favouring movies.[14] No wonder Hollywood itself paid tribute to the charisma of the *Foreign Correspondent* in a film directed by Alfred Hitchcock and released in 1940. Vincent Sheean's *Personal History* had attracted the attention of an independent Hollywood producer, Walter Wanger, who wanted to make a film about the civil war in Spain. His ideas ran into opposition from the Hays Office, which administered the industry's production code and was averse to political topics, let alone foreign ones.[15] By the time Joel McCrea starred in Hitchcock's film as a reporter sent to Europe to find out 'what was going on over there', almost the only element left from the book was its opening location, Holland; all references to Spain and to German anti-Semitism had been removed. However, the conclusion had McCrea broadcasting from a bomb-torn London: 'The lights have gone out in Europe! Hang on to your lights, America – they're the only lights still on in the world. Ring yourself round with steel, America!'[16]

H. V. Kalterborn had made the first live battlefield broadcast from Spain in 1936. At this time, NBC established a lead over CBS. Fred Bate, NBC's London chief, was a personal friend of Edward VIII and trumped CBS with very full coverage of the abdication crisis. But in the Munich crisis CBS, now led by Murrow, acquired an edge in depth of coverage and analysis and sheer number of broadcasts from Europe. At this point, a Gallup Poll showed that radio had suddenly taken over from newspapers as the preferred source of news for seven out of ten Americans – and the medium's potency was confirmed in October when Orson Welles produced his famous version of his near-namesake H. G.'s *War of the Worlds* and convinced many listeners that Martians had landed in their homeland.[17]

Murrow, initially an organiser of broadcasts by others, began to go out on shortwave direct to the US after war broke out. Before long, he was rated the 'number one' American newsman. However, interest excited by radio news helped to sell newspapers. Murrow's own Blitz reports were printed in *PM*, a New York afternoon tabloid which first appeared in June 1940, the brainchild of its editor Ralph Ingersoll, who sent Ben Robertson to cover the war in Britain and visited London himself later to convince himself at first hand that the city really was 'Taking It'.

To 'Take It' was an American expression, and its general adoption in Britain may indicate how strong the desire for American approval of its spirit was in that country. Like the 'morale' of the British themselves, the attitude of the core of the American press corps was stabilised after the fall of France and before 7 September. First, there was the colonisation of Dover Cliff. As the Battle of Britain began with the RAF trying to defend convoys in the Channel, American journalists flocked to Dover, where they stayed in the Grand Hotel by night and spent day after day watching air battles from the white cliff associated with Shakespeare's King Lear. Others drove down to join them – Murrow travelling with his friend Sheean, with Ed Beattie of United Press and Drew Middleton of Associated Press, who said 'You could be on your back, with glasses, and look up and there was the whole goddam air battle!'[18]

Ben Robertson, *PM*'s fresh-faced and idealistic young reporter, with the charming South Carolina accent and an attachment not only to rather left-wing views but to what he took to be the anti-materialistic, anti-mechanistic ethos of Deep South tradition, once saw four dogfights from the cliff in one day. His high-spirited account, published in *I Saw England* (1941), makes the atmosphere in town and on cliff seem romantically heady:

Those were wonderful days in every way – they changed me as an individual. I lost my sense of personal fear because I saw that what happened to me did not matter . . . It was not we who counted, it was what we stood for. And I knew now for what I was standing – I was for freedom. It was as simple as that . . . I understood Valley Forge and Gettysburg at Dover.[19]

There was attractive female company for Robertson – Helen Kirkpatrick of the *Chicago Daily News*, 'tall and beautiful' with a 'first class mind', Virginia Cowles, a Bostonian who wrote for the London *Sunday Times* and moved in the highest London society, and tiny Hilde Marchant of the London *Daily Express*, 'a sort of Spitfire attached to the ground . . . passionate in her belief in the common people'. One of the corps, Art Menken, a *March of Time* photographer, literally got dug in to the white cliffs, getting potatoes out of the ground 'when he was not otherwise engaged'. There were two pubs handy and more, of course, down in the town – Robertson wrote of the corps listening regularly to the views of 'the red haired woman who ran the pub in the square where David Copperfield waited for his aunt', and suggested that they were equally impressed by Josephine, the barmaid at the Grand Hotel, a brave woman whom he saw one day when 'all hell had been let loose . . . a copy of *The Grapes of Wrath* under one arm', shouting to the gunners on the beach, 'Go to it, Bofors.'[20]

Older hands, who perhaps did not in fact fully share Robertson's endearing weakness for barmaids, hotel waitresses and other young women who epitomised for him British fighting spirit, nevertheless seem to have convinced themselves that they were at the last line of defence for US democracy, now that France had fallen, and that the British were really putting up a fight. Reynolds, an occasional visitor to the cliff, wrote later that the whole corps came in July to have an 'emotional rather than a rational' faith that Britain would survive.[21] Vincent Sheean thought that the Germans were in effect winning the 'Battle of the Channel' – the corps saw dive bombers causing havoc among British convoys – but was convinced that the outnumbered RAF fighter planes 'had the best of it' in every battle against Messerschmitts which he witnessed. 'It was at Dover, I think, that the side of England became "our side" in my eyes.' Long distrustful of British imperialism, disgusted by appeasement, Sheean had, by his own account, come close to isolationism – Europeans seemed to deserve what they were getting. 'At Dover the first sharp thrust of hope penetrated this gloom . . . The flash of the Spitfire's wing, then, through the misty glare of the summer sky, was the first flash of a sharpened sword.'[22]

In August, Murrow and Fred Bate organised a joint CBS–NBC broadcast live from London town, on the 'round up' pattern, now well established, in which correspondents reported in turn from various points. To get atmospheric sound, they used techniques developed by the BBC to catch the noise of bat on ball during commentaries on cricket matches. Murrow was to kick off in Trafalgar Square, his colleague Larry Le Sueur was at an ARP station, the socialistic socialite Sheean was rather appropriately stationed on a balcony over Piccadilly Circus. Sevareid was mingling with 15,000 people at a dance hall in Hammersmith up-river, while Bate was poised to report from Buckingham Palace. J. B. Priestley (who else?) would end the programme in Whitehall, looking towards the Cenotaph.

Thirty million Americans were treated to a breakthrough in broadcasting. A light air raid was beginning. Murrow was on the steps of St Martin-in-the-Fields: there was a public shelter nearby. 'The noise that you hear at this moment is the sound of the air-raid siren . . . People are walking along very quietly. We're just at the entrance of an air-raid shelter here, and I must move the cable over just a bit, so people can walk in.' Crouching on the pavement, Murrow captured for his listeners the calm, unhurried footsteps of Londoners, despite the noise of guns conflicting with the chugging of buses as lights changed from green to red. They heard one Londoner casually ask another for a light.[23]

On 7 September, Murrow, Sheean and Robertson faced a test of their own morale. They drove down to Kent to inspect the damage in the Thames estuary and look at the air war from another angle. They saw the colossal waves of German bombers head towards the East End and set it on fire. Anticipating the Luftwaffe's return, they decided to spend the night in the open. As Murrow would tell America next day, 'Vincent Sheean lay on one side of me and cursed in five languages; he'd talk about the war in Spain. Ben Robertson lay on the other side and kept saying over and over in that slow South Carolina drawl, "London is burning, London is burning."' Robertson hadn't realised he had been doing this until Murrow told him later. He remembered the East End fires as 'the most appalling and depressing sight any of us had ever seen'.

As they returned, half dazed, to London next day, Sheean was impressed with the 'patient and orderly' behaviour of frightened, homeless 'refugees'. Robertson got back to his bed in the Waldorf Hotel in time for the next night's repetition of Blitz. Next morning, the head waiter had lost his home, but was on duty, and 'Ivey the cleaner' came to work after being buried for three hours in a basement. 'The civilians had become an army.' They cleared up one night's wreckage and waited for the next. 'They knew they had to keep the streets open, the lights on, the water flowing, the food coming in.'[24]

The three US radio networks shared one small studio, B-4, in Broadcasting House with three censors, who sat through broadcasts with finger on switch, ready to turn the microphone off if a correspondent departed from an approved script. Murrow, Bate and Arthur Mann of Mutual went out live: though recordings were sometimes surreptitiously used by CBS and NBC correspondents, it was still believed in the US that these would be subject to doctoring and thus unreliable. R. T. Clark would be close at hand in the cubicle where he worked and slept: the BBC Home News existed in virtual symbiosis with US foreign news. Usually, though not invariably, Murrow dictated the scripts of his newscasts, so that the words would suit the rhythms of speech rather than fall into the patterns of written prose.

In his absence, Murrow had been 'scooped' on the 7 September raid by John MacVane of NBC. Reporting on his trip to Kent, he minimised the risk to himself, Robertson and Sheean and concentrated on the behaviour of local people, such as a 'toothless old man of nearly seventy' who came into a pub and asked for a pint of mild and bitter, confiding that 'he had always, all his life, gone to bed at eight o'clock and found now that three pints of beer made him drowsy-like so he could sleep through any air raid'. This was to remain Murrow's approach in the days which followed. His reporting was unsensational and made weighty by near impersonality. On 9 September, of the East Enders, he said flatly, 'These people are exceedingly brave, tough and prudent. The East End, where disaster is always just round the corner, seems to take it better than the more fashionable districts in the West End . . . This night bombing', he concluded, 'is serious and sensational. It makes headlines, kills people and smashes property; but it doesn't win wars.' Next day, he reminded listeners that London was a huge 'sprawling city' and the rain of bombs wasn't continuous. As for morale:

The politicians who called this a 'people's war' were right, probably more right than they knew at the time. I've seen some horrible sights in this city during these days and nights, but not once have I heard man, woman or child suggest that Britain should throw in her hand . . . After four days and nights of this air

Blitzkrieg, I think the people here are rapidly becoming veterans, even as their army was hardened in the fire of Dunkirk.

On 12 September he pitched into Dorothy Thompson's broadcast from America to Britain that night, in which she had told the British that the poets of the world were behind them:

> They don't consider themselves to be heroes. There's a job of work to be done and they're doing it as best they can. They don't know themselves how long they can stand up to it . . . Most of them expect little help from the poets and no effective defence by word of mouth.

He had said the rich in London had better shelters than the poor; he refused to give such significance as others did to the bombing of Buckingham Palace. It hadn't been needed to convince people that 'they are all in this thing together . . . The King and Queen have earned the respect and admiration of the nation, but so have tens of thousands of humble folk who are much less well protected.'[25]

On 21 September, after much hesitation (they even auditioned him to make sure he wouldn't give away useful information to the Germans), the BBC allowed him to report a raid in progress from a rooftop, directly to America. (Bate later shared this concession.) Murrow was drawing his public deeper and deeper into the Blitz and communicating his own view of it in the process. This view amounted to saying that class-ridden England was undergoing moral revolution.

Sheean's pre-war mistrust of Britain has been mentioned. Quentin Reynolds was rather unusual among the American press corps when he confessed to being a lover of London *before* the Blitz. Sevareid, a markedly left-wing young Midwesterner, had been appalled by London on his first visit in 1937 – 'incredibly cramped and mean', with primitive heating and hygiene. The English depressed him – they were 'unable to express themselves . . . They cannot talk to one another'. Class was a different, much worse phenomenon than social inequality in the States. The lower-class English accepted their own inferiority. He nevertheless became convinced in 1940 that Britain was 'a bright beleaguered citadel of courage'. He himself candidly admitted to constant fear under bombing, 'unable to tolerate the shaking room', and saw Londoners who were also afraid. Yet overall, the British were truly 'brave and heroic'. The upper class, whatever their faults, were 'not very "soft" people' – they had a 'tradition of physical courage'. The very fact that the British 'were still afraid of each other', Sevareid thought, helped to prevent public panic. 'One could panic in his heart, but two together could not show it, nor a hundred in a group.' However, people were now losing their reserve, talking to strangers:

> We would talk about this, Ed and I, Scotty Reston and others, when sleep was not to be had for the trying, and we thought that perhaps a wonderful thing was happening to the British people: some kind of moral revolution was underway, and out of it would come regeneration of a great people.

It seemed to him important that ARP men *working with their hands* were now admired as heroes: 'The country realised abruptly that a broker in the city was of scant value compared with the man who could fashion an aircraft propeller.'[26]

Murrow's conversion to anglophilia probably owed more to calculation: well before the war he had seen Britain's significance as a potential fighter against fascism and Nazism. In a valedictory BBC broadcast when he left the country at last in 1946, he described his reactions on early visits before he settled in London: 'You seemed slow, indifferent and exceedingly complacent – not important. I thought your streets narrow and mean, your tailors overadvertised, your climate unbearable, your class-consciousness offensive. You couldn't cook. Your young men seemed without vigour or purpose.'[27] But by 1940 he was a devoted admirer, perhaps rather surprisingly, of the House of Commons and its procedures. He was deeply impressed, as he told America, when in May 1940, he saw it pass in a day the Emergency Powers Act, which took away citizens' right to private property: 'During most of the pre-war period this country has been ruled by . . . an oligarchy which has believed in its right to rule . . . But this country is now united and it is important that a lifelong Socialist [Attlee] introduced that revolutionary bill today.'[28]

Enthusiasm for the idea that Britain's 'moral revolution' involved the elevation of life, labour and freedom over money was shared by other members of the American press. It is not surprising that the romantic Ben Robertson was pleased: 'People were talking more about the Empire's ability to produce, rather than about its ability to pay in pounds and pence. After the blitz really began I one day became aware . . . that not once had I heard anyone say a hundred-thousand-pound building had been hit. The British seemed, at least for the time being, to have lost their sense of property.'[29] Nor that the left-inclined Farson should quote a bombed-out London woman as saying with a smile, 'When you've nothing left, you have nothing to worry about, have you?' – and believe that she meant it.[30] It was less predictable that Walter Graebner of *Time* magazine would look calmly upon the movement of the British towards a form of socialism: for them 'Winning the war – keeping Hitler from setting his bloody feet on British shores', was 'infinitely more important than pounds, shillings or pence', and post-war education would probably be more egalitarian, with the power of the old school tie broken.[31]

It now seems rather amazing that James B. ('Scotty') Reston of the *New York Times*, contemplating the bombing of the City of London, Britain's financial centre, nightly from his office in Fleet Street, and admiring the unscathed dome of St Paul's, should be moved to moralise about 'the utter uselessness of money under certain circumstances. What was the use of it, piled row upon row in the vaults of Throgmorton Street? What was the good of it until it was finally brought out and turned into guns and tanks and airplanes for the Cockneys to use?'[32]

When Ralph Ingersoll of *PM* was in London (for only two weeks) 'a cynic' remarked to him that 'the most terrible thing that could happen to England was to have the Germans stop bombing it'. Ingersoll thought there was some truth in this. As long as bombs fell, snobbery would continue to break down: 'A nation cannot sleep wherever it finds itself at night, and with whomever happens to lie down next to it and not have things happen to its class distinctions.'[33] One might add to this familiar point the less well-worn one that US journalists could not endure bombing night after night, with all the strain and risk entailed, without undergoing some personal changes in attitude. Perhaps Reston's ideas about money represent such a genuine change of opinion.

The US press were courted by Britain's élite of rich and powerful people. The democratic Robertson did not spurn the hospitality of the famous society hostess Sybil Colefax. (He told the world admiringly that she shared a shelter every night with her maids and several working-class people.) Even the austere Murrow mixed on occasion in upper-class circles. American broadcasters to Britain – Raymond Gram Swing, Dorothy Thompson – were received when they came like visiting royalty. David Bowes Lyon, the Queen's brother, gave an afternoon party for the US press (favouring youngsters and leaving out such a star as Quentin Reynolds) so they could meet his sister, real royalty. Ingersoll was convinced that the friendly staff in the MoI were not trying to sell him anything, and was shown the secret Home Intelligence reports on morale, the 'frankness' of which 'amazed' him. Interviews with Churchill and Bevin were laid on for him.[34]

The US press stayed in comfortable hotels or well-appointed flats. But this did not mean they were exempt from Blitz. One study points out that the homes of six reporters working for news agencies (INS, UP, AP) were wrecked by bombs.[35] Fred Bate was seriously injured in December 1940 while preparing a broadcast in the NBC office. The nearby CBS office was also demolished: this was one of three occasions when Murrow had to find new premises for that reason. He himself had been in Broadcasting House a few days earlier when a bomb falling on the building had killed six people. And so on. Sevareid found that he literally could not Take It and left before the end of 1940. Sheean left also. When he came back in April and met Murrow, Ben Robertson and Bill Stoneman of the *Chicago Daily News* in Claridge's, he was shocked at their haggard appearance. Murrow had aged visibly. 'The epic days were over, they told him, public morale near rock bottom.'[36]

John MacVane of NBC, who had, aged only twenty-eight, to take charge after Bate's injury, recalled later:

> Life seemed very tenuous indeed . . . London's ordeal was an easy story to write – one could almost have written it by sitting in a basement night and day and reading the papers – but we broadcasters had so identified ourselves with the people of London that we did not feel we could shirk any of their experiences . . . Our country was neutral, but we ourselves, for that reason, had to prove to our British colleagues and the people with whom we lived that we were willing to share their lives completely.[37]

The outcome of the press corps' experience was all that the MoI could have wished. The exactness with which US reporting by and large suited British propaganda requirements is exemplified by *Life*'s coverage of the early days of Blitz. The magazine featured a classic image of St Paul's riding the flames (by John Topham) and deftly identified the Nazi raiders as child murderers. On 9 September it featured a two-year-old baby, Margaret Curtis, with a bandaged head and 'about to die', whose mother was said to have been killed shielding her from a bomb with her body. (Actually, both survived, but so did the impression made by the story.) Two weeks later *Life*'s cover photograph was by Cecil Beaton, the brilliant English artist: it showed Eileen Dunne, a little girl in hospital, 'AIR RAID VICTIM', nursing a doll or teddy and staring poignantly at the camera.[38]

The British public were not ungrateful. They made one American

pressman and broadcaster a national hero – set him alongside
Priestley. This was not Murrow, frequently though he was heard on
British airwaves. It was Quentin Reynolds, whose book, *The
Wounded Don't Cry* was very popular in 1941, from which one infers
that the British thought that Reynolds had described their Blitz
behaviour truthfully.

Though he mingled frequently with the rest of the press corps, seems
to have been popular with it, and was certainly regarded as a leading
personality, Reynolds in some respects was an odd man out. His
background was not like that of the men who had grown up with
radio and become polished professionals, or the experienced news
reporters and foreign correspondents. One of a family of seven from
long-established Irish Catholic stock, he was born, in 1900, in the
Bronx, and had a voice to prove it. (In spite of his Irish blood, he
despised Eire's neutrality and seems to have found the British
Empire a less bothersome entity than did most US pressmen.) The
son of a high-school principal, he graduated at Brown University.
But in his senior year he secretly played professional football for the
New York Giants; as a sports writer, down on his luck during the
depression, he was recommended to William Randolph Hearst's
International News Service by the great Damon Runyon. INS sent
him to Berlin in 1933 when their feature writer was expelled by the
Nazis. A particularly revolting display of Nazi anti-Semitism in the
streets of Nuremberg alienated him from Germany's new rulers,
though he had a certain respect for their youth policy. His first article
for *Colliers Weekly Magazine* – one of 384 over fifteen years – was
about German youth and militarism and was called 'Trained to Take
It': he did not doubt later that the Germans, if bombed, would Take
It. *Colliers* soon hired him full-time – for the next six years he
wrote for the magazine about almost everything except the rise of
fascism. But in March 1940 it decided to send him to Europe, at
which point, applying for a visa for Germany, he found that the
Nazis had blacklisted him. Wearing the uniform of an 'American
War Correspondent', Reynolds saw action on the French Front in
May and then drove to Bordeaux through the hordes of refugees:
thence he arrived in London.

He got on extremely well with British pressmen. Arthur
Christiansen, editor of the most successful British daily, the *Express*,
became a close friend and slept in Reynolds's flat during the Blitz.
Reynolds rather slavishly admired Christiansen's proprietor, Beaverbrook, and claimed to be on good terms with him socially. Quite
how seriously the British Establishment took him before the arrival

of Beaverbrook's crony Brendan Bracken as Minister of Information in 1941 is not clear; he certainly did not, during the Blitz itself, get chances to meet Churchill such as were accorded to Ingersoll and Murrow. But he identified sturdily with the British case, despite the opinion of his magazine's proprietor that America should not be drawn into war: when the editor of *Colliers*, Charles Colebaugh, received a Reynolds story called 'England Can't Lose', he cabled: 'YOU ARE PROBABLY CRAZY BUT CALL SHOTS AS YOU SEE THEM. WE WILL PUBLISH EVERYTHING YOU WRITE.' And they did.[39]

Reynolds became a close friend of Sidney Bernstein, Deputy Director of the film division of the MoI. When a New York agent cabled him that Dutton would publish a book moulded out of his *Colliers* articles, Reynolds took advantage of doctor's orders – a week in bed after he had broken two ribs falling over a table in his flat when it had no electricity – to retreat to Bernstein's farm in Kent (he managed to get an official Admiralty car to take him), and there worked away with scissors, paste and a part-time secretary from the village. The result, a few months later, topped the US best-seller lists: he called the book, with flamboyant unconcern for accuracy, *The Wounded Don't Cry*.

Meanwhile he had scripted and narrated, at Bernstein's suggestion, a seminal short documentary called *London Can Take It*. Though made to MoI requirements by the Crown Film Unit (as Grierson's GPO Unit was renamed in August 1940), it had been released in the USA as 'by Quentin Reynolds', with no mention on screen of its official, propagandist provenance. It had been highly successful. When Reynolds returned to New York early in 1941 he was surprised to be met at the harbour by fellow pressmen anxious to interview him. A country-wide lecture tour in favour of British war relief had been arranged for him. In clubs, churches, schools and so on, Reynolds found audiences rather apathetic – it was still not their war – but generous: he raised nearly $200,000 dollars for the charity. Warner Brothers backed *London Can Take It* for nationwide release. (Ben Robertson, who had travelled back with him, was meanwhile making speeches and broadcasts on behalf of the British cause all the way from Boston to Georgia.[40])

After his return to Britain, where his book was selling well, Reynolds improved his establishment contacts: he had not previously met Nancy, Lady Astor, but was now invited to lunch at her mansion, Cliveden, famous as the haunt of a 'set' of pre-war appeasers. He wavered about going: not only had her 'set' let the free world down, she was also a 'militant prohibitionist'. But Murrow, also invited, talked him into it: 'You may meet people there who can be helpful to you.' Indeed, Duff Cooper was there, as well as his soon-to-be successor at MoI, Bracken, and MoI's influential Walter Monckton, to enjoy the delicious salmon sent to Lady Astor by friends in Scotland. Soon after, at Bernstein's suggestion, Duff Cooper agreed that a Postscript by Reynolds would pep up the regular series. Reynolds penned an abusive open letter to Goebbels, ridiculing the latter's boss as 'Mr Schickelgruber'. Delivered on 29 June 1941, it became front page news. Reynolds's friend Christiansen printed the full text in the *Express*. The BBC forwarded 7,000 letters to Reynolds in the next few days – one of them from Churchill, who thought the broadcast 'admirable', and one which said, 'God bless you, Yank . . . You had the whole Elephant and Castle Underground Station roaring.'[41]

Reynolds soon followed the war to Russia, though he could certainly have prospered in Britain as a result of the public's affection for him. After Murrow, he must be seen as the most influential US contributor to the Myth of the Blitz. Before discussing *London Can Take It*, it is worth looking at *The Wounded Don't Cry*, published in Britain with extra sections denied to the avid US public, by Cassell's, the publishers Reynolds shared with both Churchill and Murrow.

The first Reynolds offering accepted by *Colliers* had been a short story, and he had continued to work at times in that genre. There is no doubt that he shaped his Blitz stories for literary effects of the kind which Murrow would have spurned as untruthful and sensationalist. Bernstein would reminisce that 'Quent was very popular in a different way from Ed . . . He was a good drinker and so on.'[42] A predilection for darts and pints in pubs and drinking sessions with young servicemen is a well-advertised part of Reynolds's authorial persona. Unlike Murrow, this crony of Ernest Hemingway's made his own personal participation and reactions central in his war reportage. Comparing his post-war autobiography (1964) with his wartime books, it appears that, by his own tacit admission, he invented a good story about meeting Roosevelt's advisor Harry Hopkins at 10 Downing Street.[43]

It is more puzzling, at first sight, that he should have manipulated the events which gave him one of the effective, vivid 'short stories' in *The Wounded Don't Cry*. As he tells it in the wartime book, he is out with women working in the London Auxiliary Ambulance Service. Three dead women, sisters, are brought out of a burning house, then the child of one of them, three years old, her long golden curls 'strangely untouched by fire'. The effort to resuscitate her fails, giving rise to a peroration typical of Reynolds's burly rhetoric:

I know this isn't a pleasant story to read. It isn't a pleasant one to write. It's much better to read and write about the fighter pilots, the 'gay, laughing-eyed knights of the air'. Sure, that's what war is. Glamorous and exciting . . . But that isn't the war I see in London every night. This is the war I see. If you want a front seat to the war, come and stand over this three-year-old child with me. Don't be afraid of the bombs that are falling close, or the spent shrapnel that is raining down on us. You want to see what war is really like, don't you? Take another look at the baby. She still looks as though she were asleep. This is war – full style, 1940. This is the war that Herr Hitler is waging.[44]

The event in question evidently did move Reynolds, so greatly that he returned to it in his autobiography. From the later book, it appears that the driver of the ambulance was not the woman in charge of the ambulance station, but a girl, Ethel, who features in the wartime report as coming on duty despite losing her home and family the night before. As well as altering this important detail, Reynolds increased the number of women killed in the cellar from two to three, and made them sisters. The victims, it seems, were in fact mother, daughter and granddaughter, Gloria. The baby's father had been lost at Dunkirk – in *The Wounded Don't Cry* he is merely described as 'in the army'. In that book, a kind of 'punch line' is offered. The doctor in attendance says of the three-year-old, 'Maybe she's better off dead', and Reynolds himself ripostes 'Nobody's better off dead.' If we believe the later memoirs, it was Reynolds, thinking of Gloria's dismal future in an orphanage, who spoke the first line, and the freshly bereaved driver, Ethel, who made him repeat it and, with 'contempt in her eyes', said, 'harshly' – making him 'feel very small' – 'Nobody's better off dead.'[45]

If we assume that only original notes or a very vivid memory could have permitted Reynolds, over twenty years later, to change a tale already committed so effectively to print, we must conclude that either literary considerations, or propagandist ones, influenced his original handling.

Perhaps both can be detected. Reynolds's persona, that of the tough, optimistic, angry reporter, as always in the thick of the action, is given force by his retort to the doctor, and would be compromised by reference to the sentimentally pessimistic, almost defeatist feeling admitted in the later account. But it may also be the case that Reynolds felt he should make the episode harrowing – the Nazis, aiming at a hospital, kill yet another small child nearby – but not too completely disturbing. Ethel, in the wartime version, represents bravery, 'taking it' and 'carrying on'; but her emotion, expressed at the climax, would distract attention from the image of the dead child. The fact that the British Expeditionary Force lost many men in its retreat to Dunkirk and at the port was not a useful topic to allude to in the autumn of 1940. But why *three* grown women? Why *sisters*? Is Reynolds deliberately or unconsciously delving into the myth-kitty, where three is a more folkloristic number than two (there are three little pigs and three bears)? A trio of sisters vaguely echoes myth and legend. A last, prosaic explanation might be that he wanted to spare any friends or relatives of the victims possible emotional harassment arising from publication of their stories with detail which might serve to identify them. But the bereaved ambulance worker is presented in such detail . . .

Anyway, bluff, jovial, honest Quent was not quite the straightforward fellow he seemed, and, as we have seen, *London Can Take It* was not the personal creation of a 'neutral' reporter which American audiences, if sufficiently gullible, were lured into taking it to be.

11

Filming the Blitz

Despite the clouds of war, propaganda was still a dirty word in Britain, and advertising was considered vulgar . . . So, while desperate efforts were being made elsewhere to catch up with the lethargy and neglect of the thirties, practically nothing was done to plan or prepare for the dissemination of official information . . .

Somebody must have been thinking ahead, however, because . . . about ten days before the actual declaration of war, we were ordered to make a short instructional film, based on an official handbook, called *If War Should Come*. This was just a straightforward statement of what the public should do when the air raids sounded . . .

The fatal Sunday of 3 September 1939 came, and immediately after Chamberlain's speech, saying war had been declared, the sirens went off. To this day, no one seems to know with certainty whether it was a genuine warning or a mistake. What was certain was that nobody behaved the way they were supposed to in our film. Everybody just went into the streets and gawped at the sky, delighted in the balloons, laughed at the air raid wardens, and chatted with each other in the new-found camaraderie that – alas – makes people so nostalgic about wars. The authorities obviously thought again, our little film was canned, and the thousands of copies presumably scrapped.

Harry Watt, *Don't Look at the Camera*

VIRTUALLY everyone in Britain must have seen a fairish proportion of *London Can Take It*, whether or not they have been told what they were watching. Film of the Blitz is surprisingly rare. At that time, as many now don't realise, it was impossible to film events spontaneously and synchronously. A film-editor, Dai Vaughan, explains why in his fine book about Stewart McAllister and Humphrey Jennings: 'Slower emulsions demanded bulky lighting. 35mm synch cameras could not be hand-held; and sound recording equipment, rather than being something you slung over one shoulder, was something you drove around in.'[1] Hence effective

228

sequences of Blitz-in-progress were likely to be very rare. The aftermath of Blitz was easier to film. Some efforts by amateurs raise subversive questions about the representative quality of certain magnificent photographs which show defiant 'Cockneys' coming out of the ruins, or stricken 'Cockneys' being lifted out by rescue workers. Rosie Newman, a lady who happened to have colour film, a camera and time on her hands, filmed post-Blitz scenes in London. The effect of colour, when one sees her work, is disturbing: the Blitz is a black-and-white story in the classic photographs. Rescue work in progress seen in the middle distance looks like a street-mending operation and yields no discreet reminders of painted Renaissance Pietàs.

So the images provided for Reynolds to script over in *London Can Take It* have been recycled almost every time events in 1940 have been narrated on TV. J. B. Priestley, for instance, used most of the film in *1940: A Reminiscence*, screened by the BBC in 1965. He did duly acknowledge that this was a 'documentary' featuring Reynolds. He did not comment on the provenance of certain other elements in his compilation, perhaps because the producer, Ed Rollins, didn't remind him where they came from. Shots of women factory workers singing 'Yes, My Darling Daughter' and of Myra Hess playing Mozart in one of her famous lunchtime concerts in London's National Gallery are used to support as factual assertion what Priestley had hoped for in a Postscript quoted earlier (p. 203). There was, he states a quarter-century on, a 'sudden demand for music and the arts' in the summer of 1940 – people demanded 'at last, a higher quality of life'. In fact, the images used were filmed by Humphrey Jennings in the summer of 1941, for the masterpiece *Listen to Britain*, credited jointly to himself and McAllister.

I once sat discussing with a TV producer a planned series (it was, eventually, a good one) on Britain during the Second World War. He poured scorn on the work of the Crown Film Unit. Its importance had been greatly exaggerated. The public of the day liked feature films – who watched those worthy propaganda documentaries? In due course, it was with wry amusement that I noticed how, presenting the Blitz, his team had lifted an admittedly wonderful shot (of a fireman filthy after a night attacking a conflagration) from Jennings's film *Fires Were Started*, made in 1942 and reconstructing the heyday of the Blitz.

The truth is that Crown Film Unit material, especially Jennings's, has always been used to fill a gap. It took months to produce, for *Fires Were Started*, a vivid impression of what it had been like to fight great Blitz blazes. It was – and, as Boorman's *Hope and Glory* shows, remains – the case that portraying Blitz in continuous sequences, rather than through a series of cuts between shots filmed separately, is very expensive.

Lots of British wartime feature films included short Blitz episodes. Jane Fisher argues that 'the Blitz motif' was used again and again to evoke key propaganda themes for British and US audiences. The Blitz proved that the British Had All Been In It Together (which was 'democratic') and had Taken It (which showed their strong moral backbone) and had Carried On (working towards well-deserved victory). She refers to the 1943 feature *Demi-Paradise*, aimed at the Home Front audience and designed, not very surreptitiously, to prove the superiority of the British way of life over Soviet communism, which had by this time strong appeal for the British 'masses'. A young Russian, Ivan, visits a British shipyard which is making a propeller to his design; all his prejudices against Britain are swept away when he witnesses how people behave during a German raid on the yard.[2] In Noël Coward's *In Which We Serve* (1942), the survivors of *HMS Torrin*, sunk off Crete, cling to a raft. At one stage they sing 'Roll Out The Barrel' to cheer themselves up – this ditty was identified with cheery community singing in shelters. We learn about the men through flashbacks. We see the pregnant war bride of Shorty (John Mills) in Plymouth refusing to move down to the shelter in a raid; she goes instead to a chair under the stairs. When a bomb scores a direct hit, Freda survives and gives birth to a seven-pound son. But Kath, wife of Walter (Bernard Miles), Shorty's fellow crewman, is killed. When Shorty gets a letter and breaks the news to Walter, the latter exhibits profound British restraint: 'I think I'll just go out on deck for a bit. I'm glad Freda's all right.' The experience of the sailors, dive bombed by JU 88s, strafed in the water, is matched by that of civilians like Freda in Plymouth (a point which would not appeal to Nicholas Monsarrat). The splendid performance of Coward himself as robust but humane Captain Kinross is matched by that of Mills as a mere able seaman. 'Class' is a factor in naval life – the film would have been implausible if it had been suppressed – but the officers, apart from Kinross, are less fully and sympathetically presented than men from the lower decks. Class is sublimated in 'service' to a common cause, which is all very Myth-of-the-Blitz-like. The ship transcends the men, the Royal Navy transcends the individual ship – England transcends all.

However effective the Plymouth Blitz episode was in this film, or, say, the bombing of a factory in *Millions Like Us*, where it emphasises the role of women war workers as 'front-line soldiers', such clearly fictionalised items could not be easily recycled in post-

war TV programmes claiming factuality. Hence *London Can Take It,
Listen to Britain, Words for Battle* and *Fires Were Started*, all Crown
Film Unit documentaries, all involving Jennings, have continued to
provide images of British Blitz behaviour. 'Together', as Aldgate
and Richards put it, the Jennings films 'decisively shaped and defined
the image of Britain at War that was to be circulated round the world
and handed on to the generations to come.'[3]

Jennings is a man whose charisma – attested to so strongly by
friends and colleagues – seems curiously detached from the written
evidence provided by his own poems, letters and articles. Unlike
'Quent' Reynolds or 'Jack' Priestley's personalities, his does not leap
forth vividly from anecdotes told by him or about him: the
fascinating talk which friends admired has vanished, literally, into the
air. One is left with an irritatingly imprecise impression of a typical
leftist intellectual from a background in the professional classes and
Cambridge University, saturated in English literature, fascinated by
continental surrealism, who used the cameras which he directed, and
the talents of McAllister as film-editor, to express visually and aurally
perceptions and ideas which are never resoundingly uttered in his
creative and non-creative writings. Because he became the Crown
Film Unit's most admired director, there has been a tendency to
exaggerate his hand in documentaries (including *London Can Take It*)
where his part was auxiliary. The Unit went in for teamwork –
Jennings's individualism attracted the suspicion of John Grierson
before that dominie left his charges to work in Canada. 'A minor
poet', Grierson grumbled long after, 'a very stilted person . . . a little
literary. He was fearfully sorry for the working class . . . safely,
safely sorry for the working class . . . '[4]

Ian Dalrymple, who was in charge when the GPO Film Unit
became the Crown Film Unit, took a very different view. He
thought Jennings 'the most modest man alive; he never by any
chance sold himself at all'. But when shown Jennings's work for
Spring Offensive (1940), he was convinced that this director had
'something special . . . to be used in a quite different way'. Whereas
the ebullient Harry Watt was a vigorous director of action, Jennings
had, and Dalrymple liked, that quality of 'poetry' which irked
Grierson.[5]

Humphrey Jennings and Harry Watt were jointly credited as
directors of *London Can Take It*, commissioned by the MoI
specifically for screening in the USA, though Watt remembered the
whole unit being involved, with himself in charge as supervisory
director. It was September. London was three weeks into severe
Blitz. 'Everybody was sent round looking for people just carrying

on. We reconstructed quite a bit' (this of course was unavoidable – spontaneous filming was so difficult, people had to be persuaded to act, or re-enact, 'real life' behaviour). They wanted a 'bit of humour' in it and 'got the shot of the civil servant with the Anthony Eden Hat and the little attaché case and the umbrella getting a lift from the East End in a donkey cart going to Covent Garden. That was a fake, but it was true, you see . . . The famous last shot of a little Cockney working man lighting a fag was one of Humphrey Jennings's touches of genius. He shot that.'[6] Work on the film began about 26 September, and was finished by 11 October. The film was in the USA by 15 October. A version tactfully called *Britain Can Take It*, only half as long, was released in the UK as one of the five-minute films issued by the MoI to cinemas. The evidence is that the public at home liked it – the press, given its cue by Reynolds's friend Christiansen, certainly extolled it.[7]

Watt had gone to the MoI to ask for help in securing a commentator. The American division suggested Mary Walsh, who later married Hemingway. Watt hated women commentators and begged Bernstein to suggest an alternative. Bernstein put him on to Reynolds – 'an enormous, easy-going, rather drunken character' who, according to Watt, refused to come out of the underground restaurant at the Savoy during the night. He had never written a commentary before and Watt found this an advantage. Working with a cutting-copy of the film and Watt's own treatment, he wrote 'reams' of 'stuff' and let the Crown Film Unit men cut and reject it as they wanted. His big Bronx voice, though, was a severe problem when it came to recording:

He had never even broadcast on radio, so we stood him in front of the mike and told him to have a go. The first words were 'I am speaking from London.' Quent bellowed them out like a barker in a fair-ground! I said, 'That's great, Quent, great, but just take it down a bit, will you?' He did it again, and still sounded like a master of ceremonies at a banquet, so we gave him a drink and got into a huddle in the sound booth . . . Then Ken Cameron, the sound man, had the flash of intuition that was to make Quentin Reynolds famous. He said, 'Look, he's a big bugger with an enormous belly. Let's sit him down in an armchair, stick the microphone nearly down his throat, and let him whisper.' We did this, and rumbling out of that belly came the famous deep Quentin growl, that was destined to be listened to throughout the Allied world.[8]

Reynolds's script was successfully published as a booklet in 1941. His foreword contained a frank admission that the film's subject matter and objectives were determined by the MoI, and also the statement that he had refused payment for his work on the film, which had already been shown in 'twelve thousand' American cinemas. It is a sturdy piece of propaganda praising 'the greatest civilian army ever to be assembled' – the volunteers serving in Britain's ARP – asking viewers if they detect 'any signs of fear' in the faces of 'the very young and the very old' sleeping in the shelters; praising Britain's 'surging spirit of courage the like of which the world has never seen'; stressing that after a night of Blitz, Londoners 'manage to get to work on time – one way or another'. In Reynolds's peroration he growls out, 'I am a neutral reporter . . . I can assure you there is no panic, no fear, no despair in London Town . . . London can take it.'[9]

It is hard to believe now that such blatantly propagandist assertions were ever accepted as the factual observations of a neutral. They are in piquant tension with the film directors' sometimes witty, sometimes delicate images. But Jennings wrote to his wife that using Reynolds's commentary had been 'terrific luck'.[10]

The film stands out among short propaganda efforts from British film studios early in the war for the clarity of its propaganda and the brilliance of its cutting (in which Stewart McAllister collaborated). Delighted, the MoI followed it up with another short film narrated by Reynolds and produced by Crown, *Christmas Under Fire*. Reynolds speaks to camera in this one, which deals with British difficulties in maintaining festive traditions: 'This year England celebrates Christmas underground . . . The stable in Bethlehem was a shelter too.' The nation is resolved that its children will not be cheated. Deep England is invoked as the film cuts between blitzed London and a rural village: 'Today in England even the shepherds are in some kind of uniform.' England, 'unbeaten, unconquered, unafraid', still holds the 'Torch of Integrity' given to her by 'destiny' as the King's College, Cambridge, choristers sing, 'Come Let Us Adore Him'. This is a deeply Christian nation.

The films which Jennings directed alone with Stewart McAllister as editor were also propaganda, produced to meet the requirements of MoI policy. They were successful at the time with British and American audiences, so in MoI's terms they were efficient propaganda. They may have owed some of their success to the fact that their artistic quality captivated people who were in a position to get them shown. Thus, Roger Manvell, who would be one of the best-known British authorities on cinema in the early post-war years, was an MoI film-officer, first, from 1940 to 1943, in south-west England, then, for the rest of the war, in the north-west. He organised over 25,000 showings and claimed that in most of these he had included films by Jennings. Two or three 'shorts' might be seen in a factory during a meal break, up to six in a longer programme for a more general audience in a public hall (for instance, a screening for a Women's Institute). There were also special screenings, often on Sundays, in local cinemas.

Manvell included Jennings's material in 'virtually all' his 'general screenings' because of 'the poetic and emotional lift they gave to the programmes as a whole. I do not exaggerate when I say that members of audiences . . . (especially during the earlier, more immediately alarming years) frequently wept as a result of Jennings's direct appeal to the rich cultural heritage of Britain, going back . . . to Shakespeare and the Elizabethans, to Purcell and Handel.' The only comparable effects, according to Manvell, were achieved by 'the beautiful films of life in the English countryside made by Ralph Keene'.[11] It is perhaps unfair that while Keene is forgotten, Jennings is still celebrated.

Frank Humphrey Sinkler Jennings was born in 1907 in Walberswick, a fishing village in Suffolk. His father was an architect, his mother a talented painter who ran what we would now call a 'boutique' in the village, selling imported French pottery and textiles. The place had an appeal to artists, and when Jennings was a small boy, the great Glaswegian architect, designer and painter Charles Rennie Mackintosh lived there for a time. There is no record that Jennings noticed, on 'Toshie's' characteristic progress from a taciturn drink in one village pub to an equally silent drink in the other, that remarkable man whose career, one of huge achievement followed by frustration, had something in common with his own.

What Jennings did remember, in his own *annus mirabilis*, 1943, was the village's history of 'disaster – fire, flood, encroachments of the sea, poverty, oppression, decline, war and the military, destruction of common rights'. Another major artist whose work was fraught with enigma and ambivalence, Benjamin Britten, grew up and died in Aldeburgh, a nearby coastal village: in his *Peter Grimes*, first produced in 1945 just before the end of the war, this pacifist and homosexual projected village people less than favourably, as persecutors of the non-conformist Grimes. But Jennings, at the height of a People's War, conceived Walberswick folk as representatives of People in general:

Unwritten the story of the people's resistance, uncelebrated in word their struggle and labour. But the church towers from the past, the jetties and piers, the mills and lighthouses, the farms and cottages, the roads and the ridiculous railway – in whatever state they may be now – we must never forget that they were made and built and created and tended by the people – not by those powers for whom they were put up or whose names they bear or whose money allowed them to call them theirs – into the actual making they had little or no part – it was the people and the people alone who had the knowledge and strength and skill and love to fit the sails in the windmill, the thatch to the barn, the wings to the wooden angels, the flashing reflector to the lighthouse lamp.[12]

His parents, being 'progressives', attached to folk art and guild socialism, sent him to the Perse School, Cambridge where the work of W. H. D. Rouse, the headmaster, had been praised by A. R. Orage in *The New Age*. Here, Jennings took part in and designed scenery for plays, and he carried this on when he proceeded to Pembroke College, Cambridge, where he took a Double First in the recently set up English Tripos, and became part of a remarkable undergraduate milieu which combined rediscovery of good English things with an interest in new developments on the Continent, particularly in surrealism. (It was typical that Jennings saw Marx Brothers films as 'surrealism for the millions'.)

A postgraduate thesis on the poetry of Thomas Gray petered out as Jennings drifted into odd jobs and attempts to be a painter. Probably in mid-1934 he began to work with the GPO Film Unit. Early collaborations were with the Brazilian Cavalcanti, who had come to Grierson from the Parisian world of the young Buñuel, and the extraordinary New Zealand artist Len Lye, then experimenting with film animation. Jennings joined the organising committee of the famous International Surrealist Exhibition which shocked (or amused) Londoners in 1936 – other members were André Breton and the young Roland Penrose.

Certain events towards the end of 1936 set Jennings and friends in the Film Unit and literary Bohemia talking about what became Mass-Observation. The burning down of that great Victorian inspiration the Crystal Palace intrigued the surrealist mind as much as the way in which the abdication crisis exposed the primitive, pre-rational character of British attachment to monarchy. The story of Mass-Observation's founding has now been recited often: Jennings and his friend Charles Madge, a poet, by the sort of coincidence dear to surrealists, were brought into touch with Tom Harrisson, and the trio appealed in the columns of the *New Statesman* for volunteer 'Observers' to come forward to help them investigate the bases of mass consciousness through the study of such phenomena as 'Shouts and gestures of motorists . . . The aspidistra cult . . . Bathroom behaviour . . . Distribution, diffusion and significance of the dirty joke'.[13]

Jennings's involvement in what seemed to many a jokey fad was later held against him by serious-minded people in the documentary film movement. Yet, while brief, it was almost absurdly serious-minded: Jennings's main contribution to Mass-Observation was to edit, from a mass (or morass) of observations by individuals in London and throughout Britain, an account of *May 12th* 1937, the Coronation Day of George VI. The interest in relation to Jennings of this abortive (though fascinating) attempt to plumb the English psyche is that the book involved 'cutting' techniques analogous to those of cinema. Its failure is one of many pieces of evidence suggesting that Jennings, whose surrealist paintings are bare of lively interest and whose poems and essays veer between the naïve and the portentously opaque, needed, to fulfil his talents, a medium in which natural and human images were both 'given' and carefully selected, '*trouvé*' and complexly organised for instant effect.

While Mass-Observation developed into a serious (though ultimately unsuccessful) rival to the new British Institute of Public Opinion set up by Dr Gallup, and even the poet Madge swiftly gravitated towards 'hard', statistical methods of social investigation, Jennings soon lost interest. If we agree with Geoffrey Nowell Smith that Jennings had seen Mass-Observation as providing means of 'democratising the discoveries of Surrealism and . . . representing popular subjectivity dialectically and in unromanticised form', then work for the GPO Film Unit offered a better way forward.[14]

Grierson's contempt for his most brilliant recruit (as shown, for instance, in his notorious remark to a colleague, 'Let's go down and see Humphrey being nice to the common people') is not without paradox. There was a political agenda rather like Mass-Observation's underlying Grierson's didactic view of film – as Dai Vaughan summarises it: 'if only our social interconnectedness and our mutual dependencies could be made manifest, politics would take care of itself'.[15] It is implicit in *Night Mail* that the labour of postal workers as seen in the film – taxing, skilful, co-ordinated – helps to hold society together, and explicit in Auden's poem that letters link individual subjectivities which would otherwise be bereft, lonely. Jennings's wartime films represent Britain as an island of linked subjectivities, 'mutual dependencies'.

His development coincided with the development of a distinctive and impressive British style in feature-film narrative which was heavily influenced by the pre-war work of Grierson and his Unit. Charles Barr, in a characteristically elegant discussion of this matter, cites Grierson, in 1930, imploring the brilliant young Alfred Hitchcock, who had directed at this time *Blackmail* and *Murder*, to 'give us a film of the Potteries or of Manchester or of Middlesborough, with the personals in their proper place and the life of the community instead of a benighted lady at stake'. In the Second World War, Barr goes on, the life of the community *was* 'at stake', and the classic feature films of those years – *In Which We Serve*, *Millions Like Us*, *San Demetrio London* – subordinate individual desire and ambition to the team and the job, so that audience pleasure comes from seeing the maintenance of group effort. A 'central and very moving motif' in such movies – I have cited an instance from *In Which We Serve* – is the individual's choking back of grief over the death of a loved one and resumption of teamwork towards victory.[16]

Watt and Cavalcanti brought documentary and narrative together (and both moved into the mainstream film industry, with Ealing Studios, during the war). The result was a British version of 'realism' which can be distinguished from the 'neo-realism', presenting ideological and class conflict, which was emerging in Italy among left-wing film-makers even before allied invasion, and from the 'socialist realism' of the Soviet Union.

The hope of a better world after the war was idealistically expressed in direct statements made in documentary films and feature films alike, in films about battle and in films about civilian life. And Priestley's insistence that virtually all of Us, the People, could get on with the war best by shrugging off Them, the Old Gang of Conservative politicians and bureaucrats – matched by Orwell's now famous assertion of 1941 that England was a 'family with the wrong members in charge' – implied that class conflict, as between management and workers, could be superseded, just as the conflict of both groups with owners would disappear in the new era of state-controlled, state-planned industrial development.

In 1942–3 Jennings produced two 'classic' narrative feature films in *Fires Were Started*, and *The Silent Village*. But his famous 'poetic' documentaries of 1941 were works not of narrative, but of montage.

Listen to Britain, in particular, involves across-the-board harmonisation – of modernism (in technique) with traditional values, and of ideological contradictions and regional differences in British culture. To quote Nowell Smith again, Jennings's films express the idea of 'an industrial nation, still attached both nostalgically and projectively to rural values; a nation divided regionally and by differences of class and culture; but also one capable of holding together its contradictions and divisions in the face of external threat'. He instances that very famous cut 'on a chord' between the Jewish entertainer Bud Flanagan singing in a works canteen and the Jewish classical pianist Myra Hess playing Mozart's Piano Concerto K453 in G Major before the Queen (and lots of ordinary people) in the National Gallery. This shows, he points out, how Jennings's technique, unlike the rhetoric of Churchill, can present awareness of instability as well as suggesting how the nation holds together: 'The union of popular and high culture and their possible divergence' are 'held in the balance, possibilities glimpsed rather than realities asserted'.[17]

Jennings's biggest pre-war film for Grierson's Unit had been *Spare Time* (1939). Often, misleadingly, called his 'Mass-Observation' film, it presents the leisure activities of working-class people in three British industries: steel (Sheffield), cotton (Lancashire) and coal (south Wales). It anticipates *Listen to Britain* in its emphasis on music, much of it performed on screen, which dominates the soundtrack. The most famous sequence shows a 'kazoo band' in Lancashire: girls in a uniform which suggests a strange variant of industrial clothing march, with no audience, in a bare arena, playing their harsh, limited instruments. There is a version of 'Rule, Britannia'; one of the girls is dressed as Britannia. Orthodox Griersonians were outraged by Jennings's 'condescending' attitude towards working-class culture in this sequence. In fact, he was appalled by the 'desolation' and 'human misery' he found in Lancashire: 'At Manchester there was a sort of thin wet sunlight which makes it look pathetic', he wrote to his wife. But he went on, 'It has a grim sort of fantasy. And a certain dignity of its own from being connected with certain events in history.'[18]

'Fantasy' – the truly bizarre kazoo band – and 'history' – signified by Britannia – intersect in one face seen in particular, at a point expressive of 'dignity', in a way peculiar to this director, perhaps the key to his success as mythologist. There is a term, 'absorption', used by art historians (about, say, figures in Chardin's paintings) which is relevant to this face. A kazoo player with her cap at an angle identical to that of her instrument (both tilting on the right of her face) stares at the camera (at us) with the concentration (partly suggested by her strong eyebrows) of someone not looking 'at us' but inwardly preoccupied with some resource inside her which relates to the national essence, to 'history'. Because 'absorption' is present to this effect in *Spare Time*, I cannot buy Dai Vaughan's argument that this stylistic hallmark derives from Stewart McAllister's influence in the cutting room.

But I defer to Vaughan's expert analysis (as a film editor himself) of how this effect might be achieved. We must remember that it was impossible at that time for a documentarist to capture people *spontaneously* on film in a scene of any complexity and significance. People had to be cajoled by the director into 'acting themselves'. Now Vaughan:

> McAllister has used precisely the segments which most editors would have gone out of their way to avoid: those segments where the subjects demonstrate, albeit fleetingly, their awareness of the camera. And my own experience tells me that, a frame or two after he has left them, they will have succeeded in composing themselves into that expression of earnest attentiveness or subdued yet eager endeavour for which the camera operator, habitually, professionally, waits.[19]

As Vaughan's further analysis brilliantly suggests, it is precisely this *awareness* of the camera which detaches Jennings's cutaway-faces *from* the camera. These shots give us a sense of 'the "autonomy" of their subjects: their independent existence in a timescale, a history, a structure of motivations and meanings other than that whereby they take their place in the film'. Vaughan characterises the effect as involving a sense of 'that "self-absorption" by which is meant virtually the opposite – absorption in something outside the self – since it does not recognise the outside as a threat'. I do not quite go along with his film-maker's perception that we are aware of awareness of the camera and of trust in the crew. (Though, as he points out, even audiences in the forties might know perfectly well that documentary shots were faked – British Lion, the UK distributors of *Listen to Britain*, actually boasted in their 'campaign book' about how the Queen 'graciously' returned to the National Gallery auditorium for retakes and about how 'spontaneous' she nevertheless seems.[20]) The expression of simultaneous inwardness and trust takes us well beyond the immediate context of filming. It creates a much more general sensation of English (or British) character as one of deep goodwill, earnest or smiling innocence, typified most beautifully in the face of one of the girls singing 'Yes My Darling Daughter' in the great *Listen to Britain* sequence showing women at work in a factory. This is the face of the harmonious 'new order' swimming out of a depth of British tradition so profound that it could not otherwise be suggested than by Jennings's (as it were) bathyscope. The effect is always very moving, even after a dozen viewings.

Listen to Britain, so often casually pillaged by TV producers evoking Blitz, was in fact filmed in the early summer of 1941, when the bombing had almost stopped, after its horrific climax in London, Belfast, Clydeside, Merseyside and Plymouth. No one could be sure that the Luftwaffe wouldn't return in force; Russia hadn't yet been invaded. Britain still had no Great Power allies. Dai Vaughan says that the film grew 'like fireweed on a bombsite' out of Blitz experience.[21] But it cannot be retained within the 'moment' of its filming as he suggests – *Listen to Britain* can't simply be projecting the pride of a people standing up to Nazism but still all on their own. Its optimism must be flavoured by the post-filming, pre-editing sense of relief that the Soviet Union, after 22 June, was on Britain's side and was standing up, as Poland and France hadn't, to the 'Nazi war-machine'.

According to Joe Mendoza, assistant director of the film which was eventually credited to McAllister and Jennings as co-directors, *Listen to Britain* initially was to be 'Lunch Hour', about the famous National Gallery concerts, and it was Mendoza who not only argued successfully that Bach's music would be too intellectual, but provided an analysis of the musical structure of the Mozart chosen, on the basis of which Jennings prepared a script. Then came Reynolds's famous Postscript of 29 June – 'Dear Doktor' – and material filmed for a documentary related to that alone found its way into *Listen to Britain*, as well as out-takes from other Crown Film Unit documentaries. In August 1941, Jennings spent a week with McAllister in the latter's native Lanarkshire.

A colleague claimed that McAllister was 'one of the few people who actually liked' Jennings – 'most people admired Humphrey, but very few liked him'. They were remembered as fighting 'like cats' over the editing process, but clearly this was because they both cared so deeply and possessively about the material. McAllister (1914–62) had begun as a promising painter, a student at the Glasgow School of Art, who had got involved in the city's amateur film movement with the remarkable animator Norman McLaren. Of middle-class origins, McAllister seems to have had a socialistic view of life and film, despising commercialism. But his obsession with his work was his most obvious characteristic – he virtually lived in his cutting room, working all night until dawn, then sleeping all day. He would brood over film possessively before he cut it, emerging only to fall absurdly and impractically in love with any woman in sight.[22]

Listen to Britain is structured (like *London Can Take It*) on a twenty-four-hour cycle, but also on the form, as provided by Mendoza, of classical symphony: allegro, then the adagio of night, the scherzo of morning, a lunch-hour finale. 'People's War' imagery is transfigured into a unique and still delightful work of art.

Words for Battle, however, has 'dated', interesting though it remains. Filmed earlier in 1941, while London was still being raided, it is a 'five-minute short' for the MoI which expanded to eight minutes. Its propagandist purpose is to show what Britain is fighting for. Each of its seven sections consists of a text, read by Laurence Olivier, with related or contrasting images. An excerpt from Camden's *Description of Britain* is followed by one from Milton's defence of freedom, *Areopagitica* – the poet's image of England as 'an eagle' is matched with a shot of a Spitfire and airmen. After Blake's 'Jerusalem' and Browning's 'Home-Thoughts, from the Sea', we are surprised by Kipling's 'The Beginnings', about 'when the English began to hate', read over post-raid shots and a funeral procession down a ruined street. With Churchill's speech of 4 June 1940, an image of the dome of St Paul's comes up under 'we shall never surrender'. In a characteristic sleight of British propaganda, determined to imply that the spirit of British government is identical with US democracy, Big Ben and Parliament illustrate 'government of the people, by the people and for the people' in Lincoln's Gettysburg Address. This is the last and climactic text before tracking shot carries the film jauntily away, accompanied by Handel's 'Water Music'.[23]

It is said that Jennings was not altogether happy with the choice of texts for *Words for Battle*, which is consistently unsubtle. So it would be unfair to deduce from the film that Jennings's literary training and interests were liable to take over his work on occasions and spoil it. Some people find intrusive the 'literary' parts of *Fires Were Started*, when a Scottish fireman, 'Rumbold', recites to his mates first Ralegh's address to 'eloquent, just and mighty death', then, much later, a passage from Shakespeare's *Macbeth*. But the effect is utterly different from *Words for Battle*. If Ralegh's sardonic, rolling praise of Death – 'whom all the world hath flattered, thou hast cast out of the world and despised' – has some superficial consonance with People's War ideology, it also suggests a 'universal' truth obliterating all difference between Briton and German, democrat and Nazi. The *Macbeth* quotation ('Ay, in the catalogue ye go for men . . . ') conflates humans with dogs and suggests that the broad category 'men' includes differences as great as those between spaniels and 'demi-wolves': each man has a distinct aptitude. This works against the ethos of communal teamwork, suggesting instead the mode of epic, with individual heroes. There are other ways, of course, of explaining how these passages relate to the film as a whole, but they certainly represent that precious element of 'instability' which Nowell Smith praises: their use is certainly not 'propagandist' in any simple, direct way.

Fires Were Started, however, began with a clear propaganda remit. Those concerned with public relations on behalf of Civil Defence wanted a film which would celebrate voluntary teamwork. Harry Watt had prodded Ian Dalrymple, the head of the Crown Film Unit, to get Jennings to make 'an action picture, because everything is so static with Humphrey'. Jennings began work on the script in the early autumn of 1941; by the time the final, detailed, 'shooting' version was ready in January 1942, the London fire service had become used to relative inaction over nearly nine months since the last big raid and what we now see as the end of the Blitz.

The story is very simple. Bill Barrett, an advertising copywriter, joins, as volunteer, a fire station in working-class east London. Soon he is called out with his colleagues to deal with a fire at a blazing warehouse which threatens a ship in the Port of London laden with ammunition. After an all-night struggle, the ship is saved and can sail on its war-winning way, but one fireman, Jacko, has died in the blaze and his funeral counterpoints the ship's departure. The story eliminates all conflict except that of men (with women helping) against fire. There are hints of dramatic dissonance to begin with – why does the rather foreign-looking wife of Jacko the shopkeeper seem so sulky (sexual frustration)? will middle-class Barrett be accepted by his mates (class conflict)? These are red herrings, though useful enough in generating sufficient narrative suspense to keep going what ('poetry' apart) is essentially a film geared to one familiar objective of Griersonian documentary – the full and clear illustration of how a complex job of work is done.

The actors were all 'real-life' – but full-time – firemen. William Sansom, a well-known fiction writer then in the fire service was cast as Barrett. Johnny Daniels was acted by an ex-taxi driver, Fred Griffiths, who went on to play similar working-class roles in some two hundred more films. A romantic account of the film's making has Jennings improvising all the way through, making up dialogue on the spot. The truth seems to be less remarkable – that he incorporated interesting details which turned up by accident during filming, like a street penny-whistler discovered in an East End square. He called on Sansom to improvise at the piano, so the glorious sequence where the firemen enter one by one to the singing of 'One man went to mow . . . two men went to mow' – by implication like agriculturalists on their way to scythe the meadow of fire – may owe its freshness to not being quite foreseen. Sansom recalled the atmosphere thus: 'Democracy the rule. Christian names all round, discussion and beer together after work. He gave us the sense of making the film *with* instead of for him.'

But the superbly 'surreal' moment when a frightened horse passes the flames was carefully foreplanned – as everything to do with the fire had to be, for obvious reasons. (Despite this, most of those involved got burnt at one time or another.) Filming lasted for several months from February 1942. A real warehouse in St Katherine's Dock was ignited to provide the fire (which shows how blackout regulations no longer needed to be stringent, with visits from the Luftwaffe now so rare). Interiors were shot in Pinewood Studios, home base of the Crown Film Unit. The original title, *I Was a Fireman*, was changed after wrangles with distributors, who also insisted on a cut of several minutes in length. We now see the full seventy-five-minute version, but with the revised title – which takes a common phrase from news bulletins and has the effect, because of its passive tense, of underlining the most remarkable feature of the film, regarded as propaganda – the virtual absence of the enemy. The fire is like those natural disasters which Jennings thought typical of Walberswick life down the ages: the agents who started it are of no interest compared to the courage and resourcefulness of the people who put it out.

Even the Griersonite *Documentary News Letter* was for once (like the rest of the press) full of praise for the film when it was released in 1943, applauding Jennings for 'the best handling of people on and off the job that we've seen in any British film', though characteristically deploring 'three or four occasions when, with somebody playing the piano or reading or reciting poetry (in his worst *Words For Battle* manner), he goes all arty for a moment'.[24]

This was the Myth brought to ultimate refinement by a director who himself believed that the bombs had awakened a wonderful spirit of 'unselfishness' in London, and who worked in a tradition, of which *Night Mail* was a distinguished example, which was skilled in analysing and depicting working processes. The contributions of McAllister and the composer William Alwyn seem to be wholly subordinated to Jennings's own master conception. He wrote to his wife, on 12 April 1942:

It has now become 14 hours a day – living in Stepney the whole time – really have never worked so hard at anything or I think thrown myself into anything so completely. Whatever the results it is definitely an advance in film making for me – really beginning to understand people and making friends with them and not just looking at them and lecturing or pitying them. Another general effect of the war.

. . . Painting etc. I am afraid I haven't touched for months now . . . Reading nothing. Life concerned with a burning roof – smoke fire water – men's faces and thoughts: a tangle of hose, orders shouted in the dark – falling walls, brilliant moonlight – dust, mud, tiredness until nobody is quite sure where the film ends and the conditions of making it begin: a real fire could not be more tiring and certainly less trouble. But what one learns at midnight with tired firemen . . .[25]

That was it then: real fire, real team spirit. But no actual bombs. So far from 'beginning to hate' as in Kipling's poem the English in the film represent nothing but mutual self-sacrificing love. London's Blitz is purged of any connection with the now much-advertised nightly raids of RAF Bomber Command over Germany, where 'fires were started' in Hamburg which Bill Barrett and his mates couldn't have coped with and which more resembled apocalypse than natural disaster. A very clean propaganda film, eminently suitable for export. But also an extremely beautiful film, replete with intimations of a classless new order. 'History', as T. S. Eliot was writing while Jennings was at work on his film, was 'now and England'. And, as Eliot's 'Little Gidding' declared at the moment of its publication, which coincided with victory (at last) in North Africa and with the publication of the Beveridge Report, 'All shall be well/And all manner of thing shall be well.' The Fire and the Rose of England were one.

Hollywood could not have been expected to deal with the Myth in such profoundly felt ways. *Mrs Miniver*, directed by the distinguished William Wyler, was an Oscar-winning success in 1942. Starring the popular Greer Garson as the eponymous heroine, it went down well in Britain, even though some reviewers and cinema-goers thought its view of Britain bogus.[26] It represented Village (and also commuter) England, with a silly old feudal Lady deflated at the end, the middle classes (Miniver and her husband) Carrying On bravely at Dunkirk and under bombing, and the younger generation showing fine, classless, war-winning spirit. At the end, after planes have killed villagers, the vicar preaches in the bombed church. Henry Wilcoxson, acting the clergyman, apparently rewrote the sermon with Wyler so as to emphasise that 'this is not only a war of soldiers in uniform, it is a war of the people – of all the people – and it must be fought not only on the battlefield but in . . . the heart of every man, woman and child who loves freedom'. Six million dollars grossed in the US alone proved that these sentiments were widely acceptable, and also, presumably, that the English middle classes, being now one with 'the people', were acceptable allies in the cause of freedom.[27]

Explaining the war to US servicemen in terms of how enemies and allies related to the cause of freedom became the remit of one of Hollywood's finest and most successful directors, Frank Capra, famous for such populist pre-war movies as *Mr Deeds Goes to Town*, *Mr Smith Goes to Washington* and *Meet John Doe*.

'Documentary' film had a different, and perhaps less impressive, history in the USA: no figure like Grierson had emerged as prophet. Newsreel was a form common to both countries, but in the US, the *March of Time*, which had begun with a newsreel format, handling six or ten subjects per film, had gone over to presenting first two, then only one 'in-depth' presentation per issue. The US Film Service, set up in 1938 by FDR to make documentaries, had been quashed by anti-New Dealers in Congress two years later. The integrating control over both feature films and 'documentary' propaganda exercised in Britain by MoI would not be possible in the USA, though the Office of War Information, set up in June 1942, had the brief to produce movies, as well as attempt to bring Hollywood into line, and did so until Congress slashed its budget. Meanwhile, since 1936 the Signals Corps had been responsible to the War Department for producing training films. When it was decided after Pearl Harbor that 'orientation' films were also needed, Capra was brought in to head a special production unit within the Signals Corps. The aim was to inform and inspire the recruits flooding in to the US army, where over a third of the troops had no high-school education.[28]

'To me', Capra would write in his lively memoirs, 'documentaries were ash-can films made by kooks with long hair.' In an hour-long briefing, General George Marshall, US Chief of Staff, told him his job was to counter – in a US army of 8 million where civilians would outnumber professionals by fifty to one – the 'superman incentive' which kept the Germans and Japanese going: to 'win the battle for men's minds'. When Capra objected that he'd 'never even been near anybody' who had made a documentary, Marshall replied testily, 'Capra, I have never been Chief of Staff before. Thousands of young Americans have never had their legs shot off before.' So Capra responded, 'I'm sorry, sir. I'll make you the best damned documentary films ever made.'[29]

His unit, set up on 2 May 1942, produced three series of

'orientation' films – *Why We Fight, Know your Ally* and *Know Your Enemy* – as well as the *Army-Navy Screen Magazine* and a film on *The Negro Soldier in World War II*. Though the first *Why We Fight* film won an Oscar as the best documentary of 1942, there was considerable (and well-founded) jealousy in Hollywood of the superior quality of British war documentaries, suggested by the popularity of *Desert Victory* in the USA.[30] So Capra moved on from his '834th Photo Signal Detachment' to become commander of a Signal Corps special coverage section intended to bring US combat filming up to and past British standards. Eventually, he received the Distinguished Service Medal, the highest award the army could bestow outside actual combat.

For Capra, the American Dream had become reality. Brought to the USA, aged six, in 1903, he was the son of a Sicilian peasant. He had worked to pay his own way through high school and college while his brothers and sisters had remained illiterate. His famous films of the thirties had shown 'little people' overcoming evil. The *Why We Fight* series of seven films projects a contrast between the 'free world', characterised almost throughout in terms of 'the people', and the 'slave world', where wicked leaders scheme world conquest, rant and rave. Churchill walks through the streets of London shaking hands with workers – but Hitler's conquest of Europe has given him, personally, more than a hundred million 'slaves'.

The *Why We Fight* series told soldiers the history of the war they were now engaged in. According to Capra, as a novice in the documentary form, he sat down to watch Leni Riefenstahl's famous pre-war Nazi movie, *The Triumph of the Will*. It occurred to him that such enemy footage could be used to prove to US soldiers that the German cause was evil, theirs was just. At this point there breezed into his life Eric Knight, 'a red-moustached American captain with a British accent'. Knight was a Yorkshireman by birth, now a US citizen, a 'rollicking boon companion', creator of 'Lassie', an accomplished novelist, and a man with links with the British documentary film movement. Before his premature death in an aeroplane, he made a famous documentary, *World of Plenty*, with the English director Paul Rotha. Knight agreed with Capra's brainwave, and Capra commandeered all the German and Japanese propaganda footage he could find in Washington.[31]

His film unit was established, with what seemed to Capra very primitive equipment, in a 'falling apart borrowed studio' in Hollywood. It could draw on the services, paid or unpaid, of much of Hollywood's most distinguished talent. For *Why We Fight*, Walter

Huston, for instance, did much of the narration, Walt Disney (under a commercial contract) provided maps and drawings, and Dimitri Tiomkin took charge of all the music. Capra himself, with Anthony Veiller, finalised most of the *Why We Fight* scripts, but besides Eric Knight – given primary credit for all the scripts by one scholar – there was help from such hands as James ('Lost Horizon') Hilton and William Shirer, the former foreign correspondent and CBS colleague of Ed Murrow. The whole team – some forty Signals Corps officers and enlisted men under Capra, plus Hollywood collaborators – worked 'more or less concurrently' on all the seven *Why We Fight* films, each of them fifty minutes long. Capra personally 'directed' the first three, merely 'supervising' the remaining four, but this seems to be a rather unimportant distinction, since the shape of all of them depended on the 'editing principle' which he had conceived.

The stages seem to have been as follows. A script was produced, outlining the story, making the propaganda-instructional points. Then newsreels, allied and enemy propaganda films, and, if needed, Hollywood feature films were ransacked for footage which would tell the story and support the points. About 80 per cent of each film came from such sources – the rest was composed of animated maps and drawings provided by Disney, and 'production shots' made in Hollywood. After the script was finalised and the footage obtained, everything went to Capra and his crew of cutters, headed by William Hornbeck, an Academy Award Winner.[32]

The result would be a precision-built artefact, nothing like Griersonian 'documentary'. But it would anticipate the characteristics of post-war 'documentaries' which narrated over and over again the war's stories on television, British as well as American. This is one reason for concluding this chapter with a look at *Why We Fight* no. 4, *The Battle of Britain*. Another is that no film about the events of 1940–41 in Britain reached such a vast audience. It was shown to all US army personnel in 1943 – attendance was compulsory. Navy and air-force men were not forced to watch it, but some did. With commentary translated into French, Spanish, Portuguese and Chinese, it was screened to allied armed forces. In enemy countries occupied after the war the *Why We Fight* films raised (Capra could boast) at 10 cents a viewing, six times more than their original cost.[33]

Most significantly, *The Battle of Britain* was screened, more or less on Churchill's personal orders, in British cinemas, going on general release in the autumn of 1942 after opening at two London venues. It was prefaced by film of Churchill himself saying, apropos of the *Why We Fight* series in general:

I have never seen or read any more powerful statement of our cause or of our rightful case against the Nazi tyranny . . .

The story is told in vivid scenes, but facts and figures are carefully and accurately recorded, and it will surprise many people who have lived through these tremendous years to see, for the first time, laid out in order, what happened and why . . . As an Englishman, and as a subject of the King and a citizen of the British Commonwealth, I naturally feel deeply grateful to the generous manner in which the part we have played in this world drama has been treated. Things are said about what we have done and how we behaved, which we could never have said about ourselves . . .[34]

This was not a wholly ingenuous statement. The shot list of *Battle of Britain* held in the Imperial War Museum shows that the British Information Services in New York provided no fewer than thirty-five propaganda documentaries from which Capra and his team drew much of their material. Not surprisingly, shots from *London Can Take It*, *Christmas Under Fire*, *Words for Battle* and *Listen to Britain* were used at salient moments. German material in the possession of the US government was also heavily used. Clips from Hollywood features were cut in. And – uniquely in the *Why We Fight* series – a lot of 'production shots' were used, British in origin, which involved fictional dialogue between British citizens played by actors: scenes in an air-raid shelter, men caught in an air raid (humorous Cockneys, of course), two air-raid wardens and an old couple entering their bomb-shattered home. Some purists objected at the time to the use of 'faked' material. But the *Why We Fight* project was predicated on the idea that there was a true story about the war: in getting this truth over, it was perfectly in order to select any shots which made it vivid.[35]

The Battle of Britain does not bother much with stock anglophile conceptions of England as a green and pleasant land, but it is suffused with a conception of English character, according to which the islanders are quiet, modest folk who don't like raising their voices. (A Spitfire pilot, reporting several kills, is almost inaudible: the shot, of course, came from a British propaganda film.) The story of Battle and Blitz is brilliantly simplified so as to create a visual narrative with an easily extracted moral. Thus, on 7 September the frustrated Nazis resort to bombing London, apparently chiefly by day. It is on 5 October, according to Capra, that they switch to night bombing, and only after this are RAF bombers seen at work, *accurately* bombing a submarine yard in Bremen. *So*, Hitler retaliates *indiscriminately* against Coventry, *but*, after shots of devastation and mass mourning (thirty-two feet from *Words for Battle* are cut in amongst many more from Pathé News), the people of Coventry get back to work making planes. *Then* the British impudently celebrate Christmas (Quentin Reynolds's second film is drawn on here), *so* Hitler sets the City of London on fire, *but* it's too late, he has lost, freedom has won, *because*, under the flames, shelterers in the tubes Carry On calmly: 'They knew this was a people's war, and they were the people – and a people who didn't panic couldn't be beaten.' Churchill is cheered in the street. 'For the first time it was the Germans who had tasted the bitter dirt of defeat . . . A *regimented* people met an equally determined *free* people . . . The British did more than save their country – they won for the world a year of precious time.' The film ends with the song 'There'll Always Be An England', and with 'God Save the King' (George VI has appeared several times, but has never been identified by name, because this is the *People's* War).

From the early shots in which Hitler stares through a telescope, purportedly at the English coast – 'The chalk cliffs of Britain rose sheer and white out of the choppy water' – *The Battle of Britain* is brilliantly fast-moving. Filmed images are reinforced by Disney's animated diagrams, displaying the supposed German strategy of World Conquest (which ultimately involves getting control of the seas and dominating the USA). Statistics are snappily and authoritatively presented. The RAF is outnumbered 'ten to one' both in men and machines. As Fighter Command (largely represented by shots from the Twentieth Century Fox feature film *A Yank in the RAF*, released in 1941 and starring Tyrone Power) go up to meet the Luftwaffe, they face odds of six, eight, ten to one. In 'twenty-eight days' (precisely) of 'terror' from the beginning of heavy raids on London, 7,000 civilians are killed but the Nazis lose 900 planes . . .

There is no reason to suppose that Capra, hardly an expert on current affairs, himself knew that this film contained statements which, though convenient, were false. He came to believe that *Why We Fight* had revolutionised 'not only documentary film making throughout the world, but also the horse-and-buggy method of indoctrinating and informing films with the truth'.[36] But to what extent could Churchill have persuaded himself, as he sought to persuade the British public, that *Battle of Britain* was a film in which 'facts and figures' were 'carefully and accurately recorded'? Leaving aside (for instance) the deft positioning of the 'raid on Bremen', so that it appears that the British bombed only in retaliation, what did the Great Man privately make of the statement, 'In a democracy it is not a government that makes war, it is the people . . . To lead them the people had chosen Winston Churchill as Prime Minister'? *Battle of Britain*, with its straightforward opposition of 'people' and 'freedom' to one-man tyranny, its readily intelligible, because radically simplified, fusion of chronology and causation, and its unqualified assertions about British will to fight and British morale, created a version of the Myth of the Blitz which Americans could believe, presented with Hollywood finesse. Britons were happy to accept it also. It gave due praise from a powerful ally – an ally which had brought to the war industrial and military might far exceeding that of their own country, but which could never match the moral authority represented (of course Capra's team used it!) by the image of St Paul's dome above the ruins.

What did St Paul's represent? English creative genius, of course, since the great architect Wren had designed it. Christianity, still more obviously, triumphant over neo-paganism. Also, London's metropolitan role – within Britain, within the British Empire (though perhaps relatively few people realised that its crypt contains a British pantheon of the tombs of imperial military and naval commanders, surpassing even the copious imperial hagiography which one finds in other British cathedrals). The Palace of Westminster had not been unscathed, but Big Ben had survived, proudly erect, a more fitting symbol for the Father than for the 'Mother of Parliaments'. The monarchy, with its essential, mystified role in the unwritten and literally incomprehensible British Constitution, had been given new stature by the comportment of George VI and his smiling Queen as they toured the ruins. (After a few months, the MoI decided that 'London Can Take It' propaganda to home audiences was becoming counterproductive. Horrific footage of Coventry alone came to represent the 'provincial Blitz': film of visits by royalty was the reward of other cities for their sufferings.[37]) British institutions representing Nation and Empire, Democracy and Tradition, had come through the Blitz with enhanced credit. Whatever the Treasury's national balance sheet said, Britain was still great.

Epilogue

ALMA: Do you think it would be better for us if we had won the Battle of Britain?

FRED: Of course I do.

ALMA: I don't.

FRED: Mrs Boughton!

ALMA: It might have been better for America and the rest of the world, but it wouldn't have been better for us.

FRED: Why not?

ALMA: Because we should have got lazy again, and blown out with our own glory. We should have been bombed and blitzed and we should have stood up under it – an example to the whole civilised world – and that would have finished us.

Noël Coward *Peace In Our Time*

Noël Coward's surprising play, seen in London in the summer of 1947, when glorious weather and the amazing cricketing feats of the 'Middlesex Twins', Compton and Edrich, at Lord's must have provided unfair competition, has now been completely forgotten. *Peace In Our Time* is a tale of the British resistance, set in a pub in Kensington between November 1940, just after the Nazi conquest, and May 1945, when allied forces are liberating the island. As one would expect from Coward, it is very cleverly constructed, avoiding overstatement at every point, with only two important German characters and a wide range of English types among the regulars to provide humour and small-scale drama. Only one English person is shown as a collaborator (if one excepts a certain prostitute). That is Chorley Bannister, a homosexual, like Coward himself, but the target for Coward's ire against petty London littérateurs with no backbone, a vein of invective which Priestley and Orwell had mined already. So the play affirms, as the Myth does, the quiet heroism of the People across the classes (though in this case mostly middle).

But the passage quoted above shows that Coward, one of the war's most efficient filmic mythologisers, had done some thinking in the drab aftermath. Perhaps he had spotted that French culture had re-emerged after liberation in 1944 with enhanced intellectual and moral prestige – his projection of occupied Britain certainly seems to replicate the idealised and essentially very false notion that in occupied France only tarts and a few twisted intellectuals had had any time for the Germans. Fashion in dress, films and painting and even in drama and ideas, was increasingly dictated by Paris. In any case, it is pertinent that the astute assessment which Coward gives to Alma of the harm which the Myth of the Blitz might do to Britain is subtly mixed with resentment of the USA. It is implied that Britain is liable to suffer for having saved America.

American journalists who had collaborated in the creation of the Myth would not all look back with unmixed gratification to 1940. The distinguished Drew Middleton would affirm, in an account of the Battle of Britain published in 1960, that 1940 taught a 'lesson . . . Despite its fumbling and uncertainties, democracy by its representation of the mind and spirit of all the people can in hours of trial exhibit a resiliency and morale that can be extirpated but that cannot be broken.' But after that thinking man's version of *Why We Fight*, Middleton admits that, 'To the survivors of the blitz that second autumn of the war is a dark memory to be locked away at the back of the mind.'[1]

Eric Sevareid, as we have seen, was prepared to admit freely, in memoirs published just after the war, that unlike his fearless CBS colleague Ed Murrow, he had found the Blitz intolerable. On his way out of London that autumn, he gave a last broadcast from the city, praising its spirit – London, which was not 'England' but which was 'Britain', had become 'a city state in the old Greek sense'. He couldn't hold his voice steady and feared the broadcast was mawkish. But in the USA a businessman told him that he 'had listened while driving and had had to stop his car for a moment', and a professor of history that he 'had heard it in his bedroom and had had to bathe his eyes before he went down to dinner'.[2]

Back in Britain in 1944, Sevareid didn't like the arrogant and ignorant behaviour of US GIs. He thought that the intellectuals of the Labour Left – Foot, Strachey, Bevan – were 'bringing political journalism to its greatest flourishing in the English-speaking world'. He was certainly not an anglophobe. Even so, much in the British mood disgusted him. People seemed to have abandoned any rational approach to history. He told an intelligent British friend that the US navy after the war would not only be the world's biggest, but also the only one with really large-scale battle experience. His friend's face darkened, his hands shook, his voice choked; he was as indignant 'as if I had insulted his honour'. To British critics a bad American film was a 'typical Hollywood product', a bad British one was 'merely an unfortunate effort'. The 'Beaverbrooks of London' used 'glaring headlines to demonstrate to the people that the B-29 was not up to the capacity of one of their own heavy bombers':

> Churchill and others in the Parliament and press went out of their way whenever there was opportunity to remind the people of those old days 'when we stood alone in this island', in tones that indicated nostalgia for the moment of exclusive glory, now somewhat unfairly smothered by the avalanche of strange events and strange men who ignorantly seemed to prefer their own achievements and were no longer awed by the Battle of Britain, El Alamein, or even Dunkirk. It was as if in the British mind the Americans were a kind of mass army of robots . . . an inhuman Goliath who happened now to be on the side of England who was David.[3]

By the end of the forties, Britain, though in American eyes 'socialist', would be in military and geopolitical terms a satellite of US power. But even in the nineties, many Britons would retain the habit of thinking that Fighter Command and the Cheery Cockney had saved democracy, and that America had entered the war late, to claim the credit unfairly and to reap the benefits. After all, that, virtually, was what Frank Capra had told them . . .

As Louis MacNeice showed, it was possible for an Irish person in wartime London, completely committed to beating the Nazis, to see through, or round, the Myth with a vision which detached behaviour from British history as the Myth reconstructed it and which could discover human traits by no means defined by this Moment or Finest Hour, or confined to Londoners Taking It. Elizabeth Bowen was another case in point. Created a Commander of the British Empire in 1948, in due recognition of her loyalty and distinction, she had nevertheless published during the war short stories which presented the current scene in anything but a mythical fashion – though perhaps it should be admitted that her own post-Yeatsian mythology of the Anglo-Irish 'aristocracy', to which she belonged, and its great houses is implicated in her cool view of bombed London, concerned as it tends to be with damage to graceful architecture and to the comforts of upper-class civilisation.

Bowen's 'In the Square' first appeared in Cyril Connolly's *Horizon* in September 1941. It seems clearly to be set in the July of that year. It is a brilliant evening. A fashionable London square has lost three houses to bombs. 'The grass was parched in the middle; its shaved surface was paid for by people who had gone . . . Most of the glassless windows were shuttered or boarded up, but some framed hollow inside dark.' One house is occupied. Rupert, who has not been here for two years, comes to see Magdela, whose parties he once attended. The door is opened by 'an unfamiliar person, not a maid'. She studies him 'with the coldly intimate look . . . new in women since his return'. This is the former secretary and, we learn, mistress of Magdela's husband, who has stayed in 'the north' since the war started. But we infer, from Magdela's response to a telephone call, that she herself must have a lover, one reason, perhaps, for her coming back to London during the Blitz.

At one point Rupert looks at the 'empty pattern' of chairs around them and realises that he and she cannot 'be intimate without many other people in the room'. They stand at the window. The square beneath them has become a resort for lovers. 'Now the place seems to belong to everyone', Magdela says. 'One has nothing except one's feelings. Sometimes I think I hardly know myself.' She tells him she is 'happy', and, as the story ends, begs him to tell her how things strike him, 'coming back to everything . . . Do you think we shall all see a great change?' Things, of course, have already changed: the square is contestable space, not a fortress of privilege.[4]

This story depends completely for its point on the precise time and place of its setting. So does 'Mysterious Kor' (1944), set perhaps rather later in wartime London, in which one of three very disparate young people who have been thrown into uncomfortable proximity in a tiny flat escapes into a vision, prompted by the city under brilliant moonlight, of Kor, a dead city, forsaken, uninhabited, perfect, with 'wide, void, pure streets'. It is the combination of full moon and wartime blackout which makes her imaginings more than trivial, whimsical. In both stories the somewhat helpless individuality of lone people whose lives have been disrupted is associated with scarred, but in certain lights beautiful, London townscapes.[5]

Not all of Bowen's sixteen wartime stories are so dependent on the moment evoked: some involve their pasts 'catching up' with people as might have happened in other circumstances. But one remarkable story, 'Summer Night', set in Ireland at the time of the Battle of Britain and published in 1941, can be read as commenting on the

Myth of 1940 in a surprising, refreshing way. Again, light is important. On a glorious evening, Emma speeds sixty miles through the countryside to her lover's house. She has told a lie to escape from her sad husband, a major without a war, and her daughters Di and Vivie. The 'hotel woman' where Emma stops to make a call looks at a newspaper and says, 'with a stern and yet voluptuous sigh', that there is an 'awful air battle. Destroying each other.' Meanwhile, Emma's lover Robinson, a factory manager, has had an unexpected visit from Justin, a Dubliner deprived of his annual European holiday by the war, and Justin's deaf sister Queenie, who lives in the small town. Justin pretentiously argues with Robinson over the crisis as an intellectual in neutral Ireland sees it, generalising vacuously: 'We're confronted by the impossibility of living – unless we can break through to something else.' On their belated way out, they see Emma, just arrived, pulled up in her car at the gate. Her mood of manic, guilt-haunted excitement breaks down against Robinson's cool authority and matter-of-factness. Justin, agonised by the realisation that he has been *de trop*, writes to Robinson pompously, expressing contrition and saying that he will avoid him during the brief remainder of his stay. But the deaf Queenie is happy: Robinson, on this beautiful night, has stirred romance in the good heart of this unmarried, yet beautiful, middle-aged woman . . .

Such reductive summary does no justice to a story of Chekhovian richness and subtlety. Of all the elements essential to the structure of its narrative, only Justin's presence is causally related to the war. A reader wholly ignorant of the events of summer 1940 should be able to 'understand' the story as one about human relationships set in peaceful Irish landscape. Yet imagery and implications are enriched if one thinks of the Battle of Britain. Emma drives with the passion for speed of a Spitfire pilot. Her eyebrows are 'wing-like' – she has an 'animal' nature, like her daughter Vivie, who is naughty in her absence, moving her religious Aunt Fran, who catches her, to thoughts about the war being everywhere: 'Each moment is everywhere, it holds the war in its crystal; there is no elsewhere, no other place . . . Emma flying away – and not saying why or where. And to wrap the burning child up did not put out the fire. You cannot look at the sky without seeing the shadow, the men destroying each other. What is the matter tonight – is there a battle?'

If Emma represents animal pleasure in the speed given by modern technology, Robinson, in his up-to-date 'electric house', represents both the practical face of technology and the aura of romance which this moment has given to its apparent masters. Bowen, it seems to me, subtly works on a paradox implicit in the Myth of the Battle of

Britain: that the manic abandon of Knights of the Air depends on the skills of engineer, manager and mechanic. Wartime mythologisers found ways (as in Leslie Howard's *First of the Few*) of presenting technical men as heroic. But when Emma's romantic mania confronts Robinson's calm her 'adventure' dies 'at its root, in the childish part of her mind'. The Battle of Britain, by implication, is an episode in the history of the human imagination's difficulty in coming to terms with new technology, with electricity and petrol-fuelled rapid travel.[6]

Angus Wilson, introducing Bowen's *Collected Stories*, begins by stressing her near-uniqueness as a writer who could convey 'what life in blitzed London was like', as if a handful of stories in a volume of nearly 800 pages represented her peak of achievement, with her 'moments of sudden vision just as the bombs themselves exploded London's surface beauty or squalor to reveal long-forgotten depths beneath'. He links the stories with her post-war novel *The Heat of the Day*, published in 1949.[7]

Impressive though much of this novel is, it surely cannot compare, in sustained artistry, with 'A Summer Night' or 'Mysterious Kor'. Bowen has trouble with lower-class characters, cannot approach them except with *noblesse oblige*, and unfortunately she seems to have believed that in an ambitious war novel she must perforce do so. Thus the story of Stella Rodney – intelligent upper-middle class with Irish connections – intersects with that of Louie, a lower-middling young woman married to a soldier serving in India, who has lost her parents in the bombing of a south-coast town. Louie is not, when it comes to intellectual limitation, as extreme a case as the idiot Benjie in *The Sound and the Fury*, but at times Bowen's attempt to create processes of thought and feeling for her character suggest such theoretical calculation as must have underlain Faulkner's far more powerful creation.

Under the influence of the sharper Connie, an ARP warden now (it is 1942) underemployed in her job, with whom she shares a flat, Louie discovers newspapers. They give her 'peace', we are told, because they tell her what she thinks. She has felt as if the bad war news over the last few months 'could only in some way have been her own fault'. Now:

For the paper's sake, Louie brought herself to put up with any amount of news – the headlines got that over for you in half a second . . . As far as she could make out, the same communiqués were taken out and used again and again. As against this, how inspiring was the variety of the true stories, which made the war seem human, people like her seem important and life altogether more like it was once. But it was from the articles in the papers that the real build-up, the alimentation came – Louie, after a week or two on the diet, discovered that she *had* got a point of view, and not only *a* point of view but the right one. Not only did she bask in warmth and inclusion but every morning and evening she was praised. Even the Russians were apparently not as dissatisfied with her as she had feared; there was Stalingrad going on holding out, but here was she in the forefront of the industrial war drive. As for the Americans now in London, they were stupefied by admiration for her character. Dark and rare were the days when she failed to find on the inside page of her paper an address to or else account of herself. Was she not a worker, a soldier's lonely wife, a war orphan, a pedestrian, a Londoner, a home and animal-lover, a thinking democrat, a movie-goer, a woman of Britain, a letter-writer, a fuel-saver and a housewife?[8]

This is interesting in its anticipation of Louis Althusser's thoughts about ideology, and amusing in its satire of the propagandist efforts of the wartime press. But it is not convincing as an 'inward' account of mental processes, and its near-sarcasm creates problems in relation to the form of the book, which not only begins with Louie, out of her depth at an open-air concert, but ends with her, after D Day, wheeling a pram along a canal path: her baby, though son of a casual lover, not of her husband, Tom, who was killed in action before he could learn of her infidelity, is named 'Tom' and represents, however wryly, the future of the People. If Bowen despises (like Evelyn Waugh) the idea of a People's War, why does she give a lower class 'war worker' such salience? And if Louie is meant to represent a patriotic positive, or at least the endurance of the 'common stock', why has she, in effect, mocked her?

A defender of the novelist could argue that Bowen is seeing round the Myth of People's War: Louie represents nothing but a certain kind of person who happens to be involved in the struggles and temptations of wartime. But the relationship between Stella Rodney and her lover Robert is given the dignity accorded to those in 'Summer Night': so modes jar against each other to no useful or amusing effect.

Two points about the Stella–Robert relationship are of significance to the theme of this book. They met, two years previously, during the Blitz. And Robert, as Stella gradually learns, is a pro-Nazi traitor, whose eventual death, in effect suicidal, spares him from arrest and a bad end.

Both Stella and Robert are engaged in white-collar 'war work' so hush-hush that we have no idea what they actually do. This gives their characters an artistically acceptable insubstantiality: in such wartime circumstances, people cannot be fully known as in more normal years. But Robert's involvement in the British Expeditionary Force débâcle, in Dunkirk, has left him with a limp and clearly helps to explain his conviction that the Nazis deserve to win. Only contingently, however: 'I was born wounded; my father's son. Dunkirk was waiting there in us – what a race! A class without a middle, a race without a country. Unwhole.' Robert's 'class' is Home County, 'stockbroker belt', wealthy, commuting upper-middle. Bowen seems to set, with impressive astringency, the fragility of the public-school-educated Englishmen who conceived themselves to be the vanguard of their race against the more enduring values *rooted* in Irish life.

Bowen's ten pages describing the meeting of Stella and Robert in London in September 1940 have a subtlety and complexity which cannot be brought out here. The heightened feelings of survivors of the Blitz in that autumn are evoked: 'Never had any season been more felt; one bought the poetic sense of it with the sense of death.' Bowen presses home the intensity of the moment with detail after detail: while each yellow leaf on London's trees 'blazoned out the idea of the finest hour', strain was constant: 'To work or think was to ache . . . fatigue was the one reality.' Survivors were haunted by the nightly 'shoals' of victims; instinctively realising how little they had known about those now noticed as absent, they moved 'to break down indifference while there was still time. The wall between the living and the living became less solid as the wall between the living and the dead thinned.' In the context of Stella's first encounter with Robert, society had 'become lovable; it had the temperament of the stayers-on in London . . . This was the new society of one kind of wealth, resilience, living how it liked – people whom the climate of danger suited . . . The very temper of pleasures lay in their chanciness . . . to and fro between bars and grills, clubs and each other's places moved the little shoal through the noisy nights.'

Bowen's analysis of 'morale' (basically, of upper- and upper-middle-class morale) is brilliantly vivid and convincing: it is easy to relate it to the accounts by American pressmen of their socialising with London's élite. Her details can be selectively used to enrich the Myth. Taken overall, though, they undermine it. Blitz society is febrile, unsound. The liaison between Stella and Robert is a product of animal attraction in a phase when people are living day-to-day. The Blitz spirit is not one of orderly 'carrying on'; rather, irrational reflexes determine behaviour. The price which Stella pays for her excitement under bombardment is the ultimate realisation, in the glum middle of the war, that Robert has made her part of a double life.

British readers and film watchers were predisposed by their taste for detective stories and spy thrillers to enjoy tales about traitors at work in Britain – Bowen's novel was a best-seller. In a whodunnit a most respectable person would prove to be a calculating murderer. So why shouldn't the village squire be a fifth columnist? British home propaganda stressed that one shouldn't trust anyone at all with information which might be useful to the enemy. While in fact Germany had totally failed to create a useful spy network in Britain, everyone believed that such a thing existed: its ubiquitous presence was assumed in *Next of Kin*, a film directed by Thorold Dickinson at official instigation, which showed the dangers of 'careless talk' and enjoyed box-office success.

Another wartime film which played on public belief that there was an active fifth column was *Went the Day Well*, directed by Cavalcanti for Ealing Studios and released in 1943. It was loosely based on a short story, 'The Lieutenant Died Last', written by Graham Greene, then working for the MoI, and deliberately lodged in *Colliers Weekly Magazine*, which published it at the end of June 1940: the aim was to counteract American views that the British lacked determination and weren't really democrats. German parachutists drop on an English village and are thwarted by everyday country folk. (The success of this initial connection with *Colliers* perhaps helps to explain why Quentin Reynolds, later, was in turn so successful in getting facilities through the MoI.[9])

Cavalcanti's film has sixty Germans driving into a Deep English village, Bramley End (idyllic landscape, thirteenth-century church), impersonating ordinary British Tommies. They link up with their fifth columnist ally, none other than Squire Welsford, leading light of the local Home Guard. With his help, the intruders terrorise the village into silence while they set about their nefarious schemes to aid the coming general invasion. Various brave villagers, including the vicar, attempt resistance and meet horrible deaths, but the situation is saved by the enterprise of a naughty little boy, George, who escapes and gets word to the next village. Before help can come from there, the villagers seize arms themselves and begin to pick off Germans. During the final battle, which costs numerous British lives, the treacherous squire is shot by his patriotic mistress, and his manor is largely ruined. No motivation for Welsford's treachery is spelt out. There are no other traitors among the villagers. The mere fact that he is upper class seems (at the height of a People's War) to be sufficient, implicit explanation of Welsford's unique wickedness.

It is hardly possible to believe that German invasion would have met with such near-uniform sturdy resistance as is suggested in Cavalcanti's film and, more soberly, in Coward's *Peace In Our Time*. The history of the Channel Islands, British territory under German occupation, suggests that timid people, lookers-after-number-one and easy-lifers would have collaborated in considerable numbers, and the undoubted prevalence of anti-Semitism in various British milieux suggests that co-operation with the Final Solution would have been quite amply forthcoming. (Anyone who thinks these remarks to be a libel on the British character is required to prove that almost all Britons would have reacted quite differently from other Europeans in such circumstances.)

Nevertheless, the British people, never invaded, could believe that virtually no one would have succumbed. This, combined with sheer exhaustion and with Labour's victory in the 1945 general election, helps to explain the horrid inertia of English culture in the decade after victory. With Labour constructing, if not a New Order, then a welfare state, and with a middle-class backlash against fair shares and austerity in full swing, the leftist critics and experimenters of the thirties, already mostly co-opted into the wartime propaganda effort, were stranded as weary and rather puzzled defenders of the new Establishment composed of Labourites, statist 'liberals' and Planners. The career of Humphrey Jennings after *Fires Were Started* is sadly symptomatic.

His next film was a neglected masterpiece, *The Silent Village*, in which the story of the Nazis' destruction of the Czech village of Lidice was transposed to the Welsh coalfields. Jennings – who stayed with miners while filming and was overwhelmed by the way they seemed to live by Christian and communistic principles – knew perfectly well that Wales wasn't England and that the Welsh still nursed sour memories of English conquest. The Nazi attempt to suppress the Welsh language is a vivid issue in his film. To the film's main propagandist intention of inspiring will to fight against Nazism may have been added, in some official minds, the hope that it would encourage Welsh miners, in a vital industry prone to strikes and absenteeism, to put their backs more fully into it. But resistance by trade unionists to injustice is emphasised in Jennings's story, and the film might well have had the effect of encouraging a Welsh combination of pride, paranoia and class war. The ideological 'instability' of *The Silent Village* is very satisfying.

If Jennings's *Diary for Timothy* (1945) is less successful (though more often seen), this cannot merely be because McAllister was no longer his editor. A month by month account of the final phases of the war is narrated for the infant Tim, born exactly five years after its outbreak. We follow the activities of Goronwy, the Welsh miner, Alan the farmer and Bill the engine driver, 'all fighting in their ways'. Continued danger, austerity and trepidation are emphasised. The script, by E. M. Forster, produces a left-of-centre message, but in such a way as to suggest doubt rather than hope. Towards the end, Goronwy remembers unemployment after the last world war: 'Has all this really got to happen again?' After the three representatives of the People have gone 'back to everyday life and to everyday danger', the film concludes with a diatribe against 'greed for money and power'. But the film's generally downbeat, rather depressing, character is highlighted by shots of Myra Hess playing sombre music at a concert. Compared to counterparts in the Hess sequence in *Listen to Britain*, the faces in the audience are both more relaxed and sadder. Radio news of the abortive British airborne operation at Arnhem is cut in. It seems that the effort of building a better world must now proceed by dogged, unspectacular effort and rather stale principle, not by heady, Blitz-inspired, hope.

Reviewing a book on *The English* by Ernest Barker in the *Times Literary Supplement* in 1948, Jennings demonstrated that he still could not achieve in prose the sense of clear and ample statement present in his best wartime films. Rather petulantly, he exclaims that the English aren't 'mild', as they like to think they are. Ask the Scots and the Welsh – 'It would be inadvisable to ask the Irish.' He asserts that the English are 'in fact a violent, savage race' though 'They have a power of poetry which is the despair of the rest of the world.' (Sample surveys of the intelligentsia in Spanish-, Russian-, Urdu- and Chinese-speaking milieux might have caused him to retract this statement.) But, like Attlee's government – which, in the interests of ill-fed Britain and of British world power greatly increased commitment to the colonial Empire, presided over a spate of new colonisation in Africa and sought to exploit the Empire's resources more efficiently – Jennings favoured a new English expansion: only so could England retain Great Power status.[10]

Working, through Ian Dalrymple's Wessex Films ('Deeply English Films') for the Central Office of Information, which had succeeded the MoI in peacetime, Jennings directed *Dim Little Island* in 1949, a strange film brooding over British decline and trying to cheer people up. Four men 'Speak for England' to camera. Osbert Lancaster, cartoonist and expert on architecture, contends that the English have always 'thank heavens' remained 'deaf to the appeals of reason' – hence the glory of Dunkirk. James Fisher, the naturalist, celebrates British birds, and explains, Priestley-wise, that 'For five bob you can get from almost any industrial city of the North' into beautiful countryside. Vaughan Williams goes on about English folk-tunes. The remark in the film which, in retrospect, is saddest is made by John Ormiston of the engineering firm Vickers Armstrong: the British are no longer the best shipbuilders in the world, but are still the best sailors and can still compete.

Jennings's last film, *Family Portrait* (1951), was directed for Wessex Films 'on the theme of the Festival of Britain'. This expo on the South Bank of the Thames had been planned by great and good members of the Lab.–Lib. post-war establishment as an arena of reaffirmation, a successor to the vainglorious Empire exhibitions of 1924 and 1938, which would be exempt from charges of jingoism. It was quite good fun, especially the associated Battersea Fun Fair. The incoming Tory administration of 1951 ensured that nothing remained for posterity except the valuable new Festival Hall. Jennings's film is choppy, sentimental and confused. The script, by Jennings himself, tells us that the Festival is 'a kind of family reunion . . . We still *are* a family . . . A very mixed family . . . but nevertheless we have resisted . . . invasion for nearly a thousand years.' The diversity of people is matched by diversity of landscape and weather. After invoking Shakespeare, the film tells us that 'for centuries the family has mixed poetry and prose together'. Jennings's inconclusive fascination with the Industrial Revolution yields, after a celebration of James Watt (Scots are part of this family), the perception that it created 'a new kind of poetry and a new kind of prose'. It is saddening to see the erstwhile surrealist hop round British history echoing clichés about English character. The family are innovators who love tradition, cherish domestic life but love pageantry. They have learned the 'trick of voluntary discipline' and their parliamentary system embodies compromise. Naturally, the Myth of the Blitz features here: 'The Elizabethan journey ended with the Battle of Britain.' That matchless invention radar involved 'Prose and poetry again, but put together in a new way . . .'

One sees all the more clearly how impressive is Bowen's presentation of the poetry–prose, romance–technology dichotomy, in 'Summer Night'. Lindsay Anderson's acerbic but just dismissal of *Family Portrait* is worth quoting:

He found himself invoking great names of the past (Darwin, Newton, Faraday and Watt) in an attempt to exorcise the demons of the present. Even the fantasy of Empire persists ('The crack of the village bat is heard on Australian plains . . . '.) The symbol at the end of the film is the mace of Authority, and its last image is a preposterous procession of ancient and bewigged dignitaries. The Past is no longer an inspiration, it is a refuge.[11]

Jennings's last remit was to make a film for the European Economic Commission on 'health', as part of a series on *The Changing Face of Europe*. He looked at possible locations in France, Switzerland, Italy and finally Greece, where he slipped on the Island of Poros, fell from a rock and died. It is very sad that death came just as he was preparing to step outside the ideological paradigms of the 'dim little island' and perhaps to reactivate his youthful internationalism. But it could be that for his generation, or most of them, these paradigms and the Myth of the Blitz were ultimately inescapable. The most vital films coming from any British studio at the end of his life were, after all, the Ealing Comedies, which profoundly influenced the styles and themes of comedy in the rising medium of television.

Charles Barr's brilliant analysis of the output of *Ealing Studios*, published in 1977, is, or should be, well known. Perhaps its most important point, in terms of the Myth of the Blitz, is its first:

> Asked to invent a typical Ealing comedy plot, one might produce something like this. A big brewery tries to absorb a small competitor, a family firm which is celebrating its 150th anniversary. The offer is gallantly refused, whereupon the boss's son goes incognito from the big firm to infiltrate the small one and sabotage its fortunes. Gradually, he is charmed by the family brewery and by the daughter of the house, saves the company from ruin, and marries into it. Officials and workers unite at the wedding banquet to drink the couple's health in a specially created brew.
>
> To make this really Ealing, lay on the contrasts. The brewery names; Ironside against Greenleaf, grim offices and black limousines against country lanes, ivy-covered cottages, horses, bicycles. Autocratic rule against the benevolent paternalism of a grey haired old man who collects Toby jugs. The beer itself: quantity against quality, machines against craftsmanship.[12]

Barr can now reveal that this scenario was actually realised at Ealing Studios. But, whereas Ealing Comedy is thought of as a post-war phenomenon, *Cheer Boys Cheer* was released in August 1939. Again we see how the Myth of the Blitz was all but forged before May 1940. The country lanes and friendly manners of the Greenleaf English would confront the mechanised might of the Ironside Germans and win. At one point in *Cheer Boys Cheer*, the bullying chairman of Ironside is seen reading *Mein Kampf* . . .

Michael Balcon, who from 1938 until they were taken over for television in the late fifties ran Ealing Studios much like a family business in a site on the village green of a London suburb, was the son of poor Jewish immigrants. He shared with Leslie Howard that special patriotic fervour which only assimilated outsiders feel. He believed that British films should be 'absolutely rooted in the soil of this country', and after he bought an estate in Sussex grew willow for cricket bats along the river. Charles Frend, who directed for Ealing the important wartime films *The Foreman Went to France* and *San Demetrio London*, and, in the early fifties, *The Cruel Sea*, seemed to Balcon 'the ideal man to deal with any subject concerning the traditional English values' – Frend was 'born in Kent, educated at King's School Canterbury, an expert on Kentish beer, with his roots firmly planted in the soil of this country . . . '.[13]

Balcon's patriotic commitment to supporting MoI policy was never in doubt – indeed, Ealing was ideally orientated towards the expression of one propaganda theme in particular. The slogan on the office walls was 'The Studio with the Team Spirit', and in such movies as *The Bells Go Down* (about firemen at war), *Nine Men* (an army patrol in Africa) and *San Demetrio London* (Merchant Navy men salvage their stricken tanker), all released in 1943, Ealing celebrated wartime teamwork. It was significant that in the first two the British teams were led by sturdy Scots, while *The Foreman* (who) *Went to France* (1942) was a Welshman with Scottish and Cockney sidekicks – their mission to rescue their firm's plant from a factory in the path of German advance. Ealing teamwork was pan-British, and class-free.

Balcon said in interview about his close-knit team (six out of ten Ealing features during his twenty years as captain were the work of just half a dozen directors), 'By and large we were a group of liberal-minded, like-minded people. We were middle-class people brought up with middle-class backgrounds and rather conventional education . . . We voted Labour for the first time after the war: this was our mild revolution.'[14] Ealing had a strong affinity with J. B. Priestley, who had produced the story of *The Foreman Went to France*, and when Priestley's dramatic allegory calling for a future of co-operation rather than greed, *They Came to a City*, was filmed in 1944, it was Ealing which did the job. Cavalcanti and, over a longer period, Harry Watt provided a direct link with Griersonian documentary. The ethos of People's War was imprinted on all the studio's work.

After the war Balcon characteristically proclaimed the aim of asserting British 'greatness' through Ealing movies. But *Scott of the Antarctic* (1948) celebrated the amateurishness which caused the British hero to fail in his race against the Nordic professional Amundsen. And the studio's best earners, abroad as well as at home, were the quirky, delightful, 'Ealing Comedies'.

These are very diverse films made by directors of markedly varied proclivities. *Passport to Pimlico* (1949) was the only Ealing film directed by Henry Cornelius, a South African, but it was scripted, like several later comedies, by T. E. B. ('Tibbie') Clarke. Clarke, eventually an Oscar winner, had no reason to be nostalgic about the Blitz: he was discharged from service in the wartime police force after a recurrence of nervous asthma, not experienced since his childhood: he had loathed the 'cruelty and horror . . . sickening destructiveness . . . white dusty filth . . . peculiar stink of fresh decay' with which the Luftwaffe's raids on London had assaulted his senses.[15]

But *Passport to Pimlico* reworks the Myth of the Blitz in a peacetime context. What does a close-knit London 'village' community want to do with the huge bombsite which dominates its area? Shopkeeper Pemberton wants to make it a playground, the majority on the local council want to sell it at a profit for private development. The conflict is cast in Priestley-esque terms – fun-and-games and community spirit against private greed. When an unexploded bomb is set off by local boys, an underground cave is discovered which contains a treasure trove, together with medieval documents which prove that Pimlico is legally part of Burgundy. Pemberton, former air-raid warden, can reassume his authority of Blitz days. The community, as Barr puts it, can 'go on being *itself* as it was in the war'. Eventually, of course, Pimlico is reintegrated into Britain, but not before, as Burgundy, it has abolished food rationing and pub licensing hours and given British cinema audiences sick of austerity and bureaucracy a vision of release.[16]

Whisky Galore, directed by the brilliant young Scot Alexander McKendrick, presenting the theft of a cargo of precious spirits from a wrecked vessel by clever Hebridean islanders who totally outwit authority in the person of an honourable but stupid Englishman, has no Blitz bearings whatsoever. Nor does *Kind Hearts and Coronets*, Robert Hamer's elegant and sadistic period comedy. The core of 'Ealing', Barr argues, is found in films scripted by Clarke. In *The Blue Lamp*, PC George Dixon (later to have a lengthy posthumous career from 1955 to 1976 as TV's *Dixon of Dock Green*) is murdered by a young criminal so obnoxious that even the decent criminal fraternity help the police to track him down. Paddington police station houses a family. Dixon, the good bobbie, represents communal interests. The young assassin stands for a new, post-war type, disrupting the national family which won the war. Clarke's *Titfield Thunderbolt* (1953) marks the moment where Ealing's inbuilt tendency to identify with tradition and local identity degenerates into anti-modern fantasy. It has to do with the efforts of enthusiasts to keep a small railway branch line open. The 'Thunderbolt' which serves it is antiquated and picturesque. The implication is that old-fashioned steam trains represent, by their very impracticality, something very English, like Priestley's uninhabited English cottage. Modernisation threatens such precious things. McKendrick's *The Maggie* (1954), scripted by an American, William Rose, provides a Scottish equivalent, in which a picturesque old 'Clyde puffer' is saved from the scrapyard.

By 1958, when Balcon gave up and moved on, his studios had clearly run out of capacity to cope positively with British life. *Dunkirk*, released in that year, shows, as Barr puts it, 'a dispirited, sluggish country blundering its way to disaster'. The final, conventional assertions, made in commentary, that 'Dunkirk was a great miracle . . . A nation had been made whole' had not been vivified in the film.[17]

Little of note was done with 1940–41 on the big screen thereafter until Boorman's *Hope and Glory*. Nostalgia for the war was somewhat submerged in the essentially optimistic and forward-looking Britain of affluence and permissiveness. In the bad-tempered Britain of the seventies – a country skidding at terrifying pace towards second-rate status – angry left-wing dramatists turned to the war years, on stage and TV, to find the origins of present crisis in the betrayal of the people after 1945. Ian McEwan's *Imitation Game* and David Hare's *Licking Hitler* both focused on secret war work – by scientists and propagandists respectively. They bring out the retrospective irony of the term People's War, but don't bear centrally on Blitz. Nor does Trevor Griffiths's *Country*, which shows the Old Gang of moneyed Tories manoeuvring successfully to adjust to Labour's 1945 election victory.

Howard Brenton's *The Churchill Play*, first produced in 1974 in

Nottingham by Richard Eyre (who also encouraged the writers named above to dramatise the war), was revived by the Royal Shakespeare Company in 1978. Brenton wrote in a preface of 1986 that the play was 'at its root a satire against the erosion of civil liberties and union rights that began under Edward Heath's Government and spread apace under Margaret Thatcher's'.[18] Therefore, alas, it remained pointful.

In the Orwellian year, 1984, Brenton's Britain has dozens of internment camps to accommodate strikers and other dissidents. Some inmates of one of them, encouraged by the camp recreation officer, who is a queasy middle-class, ex-public school liberal, put on a play. In this, Churchill rises from the coffin in which a grateful nation buried him in 1965. When it is performed before two MPs from the parliamentary select committee concerned with the camps, the actors use it as a springboard for an attempted breakout.

Brenton is not totally unsympathetic towards Churchill, seen as a lonely depressive, the son of a tragically syphilitic father. But his role as imperialist adventurer in Africa is related to his actions, as pre-1914 Home Secretary, against Welsh miners: both are used to undermine his heroic status. He is confronted by antagonistic voices from blitzed Clydebank, blitzed London. The MPs who witness the play are respectively a smooth 'Conservative-Labour' government man and a guilt-ridden drunk labelled 'Socialist-Labour', so Brenton's target is wider than his retrospective preface suggests. Post-war 'consensus', Labour 'sell out', Tory 'compromise' are all implicated in a tyranny which betrays the professed aim of People's War.

The brilliant film *The Long Good Friday*, originally conceived by its scriptwriter Barrie Keeffe in 1977, finally-released, as directed by a Scot, John Mackenzie, in 1981, makes, though obliquely, a subtler commentary on the relevance of the Myth of the Blitz in the era of Callaghan–Thatcher.

Harold Shand, the central figure of this very violent film, wonderfully acted by Bob Hoskins, is seen by Keeffe, in his own words, as 'a Thatcher man gone mad – the ultimate self-made capitalist and utterly patriotic'. This gangster boss owns a yacht, possesses a posh mistress (named, piquantly, 'Victoria') and has the police and local authorities in his pocket. He is planning a major property development in the East End Docks area and is forging links with the US Mafia, whose chief envoy is Charlie, 'the kid from New Jersey' (played by Eddie Constantine).

At a party aboard his yacht, attended by local government bigwigs and the Mafia men, Harold tells his guests that he is a 'business man . . . with a sense of history . . . Our country's not an island any more

– we're a leading European state. And I believe . . . that this is the decade in which London *will* become Europe's capital, having cleared away the out-dated.' Yet, passing the docks later, he says to Charlie, 'There used to be eighty or ninety ships in this dock at one time. They used to queue to get in.' Charlie replies, 'Don't get nostalgic . . . Remember, you're thirty-five miles from Europe here.' Keeffe has detected a contradiction at the core of both Labourism and Thatcherism – a commitment to modernisation conflicts with patriotic nostalgia.

Shand epitomises further contradictions. He is casually racist. Going to Brixton with its large Caribbean population, he says, 'This used to be a nice street, decent families, no scum.' But he is sentimental about the poor. After torturing a 'grass', he cruises down a Brixton side street where a mother and child in tatty clothes are sitting on the doorstep of a decaying house, and remarks, much as George VI's Queen once did apropos of blitzed Londoners, 'These people deserve something better than this.'

He takes Charlie proudly to a pub which he bought, with true Ealing spirit, 'To stop the big breweries turning it into a slum. It's got Charles Dickens links, historical – very "olde London". You'll love it.' As they approach the pub it blows up.

This explosion is the work of the IRA, now fatally interested in Harold's affairs as a result of the indiscretions of certain subordinate gang members. As the mayhem escalates, the Mafia pull out. 'Harold', Charlie says, 'this is like a bad night in Vietnam.' His sidekick Tony snaps, 'This country's a worse risk than Cuba was. It's a banana republic. You're a mess.' But Harold fights back verbally, calling them 'wankers':

> Us British . . . we're used to a bit more vitality . . . imagination . . . touch of the Dunkirk spirit – know what I mean? . . . What I'm looking for is someone who can contribute to what England has given the world . . . Culture . . . sophistication . . . genius . . . A little bit more than a hot dog – know what I mean? Look at you . . . the Mafia. I shit 'em.

The last we see of Harold, he is in the hands of the 'Micks', the IRA, who are driving him away to be murdered.[19]

Harold, as representative Cockney, has survived into a situation where wisecracks, sentiment and a sense of History cannot save him. As played by Hoskins, he is not 'tragic' but sympathetically comic, in spite of his propensity to bully and torture. He is a monster spawned in the ruins of blitzed Stepney, who finds that the

Americans are no longer admiring and patient and the Celts can no longer be overawed. His only interest in 'Europe' is in leading it. In terminal crisis, the Dunkirk Spirit is the talisman by which he preserves self-esteem. His type, he believes, are never really beaten. He is wrong.

Keeffe might claim to have anticipated, in his Harold Shand, the outbreak of atavism among British politicians of most complexions which marked the decision to fight Argentina over that country's occupation of some islands, known either as the 'Malvinas' or the 'Falklands', which successive British governments, Labour and Tory, had been trying to hand over to Argentina for years.

In retrospect the 'Falklands factor' was much less important than it seemed at the time in securing Mrs Thatcher's re-election (with a slightly decreased share of the poll) in 1983. Inept and divided Labour leadership, together with the split in the opposition vote created by the rise of the Liberal–SDP alliance, would surely have made her return certain anyway.

To judge from speeches in the House of Commons, the opposition were fully as anxious to exploit whatever 'Falklands factor' there might be as the Iron Lady herself. Her image as Elizabeth I Redivivus, or Female Churchill, following her dispatch of the task force to oust the Argies from 'our soil', because it was inherently ridiculous, probably contributed to the intense dislike of her felt by a very large proportion of the electorate, whose views could not be adequately represented because of the antiquated 'first past the post' system by which the Mother of Parliaments was elected to serve under the inscrutable British Constitution.

Anthony Barnett, however, promptly showed, in a very lively analysis, that the Falklands affair was deeply revealing in regard to British political history since the war.

The invasion should clearly have been anticipated and prevented. Once it had happened – at the direction of a particularly brutal military régime with which British governments had previously cultivated good relations – Thatcher was in some difficulty when the House of Commons met to discuss the invasion on 3 April 1982, the day after the islands were overrun. Michael Foot, the Labour leader – erstwhile co-author of *Guilty Men*, Beaverbrook journalist, friend of the wartime US press corps – was possessed by the spirit of 1940, and by that noble tradition of liberal imperialism which conceived Britain to be moral leader of the whole world. He reminded the Commons of:

the claim of our country to be a defender of people's freedom throughout the world, particularly those who look to us for special protection, as do the people in the Falkland Islands . . . Even though the position and the circumstances of the people who live in the Falkland Islands are uppermost in our minds . . . there is the longer term interest to ensure that foul and brutal aggression does not succeed in the world. If it does, there will be a danger not merely to the Falkland Islands, but to people all over this dangerous planet.

Foot's effusion was promptly acclaimed by a leading Conservative backbencher, Edward du Cann – 'the Leader of the Opposition spoke for us all'. Another Conservative, Raymond Whitney, who had quite recently worked in Argentina for the Foreign Office and therefore knew something about the history of the crisis, was heckled and interrupted from his own benches as he tried to suggest that the interests of the islanders might best be protected by negotiation. A former Labour minister, Douglas Jay, said later in the debate that the Foreign Office was 'a bit too much saturated with the spirit of appeasement'.[20] So Thatcher was incited by opposition leaders as well as jingoistic Tories to liberate the 1,800 Falklanders (who had enjoyed no democratic rights, in fact, as UK citizens) by sending a mighty expedition.

As Barnett points out, 'The stubborn, militaristic determination' evinced by the Thatcher government, her instant creation of a 'War Cabinet' that met daily, was a simulacrum of Churchillism. So too was the language Britain had used to defend its actions. Both rhetoric and policy were rooted in the formative moment of contemporary Britain, the time when its politics were reconstituted to preserve the country as it 'stood alone' in May 1940.[21]

The rhetoric of the 1940 coalition, involved as it was with what Barnett called 'Churchillism', was the creation of many elements in British politics, rallying behind the new Prime Minister. As this book has tried to show, by mid-1941 – and still more by 1943 – it was a rhetoric in which Left had a bigger stake than Right, because the Left was sympathetic to New Deal America as the Right, on both nationalistic and doctrinal grounds, could not be; it could therefore translate into its own terms the Atlantic Charter and the idea that the war was being fought for 'democracy' by the People. Deep at the core of Churchillism itself was collaboration between capital and labour: Churchill became Prime Minister because the Labour Party agreed to serve in his government, and his summoning of Bevin into the Cabinet put him, in effect, into a position where he could not resist trade-union claims and aspirations. But in return Labour and Liberal supporters of the coalition were committed – for the most part willingly – to elements in Churchill's personal philosophy: to his majestic but simplistic view of English (British Empire) history culminating in a Finest Hour, to the nationalism which would make him describe the Eighth Army's victory at El Alamein in the autumn of 1942 – rather than that of the US fleet at Midway some months earlier or the truly decisive Soviet victory at Stalingrad soon after – as the 'Hinge of Fate' in the Second World War; to his uncritical devotion to the Mother of Parliaments which Foot, above all, would come heartily to share.

Thatcher was able (albeit with only temporary and limited success) to clarify at last what the Tories wanted from Churchillism – not the whole forties package, which included consensus and commitment to social amelioration under state direction; just the rhetoric which had Britain standing alone in defence of freedom world-wide, recovering from an early reverse (for Dunkirk read 'unforeseen Argentinian action') and sweeping on to ultimate victory through the selfless courage of 'her boys'. Foot obligingly offered her much of this rhetoric in his own inimitable oratorical manner. But it now seems as if Thatcher's appropriation of parts of the Myth for Party advantage in 1982 may have helped to reduce the potency of the whole paradigm. The apparent growth of some real enthusiasm for British participation in the European Community by the later eighties and the strength of the economic and political pressures driving the country towards European union, suggest that recent British history will, by the end of the century, have been re-interpreted in such a way that the Myth of the Blitz will be recognised as a *fact* rather than asserted as a *truth*. This can be argued despite crude 'anti-Kraut' headlines in tabloid newspapers and the nationalist rhetoric of many active Conservatives. The mood of the populace during the Gulf War of 1991 was by and large 'patriotic' but not jingoistic. Suspicion of Myth-making media was widespread, not least in the media themselves.

Now that it seems that the Myth of the Blitz may be losing its magical hold, and that rational discussion even of the British Constitution which the Myth sanctifies will be encouraged by British concessions of sovereignty to European institutions, perhaps it is time to remember its better features? Sentimental as it may seem to present the English as mild, quiet people with great reserves of patience and tolerance, there was a lot to recommend this national ideal over any encouraged, between about 1850 and 1918, by proponents of imperial expansion. The Myth, while it dealt tenderly with antiquated elements in the British social structure, was firmly orientated against snobbery, selfishness and greed and could be given a forthrightly egalitarian emphasis. Involving the notion that the heroism of a united people deserved reward, it helped to promote the creation of a National Health Service after the war. If a disastrous conflation of state with community produced an excessively bureaucratic welfare state out of control by the People whom it professed to serve, at least the Myth had fostered the notion of the mutual responsibility of all for the welfare of all. Surveys of public attitudes half a century after Dunkirk would indicate that more than a decade of Thatcherism had not rooted out a preponderant attachment to public services involving public spending, and to the values of caring above those of moneymaking. The shades of Priestley and Murrow, Jennings and McAllister, if they attend to presentday Britain, need not feel disheartened with the legacy of their hectic, at times desperate, labours to seize from a frightening, often horrific war images useful for making a juster and friendlier society.

Bibliographical Note

An enormous number of titles have been published which are relevant to the topic of this book, and huge reservoirs of archival material exist. No bibliography could be comprehensive, and my own reading has necessarily been rather opportunist and random. The references which follow will suggest, *verb. sap.*, lines of further exploration. I am grateful for having had access to the resources of the Mass-Observation Archive, Princeton University Library and, as always, the National Library of Scotland.

Notes

1 Myth Making

Epigraph: A. Stevenson, *The Fiction-Makers*, OUP 1985, 9.
 1 J. Keegan and R. Holmes, *Soldiers*, Hamish Hamilton 1985, 130.
 2 T.H. O'Brien, *Civil Defence*, HMSO 1955, 386.
 3 R. Barthes, *Mythologies*, Granada 1973, 142–3.
 4 M. Brearley, *Phoenix from the Ashes*, Unwin 1983, 175.
 5 See Keegan and Holmes, op. cit., 243.
 6 Barthes, op. cit., 130.
 7 R. Lacour-Gayet, *A Concise History of Australia*, Penguin 1976, 297.
 8 Quoted ibid., 298.
 9 G. Dallas and D. Gill, *The Unknown Army*, Verso 1985, 137.
 10 J. Munson, ed. *Echoes of the Great War: The Diary of the Reverend Andrew Clark 1914–1919*, OUP 1985, 199–200.
 11 Ibid., 208–9.
 12 R. Ward, *The Australian Legend*, OUP 1958, 1–2 et seq.
 13 As argued, for instance, by Dr Adrian Graves in the Trevor Reece Memorial Lecture at the University of London, on 30 January 1986: 'Race and Immigration: The White Backlash in Britain and Australia'.
 14 A. Thomson, 'Gallipoli – A Past That We Can Live By?' in *Melbourne Historical Journal*, 14, 1982, 56–72.
 15 A. Bryant, *Years of Victory*, Collins 1944, 206–7, 333–4, 355.
 16 T. Wintringham, *New Ways of War*, Penguin 1940, 125, 127–8.
 17 P. Wright, *On Living in an Old Country*, Verso 1985, 16.
 18 Ibid., 23.
 19 Ibid., 24.

20 Ibid., 83–4.
21 J.A. Williamson, *The Age of Drake*, A. & C. Black 1938, 316.
22 W.G. Hoskins, *The Making of the English Landscape*, Penguin 1970, 13.
23 C. Royster, *A Revolutionary People at War: The Continental Army and American Character, 1775–1783*, University of North Carolina Press (Chapel Hill) 1979, 3–24.
24 W. Churchill, *Into Battle . . . War Speeches*, Cassell 1941, 234.
25 J. Keegan, *The Face of Battle*, Vintage (NY) 1977, 257–60, 263, 283.
26 Quoted in S. Hynes, *The Auden Generation*, Bodley Head 1976, 191.
27 P. Fussell, *The Great War and Modern Memory*, OUP 1975, 139, 169, 174–9.
28 Ibid., 179–83.
29 Ibid., 188.
30 Ibid., 119.
31 V. Hodgson, *Few Eggs and No Oranges*, Dennis Dobson 1976, 92–3.

2 'Finest Hours'

Epigraph: B. Brecht *Poems 1913–1956*, ed. J. Willett et al., Eyre Methuen 1976, 350.
1 R. Kee, *The World We Left Behind: A Chronicle of the Year 1939*, Weidenfeld & Nicolson 1984, 300–1.
2 Ibid., 307–10.
3 Churchill, op. cit., 156.
4 Ibid., 183.
5 J. Terraine, *The Right of the Line: The Royal Air Force in the European War 1939–1945*, Hodder & Stoughton 1985, 115.
6 P. Addison, *The Road to 1945: British Politics and the Second World War*, Cape 1975, 93–8.
7 J. Keegan and R. Holmes, *Soldiers*, Hamish Hamilton 1985, 189–90.
8 Addison, op. cit., 75–9.
9 C. Graves, *The Home Guard of Britain*, Hutchinson 1943, 13–14.
10 M. Thomson, *The Life and Times of Winston Churchill*, Odhams n.d. (1945), 267.
11 P. Guedalla, *Mr Churchill: A Portrait*, Hodder & Stoughton 1941, 294–5.
12 *The War Illustrated*, vol. 2, no. 41, 14 June 1940, 622–3, 626.
13 Churchill, op. cit., 215–23.
14 L. Thompson, *1940: Year of Legend, Year of History*, Collins 1966, 138–40.
15 Churchill, op. cit., 215–23, 225–34.
16 Terraine, op. cit., 169–70; George Orwell, *Collected Essays, Journalism and Letters*, vol. 2, Penguin 1970, 50; Vera Brittain, *England's Hour*, Macmillan 1941, 62.
17 V. Hodgson, op. cit., 36.
18 Churchill, op. cit. 252–62.
19 Brittain, op. cit., 115.
20 Terraine, op. cit., 222.

21 H. Asquith, 'Youth in the Skies', *The Best Poems of 1941* (sic), ed. T. Moult, Cape 1942, 28.
22 M. Panter-Downes, *London War-Notes 1939–1945*, Longman 1972, 98–101.
23 C. Ritchie, *The Siren Years*, Macmillan 1974, 61.
24 Panter-Downes, op. cit., 102, 105, 106.
25 Ibid., 110–12.
26 Ritchie, op. cit., 74–5.
27 Hodgson, op. cit., 95–7.
28 W. Churchill, *The Second World War*, vol. 3, *The Grand Alliance*, Cassell 1950, 539–40.
29 Terraine, op. cit., 485–8.
30 Ibid., 488, 505–11, 513.
31 Ibid., 545–8.
32 Ibid., 554–7.
33 C. Bielenberg, *The Past is Myself*, Chatto & Windus 1968, 125.
34 M. Balfour, *Propaganda in War 1939–1945*, Routledge & Kegan Paul 1979, 378.
35 D. Botting, *In the Ruins of the Reich*, Allen & Unwin 1985, 64.
36 J. Stevenson, *British Society 1914–45*, Allen Lane 1984, 448–9.
37 M. Middlebrook and C. Everitt, *The Bomber Command War Diaries*, Viking 1985, 663–4.
38 T. H. O'Brien, *Civil Defence*, HMSO 1955, 677.
39 Middlebrook and Everitt, op. cit., 708.
40 A. Harris, *Bomber Offensive*, Collins 1947, 267.
41 Churchill, *Into Battle*, 259.
42 Terraine, op. cit., 538–9.

3 No Other Link

Epigraph: R. Skelton, ed., *Poetry of the Forties*, Penguin 1968; 93–4.
1 *Index on Censorship 14:8*, December 1985, 7–10.
2 Ibid., 21.
3 Correlli Barnett, *The Audit of War*, Macmillan 1986, 144.
4 A.J.P. Taylor, *English History 1914–1945*, OUP 1965, 513.
5 Barnett, op. cit., 144–5, 88.
6 Taylor, op. cit., 495.
7 Churchill, *Into Battle*, 223.
8 Ibid., 232, 234.
9 Ibid., 249–51.
10 Ibid., 262.
11 C.W. Dilke, *Greater Britain*, vol. 2, Macmillan 1868, 406.
12 A.J.P. Taylor et al., *Churchill: Four Faces and the Man*, Penguin 1973, 39–40.
13 C. Thorne, *The Issue of War: States, Societies and the Far Eastern Conflict of 1941–1945*, Hamish Hamilton 1985, 226–7.
14 Quoted in V.G. Kiernan, *America: The New Imperialism*, Zed 1978, 193.

15 Mass-Observation, *Change No 2: Home Propaganda*, Advertising Service Guild (1941), 18.
16 I. McLaine, *Ministry of Morale*, Allen & Unwin 1979, 223–4.
17 J. Mackenzie, *Propaganda and Empire: The Manipulation of British Public Opinion 1880–1960*, Manchester UP 1984, 253–8.
18 Ibid., 235–8, 90.
19 McLaine, op. cit., 263–8.
20 Mass-Observation File Report, 1095, *Opinion on America*, 16.3.42 (Mass-Observation Archive).
21 H. Pelling, *America and the British Left*, A. & C. Black 1956, 130–46.
22 Laski in Pelling, loc. cit.; N. Branson, *History of the Communist Party of Great Britain 1927–1941*, Lawrence & Wishart 1985, 214–15.
23 J. Strachey, *A Programme for Progress*, Gollancz 1940, 169, 230 etc.
24 W. Willkie, *One World*, 1943.
25 J. Stevenson, op. cit. 457–8.
26 A. Marwick, *Britain in Our Century: Images and Controversies*, Thames & Hudson 1984, 114.
27 James E. Cronin, *Labour and Society in Britain 1918–1979*, Batsford 1984.
28 Terraine, op. cit. 11–13.
29 T.L. Crosby, *The Impact of Civilian Evacuation in the Second World War*, Croom Helm 1986, 31–3.
30 Ibid., 33–5.
31 Ibid., 46–8, 50.
32 Ibid., 50–8.
33 Ibid., 35.
34 B.S. Johnson, ed., *The Evacuees*, Gollancz 1968, 38–41.
35 Kenneth O. Morgan, *Labour in Power 1945–1951*, OUP 1984, 328.
36 J. Lee, *My Life with Nye*, Penguin 1981, 188–90.

4 Celts, Reds and Conchies

Epigraph: Hugh MacDiarmid, *Complete Poems*, vol. 1, Martin Brian & O'Keeffe 1978, 603.
 1 R. Kee, op. cit., 101–3, 241–2, 283–4.
 2 A. Briggs, *History of Broadcasting in the United Kingdom*, vol. 3: *The War of Words*, OUP 1970, 315; F.S.L. Lyons, *Ireland Since the Famine*, Fontana 1973, 557.
 3 M.M. Postan, *British War Production*, HMSO 1952, 221.
 4 J.W. Blake, *Northern Ireland in the Second World War*, HMSO (Belfast) 1956, 206–49; Lyons, op. cit., 556–7, 728–37.
 5 Tom Nairn, *The Break-Up of Britain*, New Left Books 1977, 207.
 6 Balfour, op. cit., 138–9; Briggs, op. cit., vol. 3, 221–33.
 7 J. Stevenson, op. cit., 269–73.
 8 Kenneth O. Morgan, *Rebirth of a Nation: Wales 1880–1980*, OUP 1981, 206–9, 254–7.
 9 Gwyn A. Williams, *When Was Wales?*, Penguin 1985, 253, 261–72, 274–5.
 10 Morgan, *Rebirth of a Nation*, 295; A. Calder, *The People's War*, Cape 1969, 245.

11 Addison, op. cit., 76.

12 M. Foot, *Aneurin Bevan*, vol. 1, *1897–1945*, MacGibbon & Kee 1962, 320–21.

13 W. Knox, ed., *Scottish Labour Leaders 1918–39: A Biographical Dictionary*, Mainstream (Edinburgh) 1984, 119.

14 R.J. Morris, review of I. McLaine, *The Legend of Red Clydeside*, in *Scottish Economic and Social History*, vol. 4, 1984, 90–1.

15 C. Harvie, *No Gods and Precious Few Heroes: Scotland 1914–1980*, Edward Arnold 1981, 15–23, 32.

16 R.P. Arnot, *A History of the Scottish Miners*, Allen & Unwin 1955, 247, 252, 257: Knox, ed., op. cit., 252–3.

17 John McNair, *James Maxton – The Beloved Rebel*, 1955, 289; A. Calder, *The Common Wealth Party 1942–1945*, University of Sussex D Phil. Thesis, 1968, 80–2.

18 C. Harvie, *Scotland and Nationalism*, Allen & Unwin 1977, 46–54; Knox, op. cit., 217–21.

19 Harvie, *No Gods . . .* , 103.

20 E. Muir, *Collected Poems*, Faber 1959, 97–8.

21 R. Watson, *The Literature of Scotland*, Macmillan 1984, 367–73.

22 Briggs, op. cit., vol. 3, 232–3.

23 Ibid., 235.

24 Emile Burns, quoted in N. Branson, *History of the Communist Party of Great Britain 1927–1941*, Lawrence & Wishart 1985, 139.

25 A. Marwick, *Britain in the Century of Total War*, Bodley Head 1968, 249.

26 A. Marwick, *The Deluge*, Bodley Head 1965, 81–3.

27 A. Calder, *The People's War*, 52, 494–8.

28 P. and L. Gillman, *Collar The Lot!*, Quartet 1980, 84–6.

29 Branson, op. cit., 191, 275, 285.

30 McLaine, *Ministry of Morale*, 55–9.

31 J. Hinton, 'Coventry Communism: A Study of Factory Politics in the Second World War', *History Workshop* 10, 1980, 93.

32 *Tribune*, 8.9.39, 22.9.39, 1.12.39, 8.12.39.

33 *Left News*, 4, 40.

34 *Left News*, 7, 40; J. Strachey, *A Faith to Fight For*, Gollancz 1941, 121.

35 F. Brockway, *Bermondsey Story*, 1949, 221.

36 *Labour Discussion Notes*, 6, 40. Three future Labour MPs were members of *LDN*'s 'Publication Committee' – Patrick Gordon Walker, Austen Albu and William Warbey.

37 N. Mitchison, *Among You Taking Notes*, Gollancz 1985, 62–6.

38 H. McShane and J. Smith, *No Mean Fighter*, Pluto 1978, 231.

39 Branson, op. cit., 265–71.

40 Ibid., 271–4.

41 Ibid., 287–90.

42 Ibid., 290–301.

43 Ibid., 301–6.

44 Hinton, loc. cit., 94–5.

45 McShane, op. cit., 233; Branson, op. cit., 306–8.

46 T. Harrisson, 'Public Opinion About Russia', *Political Quarterly 12:4*, 1941, 353–9.

47 See D.N. Pritt, *Choose Your Future*, 1941.

48 *The People Speak*, People's Convention 1941, 40, 50–1, 58–9.

49 A. Calder and D. Sheridan, eds, *Speak for Yourself: A Mass-Observation Anthology 1937–49*, Cape 1984, 199–202.

50 *Tribune*, 17.1.41; *New Statesman*, 18.1.41.

51 Branson, op. cit., 315–19, 322–3; P.N. Furbank, *E.M. Forster: A Life*, vol. 2, OUP 1978, 241–2.

52 C. Cockburn, *Crossing The Line*, McGibbon & Kee 1958, 72.

5 Standing 'Alone'

Epigraph: Quoted in K. McCormick and H. D. Perry, eds, *Images of War*, Cassell 1991, 6.

1 Taylor, op. cit., 468–9.

2 Addison, op. cit., 86–91.

3 Ibid., 104, 125.

4 H. Nicolson, *Diaries and Letters 1939–45*, Collins 1967, 85, 93; A. Calder, *The People's War*, 86.

5 N. Harman, *Dunkirk: The Necessary Myth*, Coronet 1981, 17.

6 Ibid., 58–60.

7 Ibid., 60–5.

8 Ibid., 86–96, 106–7.

9 Ibid., 112–37.

10 'Cato', *Guilty Men*, Gollancz 1940, 11–12.

11 H. Marchant, *Women and Children Last*, Gollancz 1941, 42–3.

12 Harman, op. cit., 181–3, 187–8.

13 Ibid., 201–4.

14 Ibid., 263–4; L. Deighton, *Fighter*, Granada 1979, 61–4.

15 Terraine, op. cit., 187, 219–20.

16 Thompson, op. cit., 139; Deighton, op. cit., 244.

17 Terraine, op. cit., 190–1.

18 Lee, op. cit., 148–52.

19 Terraine, op. cit., 191–2.

20 A. Calder, *People's War*, 117–18; A. Bullock, *The Life and Times of Ernest Bevin*, vol. 2, *Minister of Labour 1940–1945*, Heinemann 1967, 80–1.

21 Lee, op. cit., 151–2.

22 Mass-Observation, *People in Production*, John Murray 1942, 55–6, 244.

23 Terraine, op. cit., 222.

24 P. Townsend, *Duel of Eagles*, Weidenfeld & Nicolson 1970, 343–4.

25 Deighton, op. cit., 107, 181–2.

26 Ibid., 207, 227–30, 240–3, 278–9; Townsend, op. cit., 345–6.

27 Deighton, op. cit., 297–8.

28 Babs Diplock, *You Can't Really Call it Poetry!!*, Cleethorpes 1985; the final prose comment is given not as in this booklet but as in a typescript copy sent to me by Mrs Diplock.

29 Panter-Downes, op. cit., 65, 67, 70–1.
30 H. Agar, *Britain Alone June 1940–June 1941*, Bodley Head 1972, 69.
31 D. Middleton, *The Sky Suspended*, Secker & Warburg 1960, 75.
32 Ritchie, op. cit., 55.
33 Brittain, op. cit., 92–7.
34 P. Mayhew, ed., *One Family's War*, Hutchinson 1985, 66, 82–3.
35 Thompson, op. cit., 134–8.
36 McLaine, *Ministry of Morale*, 80–4.
37 Gillman, op. cit., 45–6.
38 Ibid., 73–80.
39 Ibid., 101–5.
40 Ibid., 115–29.
41 Mitchison, op. cit., 65.
42 Gillman, op. cit., 185–201.
43 C. Perry, *Boy in the Blitz*, Colin A. Perry 1980, 13–14.
44 T. Johnston, *Memories*, Collins 1952, 139.
45 Gillman, op. cit., 243–55; P. Grafton, *You, You, and You: The People Out of Step with World War II*, Pluto 1981, 20–3.
46 R. Stent, *A Bespattered Page*, André Deutsch 1980, 156–85.
47 F. Lafitte, *The Internment of Aliens*, Penguin 1940, 173 and title page.
48 Stent, op. cit., 248.
49 Lafitte, op. cit., 156.
50 Ibid., 170.
51 *Daily Mail* 12.7.40, quoted in Lafitte, op. cit.

6 Day by Day

Epigraph: R. Fuller, *New and Collected Poems 1938–1961*, Secker & Warburg 1985.
1 For convenience's sake, I have used the series of Daily and Weekly Reports, with related documents, to be found in the Mary Adams papers in the Mass-Observation Archive at the University of Sussex. The reports have long been available in a 35 mm. microfilm edition produced by Harvester Press (Brighton), as well as in the archive held by the Public Record Office and well mined by Ian McLaine for his *Ministry of Morale*, Allen & Unwin 1979.
2 The Mass-Observation Archive is intricately filed and catalogued. Remarks in the main text should be enough to guide any enquirer to the right place – in this case, Box 180, 'Air Raids'.
3 Some of this is printed in A. Calder and D. Sheridan, ed., *Speak for Yourself: A Mass-Observation Anthology 1937–49*, Cape 1984, 76–83.

7 Formulations of Feeling

Epigraph: L. MacNeice, *Collected Poems*, Faber 1979, 203–4.
1 T. McKendrick, *Clydebank Blitz*, no publisher, Clydebank 1986.
2 Bert Hardy, *My Life*, Gordon Fraser 1985, 40.

3 MacNeice, op. cit., 196, 217–18.
4 A. Calder, *T.S. Eliot*, Harvester Press 1987, 131–60.
5 T. S. Eliot, *Collected Poems 1909–1962*, Faber 1963.
6 J. Masefield, *The Nine Days Wonder*, Heinemann 1941, 58.
7 T. Moult, ed., *The Best Poems of 1941*, Cape 1942, 13, 28, 38–40, 72, 79–82.
8 I. Hamilton, ed., *The Poetry of War 1939–45*, Alan Ross 1965, 164–5.
9 Fuller, op. cit., 42–5.
10 Skelton, ed., op. cit., 19.

8 Fictions

Epigraph: Norman Lewis, *Naples '44*, Pantheon (New York) 1978, 100.
 1 Ibid., 124.
 2 L. Wigmore, *The Japanese Thrust*, Australian War Memorial (Canberra) 1959, 287–8.
 3 H. Klein *et al.*, eds., *The Second World War in Fiction*, Macmillan 1984.
 4 Masefield, op. cit., 51.
 5 L. Thomas, *The Dearest and the Best*, Penguin 1985, 179–218.
 6 R. Hillary, *The Last Enemy*, Macmillan 1942, 221.
 7 Ibid., 11.
 8 Ibid., 19–23.
 9 Ibid., 52–4, 96–9.
10 Ibid., 70–1, 124–8.
11 Ibid., 135.
12 D. Robinson, *Piece of Cake*, Pan 1983; Author's note, 668–72.
13 A. Munson, *English Fiction of the Second World War*, Faber 1989, 79.
14 N. Monsarrat, *The Cruel Sea*, Reprint Society, 1953 edn, 481, 508.
15 Ibid., 367–8.
16 Ibid., 314.
17 Ibid., 228–9.
18 Raynes Minns, *Bombers and Mash*, Virago 1980, 61.
19 H. Forrester, *Three Women of Liverpool*, Fontana 1984, 256.
20 R. Fisk, *In Time of War: Ireland, Ulster and the Price of Neutrality 1939–45*, Granada 1985, 478–508.
21 Brian Moore, *The Emperor of Ice Cream*, Mayflower 1967, 175–6, 181, 189–90.
22 R. Jenkins, *Fergus Lamont*, Canongate (Edinburgh) 1979, 287–93.
23 R.F. Delderfield, *The Avenue Goes to War*, Coronet 1971, 116, 132, 168.
24 J. Boorman, *Hope and Glory*, Faber 1987, 6–9.
25 Ibid., 47–9.
26 R. Westall, *Children of the Blitz: Memories of Wartime Childhood*, Viking 1985, 77.
27 R. Westall, *The Machine-Gunners*, Penguin 1977, 186.

9 Deep England

Epigraph: M.-L. Jennings, ed., *Humphrey Jennings: Film-Maker, Painter, Poet*, British Film Institute 1982, 25.

1 C. Chant, ed., *Science, Technology and Everyday Life 1870–1950*, Open University Press (Milton Keynes) 1989, 180.
2 W.J. Keith, *The Rural Tradition*, Harvester Press (Brighton) 1975, 238–40.
3 H.J. Massingham, *Chiltern Country*, Batsford 1940, 27.
4 Ibid., 6–7, 14.
5 H. Newby, *Green and Pleasant Land? Social Change in Rural England*, Wildwood 1979, 39.
6 Ibid., 14–16.
7 A. Potts, '"Constable Country" Between the Wars', in R. Samuel, ed., *Patriotism: The Making and Unmaking of British National Identity*, vol 3, *National Fictions*, Routledge 1989, 160–86.
8 J.B. Priestley, introduction to *The Beauty of Britain*, Batsford 1935, 1–10.
9 I. Brown, *The Heart of England*, Batsford 1935, vi, 65–70.
10 Ibid., 94.
11 H. Kingsmill, ed., *The English Genius*, Eyre & Spottiswoode 1938, 4–5.
12 H.J. Massingham, *The Fall of the Year*, Chapman & Hall 1941, 54–5.
13 W.H. Auden, poem XXIII from *Look, Stranger!*, Faber 1936.
14 W.H. Auden, 'Letter to Lord Byron' from *Collected Longer Poems*, Faber 1968.
15 D. Mitchell, *Britten and Auden in the Thirties: The Year 1936*, Faber 1981, 33ff.
16 Ian Jeffrey, *The British Landscape 1920–1950*, Thames & Hudson, 1984, 7–8.
17 Barbican Art Gallery, *'That's Shell – That Is!': An Exhibition of Shell Advertising Art . . .*, BAG and Shell UK 1983, 9.
18 C. Harrison, *English Art and Modernism 1900–1939*, Allen Lane 1981, 321.
19 A. Howkins, 'Greensleeves and the Idea of National Music' in Samuel, ed., op. cit., 89–98.
20 J.B. Priestley, *Margin Released: A Writer's Reminiscences and Reflections*, Heinemann 1962, 218–19.
21 Asa Briggs, *The History of Broadcasting in the United Kingdom*, vol. 3, *The War of Words*, OUP 1970, 210–11.
22 Mary Adams Papers, Mass-Observation Archive.
23 Briggs, op. cit., 320–2.
24 Priestley, op. cit., 2, 68.
25 J.B. Priestley, *Postscripts*, Heinemann 1940, 1–4.
26 Ibid., 5–8.
27 J. Strachey, *Post D*, Gollancz 1941, 134–5.
28 *Postscripts* 9–13.
29 Ibid., 15, 17.
30 Ibid., 19–23.
31 Ibid., 73, 83.

32 Ibid., 49–53.

33 Ibid., 36–8, 43, 98–100.

34 A. Mee, *Nineteen-Forty: Our Finest Hour*, Hodder & Stoughton 1941, 66, 121.

35 *Arthur Mee's Book of the Flag: Island and Empire*, Hodder & Stoughton 1941, 19–34.

36 *Dandy Monster Comic*, D.C. Thomson (Dundee) 1941, 76–7.

37 A. Aldgate and J. Richards, *Britain Can Take It: The British Cinema in the Second World War*, Blackwell (Oxford) 1986, 54.

38 Ibid., 51–72.

39 L. Foreman, ed., *From Parry to Britten: British Music in Letters 1900–1945*, Batsford 1987, 240–2.

10 Telling It To America

Epigraph: Ben Robertson, *I Saw England*, Jarrolds 1941, 134.

1 N. Farson, *Bomber's Moon*, Gollancz 1941, 148.

2 Q. Reynolds, *The Wounded Don't Cry*, Cassell 1941, 216–27.

3 C.R. Koppes and G.D. Black, *Hollywood Goes to War*, I.B. Tauris 1989, 230–3.

4 A. Duer Miller, *The White Cliffs*, Methuen 1941, 23, 59.

5 Unpublished paper by Nicholas J. Cull, 'Propagandising Uncle Sam – An Outline of the Origins and Evolution of British Publicity Structures in the United States during the Second World War'. I am very grateful to Mr Cull for sight of this paper.

6 Cull, loc. cit.

7 D.H. Hosley, *As Good as Any: Foreign Correspondence on American Radio 1930–1940*, Greenwood Press (Westport, Conn.) 1984, 76.

8 R. Franklin Smith, *Edward R. Murrow: The War Years* (Kalamazoo, Mich.) 1978, 37, 39, 49.

9 A.M. Sperber, *Murrow: His Life and Times*, Michael Joseph 1987, 184–5, 189.

10 Eric Sevareid, *Not So Wild a Dream*, Athenaeum (New York) 1976, 82–3, 176–8.

11 Vincent Sheean, *Between the Thunder and the Sun*, Random House (New York) 1943, 210.

12 Sperber, op. cit., 182–3.

13 Ibid., 100–4, etc.

14 Hosley, op. cit., 4, 43.

15 Koppes and Black, op. cit., 26–7, 30–1.

16 Colin Shindler, *Hollywood Goes To War*, Routledge & Kegan Paul 1979, 21; John Russell Taylor, *Hitch: The Life and Work of Alfred Hitchcock*, Faber 1978, 163–8.

17 Hosley, op. cit., 59–62.

18 Sperber, op. cit., 160–2.

19 Robertson, op. cit., 79.

20 Ibid., 86–92; Sheean, op. cit., 195–6.

21 Q. Reynolds, *By Quentin Reynolds*, Heinemann 1964, 174.
22 Sheean, op. cit., 200–1.
23 Sperber, op. cit., 162–3; A. Kendrick, *Prime Time: The Life of Edward R. Murrow*, Little Brown (Boston) 1969, 173–6.
24 Sheean, op. cit., 218 ff; Robertson, op. cit., 105–8, 110–11; E. R. Murrow, *This Is London*, Cassell 1941, 173.
25 Murrow, op. cit., 171–91.
26 Sevareid, op. cit., 79–80, 166, 169–74.
27 E. Bliss Jr, ed., *In Search of Light: The Broadcasts of Edward R. Murrow 1938–1961*, Macmillan 1968, 1–2.
28 Sperber, op. cit., 153.
29 Robertson, op. cit., 65–6.
30 Farson, op. cit., 74.
31 S. Laird and W. Graebner, *Hitler's Reich and Churchill's Britain*, Batsford 1942, 27.
32 James B. Reston, *Prelude to Victory*, Heinemann 1942, 29.
33 R. Ingersoll, *Report on England*, Bodley Head 1941, 217.
34 Robertson, op. cit., 148–9; Sheean, op. cit., 246–8; Ingersoll, op. cit., 54–5, 150.
35 R.W. Desmond, *Tides of War: World News Reporting 1931–1945*, Iowa UP (Iowa City) 1984, 135.
36 Sperber, op. cit., 192–3.
37 Hosley, op. cit., 143–5.
38 David E. Scherman, ed., *Life Goes To War: A Picture History of World War II*, Simon & Schuster (New York) 1977, 72–5.
39 Reynolds, *By Quentin Reynolds*, 175, etc.
40 Ibid., 188–92; Robertson, op. cit., 182–3.
41 Reynolds, *By Quentin Reynolds*, 196–8.
42 Sperber, op. cit., 175–7.
43 Reynolds, *By Quentin Reynolds*, 199–207; Reynolds, *Only the Stars are Neutral*, Cassell 1942, 5.
44 Reynolds, *The Wounded Don't Cry*, 234–9.
45 Reynolds, *By Quentin Reynolds*, 188–91.

11 Filming the Blitz

Epigraph: H. Watt, *Don't Look at the Camera*, Elek 1974, 125–6.
 1 D. Vaughan, *Portrait of an Invisible Man: The Working Life of Stewart McAllister, Film Editor*, British Film Institute 1983, 39.
 2 Jane Fisher, unpublished seminar paper, 'What Shall We Tell Them? British Propaganda on the Blitz and Bomber Offensive, 1939–45'. (Edinburgh University, 28.2.90).
 3 Aldgate and Richards, op. cit., 220.
 4 E. Sussex, *The Rise and Fall of Documentary*, University of California Press, Berkeley, 1975, 110–11.
 5 Ibid., 124.
 6 Ibid., 125–7.

7 Vaughan, op. cit., 63–9.
8 Watt, op. cit., 141.
9 Q. Reynolds, *Britain Can Take It: The Book of the Film*, John Murray 1941 (no pagination).
10 Jennings, op. cit., 26.
11 A.W. Hodgkinson and R.E. Sheratsky, *Humphrey Jennings – More than a Maker of Films*, University Press of New England 1982, xii–xiv.
12 Jennings, op. cit., 7.
13 Ibid., 16–17.
14 G. Nowell Smith, 'Humphrey Jennings, Surrealist Observer', in C. Barr, ed., *All Our Yesterdays: 90 Years of British Cinema*, British Film Institute 1986, 324.
15 Vaughan, op. cit., 30, 38.
16 C. Barr, introduction, ibid., 10.
17 Nowell Smith, loc. cit., 326.
18 Jennings, op. cit., 22.
19 Vaughan, op. cit., 94.
20 Ibid., 95–6.
21 Ibid., 97.
22 Ibid., 101–6, 126–8, etc.
23 See Jennings, op. cit., 28–9.
24 Aldgate and Richards, op. cit., 230–42; Hodgkinson and Sheratsky, op. cit., 60–5 – details here drawn from both.
25 Jennings, op. cit., 31.
26 See D. Sheridan and J. Richards, *Mass-Observation Goes to the Movies*, Routledge & Kegan Paul 1987.
27 Colin Shindler, *Hollywood Goes to War*, Routledge & Kegan Paul, 1979, 48–9.
28 T.W. Bohn, 'An Historical and Descriptive Analysis of the "Why We Fight" Series', University of Wisconsin, D.Phil. Thesis, 1968, 23, 50 ff.
29 F. Capra, *The Name above the Title*, W.H. Allen 1972, 326–7.
30 Ibid., 351–2.
31 Ibid., 328–33.
32 Ibid., 336–50; Bohn, op. cit., 101–7.
33 Capra, op. cit., 336; Bohn, 107–9.
34 Press release from MoI films division, in Imperial War Museum.
35 Bohn, op. cit., 112–13, 168.
36 Capra, op. cit., 336.
37 J. Fisher, loc. cit.

Epilogue

Epigraph: N. Coward, *Peace In Our Time*, Heinemann 1947, 15–16.
1 D. Middleton, *The Sky Suspended: The Battle of Britain*, Secker & Warburg 1960, 253–4.
2 Sevareid, op. cit., 179–80.
3 Ibid., 484–6.

4 E. Bowen, *Collected Stories*, Penguin 1983, 609–15.
5 Ibid., 728–40.
6 Ibid., 583–608.
7 Ibid., 7.
8 E. Bowen, *The Heat of the Day*, Cape 1949, 145–6.
9 Aldgate and Richards, op. cit., 115–20.
10 Jennings, op. cit., 43.
11 Ibid., 59.
12 C. Barr, *Ealing Studios*, Cameron & Taylor 1977, 5.
13 *Made in Ealing*, BBC TV *Omnibus* 1977; M. Balcon, *Michael Balcon Presents . . . a Lifetime of Films*. Hutchinson 1969, 137.
14 Barr, op. cit., 9.
15 T.E.B. Clarke, *This Is Where I Came In*, Michael Joseph 1974, 133, 137.
16 Barr, op. cit., 80–107.
17 Ibid., 178–9.
18 H. Brenton, *Plays: One*, Methuen 1986, Preface, 108.
19 B. Keeffe, *The Long Good Friday*, Methuen 1984, 9, 15, 17, 18, 44.
20 A. Barnett, *Iron Britannia*, Allison & Busby 1982, 20, 31–2, 40, 42.
21 Ibid., 56.

Index